WHERE THE LIBRARY HIDES

ALSO BY

ISABEL IBAÑEZ

Woven in Moonlight

Written in Starlight

"Rogue Enchantments"
(short story in *Reclaim the Stars* anthology)

Together We Burn

The Storyteller's Workbook
(with Adrienne Young)

What the River Knows

WHERE THE LIBRARY HIDES

a novel

ISABEL IBAÑEZ

WEDNESDAY BOOKS
NEW YORK

This is a work of fiction. All of the characters, organizations, and events portrayed in this novel are either products of the author's imagination or are used fictitiously.

First published in the United States by Wednesday Books, an imprint of St. Martin's Publishing Group

For information, address St. Martin's Publishing Group, 120 Broadway, New York, NY 10271.

www.wednesdaybooks.com

Designed by Devan Norman
Interior illustrations by Isabel Ibañez

The Library of Congress Cataloging-in-Publication Data is available upon request.

ISBN 978-1-250-82299-4 (hardcover)
ISBN 978-1-250-82300-7 (ebook)

Our books may be purchased in bulk for promotional, educational, or business use. Please contact your local bookseller or the Macmillan Corporate and Premium Sales Department at 1-800-221-7945, extension 5442, or by email at MacmillanSpecialMarkets@macmillan.com.

First Edition: 2024

10 9 8 7 6 5 4 3 2 1

For the readers who stayed up all night
agonizing over the epilogue in
What the River Knows*:*
This one is dedicated to you.

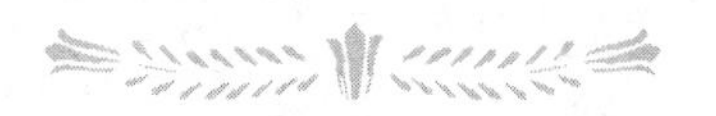

CAST OF CHARACTERS | *A REFRESHER*

Inez Emilia Olivera, *our heroine*
Elvira Gabriella Montenegro, *Inez's favorite cousin*
Amaranta Lucia Montenegro, *Inez's not-favorite cousin*
Tía Lorena, *Inez's aunt*
Tío Ricardo Marqués, *Inez's uncle and guardian; Abdullah's business partner and brother-in-law; an excavator*
Lourdes Patricia Olivera, *Inez's mother; a smuggler of artifacts and at large*
Cayo Roberto Olivera, *Inez's father*

Whitford Simon Hayes, *Ricardo's aide-de-camp*
Porter Linton Hayes, *Whitford's older brother*
Arabella Georgina Hayes, *Whitford's younger sister*
Leo Lopez, *soldier and Whitford's best friend*

Abdullah Salah, *Ricardo's business partner and brother-in-law; an excavator*
Farida Salah, *Abdullah's granddaughter; a photographer*

Kareem Ali, *assistant cook and field hand on the Philae excavation*
Sallam Ahmed, *hotel manager at Shepheard's*

Charles Fincastle, *a weapons expert and hired gunman on the Philae excavation*
Isadora Fincastle, *Charles's daughter*

Basil Digby Sterling, *a British antiquities agent*
Monsieur Gaston Maspero, *French Egyptologist and director general of excavations and antiquities*
Sir Evelyn Baring, *consul general of Egypt*

MAP OF ALEXANDRIA | 1885

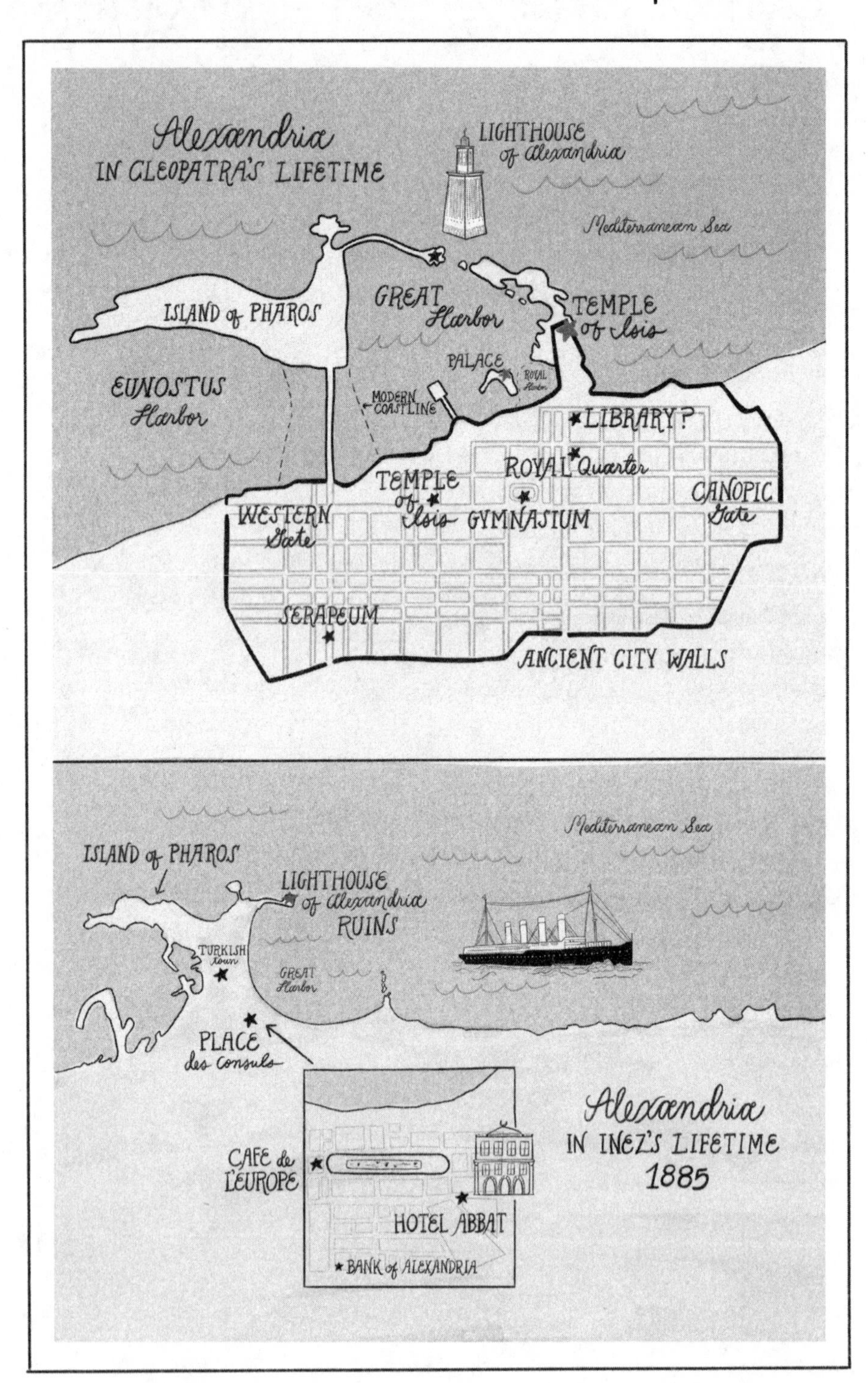

A (BROAD) TIMELINE OF EGYPT

2675–2130 BCE	Old Kingdom
1980–1630 BCE	Middle Kingdom
1539–1075 BCE	New Kingdom
356 BCE	Birth of Alexander the Great
332–305 BCE	Alexander the Great conquers Egypt; Macedonian Period
69 BCE	Birth of Cleopatra VII
31 BCE	Battle of Actium (Deaths of Cleopatra and Marcus Antonius)
31 BCE	Beginning of Roman rule
639	Beginning of Arab rule
969	Cairo established as capital
1517	Egypt absorbed into the Turkish Ottoman Empire
1798	Napoleon leads French Army to Egypt; conquers Alexandria and Cairo (discovery of Rosetta Stone)
1822	Champollion deciphers hieroglyphs
1869	Opening of Suez Canal
1870	Thomas Cook's first Nile tour
1882	English fleet bombs Alexandria and takes control of Egypt
1922	British rule abolished; discovery of Tutankhamun's tomb
1953	Egypt's independence

WHERE THE LIBRARY HIDES

PRÓLOGO

"Marry me instead."

The words ricocheted around the room, finally hitting me square in the chest, where each syllable felt like a smack.

I licked my lips, forced myself to speak through the haze. "You want to get married."

Whit kept a steady gaze on me, blue eyes searing and red rimmed, and said with no hesitation, "Yes."

"To me," I said, needing clarification. Some light to cut through the fog. I pushed away from him, and he let me go. I eyed him uneasily as I rounded the bed, needing something tangible in between us. The distance cleared my head from the scent of whiskey curling around him, smoky and rich.

Again his reply came sure and quick. "Yes."

"Married," I repeated, because clarification was *still* in order. He had been drinking and, by the look of it, not one tidy glass. "In a church."

"If need be."

"It'd have to be," I said. The idea sounded normal and sane. Unlike our conversation. Getting married in a church was something I would have done—seemingly in another life. The one I'd been groomed to live in Buenos Aires. I would marry the handsome Ernesto, a young caballero my aunt approved of, and presumably live as her neighbor, where she could keep an eye on me for the rest of my life. There would be no trips to Cairo. My days of drawing temple walls in my sketchbook would be over. Instead, my time would revolve around someone else and, eventually, my children. I could see that future as if I were already living it. My heart raced in protest, and I had to remind myself I was here in Egypt.

Exactly where I wanted to be.

Whit arched a brow. "Is that a yes?"

I blinked. "You need an answer right this moment?"

Whit swept his arm across my luxurious hotel bed, currently covered in skirts with ruffled hems and jackets with brass buttons. To my horror, several pairs of stockings were strewn over a plump pillow, next to my favorite chemise, which was practically threadbare. He followed my gaze and then, with admirable restraint, didn't remark about my underthings.

"I don't necessarily need one right now, but I'd *prefer* one, yes," Whit drawled. "For a little thing like my peace of mind."

His manner was beginning to infuriate me. This was one of the most important decisions I would make, and if he wanted me to take it seriously, then he should, too. I shoved my clothing off to the side, then bent to drag my suitcase out from under the bed and dropped it onto the cleared-off space. Without ceremony, or care for wrinkles, I began throwing in my clothing. In went my Turkish trousers, cotton shirts, and pleated skirts. I bundled up my underthings and tossed them inside.

He looked at the growing pile in my trunk with alarm. "What are you doing?"

"What does it look like?" I tossed in my satin slippers, the boots I wore while on Philae, and leather heels. I looked around the room, my hands on my hips. What else?

"We are in the middle of a conversation and you already have one foot out the door." Whit reached forward and pulled out several articles of clothing, and then he removed the pair of boots I'd dropped in.

"Excuse me, but I am packing," I said, shoving a shirt back into the trunk.

"Nowhere on this planet would anyone call what you are doing packing," Whit said, eyeing my balled-up shirt in disgust.

"Now you're being mean."

"I asked you a question, Inez."

I glared at him and held out my hand for my boots. "I need those."

"Not right now you don't." Whit dropped them onto the floor and, without taking his eyes off me, grabbed my trunk with both hands, turned it upside down, and dumped everything back out.

"Why don't you tell me what's really bothering you?" he asked.

Cielos, he was *insufferable*. "You've been drinking."

"So?"

My voice rose by several unladylike decibels. "*So?* How do I know if you mean it?"

Whit rounded the bed. Sure on his feet, his hands steady. His words weren't slurred. They came out clear and sharp edged, as if they were the last ones he'd say in front of a firing squad. "*I want to marry you.*"

I gestured to the Inez mountain sitting on top of the bedding. "Despite the mess."

Slowly, he touched the tip of his index finger to the corner of my mouth. "No one else."

"Oh."

"Well?"

From the corner of my eye, I noticed a delicate underthing had slipped off the bed and onto his shoe. I bent to retrieve it, but he beat me to it. He carefully placed it on one of the pillows.

I detected the faintest blush blooming high on his cheeks.

It occurred to me then that I'd never seen Whit blush.

I'd seen him messy and smirking, furious and amused. But never embarrassed. It was this sight that reminded me of who I was dealing with. Whit was my friend, maybe even the best one I had. He'd kissed me when we thought we'd die trapped in that tomb, the air slowly turning against us, quietly dangerous. He had held my hand in the dark and shared his biggest regret with me.

When someone had dared to hurt me, he'd ended them.

This was the man asking for my hand.

"I'd give you more time," Whit said, "but you're *leaving the country.*"

That was true—my uncle wanted me gone. For my safety, as if he could protect me still when I had already lived through the horror of seeing my cousin shot in the head, not ten feet away from me.

Elvira.

Pain stabbed my heart, and the cloud of confusion descended again. It seemed impossible that I'd never see her mischievous grin right before breaking one of her mother's many rules. Never hear her voice or read another one of her stories. Her life had been cut short, a book closed forever, the ending written as a horrifying nightmare.

I had to stay in Egypt for her.

It was my traitorous mother's fault she was gone. Grief held on to me like a tightened fist, and a sob worked its way up my throat. I ruthlessly tamped the emotion down, searching for another that wouldn't leave me on the floor.

Anger simmered in my blood, just under the surface.

More than anything, I wanted to hunt my mother down. Force her into prison where she could rot for eternity. I wanted her to tell me what she had done to my father, if he was still living, trapped somewhere and only she knew how to find him. Papá's words from his last letter to me swam in my mind.

Never stop looking for me.

I could do nothing from another continent.

I understood at once what Whit was implying. If I married him, I would have free rein over my fate. It made my head spin. A destiny uncontrolled. Access to my fortune, no longer dependent on my uncle, and as a married woman, I would no longer need a chaperone everywhere I went. Whit's offer was appealing. And there was the other thing. The thing I couldn't have predicted when I first set sail for Egypt.

I had fallen in love with Whitford Hayes.

I loved him with my whole heart, despite my head telling me to have better sense. But I loved him in a way that meant forever. I hadn't known for sure until this moment, as I stared into his face, which was somehow vulnerable and remote all at once. Terror gripped me. I'd never felt so stricken, so raw, so exposed.

Again my head said, *What you're feeling is utter nonsense.*

She sounded stern and convincing.

"Think it over, then. And let me know." He smiled faintly, and his next words sounded more like himself. "Preferably before you get on that train to Alexandria."

He left, the door closing with a measured click.

To the empty room I said, "Miércoles."

PART ONE

THE CITY OF ALL CITIES

CAPÍTULO UNO

I kept Whitford Hayes waiting.

Twelve hours later, I still hadn't made up my mind. It alarmed me how badly I wanted to say yes. If I'd learned anything from my time in Egypt, it was that I couldn't trust my own judgment. A disappointing and terrifying realization. From now on, I'd have to be on my guard, no matter what my heart wanted. Besides, what would happen if I *did* marry him? Whit had made a promise to someone else, and while it hadn't been his personal choice, he had given his word to another. He had insisted on keeping his distance, and we had agreed on a friendship, and nothing more. But then he'd kissed me when we thought we were dying, and so the scale tipped, and we lost our equilibrium.

Everything changed while we were locked up in a tomb.

Did his proposal mean he cared about me? Was he as deep in as I was?

I could have asked him, but then, wouldn't he have made some kind of declaration when he proposed? A simple *I adore you* would have been much appreciated. Now that I thought of it, Whit hadn't actually asked me the question. He'd said, *Marry me instead*, matter-of-factly. I'd been so rattled I hadn't had the time to pick through my thoughts before he'd left the room. Instead, I teetered from terror and joy. All the good things I'd ever loved had been lost to me. The family I believed I had. Elvira. The discovering of Cleopatra's tomb. All destroyed by one person.

What if Mamá somehow wrecked this, too?

I tugged on the scarf around my throat. My mother had given it to me to shrink dozens of artifacts from Cleopatra's tomb, and for some reason,

I had kept it when I probably ought to have burned it. This stretch of fabric was evidence of her betrayal. It felt like a chain, linking me to her. Maybe if I pulled on it hard enough, it'd somehow lead me to where she was hiding.

"Stop fidgeting with that scarf. Why are you dragging your feet?" Tío Ricardo asked, voice laced with impatience. "Whit will be waiting."

I winced. Ah, yes, Whit's perpetual state at the moment. "Él es paciente, Tío."

"Ha! Whit? Patient? You don't know him like I do," my uncle scoffed. "All I've eaten is broth for the last few days, y me muero de hambre. I need a hearty meal, Inez, and if you say one word in disagreement, I will start yelling."

I threw him a disgruntled look, even though he didn't see it. He was categorically not dying of hunger—I personally made sure of it. I was not a violent person, but I silently contemplated throwing something at his head. Tío Ricardo, *once again*, refused to stay in bed. One would think I were suggesting he bite into a raw onion like an apple. Instead, he tugged me along as we made our way to Shepheard's lavish dining room, one hand holding tight to my wrist. His other arm was bound up in a sling, which he periodically glared down at, resenting anything that might keep him from Philae. He also kept eyeing every person who passed us in the corridor with deep suspicion. When two gentlemen entered the hallway leading to the main stairs, my uncle forcibly moved me down another turn and waited for them to pass.

This time I didn't try to hide my exasperation. "Just what do you think will happen to me on the third floor of the hotel?"

Tío Ricardo wasn't looking at me but was focused on the retreating backs of the pair of gentlemen walking, presumably, to their room. "Have you seen them before?"

I yanked my arm free. "You ought to be resting and not casting judgment on unsuspecting tourists."

My uncle finally angled his bearded face toward mine. He towered over me, smelling of citrus soap, and his clothes, for once, were pressed, his shoes wiped clean. Direct results of staying in the hotel for the past few days. "Have you learned nothing? Lourdes's contacts could be *anyone*."

"If she wanted to kill me, she had plenty of opportunity. But she didn't," I whispered. "I'm still her daughter. Her only child."

"You have proof of how far she will go to protect her interests. Don't depend on any maternal affection she might have for you." The deep lines gathered at the corners of my uncle's mouth smoothed away. He regarded me with soft eyes the exact same color as my own—hazel, which changed hue, depending on our mood. Pity lurked deep within them, and I couldn't stand it. "Trouble follows wherever she goes. You of all people should know that."

My lips parted as a memory raced into my mind. A quick flash, like the swipe of a knife against my skin.

Elvira screaming my name—calling for me as the trigger was pulled, the bullet streaking toward her. And a moment later, her blown-up face. Unrecognizable. Blood pooling under her head, staining the golden sand.

If I could, I would give up years of my life for that memory to be struck from my mind.

"I think it's safe to go on down," he said, and resumed holding on to me, half pulling me down the hall with his uninjured arm. "We have much to discuss."

Ordinarily I would have made some retort, but his words had chilled me through. I could never forget who my mother was. Master manipulator and a shrewd strategist. A liar and a thief. A woman who could and did betray her daughter, who was hungry for power and would do anything to acquire wealth. Coldly ruthless as she sacrificed Elvira without remorse.

A woman lost in the wind.

Be on your guard, I told myself. We continued our trek to the dining room, but this time, I joined my uncle in his careful observation of our surroundings.

Hotel guests filled the dining room, sitting at round tables covered in snow-white tablecloths, while servers nimbly carried trays laden with silver teapots and porcelain cups. Whit sat across from me, dressed in a blue button-down tucked into his standard khaki trousers. His brawny frame filled up the dainty seat, broad shoulders overtaking the back of the chair's width. I didn't need to look under the table to know that he wore his favorite leather boots, laced up to midcalf. He poured his second cup of coffee, and I knew he'd forgo sugar or cream, preferring to drink it black.

I tore my gaze away, conscious of my uncle sitting not two feet from me, and lifted my teacup to hide my burning cheeks. The liquid was hot on my tongue, but I swallowed it down to buy myself time. I felt the weight of my uncle's gaze, silently assessing and watchful. The absolute last thing I wanted was to give myself away.

My uncle would not appreciate the depth of my feelings for Whit.

"We'll depart in a few days," Tío Ricardo said to him.

"Not what the doctor ordered, I'm afraid," Whit said calmly. "He instructed you to keep off your feet for another day or two and warned of too much activity at once. Certainly no traveling long distances. Too much jostling and the like."

My uncle let out a muted snarl. "Philae is hardly a long distance."

"Only several hundred miles," Whit said, still unperturbed by Tío Ricardo's foul temper. "You could pull the stitches, risk infection—"

"Whitford."

Almost against my will, my eyes flew in his direction. I couldn't help it, much like I couldn't help the soft laugh that escaped from my mouth. My uncle wasn't only irascible with me, he dumped his acerbic manner onto Whit, too.

He just handled it better than I did.

"You'll do what you want, but I did promise the doctor I'd issue his warning," Whit said, smiling faintly. "And now, at least in this instance, my conscience is clear."

You'd never know that hours earlier, he had spoken of marriage. His manner was the same as it always was, an amused air that hid a deep current of cynicism. He met my uncle's eyes confidently; his words came out with nary a wobble. His hands were steady around the handle of the coffee cup.

Only one thing gave him away.

Since I sat down, he hadn't looked in my direction.

Not once.

Tío Ricardo narrowed his eyes. "What else have you gotten yourself involved with? Or do I not want to know of the other instances?"

"I'd stay clear," Whit said before taking a long sip. He still wouldn't look at me. As if he worried that meeting my gaze might reveal all of his secrets.

My uncle pushed away his plate—he'd eaten pita bread, dipping it in hummus and tahina, and four fried eggs. Despite my frustration with him, I was pleased to see his appetite had returned. "Humph," Tío Ricardo said, but he let the matter drop. "Now, Inez," my uncle began, rummaging through his jacket pockets. "I have your train ticket to Alexandria. You'll be leaving within the week, and hopefully by then I'll have found you a chaperone for the journey. It's a shame Mrs. Acton already sailed." He threw me a vexed look. "By the way, I had a hell of a time calming her down when you walked out on her. She was deeply offended."

I'd nearly forgotten about dear Mrs. Acton, a woman my uncle had hired to escort me back to Argentina upon my arrival in Egypt. I had tricked her and escaped from the hotel where my uncle had wanted to keep me under lock and key until he could pack me off. But I couldn't scrounge up any feeling of remorse. I couldn't even form a reply.

My mind stuck on my forthcoming departure date.

Within the week.

My uncle let out an exclamation of triumph as he pulled something out of his pocket. He held up two slips of paper and then slid them to me. I glanced down, refusing to touch the sheets: a one-way train ticket to Alexandria, and one passage booked for the port of Buenos Aires.

The noise level in the room died down, the constant chattering falling to a hush. I contemplated drowning the tickets in my water glass. I thought about ripping them intro shreds and flinging them at my uncle's face. Whit's marriage proposal loomed large, a way out of my exile. He offered a lifeline, a chance to make things right. Access to independence, a way to stop my mother and her heinous behavior. My answer to Whit's question crystalized in my mind. Slowly, I lifted my face and looked in his direction.

And for the first time since I sat down, he met my gaze.

His blue eyes seared.

Whit arched his brow, a silent question that only I knew the answer to. He must have read something in my face because he lowered his coffee, pushed his chair back from the table. "I'll be out on the terrace while you work out the details."

Tío Ricardo murmured distractedly. His attention was on a dark-skinned man across the room, dining with his family. He wore a tarboosh on his head and a crisp suit pressed to perfection. Whit shot me a quick meaningful glance before striding away. My pulse raced, knowing he wanted me to find a way to meet him outside, away from my uncle.

"Excuse me a moment. I've found a friend," Tío Ricardo said. "Wait here."

"But I've finished my breakfast," I said. "I think I'll head back to my room—"

"Not without me," my uncle said, standing. "I won't be ten minutes." He fixed me with a stern glare and waited for me to agree with his demand.

It was almost too easy. I set my mouth in a mulish line and gave in reluctantly. He nodded, turning away, and when I was sure he wouldn't notice my empty chair, I walked out of the dining room, toward the terrace where Whit waited. The lobby teemed with guests from everywhere, several languages spoken audibly as I weaved through the crowd. The front doors were opened for me and I stepped outside, blinking in the sunlight. Overhead, a blue sky with nary a cloud stretched above Cairo. The city of all cities, as some renowned historians had called it, and I had to agree. Since the dawn of time, this place had been a marvel.

I hated the idea of leaving it behind me.

Whit sat at his favorite wicker table, painted a deep green, his back to the wall, facing out toward the street. From that vantage point, he could see the comings and goings. I marched right up to him, not bothering to sit. He'd observed me the second I walked out onto the terrace, of course, and he tilted his chin up in order to meet me head-on.

"Why did you kiss me in the tomb?" I demanded.

"Because I didn't want to die without having done it once," he said immediately. "At least."

I dropped into the chair opposite him. "Oh."

"For the first time in my life, I'm choosing for myself," he said quietly. "I'd rather marry a friend than a stranger."

A friend. Was that all I was to him? I shifted in my seat, trying to display the same cool nonchalance that he exhibited. In that moment, I hated his self-possession. "Won't your betrothed be upset?"

"Darling, I don't give a damn about her." He leaned forward and held my gaze. His voice dropped to a husky whisper. "I'm still waiting for your answer, Inez."

A zip of electricity went through me, and I fought to keep myself from trembling. It was a big decision—the biggest of my life. "Are you sure?"

"I've never been more sure of anything in my entire life."

"Let's get married, then," I said, breathless.

It was as if he'd been a balloon filled with worry. His shoulders dropped as the tension eased off him. Relief relaxed his features, his mouth softening, his jaw loosening. I hadn't noticed he'd been that agitated while he waited for my answer. A thrilling feeling thrummed under my skin, making my heart pulse. I'd made Whitford Hayes nervous.

But he recovered quickly and grinned at me. "Does three days from now work for you?"

"Three days? Is that even possible?"

"Certainly not impossible." He tugged at his tousled hair. "Damn complicated, though."

"Tell me."

"We need a priest, a license, a church, and a witness," he said, listing each off with his fingers. "Then I'll need to submit notice to the British Consulate Office here in Cairo, where they'll notify the General Register Office in Britain."

I raised my brows. "You've spent quite a bit of time thinking about this." Unease settled deep in my belly. "Were you so sure I'd say yes?"

Whit hesitated. "I hoped you would. It was easier to dwell on the details than the possibility of a refusal."

"Details that have to be looked into while under my uncle's nose," I said. "We mustn't get caught."

"Like I said, damn complicated." Whit never lost his smile. "But we still have three days."

I held on to the edge of the table. I couldn't believe the direction my life was taking. Exhilaration made me breathless, but I couldn't help feeling that I was missing something. Papá always wished I'd slow down to pay attention to the details I constantly overlooked. I heard his dry voice in my mind, gently chiding.

When you're moving fast, hijita, it's easy to miss what's right in front of you.

But he wasn't here. I didn't know where he was, if he was even alive. My mother said my uncle had murdered my father, but she was a liar. He could be locked up somewhere, waiting for me to put the pieces of the puzzle together. I shoved my worry aside. There were other details needing my attention. Somehow, Whit and I had to sneak off to get married without anyone knowing.

Especially not my uncle.

"What do you need me to do?"

He sat back in the wicker chair, folded his hands across his flat belly, and grinned. "Why, what you do best, Inez." His expression was warm, half-amused, half-teasing. The smile said he knew me all too well. "I need you to be exactly where you shouldn't."

WHIT

This was, by far, one of the worst ideas I'd ever had.

The Khedivial Sporting Club loomed over me, a building designed in a European style, painted in bland colors and surrounded by lush palms and trees. Distaste coated my tongue, sour like wine years past its prime. Only British military and high-ranking English civil servants were allowed within. And while my name and title met requirements, I had—dishonorably—

lost my place in the military. Britain's disgraced son who wanted to remain that way.

No one would throw the doors open in welcome.

But I needed a priest, a church, a witness, and a license. In order for our marriage to have any credible weight, I'd have to ask someone inside for the last two items on my list. Someone I hadn't spoken to in months. Christ, a year? Time had moved in a crawling blur after I was discharged. He'd been my friend, and even though I'd pushed him away, I kept up with him whenever I could, not that he knew. His parents were ranchers from Bolivia, and they had sent him to live in England when he was only eight years old. He rarely talked about his family; he never stayed still long enough to have that kind of conversation. He liked to ride and he liked to drink. He shied away from gambling but risked his life almost daily.

Fast horses, front lines, and hard liquor.

But Leo Lopez never let me fight my fights alone, except that had been when I still had my reputation.

I pushed the wooden doors open and strode inside, a knot of tension blooming along my jawline. I unclenched my teeth, forced myself to wear an expression that didn't openly display my revulsion.

The foyer was as fine as any English drawing room, with plush chairs, expensive drapery, and patterned wallpaper. Swirls of cigar smoke cast the room in a hazy, warm glow, and the sound of boisterous chatter came at me from everywhere at once. Men dressed in tailored suits and polished shoes lounged across several alcoves of comfortable seating, low coffee tables, and potted greenery. It was my father's kind of establishment. A place to hobnob with the cream of society, rub elbows with the rich and landed, while bemoaning his needy wife and her penchant for pearls and gems. I could picture my father here, stone-cold sober, assessing weaknesses and waiting to strike. He'd use everything he learned at the table later.

The door swung shut behind me with an audible slam.

I knew the moment I was recognized.

A thick quiet settled over the room, choking all conversation. No one spoke for several heartbeats. It seemed I had greatly overestimated my charm.

"What the hell are you doing here?" a man asked, swaying slightly as he stood. I blinked against the stark red of his uniform. It seemed incredible that I had worn the same one for nearly seven years. His name came to me suddenly—Thomas something or other. He had a sweetheart in Liverpool and elderly parents who liked port after dinner.

"I'm looking for Leo," I said nonchalantly. "Have you seen him?"

Several others stood, their faces turning red.

"The sporting club is for *members* only."

"Not for bloody defectors," another shouted.

"For shame," cried one.

"I'm not staying," I said over the outraged exclamations. "I'm looking for—"

"Whit."

I turned toward a doorway leading into a narrow corridor. Leo slumped against the frame, shocked, as if he'd seen a ghost. He looked the same as the last time I'd seen him, the handsome bastard. Neat as a pin, shiny boots, pressed uniform. His black hair carefully combed back. I had no way of knowing what kind of welcome he'd give me.

"Leo, hello."

His eyes flickered over the room, expression blank, but I caught his understanding of the situation. I felt, rather than saw, several of the men pressing close, surrounding me. They looked between us, assessing our degree of familiarity. Leo opened his mouth, then closed it abruptly, a calculating gleam in his eyes. I recognized it at once—was I worth owing him a favor? I was a man without country, my name worse than a muddy puddle. But he knew I had a talent for collecting secrets. I gave him a rueful smile, arching a brow slightly. My chest tightened, air caught in my lungs. All he had to do was extend a hand and I could remain, if only for a few minutes. I waited to see what my friend would do.

Leo averted his gaze.

It was another sentencing.

Rough hands reached forward, tugging at my clothes, yanking me back toward the entrance. I offered no resistance, even as someone shoved at my shoulder and another kicked at my shins. Rage pulsed in my blood.

I held my hands up as I fought to quiet the beast roaring inside. The urge to defend myself nearly overwhelmed me. I could not give in to the impulse. They'd look for any excuse to drag my ass to the Cairo prison. I'd been there once, and I still recalled the vile stench, the oppressive weight of despair, the emaciated occupants. If I went inside, I'd never come back out. I knew that was exactly what they wanted.

Reckless Whit, losing his temper. Dishonorable Whit, attacking an officer.

If I reacted at all, any chance of marrying Inez would disappear.

And I needed to get married.

The officers dragged me to the front doors and threw me out. I landed hard on my hands and knees, the scrape of stone stinging my palms. I hauled myself to my feet as the men cheered and locked themselves away, singing merrily.

Bloody hell. Now what?

The sporting club was a short walk from the hotel. I shoved my hands deep into my pockets and retraced my steps, my mind clouded with useless ideas. Leo wouldn't see me—there went my witness. The army chaplain was out of the question, as was the license. Without that, I wouldn't be able to officially register the marriage in Britain.

Shit, shit, shit.

I walked one block, mind whirring. I wasn't on good terms with any of my other countrymen in Cairo. They were all dignitaries and diplomats, staunch imperialists who looked down their noses at men who couldn't follow orders.

Footsteps sounded behind me, someone racing down the path.

"Whit!"

I stopped and turned, barely catching my grin. My old friend, coming through after all. Leo stopped, his neat hair not so neat anymore.

"That was stupid," he said. "What possessed you?"

"I'm getting married," I said. "And it needs to be aboveboard and acknowledged by the right people."

His brows rose. "Christ. Should I congratulate you? Or offer condolences?"

I clapped my hand on his back. "Decide at the wedding—you'll be our witness."

I was in another bar.

We were fighting for twelve inches of space, the stretch of mahogany overtaken by dozens of patrons at Shepheard's famous establishment. Leo had insisted he knew where to find the army chaplain, one Henry Poole, who apparently liked his beer pale and bountiful. When he dragged me back to Shepheard's, the image of my future wife swam across my mind, clear as if she were standing before me. Dark curls that wouldn't be tamed, alchemical eyes shining gold, lit by an insatiable curiosity. She was probably plotting sneaking out of the hotel without her uncle noticing. Even now, she could be learning Ricardo's schedule or asking for the aid of an employee.

One never knew when it came to Inez.

"Buy him another before asking," Leo said in Spanish from out of the corner of his mouth.

I flicked my gaze in his direction. How did he know I learned Spanish? While in the military, I had learned some phrases but nothing like how I spoke or understood the language now. It seemed like I wasn't the only one who had kept tabs.

He took a sip of his drink and shrugged noncommittally. Then he jerked his chin in the direction of the army chaplain. He stood at my elbow, a smile tugging at his mouth as he took in the riotous scene in the lavish space. I'd been here before, many times, often on a job for Ricardo. Many people came by the famous watering hole, intent on a good time and not much else.

Henry leaned forward and shouted his order for all three of us at the bartender, who nodded briskly while also taking the order of half a dozen other people. I admired the competent multitasking. The chaplain glanced over, grinning. I got the sense he didn't have too many friends and was eager for camaraderie. I had expected him to be stodgy, uptight, and ill-humored.

But he was jovial and chatty—truly bizarre for a Briton—and nearly drunk. He smiled too much and was the too-trusting sort, poor sod. The bartender pushed three more glasses toward us, filled to the brim, and I hesitated.

I had drunk two already.

"Is the gun absolutely necessary?" The chaplain hiccupped. "We aren't in any danger here, surely."

"I never go anywhere without it," I said.

Leo bent and stuck his nose close to the weapon attached to my hip. "You still have his revolver? After all this time?"

"Whose?" Henry asked, eyeing it with interest.

"General Gordon's," Leo said in a hushed voice, before raising his glass in a solemn salute.

"*The* General Gordon?" Henry asked in an awed whisper. "That's *his* gun?"

I nodded tightly, reaching for the glass. Without another thought, I took a long drag of the liquor.

"But how did you get it?" the chaplain sputtered. "I heard he was decapitated—"

"Another round?" Leo broke in.

"We just got our drinks," Henry protested.

"Something tells me we'll want another," Leo said, with an uneasy glance in my direction. He knew the full history of my disreputable time in the military, of course. I had been thrown out, with no time to say my piece or my goodbyes to the rest of them. Not that I cared—except, perhaps at times, for the way I had disappeared on Leo.

But even then, I had a feeling he would have understood, despite never being able to publicly take my side. It didn't matter anymore, because he was here now.

"Bottoms up, as they say," Henry said, between hiccups.

We raised our glasses. In for a penny, in for a pound.

As they say.

What bloody time was it? Leo's face blurred in front of me. The singing had gotten louder. Lord, *so loud.* But I had won us more inches at the bar. Victory.

"Didn't you have to ask Henry something?" Leo roared in my ear.

"Jesus," I said, wincing.

He laughed, face red, not neat anymore.

Henry went to the other end of the bar, then came back with more beer. He always had more beer. He must have been made of it.

"I need to get married!" I yelled.

"What?" Henry bellowed.

"I NEED TO GET MARRIED!" I bellowed back. "WILL YOU DO THE HONORS?"

He blinked, slopped his beer over the rim as he laid a hand on my shoulder. "'Course! I *hate* funerals."

"This calls for whiskey," Leo said, then he let out a soft, rueful laugh. "*More* whiskey," he amended.

Relief cut through the fog blanketing my mind. I had a chaplain. I had a priest.

And I would have Inez.

Thank Christ.

I raised my glass and embraced oblivion.

The lobby was quiet by the time we stumbled out of the bar. Leo made it a couple of feet before having to lean against one of the immense granite pillars. My limbs felt loose, but my mind was steeped in a thick haze, making every one of my thoughts hard to grasp.

"He said he was going to do it?" I asked, trying to recall the chaplain's exact words. He had left an hour ago. Maybe longer. I had stopped looking at the wooden clock inside.

Leo nodded and then winced. "Don't you remember screaming that you were getting married?"

"What? No." That would have been extremely stupid—no one was supposed to know of our plans. Anyone could go back to the well-known Ricardo Marqués with the news.

"You were congratulated by nearly everyone inside," he remarked. I stood a few paces from him, but even so, I could smell the hard liquor on his breath.

Even as the room spun, a feeling of unease rose. I swallowed down the taste of acid coating my tongue. We watched in silence as a parade of patrons exited the bar, some upright, others swaying, and a few who had to be carried out by friends. I was reasonably proud I was having no trouble remaining upright.

"Turn back," Leo said suddenly, his eyes fixed on a large crowd loitering not ten feet from us.

I instinctively hid behind the pillar, away from the bar entrance. I peered at the group.

"Stop," Leo hissed.

But it was too late—I'd already seen my former captain. Judging by the way he glared at my friend, it was quite clear he had seen the pair of us drinking—he might have even seen his chaplain with us.

Leo whistled sharply, and I heard several people draw near, laughing, talking loudly. I walked around the pillar, astounded to find my friend surrounded by soldiers. Several of whom had bought me rounds of whiskey. I knew Leo hoped to use their bulk to shield me from the captain's observant gaze, but it didn't work.

He approached, and the soldiers straightened, some scampering off to the hotel entrance. His decorated uniform showed off rows of ribbons and brass pins that shone brightly in the candlelight flickering around the room. The captain's light eyes moved over me, assessing, his lips tight in disapproval. He took in my dusty boots and wrinkled shirt. My too-long hair and the alcohol on my breath.

"Whitford," he said. "I heard you stopped by the club."

It seemed best to keep my mouth shut.

"You're still working for Ricardo," he said. "Does he know you're planning on marrying his niece?"

The blood drained from my face.

"I didn't think so," he said with a cold smile. "You're exactly the same, Whitford." He shook his head, contempt stamped across his stern features. "Your father deserved better." His attention turned toward Leo, who was still using the pillar to remain standing. "I'll see you in the morning."

He walked away, shoulders straight, back stiff.

Thunder roared in my ears. "How did he know it was Ricardo's niece?"

Leo let out a crack of laughter. "You said so in the bar, idiot."

For fuck's sake. There was no help for it now—Inez and I would have to marry sooner. If there was anyone who wanted to mess up my life, it would be the man who reported me to the military judge.

It was only after I said goodbye to Leo that I felt someone watching from the top of the stairs. I tipped my head back, mouth dry, eyes blurring. I stumbled on the first step and barely managed to stay upright. The figure looked familiar.

It took a minute for the shape to crystallize, the lines becoming sharper. It was a young woman, her expression hard to read. It might have been incredulous horror. She turned, walking briskly away, tying the sash of her dressing gown tight around her slim waist. Dark curls swaying around her shoulders. I recognized her at last.

Inez.

CAPÍTULO DOS

The sight of Whit drunk had speared me through. I paced my hotel room, hands flapping, wondering at what I'd seen and what it meant. I had gone to look at other exits, hoping to find another way out of Shepheard's other than the main entrance that everyone used, and had seen him standing in a crowd of *soldiers*. Something I'd never thought was possible, given how he felt about his time in the militia. Not to mention what *I* personally felt about them. But there he had been, smiling easily, staggering a little, and clearly enjoying himself. Then he spoke to someone of rank, dressed in a decorated uniform, and the sight had turned my stomach.

I couldn't make sense of it.

Whit wanted nothing to do with the military. That's what he had led me to believe. He didn't want any reminders of what had happened, and so I could hardly see him engaging in a pleasant chat. And why would any British soldier or captain engage in conversation with one of theirs who had been dishonorably discharged?

I'd left the balcony doors open, needing fresh air. The moon showed her face, the night still and quiet. I ought to have climbed into bed, but my heart pounded hard against my ribs. There was a time when I couldn't trust Whitford Hayes. When I'd believed the worst of him. But he'd shown me a hidden side of himself, and I'd had to adjust my earlier assumptions.

He made me feel safe.

Except when I saw the way he was tonight, drunk and merry with the militia, a niggling sense of dread wound its way through my heart.

What if I'd been right about him all along?

"Wake up, Inez."

I shifted under the sheets, blinking against the pillow. That had sounded like Whit. I turned, squinting through the heavy gauze of the mosquito netting. It *was* Whit.

"Look who's being inappropriate now," I said when I could find my voice.

Usually that might have earned me an amused smile or even a chuckle. But Whit's blurry frame remained silent and motionless.

"What time is it?" I asked.

"Early," came his curt voice. "Will you come out of there?"

"Something tells me I'm not going to like what you're going to say."

"Probably not."

I sighed as my stomach tightened into unruly knots. Whit pulled the mosquito netting aside, and I murmured a quiet thank-you as I slipped out from under the bedding. My nightgown was loose and long, and I tugged at it, self-conscious and shy. Whit held himself back, his expression remote and guarded. He was wearing the same clothes as the night before. He smelled like whiskey, cloves, and peat in a swirl of smoke. I wondered if he had seen his bed, or if he had stayed up with his soldier friends the rest of the night.

"I saw you in the lobby."

A muscle in his jaw ticked. "I know."

"Who were those men?"

Whit shrugged. "No one of import."

I tipped my head to the side, considering. Obviously, they were in the militia, and he had clearly known them. What I ought to have asked was why he went out drinking with them, when he was presumably busy with the preparations for our wedding. I had barely seen him since he had laid out exactly what he wanted me to do. His own to-do list had been extensive. He had made it seem like it would take a miracle to pull off a wedding in such a short period of time, all while keeping it from my uncle.

"Have you slept?"

Whit waved off my question. I took a step closer, noted the spidery red veins in his bloodshot eyes and the line of tension in his clenched jaw. His usually clean-shaven face had not seen a razor in the last twenty-four hours. Once again, I felt a prick of alarm. He seemed tense and nervous.

He was going to call off the wedding. I was sure of it.

He'd made a mistake asking—it was too reckless, an idea that should never have been spoken aloud. He was going to tell me that he agreed with my uncle, that it was for the best that I leave Egypt, and then I'd have to find someone else. People married for convenience all the time, surely. There had to be—

"We have to get married today."

I blinked. "*¿Qué?*"

He crossed his arms. "It has to be today. Too many people could interfere, get a hold of your uncle, and tell him of our plans."

My mind reeled. "But—"

"I have our witness and someone to marry us. But I need to work on securing the license." He went on as if I weren't floundering in deep water, trying to stay afloat. "Were you able to find a way out of Shepheard's?"

"Yes," I said. "I don't have a dress. It has to be today?"

"If I can get the license, then yes. Meet me at the Hanging Church when the sun goes down."

Whit turned to go and I reached for him, but he'd already crossed the room and was at the door.

"How did you get inside my room?" I asked. "I have the key."

"I nicked the spare from downstairs," he said over his shoulder. "The hotel security is appalling."

"Whit—"

"I have to go," he said hurriedly and was gone. Gone before I could get another word in, gone before I could ask him why he wasn't acting like himself, before I could demand that he *look* at me. Just once.

I stood motionless, overwhelmed and terrified. It was as if I could already feel the swaying of the boat under my feet, dragging me back home.

I wore black to my wedding, and if I were feeling sentimental, I'd let myself think of the moment when I first laid eyes on Whit, while wearing the same exact dress. But that awful raw feeling of terror clung to me like a shroud, and I could think of nothing but Whit's aloof manner earlier. I fingered the only adornment I'd chosen to wear, Mamá's brightly patterned shrinking scarf. I had thought about leaving it behind, but it gave me a reminder of why I was getting married in the first place.

I would not allow my mother to win.

A sharp yell yanked me from my thoughts. A carriage driver had narrowly avoided hitting a stray dog barking happily at several children playing in front of a small market stall. Barrels of spices scented the air: paprika, cumin, and turmeric. Next door stood Harraz, a store specializing in herbs and fragrances, where many Egyptians and tourists strolled among the varied offerings. They all came out smelling of essential oils, and I itched to sample a few for myself, but I didn't have the time. I waited for Whit at the street corner in front of the church, entertained by watching the proceedings of daily Cairo life. No one spared a glance at the widow standing alone at the end of the street corner. I had slipped through the front entrance of Shepheard's in my disguise with a confidence that I didn't feel in the slightest as the minutes dragged.

Whit was late. Very late.

The sun lowered, cool air settling over the city as the sky gradually darkened. The sound of the evening prayer rose high in the night. I usually found it comforting, but it only served as a reminder that the person I was marrying hadn't arrived.

A part of me doubted he'd show up at all.

Maybe he hadn't been able to secure the license; maybe my uncle found out about our plans and was now, in this moment, confronting Whit. A thousand reasons and explanations swam in my mind, all of them viable possibilities. But there was one reason that sat heavy in my stomach, an indigestible lump, one that shared the space with my worst fears.

Whit was just another person in my life who could easily walk away from me.

I shifted on my feet and tried not to think the worst. Except it kept rising in my mind like steam, making the back of my neck damp with sweat. Whit might have changed his mind. For the first time in my life, I wished for a pocket watch. I'd give him a few more minutes before heading back to the hotel, and in my head, I began to count seconds. By the time I'd gotten over five hundred, I finally faced the truth.

He wasn't coming.

My feet seemed to move of their own accord as I slowly began the walk back to the hotel. What was I going to do now? I thought about using my mother's scarf to shrink me down to nothing, except the magic probably wouldn't work on humans. I went to cross the street, when I heard a shout and realized with a start that someone was yelling my name.

"Olivera!"

A familiar frame appeared at the end of the path, hands stuffed deep into his pockets. Relief stole over me as he drew closer, feeling like a balm over an aching wound. I let out a shaky breath as I took in his features. Whit seemed lighter somehow, less encumbered. Hope dug its way into my heart, a determined weed.

He stopped in front of me.

"Hello," I said cautiously.

Whit grinned and pulled out a single sheet of paper. "I got it."

"The license?" I asked. "Someone actually gave us permission to marry?"

He nodded and then reached for me, tugging me close. "I didn't think we'd pull this off, Inez." One of his arms braced my lower back, and a warm feeling spread down to my toes. The soft linen of his shirt brushed against my temple and I heard his steady heartbeat under my cheek.

"Why are you shaking?" he whispered against my hair.

"I didn't think you were coming," I whispered back.

Whit moved me far enough away that he could gaze down into my face. "Why on earth would you think that?"

"You were distant earlier," I said. "It didn't feel like we were in this together. And when I saw you last night in the lobby, I worried about what it meant."

"I had to ask a friend for a favor," he said, wincing. "And I got carried away acting a part." He used his index finger to tip my chin upward. "I wouldn't change my mind about marrying you, Inez."

"This is probably a terrible idea," I said. "Isn't it?"

"Yes," he said softly. "But the best option we have, right?"

He was correct, but I hated how it sounded like it was our last resort. I glanced down at our attires. Neither of us was dressed for celebration. I wasn't wearing a new gown, with ribbons and ruffles, or enough jewelry to make me glitter like a far-off constellation. The fabric of my clothing felt heavy and cloying. I was dressed for mourning. And perhaps, a part of me did grieve. I had always thought my wedding day would be under blue skies, inside the church I knew like the palm of my hand, and followed by a lavish breakfast. Surrounded by my parents and extended family, my favorite cousin, Elvira, at my side.

But my cousin was dead, my father was still missing, and my mother was a thief.

We approached the ancient church constructed above the gatehouse of a Roman-built Babylon fortress. Whit led the way, wearing another wrinkled navy shirt tucked into his khaki pants. He hadn't changed his shoes. His lace-up boots went up his calf, and they were dusty and well-worn. His face bore the marks of our time in the tomb—a bruise had bloomed across his cheek; a shallow gash followed the line of his scruffy jaw. And his eyes were still bloodshot.

I'd done reckless things in my life, but getting married in a secret ceremony surpassed them all. I tried not to think about what Tío Ricardo and Tía Lorena would say if they could see me now. But I heard their admonishments anyway.

Thoughtless. Foolish. Rash.

At least I was taking charge of my own life. Making a decision that allowed me to do what I wanted, even if it might be a mistake. If it was, I'd find a way through. I always did. I could, at least, trust myself enough to know what I wanted.

And that was to stay in Egypt—however possible.

"Do you know why it's called the Hanging Church?" Whit said, jarring me from my thoughts. He pointed through the iron gates situated under a pointed arched roof and to the twenty-nine steps leading up to the carved wooden door. "The nave is suspended over a passageway."

"It's lovely," I said, my attention arrested by the twin bell towers flanking the arabesque entrance. It would have looked beautiful adorned in flowers and satin ribbons.

Whit strode forward, and I followed, my heart slamming against my ribs with every step we took in unison. Together we climbed, and then he pulled the heavy door open. He tossed a glance over his shoulder, meeting my gaze swiftly. His expression was unreadable in the dying light of the day. The spread of purple light swept across the sky as the evening prayer rose higher into the burgeoning night.

"Are you ready?" he asked, his voice quiet.

"Am I ready?" I repeated. "No. I can't believe we're about to do this. Ten minutes ago, you were going to marry someone else. Five minutes ago, I didn't think you were coming. But now you're marrying *me*, and we're here. When we walk through that door, this silly idea will become real. My mind feels fuzzy all of a sudden. Does your mind feel fuzzy?"

Whit let the door swing shut. His chin dropped, his attention straying to the toes of his boots. When he lifted his face again, his expression was carefully neutral. He contemplated me in the dusky light and seemed to come to a decision. "We don't have to do this, Inez. We can walk back to Shepheard's and pretend—"

"But then what?" My voice turned shrill. "Tío Ricardo still controls my fortune. I have nothing, not even a place to sleep. I must vacate the room on the tenth of January. By the way, it's the *ninth* of January, in case it's escaped your notice."

"You'll think of something," Whit said, grinning. But the smile didn't quite meet his eyes. "You always do."

"I'm tired of trying to plan six moves ahead. Pretending to be a widow and lying to my aunt so I could come to Egypt, sneaking out of the hotel *twice*, and then stowing away on the *Elephantine*—"

His voice was kind, his fist still closed around the door handle. "Olivera, I know."

"I don't have another option," I continued. "And I need to stay in Egypt. My mother—"

Whit released the handle and stepped closer. He placed his hands on my shoulders, bending his knees so that he could meet my eyes. His breath brushed against my mouth. "Sweetheart, I *know*."

The endearment felt like a soft touch, smoothing away the knot of tension pressing against my temples. He rarely used them—only when I was inconsolable or in mortal peril. His nearness overwhelmed my senses. This towering man would be my husband—if I wanted. It seemed incredible, impossible. Excitement pulsed in my blood. I wanted Whit, but I also wanted control of my life. Saying yes to Whit meant my uncle could no longer dictate my plans, my future. It meant I could stay in Egypt.

No more planning. No more stratagems. That kind of behavior reminded me of my mother. And I didn't want to be her; I didn't want to inherit something that could hurt so many people. And suddenly, I remembered that I already had.

All my machinations had led to Elvira's death.

Someone else had pulled the trigger, but it was *me* she had followed.

More than anything, I wanted to atone for my behavior. I wanted to stop my mother from selling off artifacts that had belonged to Cleopatra. I wanted to discover what happened to my father. I was filled with so much tangible yearning, each a weight on my shoulders, pressing me down into the earth. All that *want* threatened to bury me alive.

Unless I did something about it.

"Talk to me," Whit whispered. "What are you thinking?"

I shook my head, trying to focus on the here and now. On the man who stood in front of me. Sometimes, I could read him easily. When our hearts connected, and for a moment, we saw the world the same way. But more often than not, I barely understood him. I still didn't know why *he* wanted to marry *me*.

A term of endearment was just a noun and not a promise.

"I have my reasons for doing this," I whispered. "What are yours?"

He took a step back, nodding, as if he'd expected the question. His words from the day before still rang in my ear. The weight of them, said in his deep baritone, in his smooth and aristocratic accent. The breadth of his shoulders tight and sharp, his hands trembling. He had been nervous when he'd said them.

Marry me instead.

That had been then. Now that I stood before the church, I wasn't sure I had fully understood the permanence of my decision. Marriage meant forever—or at least, I wanted it to mean forever. I studied Whit, who had gone stone-still, visibly weighing his answer.

He tucked his hands deep into his pockets.

"Proposing to you was my choice and no one else's," he said. "In the utter chaos of my life, you are the only thing that makes sense. You asked me what my reasons are, and I don't know all of them yet, but I do know one important thing." He took a shaky breath, his eyes never leaving my face, and the raw emotion lurking in their depths almost keeled me over. "You're the one I want, Inez."

My lips parted.

His voice dropped to a husky whisper. "Please make me the happiest man on this earth."

And the planet tilted again, off-kilter. The ground seemed to shift under my feet, and my knees buckled. Whitford Hayes was a multifaceted prism, and I thought I had seen every side. The outrageous flirt with his equally outrageous winks, the soldier loyal to his general, the drunk with red-rimmed eyes and a flask hidden in his pocket, the adventurer who knew how to handle dynamite, the man who loved Egypt, and the brother who adored his only sister.

But I'd never seen his raw vulnerability.

That side of him left me breathless.

"Is that enough for you?" he prodded.

"Yes," I breathed.

Whit nodded, solemn and grimly determined. Sweat beaded at his hairline, and it occurred to me that he might still be nervous. He might be trying to appear calm and reassuring for my sake, but on the inside, maybe his heart was beating just as fast as mine.

He opened the door and held out his hand. I didn't hesitate, taking it with a small smile, feeling I could take on my uncle and my mother and my aunt and anyone else who stood in my way.

We walked through.

CAPÍTULO TRES

The inside of the church was even more beautiful than the exterior. At the foot of the grand room stood an altar, and beyond, lotus-shaped inlaid wooden panels decorated the walls. Three aisles divided up the space with rows and rows of wooden pews. And on the eastern end, there were three sanctuaries tucked nearly out of sight. Automatically, I began moving in that direction, curious to see the elaborate screens adorned in ebony and ivory.

Whit hooked his arm around my elbow, swinging me toward him.

"The art caught my eye," I explained. "I just want a closer look at the pattern. Perhaps I'll bring my sketchbook next ti—"

Amusement creased the corner of his eyes. "Have you forgotten why we are here?"

"Of *course* not. I was only curious—"

"Inez."

"Whit."

"We have to move quickly," he said, exasperated. "Before anyone notices we're gone. Because we're *secretly getting married*."

I grinned, and he smiled. We might have been back on Philae, examining the ancient reliefs on the walls, drinking terrible coffee, and getting our hands dirty.

"The chaplain is waiting," Whit added. "And where's . . . oh." He let out a forceful sigh. "Let me just go wake him up."

He strode off and I watched in bemusement as he approached an empty pew. No, not empty. There was a pair of boots hanging off the edge. Whit leaned forward and knocked them with his knee.

"Leo," he said. "Wake up."

I came to stand next to him and peered down at the sleeping man. His dark wavy hair flopped onto his brow, making him look quite young. I would have placed him a few years younger than Whit except for one thing: his mouth, even while reposed, was hard-edged and sardonic. He was dressed in a gleaming red coat—with a start, I realized I'd seen him before. It was one of Whit's soldiers from last night.

"Leo," Whit said again, this time raising his voice a notch.

Said Leo let out a symphonic snore.

"Typical. I can always count on him for all manner of dangerous activities, but if it's something tame? He can't be bothered to remain upright. Or awake," Whit added in disgust. "Right. Let's leave him."

"Who is he exactly?"

"Our witness."

"Ah. Shouldn't he be awake for the ceremony?"

"I think the important thing is that he's here. Come on; the sooner we're back at the hotel, the better."

I nodded. "Lead the way."

Whit kept a hold on my arm as he did so, as if he was afraid I'd wander from his sight. He called out a greeting to a man waiting at the front of the church. He was young, with a mop of brown hair and a genial smile on his face. He had kind eyes, and in his hands, he carried an old, leather-bound Bible, opened near the back of the book. But instead of looking at the holy scripture, he peered at me. He wore a long pale robe that brushed against the stone floor.

"Good evening, miss," he said as we reached him. "Before we begin, I suppose I ought to ask if you're in trouble." His voice was whisper soft. Great windows lined the sturdy wooden pews and soft light made patterned shapes across our faces, casting us in a silver glow. Candles were lit on the altar, wispy curls of smoke rising in beckoning circles.

I shook my head. "No trouble. Why?"

The chaplain cast an amused smile over to Whit. "Well . . . this is highly unusual. For one thing, where is your family? Your attendants? A maid?" He squinted. "Are you in mourning? And shouldn't a bride have flowers?"

I was about to say none of that mattered—the missing family, my black dress. But his last question robbed me of breath, and I was unprepared for the wave of sadness that washed over me. "I would have loved flowers," I whispered.

Whit glanced at me, brow puckering.

But then the chaplain spoke again, distracting me with his next words. "The groom has also brought a gun to his wedding."

My husband-to-be was armed? I rounded on him. "Whitford Hayes, you will *not* be married with a gun attached at your hip."

He laughed, removing the revolver from its holster. The familiar initials winked back at me in the soft lighting. He held it up, as if in surrender, and set it on one of the pews.

"An egregious oversight," Whit said, sounding so much like his usual self that I couldn't help but smile. "He's still waiting for your answer to his question."

"What question? Oh! Right, yes." I licked my lips. "This is my decision."

The chaplain nodded. "Then we can begin. Have you thought about your vows?"

I blinked. I hadn't given much thought to the wedding other than arriving at the church in secret. It had been hard to evade Tío Ricardo's notice. It was only after pretending to have a miserable headache that I was able to rush out of Shepheard's.

"Yes," Whit said.

"Vows?" I asked, the sanctuary growing warmer by the second.

"Well, I'm not going to write them for you," the chaplain said with a laugh. He made the sign of the cross and launched into a lengthy speech about the responsibilities of marriage. I was too focused on coming up with my vows to pay attention. Worry skittered across my skin. This was my wedding day, the only wedding day I'd ever have in my life. It wasn't what I expected or ever imagined. If nothing else, I wanted my promise to Whit to be perfect. Because one day, we could forget what the church looked like, what we wore, or maybe even the priest himself.

But I wanted to remember what I said next.

Somehow, I knew the words would stay with me for the rest of my life.

I wrung my hands and began to pace, going up and down the path before the altar, circling around the priest and Whit, and then down one of the three aisles. Dimly, I heard the chaplain's voice trail off into a long pause before asking Whit if he ought to continue.

"She's processing, but please continue until it's time for the vows," Whit said, amused. "She'll come back eventually."

"Er . . . right, then." The chaplain cleared his throat and continued in a soft drone.

I spoke out loud, sometimes in a whisper, sometimes mumbling, as I agonized over every word. The chaplain tried to follow along with my ramblings but eventually gave up. He sat in one of the pews and quietly read his Bible as I worked through my vows. Leo continued to snore, the sound echoing off the stone walls. Whit watched my progress up and down the aisle with a slight smile on his face, and when I came to stand by him again, I knew what I was going to say.

"Have you finished, then?" the chaplain asked, coming to his feet. He resumed his former position in front of the altar, the Bible propped open.

I faced Whit and took his hands in mine. I lifted my chin and held his gaze steady with mine. "I'm ready."

Leo woke with a loud groan and sat up, his head and shoulders the only thing visible from where I stood. Whit half turned. "Kind of you to join us, idiot."

Leo blinked, gazing around the church, and his sleepy eyes focused on me. "Have I missed it, then?"

"Not entirely," Whit said dryly.

"You may say your vows," the chaplain prodded. Leo stood, swaying slightly, and came to stand behind us. His presence made me curious. This was someone from Whit's past life, and a thousand questions burned at the back of my throat. I wanted to ask him every single one of them, uncover every detail about the Whit I never knew. The soldier and estranged son. Devoted brother and loyal friend.

"Stop thinking about everything you want to ask him," Whit said. "You'll have time to ask your questions after the ceremony."

"How on earth did you know what I was thinking?"

"Because I know you." He raised his brows. "Your vows?"

"Right." I cleared my throat. "Whitford Hayes, I will honor and protect you but only obey you if you're being reasonable. Actually, you might expect me not to obey you at all. It goes against my nature, and I'd prefer to begin marriage by being honest." His lips twitched in response. Fortified, I pressed on. "I will be faithful, and I will respect you—unless you do something unworthy of it, then God help you." I thought Whit would laugh, but he remained silent. "In sickness and in health, I will be yours for all the days of my life."

Whit licked his lips, his face pale in the candlelight. "Inez, I will honor and protect you and lay down my life for you. In sickness and in health, I will be by your side." He gave me a faint smile. "And I promise I will never expect obedience from you."

"Do either of you have rings to exchange?"

I looked at the chaplain in bemusement. "Rings?"

"It is customary," the chaplain helpfully explained, as if I didn't know.

But I had come to the church not knowing if Whit would show up. The matter of the rings had never occurred to me.

"We have none," Whit said.

"No? Oh well; I think it gives the situation a sense of pomp and ceremony." Whit rolled his eyes, and the chaplain hastily added, "I pronounce you man and wife." The chaplain grinned. "You may kiss the bride."

I startled, somehow forgetting what happened at the close of the ceremony. The last time we'd kissed, we thought we were going to die within an abandoned tomb. Whit leaned down and brushed his mouth against mine. I tried to memorize the moment, to capture the warmth of his lips, the almost tender look in his blue gaze. But he pulled away only after a second and then thanked the chaplain, while I stood reeling from what we had just done.

"Congratulations," Whit's friend said to me. "I'm Leo."

"I heard," I said, looking him over. He was tall and lean, with disheveled black hair and shrewd dark eyes set under stern, thick brows. His look gave the impression of a grumpy raven, impatient to take flight. "And thank you."

"You have family in Bolivia," he commented.

"Yes," I said, surprised. "How did you—" I broke off, remembering where I had first seen him. And with whom. "Whit told you."

Leo nodded. "My parents are from Santa Cruz."

But he spoke with a crisp English accent, and he fought for them, too. I opened my mouth to ask but he cut me off.

"It's a long story, and worse, it's a boring one." He looked at me curiously, and I fidgeted under his scrutiny. "You're not what I expected."

"What were you expecting?"

Leo smiled. "I pictured a demure English lady with loads of money, I'm afraid. Covered in gemstones and gleaming pearls. Wearing a pastel dress."

"Oh," I said. "How strange."

"Not really," he said, frowning slightly. "I just described his former betrothed." His expression cleared. "Don't mistake me—I'm happy he married you instead. It's just that I never thought he'd actually cut them off."

"Cut who off?"

"His parents," Leo explained. Then he reached for my hand and kissed it, before tugging Whit off to the side. They exchanged whispers back and forth, Leo gesturing wildly. Whit stood with his arms crossed, attention fixed on his boots. Whatever his friend was telling him, he didn't like it in the slightest. My curiosity nearly overwhelmed me, but I forced myself to not interfere. Leo's parting words swam in my mind.

I knew Whit hadn't wanted to marry the woman his parents had chosen for him, and subconsciously, I knew that his parents would be displeased with his marriage to me. But I hadn't realized Whit would be cutting his parents out of his life. I had been raised to value familial bonds that were governed by loyalty, and yet my time in Egypt had taught me that the human heart was quick to change. I couldn't trust or depend on my mother, despite her being my mother.

Finally, Leo turned to go; the chaplain was waiting for him by one of the pews. Leo called over his shoulder, "You owe me, Somerset."

Whit nodded and watched him leave, expression carefully blank. Then he glanced at me, the lines around his eyes softening. He walked toward me, holding out his hand. I took it, feeling the familiar calluses and rough palm. We trailed after Leo and the chaplain, unease making my breath hitch oddly. There was so much about him I still didn't know, didn't understand. I hoped I hadn't made the biggest mistake of my life. Then Whit tucked a strand of my curly hair behind my ear, and the tension seeped out of me. I remembered everything I loved about him. He made me laugh, and he was loyal. He would honor his promise to me. I was sure of it. I'd made the right decision.

We were married.

Married.

CAPÍTULO CUATRO

Scores of people crowded Shepheard's terrace, dining out in the cool open air, their conversation reaching us where we stood at the bottom of the hotel steps. Night had settled over Cairo, the stars glimmering like the ones I'd seen painted on the ceiling of the tombs we'd found in Philae. The air had turned crisp while we were *getting married*—a jolt went through me—and the breeze swept through the street, coming from the Nile River. It was a perfect winter evening in Egypt, the temperature cool enough for my heavy black dress. Whit's gaze flickered over the swell of well-heeled travelers deep into their cups, his lips flattening.

"What is it?" I asked.

"We'll have to somehow sneak inside without bumping into Ricardo. He won't appreciate seeing us together, and we've been gone for hours now."

"He ought to be recovering in bed."

Whit slanted me an amused look. "You're more like your uncle than you think."

I placed a hand on my hip. "How so?"

"Would you let an injury stop you?"

"It depends on the injury. He was shot, after all." I pulled at my bottom lip. "But probably not," I admitted.

"It must run in the family," he said with a laugh. "He told me that he was going to try to make it for dinner. Ten to one he's by the front desk right now, swaying on his feet and trying to hold a conversation. Bandage and all."

Whit and I walked side by side through the front doors, taking advantage of the swelling crowd in the lobby. But not two steps inside, I spotted my uncle. He stood scowling at several gentlemen, waving one of his hands around, clearly frustrated. He must have been in tremendous pain but somehow managed to still appear intimidating. I nudged Whit's side, hard, and loudly cleared my throat.

He let out a grunt. "A whisper would have sufficed."

"*Look*."

"I saw him before you did. I was just less dramatic."

"He looks upset."

"Well, he is bleeding all over the Turkish rug."

I gasped. Sure enough, blood stained my uncle's cotton shirt, spreading outward in a gruesome fashion. He should be in bed, and someone ought to bring him a bowl of soup or, at the very least, change his soiled bandage. But no, his voice boomed, ricocheting loudly, and he seemed unaware that he had reopened his wound. My uncle excelled at starting arguments. I took an instinctive step forward, but Whit yanked me behind one of the immense granite pillars, fashioned after the famous ones in Karnak.

"He doesn't appear to be in the best mood right now," Whit whisper-yelled. "And he specifically asked you to stay in your room and pack up all your shit."

"*Whit*," I said reproachfully.

"Belongings," Whit amended, his lips twitching. "You have so many belongings."

He pulled me closer until I was flush with the long line of his body, and I let out a protest. He looked down at me, a sardonic curve to the blunt edge of his mouth.

"I'm not going to ravish you against this column, Olivera. I just don't want you to be seen."

My cheeks flooded with heat. "I knew that."

He winked. "Sure you did, my little innocent."

"This is hardly the moment for teasing."

He took my hand. "Let's make a go for it."

"If Tío Ricardo sees us, he'll make a scene," I warned. "Your hearing will never be the same."

He peered into the crowd. My uncle stood in the dead center, as if by some instinct he knew he needed to position himself within easy reach of the grand staircase. But at least he faced the lobby entrance, his back turned to where we needed to go.

"Do what I do, and don't do anything so stupid as to trip or faint."

"I have never fainted in my life," I said in my haughtiest voice.

He pulled me around the pillar, and we slowly walked through the crowd. Whit kept a careful eye on my uncle, and I kept a careful watch on my husband.

Husband.

I swore I'd never get used to it.

Whit stopped abruptly, motioning for me to stay behind him. We stood alongside a group of four Egyptian businessmen, their tall tarbooshes concealing Whit's towering height. They puffed on their cigars, discussing cotton prices. Through the gaps, I caught my uncle's feverish gaze roaming the room. He looked so terrible with his hollowed-out cheeks and red-rimmed eyes that I wanted to usher him up the stairs myself. But then I recalled his demand that I leave the country posthaste.

My sympathy soured.

Whit squeezed my hand, and we moved forward, darting and ducking around the room as if we were game pieces on a massive chessboard. One step forward there, two steps to the side here. After taking a moment to hide behind an enormous potted plant with leaves that plumed outward like a broom, we finally reached the foot of the stairs. Whit peered down the corridor leading to the dining room.

"I'll return shortly," he said before running down the hall.

I gaped after him, scrambling behind a voluminous curtain obscuring an arched window. I peered around the thick embroidered fabric in time to see my uncle drop into a leather seat in one of the alcoves. He leaned forward and retrieved a discarded newspaper and idly ruffled through the pages.

I snapped the curtain around me, breathing hard. Where had Whit gone? And did he really need to run an errand that precise moment? Couldn't it have wait—

"I can see the toes of your boots," came an amused voice. Whit swept the curtain aside. In his left hand, he carried a bottle in the deepest green, a shade that reminded me of Elvira's eyes when she was furious. I took a closer look and corrected myself. He carried an *expensive* bottle of Veuve Clicquot champagne from 1841. Grinning, we made our escape to the upper floor, but all I could think about was that I walked beside my *husband*.

We belonged to each other now.

I snuck a glance in his direction, sure I'd imagined the whole evening. His auburn hair that couldn't decide if it was red or brown, the strong line of his shoulders, and his blue eyes that were sometimes serious, sometimes mischievous, sometimes bloodshot.

Whit threw me a sidelong look. "We make a good team, Olivera."

"It hardly seems real," I murmured as we reached the third floor.

"And yet here we are." Whit took my hand, his warm palm grazing mine, and I shivered. "Regretting me already?"

"Ask me again tomorrow."

We reached my hotel door, and I stared at it dumbly, only just realizing the part that came *after* a wedding. Whit leaned against the frame, his gaze drifting from my face down to my toes. He'd never looked at me so thoroughly. I felt naked beneath his study. We were still holding hands, but neither of us moved to reach for the handle.

"We rushed getting married," he said softly. "We don't have to rush tonight."

My cheeks flooded with color, and I shifted my feet, thinking hard. There were practical reasons to consider. There could be no room to undo what we had done. If there was a weakness in our plan, my uncle would sniff it out. "When we tell my uncle about what we did," I said slowly, "the first thing he'll do is push for an annulment."

Whit's expression darkened. "The hell he will."

"The second," I continued, "will be to bring a doctor to check if my maidenhead is still intact."

"That feels extreme."

"He'll do it to call my bluff." I cleared my throat. "I mean, if we pretended we had but actually hadn't." Heat stole over my cheeks. "I'm talking about the consummation."

I'd never been so embarrassed in my life. He could have teased me, but his expression was patient and gentle, his blue eyes soft. Slowly, my embarrassment faded, and instead I felt a bone-deep sense of rightness. Tonight with Whit was my choice. He let go of my hand and tugged a strand of my hair behind my ear, his fingers brushing against my cheekbone.

"I've always loved your hair."

"Really?" I said, raising my brows. "But there's so much of it, and it always knots, and it's forever falling down from the pins . . ." He waited patiently while I finished rambling. Dios, I was so nervous. If I were a teakettle, I'd be whistling loudly. If I were a champagne bottle, the cork would have long since popped. I lost track of the words coming out of my mouth, and my voice trailed off. I shrugged helplessly, and somehow he understood what I needed to hear.

"I don't give a damn about your uncle," Whit said. "This is about you and me and no one else. I don't want to rush you into something you're not ready for."

"And what about you? Are *you* ready?"

He gave me a slow smile, tender and rueful. "Since Philae, Inez."

Warmth pooled in my belly as dozens of memories with Whit flooded my mind. The moment when we had found Cleopatra's final resting place, and we had laughed so hard tears dripped down our faces. When he dove into the Nile to save me, giving me air when the last of my breath rushed out of me. I still remember his face through the murky blur of the river, bubbles drifting between us before he pressed his mouth to mine. And I could still hear his hushed reply after I had told him how I felt in a moment of bravery. His quiet words had sent a delicious shiver down my spine.

It goes both ways.

The mask he always wore around everyone else had been gone, and in its place was a stark vulnerability that stole my breath like the river had threatened to do.

He wore the same expression now, and it made me feel brave. I'd been falling in love with Whit slowly, under the river's surface, in a lost burial chamber, in a makeshift tent, on a boat.

By the time he held me in the dark of the tomb, it was irrevocable. "I'm ready," I whispered. "I've been ready for a long time. This is what I want. You and me."

A grin tugged at the corner of his mouth. Whit moved forward, ducked his head, and kissed me. His lips were soft against mine, moving slow but sure. He slipped his hand inside my purse dangling at my wrist, and he smiled against my mouth. Dimly, I heard the key unlocking the door. Whit tugged me inside and kicked it shut behind us. I barely heard the sound. The only thing I noticed was the way his mouth moved against mine, sweet and deep. Then he pulled me close, his left hand cradling the back of my head and his right arm banded around my waist, the bottle tight against my side.

Whit pressed his forehead against mine, and we shared the same breath for one heartbeat. Two. And then another. He stepped away and bent forward, retrieving the knife tucked inside his boot. With one strong flick of his wrist, he aimed the blade and swiped the cork neatly off. Frothy champagne spilled, and we laughed. He lifted the bottle to his mouth and took a swallow, and I watched the long line of his tanned throat.

Wordlessly, he offered me the champagne.

I drank deeply, the flavor tart and dry on my tongue. The sparkling liquid reached every corner of my body, and I felt fizzy, luxurious, and impatient for what else the night might bring. Whit led me to the green sofa and turned me around halfway so that when we sat, he was cradling me in his arms, both my legs stretched over his lap. I took another sip and offered him more. He shook his head and took the bottle away, placing it gently on the floor.

"We are going to *talk* first," he said. "Somehow, you always find out way too much about me, while I don't even know your middle name."

"It's because I ask questions."

"Too many."

I smiled. "I don't know your middle name, either."

"You first."

"Emilia. It's a family name." I nudged his shoulder. "Your turn."

"Lord Whitford Simon Hayes."

"I'm never calling you Lord Somerset."

Whit shuddered. "If you ever do, I am walking."

I thought about Whit as a soldier, fighting against all odds to save a friend, contrary to a direct command. Even with Ricardo, he displayed an innate loyalty, sometimes to a frustrating degree, but that was only when he wouldn't answer any of my questions. I leaned forward, nipped his ear. "You would never walk away from me."

All trace of playfulness vanished off his face, as if he'd snuffed a candle and all that remained was a plume of smoke. "You know me well enough to talk in absolutes?"

"Protest however much you want, and however loudly, Mr. Hayes, but you can't hide your honorability from me."

"I've done many dishonorable things, Inez," he said quietly.

"Has anyone ever told you how hard you are on yourself?"

"Has anyone ever told you that it's dangerous to believe the best in people?" he countered.

"Well, I think underneath all that cynicism, you love deeply. And you're loyal. And kind," I added because I couldn't help myself.

Whit let out a laugh. "I'm not kind, either, Inez."

"You can be," I said stubbornly. "You are."

Whit scowled in mock consternation and pinched my leg and I tried to squirm away, but he held on tight, one arm around my waist, the other draped over my legs. My dress was bunched around my ankles. I'd never dreamed I'd be in this position. We had fallen into our familiar rhythm of conversation, a fast waltz with dozens of tight spins. It left me breathless and oddly confident. Whit made it easy to be myself.

"I've only ever been truly kind to one person." He shifted me closer.

"Just one?" I slowly shook my head. "I beg to differ."

Whit smiled small. "I'll concede that I may have been kind to you once or twice."

More than once or twice. "What a concession." I paused. "Who were you talking about?"

In response, he pulled me closer and whisked his lips over mine. His scent swirled between us, a cross of the great outdoors and fresh air and the tart bite of an orange slice.

"Are we done talking, then?" I asked, breathless.

He pulled back, enough to meet my gaze. "I want to know about *you.* Your family."

So, I told him. The long years of waiting for my parents to come back from Egypt, my aunt and her grating ways, my cousin Amaranta, who knew how to behave like a lady, and then Elvira. She was my favorite. My person. Every time I glanced over my shoulder, she had been there. She saw the best in me, and I thought we'd live next door to each other, collecting kittens who grew into sassy cats.

I'd never forget the moment I lost her. That exact moment when she was still breathing and a second later, when her face was blown apart. Unrecognizable. Her mistake was to follow in my footsteps, sneaking away to Egypt like I had done. I came searching for answers, but Elvira had come searching for me. Like she always did. Now, whenever I looked over my shoulder, she wouldn't be there.

Whit gently wiped the tears from my cheeks. I hadn't realized I'd started crying. I'd lost her less than a week ago, but it already felt like an eternity. I hated that there would be more days since the last time I was with her. Days that would turn into months. Months into years. Years into decades. And time would be cruel, because it would take my memories and blur them until I'd forget the details that made her *her.*

"If I lost Arabella, I would be inconsolable," he whispered.

"Arabella?"

"She's who I was talking about."

"Your sister," I said, remembering. A girl almost grown up, who loved painting in watercolor, who was innately curious. She sounded like someone I'd want to be friends with. I pictured her with the same hair color as Whit, the same pale blue eyes.

"My sister," he confirmed. "The best of our family, and the nicest. She's like a hummingbird, flitting around the house, making the servants laugh, charming animals, painting watercolors that look like they belong in the pages of Grimms' fairy tales. We don't deserve her." His face turned somber. "There's nothing I wouldn't do for her."

"Kind *and* loyal," I mused.

Whit rolled his eyes. "Once you make up your mind about something, there's just no changing it, is there?"

I couldn't understand why he kept trying to dismiss the qualities he had that I admired. "Funny, I was going to say the same thing about you."

"I'm not a hero," he muttered, his chin pointed down. "One conversation with my parents and you'd know the truth."

"It sounds like they were hard on all their children."

He nodded. "My brother and I can take it, but Arabella can't."

"So you protected her." I slid my hand to the back of his neck and played with the ends of his hair. He tilted his head back against the sofa, eyes drifting closed. "You don't talk much about your brother," I said.

"Porter," he said. "It's because he's frightfully dull and sensible and practical."

"You're practical, too," I observed.

He made a disgusted face. "I don't want to hear such nonsense."

"I don't know anyone better prepared for what may come."

He opened his eyes. "Porter is so much worse. He brings everything—a trunk for clothes, a trunk filled with medicine, a trunk for his shoes and his guns, a trunk filled with maps of our destination, a trunk of toys for his *dog*—"

"But he's your brother, and you'd die for him."

"Such drama." Whit rolled his eyes. "But yes, I would."

That list of who he loved deeply enough to sacrifice his life for would be very short. He gave out his smiles and kisses freely, but his heart he kept safe in his fist. Draw too near to it, and he'd lash out. And yet, there were at least two people on this earth who had his heart.

I hoped I could be one of them.

"What are you thinking about?" he asked.

"Kiss me, Whit."

He tugged me closer, his lips brushing against mine, and then he deepened the kiss and groaned against my mouth. My fingers curled around the back of his neck as he parted my lips and lightly sucked on my tongue. I'd never been kissed so thoroughly. A year might have gone by, and I wouldn't have known it. In one slow pull, he took the scarf off from around my neck, the fabric a soft whisper against my skin.

"Why do you still have this?" he asked.

"It's strong magic," I said. "It might come in handy."

Whit narrowed his gaze, and I fidgeted in his lap. "You've kept it for the magic?"

I took the scarf back, lightly ran my fingers across the bright pattern. "It belonged to my mother."

"I know," he said, his voice gentle.

"I can't seem to get rid of it," I whispered. "I should, though, shouldn't I?"

"Whenever you're ready to let go of it, you will," he said. "And if that day never comes, there's no shame in keeping it."

I folded the fabric neatly, feeling the magic buzzing from every thread. Not for the first time, I wondered about the original spell and the Spellcaster who must have been wearing this particular adornment. Did they know some of the magic would latch on to something so ordinary? Were they—

"Inez," Whit whispered. "Stop thinking about the magic in the scarf."

I smiled ruefully.

"Come back to me." He splayed his hand against my lower back, while his other moved to the front of my dress, slowly working each button. My white chemise came into view, the collar held together by a silk ribbon. Whit pulled, and the knot came undone, revealing the swells of my breasts. I'd never done anything like this, and innocent terror snatched at my throat. He leaned forward, kissed me again. I knew what to expect, thanks to the scientific reading material strewn about Papá's library, but no one had ever prepared me for how this moment would feel.

A too-fast carriage ride downhill.

Spinning wildly around in circles, arms outstretched to keep balance.

A fever that spiked and threatened delirium.

My head swam from want and dizziness. I clutched at his linen shirt, bunching the fabric in my fists, desperate for something to hold on to.

"Your heart is racing," Whit murmured against my mouth.

I placed my palm over his chest. "So is yours."

Whit tucked a strand of my curly hair behind my ear. It had escaped my braid. I didn't even think to glance in the mirror. Heaven knew what I looked like.

"You're so beautiful," he said.

He stood and carried me to the bedroom. Gently, he laid me across the bed, and then he crawled on top of me, careful to keep his weight off. He bent his head and placed hot kisses down the length of my throat. The front of my dress gaped open, and he traced a finger along my collarbone.

Goose bumps flared up and down my arms.

"Are you sure, Inez?" he whispered.

"Aren't you?"

Something flashed across his face, an expression I couldn't read. He nipped my bottom lip lightly as he cupped my breast, his thumb gliding over me through the thin cotton. Warmth pooled deep in my belly, and I gasped. He kissed me again, softly at first, but it quickly turned deeper, more desperate. Every sweep of his tongue made my heart race, my head spin.

It was only much later, after Whit dragged the covers up over our flushed skin, and after he fell asleep first and I listened to his soft breathing, that I remembered he hadn't answered my question.

CAPÍTULO CINCO

Something soft brushed against the back of my neck. The slightest glide across sensitive skin. I kept my eyes closed, sure I was dreaming and that the minute I woke, the sensation would stop. But a strong arm was wrapped around my waist, tucking me close against a broad chest. I'd left the balcony open, and cool air drifted through the tight weave of the mosquito net wrapping around the bed like a cocoon. I opened one of my eyes, squinting at the gossamer fabric, making out the hazy paint strokes of dawn.

"Buenos días," Whit murmured against my hair.

I shivered, tucking myself closer to his warmth. Memories from last night played through my mind, one moment after another. The heat from Whit's hands as he explored every inch of my body. His kisses that made it hard to think, made my head spin and spin. The sharp ache when he first moved inside me, and it fading, becoming something that took over my body. Indescribable. He'd been gentle but possessive. Patient, and yet I felt his urgency in the noises he made, his soft gasps against my mouth. It seemed too incredible to be real. "Am I dreaming?" I asked in a marveling tone. "Did yesterday really happen?"

"I hope so, or I have no business being in your bed."

I smiled against the pillow. "Were you able to sleep at all?"

"Of course not." He stretched and pulled me closer and then sneezed when my hair tickled his nose. "I woke up wanting you throughout the night."

I blushed. "Oh."

Whit laughed, his thumb drawing light circles against my ribs, before slowly drifting upward. "I can't believe I have a wife." He pressed a soft kiss to my ear.

The enormity of what we'd done stretched out before me, as if our future were a ribbon unspooled. "What do you want to do?"

Whit paused, his thumb resting in the crook of my shoulder. "This minute?" He sounded amused. "The rest of the day? Or in general?"

I turned in his arms, curious and hardly believing we hadn't discussed what came after the wedding. After I dealt with my mother, we had our whole lives ahead of us. The world was our oyster, as the saying went. I smiled, and Whit stared at me, brow furrowed.

"What is going on in that head of yours?"

"The world is our oyster," I explained.

"Ah," he whispered. "Shakespeare again."

I trailed my finger along his jaw, following the hard line to his stubborn chin I drew months ago. "You've been a soldier, and a spy for my uncle. We have means now, and we can do whatever we want." I licked my lips. "What do you want to do with your life?"

"I think the better question is what do *you* want to do? It's your fortune."

"It's ours," I said, because I didn't want to start our marriage as if we were on different sides. I'd been cut off from my parents for so long, untethered and unsure of where I stood or where I belonged. All I wanted was to be a part of something he and I created together. A family. My mother had broken ours. My cousin's face flashed through my mind, and grief surfaced, potent like strong liquor. For once, I didn't want something I touched to smash into a million pieces.

"Inez, what do *you* want?"

"I want to know what happened to my father," I whispered. "I want to know if he's alive, or where he's buried. Elvira—" My breath caught in my chest, and I swallowed hard. "Elvira died because of my mother," I said. "I want her in prison. I want justice."

"None of that costs money."

"It'll cost something to track her down."

Whit shrugged. "You only need to find the right people." He rubbed his thumb across my lower lip. "What about afterward?"

There was something that I hadn't yet put into words. A feeling that stuck close whenever I walked the streets of Egypt. It was telling me to pay attention to my sense of wonder, the stimulating challenge in slowly learning a new language, the warmth and hospitality of the people here. Egypt had sunk deep into my bones, and I knew I'd miss her always. But what if . . . I called her home? What if *we* called her home? Working alongside my uncle and Abdullah had brought me joy. To work as a team and support what they were doing had given me purpose. A sense of rightness. I pushed my thoughts out into the open for the first time. "I want to stay in Egypt and fund Abdullah's excavations. Perhaps purchase a home in Cairo."

"You'd want to live here?" Whit asked, each word drawn out slowly, as if to make sure he had understood me fully. A tentative smile tiptoed across his face.

"I can't picture calling anywhere else home," I admitted. "What about you?"

"I was always supposed to return to England, so I didn't let myself hope or expect anything different. Much like I hadn't expected to be married to you."

"Married," I whispered. "Tengo un esposo."

"Yes, you do."

I'd forgotten he could understand me when I spoke my first language. A pleasant thrill sparked across my skin. This was how it would be between us. Slow early mornings and whispered conversation. He made me laugh, and he was loyal. I trusted him. "How good is your Spanish?"

Whit rose above me, guiding me onto my back. My pulse quickened, stirring my blood. His hair fell in soft waves across his brow, a tangled mess. The broad expanse of his shoulders blocked everything else. Sleepy blue eyes gazed at me, awake but not alert. A lazy smile deepened the corners of his mouth. He bent down, his soft lips gently parting mine, sinking into the kiss with a quiet ferocity, nibbling and tasting.

It was still dark in the room, and it felt like we were in a dream, until I felt his body wake up slowly, his breath coming out fast, his hand sliding down my neck and farther down still.

"Debería practicar más," he said, his mouth moving against my collarbone.

"What?" I had no idea what he was talking about. A delightful haze had swept through my mind, and I wanted to never come out of it. I would have been fine to be lost forever. No map necessary.

Whit lifted his head, grinning, and I detected a hint of smugness. He moved against me, the long line of him cradled between my thighs, and my breath caught. His smile grew, no more hinting.

I narrowed my gaze. "You're awfully pleased with yourself."

"I said," he whispered, pausing to nip my chin, and then repeated in Spanish, "that I needed to practice more."

The words were right, but his accent needed work. "You ought to speak Spanish with Tío Ricardo."

At the mention of my uncle's name, we both froze. Whit dropped lower, nearly crushing me, and groaned against my neck. Then he lifted and flung himself backward against his pillow.

His voice was flat. "Ricardo."

"We have to tell him today."

Whit stared up at the ceiling and nodded. "This morning."

"He'll be furious," I said. "He might hire a doctor; he might push for a divorce."

Whit slowly turned his head toward mine and met my eyes. His voice was a murderous whisper. "No one is going to dictate my life, Inez." He tugged me close, and I placed my ear over his heart. The rhythm was steady. "No one."

I believed him.

We walked down the stairs to the second floor without touching, without speaking. With every step, Whit changed his demeanor in subtle ways, slipping on the mask he wore in front of everyone. The careless rogue who kept a flask within reach, the charming flirt who knew how to coax smiles. This version of Whit was familiar, but I missed the one I'd uncovered in the dark. That Whit held me close, and his words lost their sharp, cynical edge.

We reached a dark green painted door, etched in curls and spirals, but before I could knock, Whit reached for my pinky with his own and held it for the length of a heartbeat. And even though he held on to me with just one finger, I felt connected to him. We were in this together.

Whit released me and opened the door, stepping through first. We were greeted by a messy sitting room. Old newspapers were stacked haphazardly on the coffee table, and there were several trays of uneaten food: pita bread and hummus, bowls of fava beans stewed in tomato broth. Empty coffee mugs littered nearly every surface area.

The room smelled of stale air and male sweat.

I wrinkled my nose. I had tried to keep up with the mess, but Tío Ricardo howled at any interference. He permitted me to sit beside him for a few minutes, but then he would order me from the room to pack.

Whit knocked on the bedroom door, and my uncle's grunt sent my nerves into a tailspin. My breath shuddered, and Whit must have heard because he pulled me back from the closed door.

"I can tell him on my own," he whispered. "You don't have to be here."

"We're a team," I said.

"I can handle it."

"I know you can," I said, rising on my tiptoes. I pressed a soft kiss on his cheek. "But you shouldn't have to."

He held my hand. "Together, then."

Whit opened the bedroom door and stepped through. If the sitting area was a mess, the state of my uncle's bedroom was a catastrophe. Clothes were strewn everywhere, his boots had been flung near the window, and scores of books were scattered on the bed. Several empty mugs lined the windowsill, and there was a plate of uneaten toast on the nightstand. I grimaced and made a mental note to tidy up the space.

"Oh, good. You left your tickets on the table. They're in an envelope over there. Have you packed yet?" my uncle asked, focused on a stack of papers in his lap. He hadn't shaved in days, giving him the look of a surly grizzly bear. He wore striped pajamas that were faded, the cuffs frayed. It looked like something my mother would have given him. She liked to look after him because he would never do so himself. At the thought of her, fury rose like a billowing sand cloud. I couldn't think of her without remembering Elvira.

I shoved Lourdes far from my mind.

Whit opened his mouth, but I beat him to it.

"As I've told you, I'm staying in Egypt."

"And as I've repeatedly told *you*," my uncle said, lifting his gaze to meet mine. He threw the pile of papers off to the side, and the sheets fanned in every direction, a few falling off the bed. "I'm your guardian, and you'll do as I say. I would prefer not to send another coffin back to Argentina." He opened his mouth to say more but froze. His attention had drifted down to our clasped hands. All the color left his face, leaving him stark pale. His expression turned to astonished rage. "*Whitford*."

"We have news," Whit said, and for once he wasn't smiling or winking. His manner had the seriousness of a man walking through a cemetery, grave and respectful.

"Step away from her."

Whit tightened his hold. My uncle registered the movement and swung the bedding away, feet coming down hard on the rug. He stood, swaying slightly, but then stumbled around the bed.

"No, don't—" I exclaimed.

Whit maneuvered me behind him as Tío Ricardo raised his fist. Whit didn't try to stop the hit—I heard the loud smack as my uncle punched my husband in the face. Whit staggered, and it took both of my hands to keep him upright.

"What have you done?" Ricardo boomed. "You promised me you wouldn't—"

"He made me a promise, too," I said.

"Inez," Whit warned, wiping the blood from his lip. "Not yet—"

Ricardo's hazel eyes widened. "Carajo," he said just as I trilled, "We're married!"

The words boomed like cannon fire, exploding all around us. I was amazed the walls didn't tremble, that the floors didn't crack.

"No," Ricardo said, dropping onto the bed. "*No.*"

Anger radiated off him in strong waves. He launched to his feet, one hand raised—but Whit sidestepped and used my uncle's momentum to whirl him around and away from us.

"It's done," Whit said.

"It isn't," Tío Ricardo spat out. "I'll have it annulled."

"Too late," I said cheerfully. "I'm ruined."

"Inez." Whit groaned. "Bloody hell."

Tío Ricardo swung around, his eyes wild. "You're lying—another one of your tricks!" He came toward me, hands outstretched as if he wanted to throttle me.

But Whit stepped between us. "You can yell at me," he said quietly. "You can be disappointed, feel betrayed. But you do not raise your voice at my wife. If you want someone to battle, you battle with me, Ricardo."

"I'll send for a doctor," he said, jabbing his index finger in my direction. "See that I won't! You're bluffing."

"Do it," I said, lifting my chin. "But you won't like the results."

My uncle appeared thunderstruck. Slowly, the angry bafflement cleared from his expression, leaving total desperation. I instinctively guessed that he was recalling every time I had put him through hell since I'd arrived in Egypt.

There were several occasions.

"Oh my God," Tío Ricardo said. "*Dios.*" He fell back onto the bed, his shoulders shaking. When he spoke again, his voice was flat and devoid of any emotion. "I will undo it."

"I could be pregnant," I said, this time less cheerfully.

The blood drained from Whit's face. "Good God, Inez."

My uncle pinched the bridge of his nose, clearly fighting for some semblance of control. I hadn't expected the news would actually wound him. I expected his fury, but not his profound concern. In my anger, I'd just assumed this was about control. But I'd been mistaken. My uncle cared for my well-being, and he genuinely didn't want to see me hurt. Whether by my mother's machinations or by Whit.

Whit shot me a look, exasperated. "Could you try for tact?"

"He doesn't understand tact," I said, forcing myself to remember my uncle's high-handedness. If he hadn't pushed me, then I wouldn't have married Whit in secret. It was his domineering behavior that had left me with no recourse. I'd only had two real choices.

Leave Egypt or marry.

"Maybe if you could try not to terrify everyone in this room, *me included*, the conversation might move in a more productive direction."

I faced my uncle. "You'll have to accept it."

"He doesn't deserve you. Whit doesn't have a penny to his name, and when I found him, he was a drunk. He didn't know what year it was."

"He told me," I said, which wasn't exactly true. I hadn't precisely known my new husband was penniless, not that it mattered. I needed his name. A husband.

"Whitford shares enough of himself to let you think he's being vulnerable," my uncle said wearily. "But he only lets you see what he wants you to see."

I felt as if I were standing atop a tower, and with every sentence, my uncle was removing a block. If he kept going, the whole structure would crumble. And I'd be buried underneath the rubble.

"I know enough," I said, my voice warbling at the edges. Whit had talked to me of his family, his past, the friendship he'd lost, and his disillusionment with his years in the militia. I snuck a glance at him, startled to find him completely stone-faced and withdrawn.

"You don't *know* him." Tío Ricardo jabbed a finger in the direction of my husband. "Tell her I'm right."

I flinched, his words grating against my skin. I didn't know how to protect myself from them because a small part of me worried about the same exact thing. Our marriage was like shifting sand in my palm. Our tenuous connection might slip through my fingers.

With visible effort, Whit met the criticism with a grin that reminded me of the sliver of light reflecting off the surface of his gun. He wore it like a weapon. "I didn't know you thought so little of me."

My uncle might never realize how he'd hurt Whit with his careless words, but I did. Now that I knew where to look, I could see the subtle display of pain in his tightened jaw, the rigid shoulders. A muscle jumped in his cheek. But he would not defend himself. He'd take every accusation, every blow to his character and honor with a detachment that was painful to watch.

This was how Whit survived.

He shut himself away and buried his wounds. Hid behind a bottle of whiskey, a quicksilver grin and caustic wit, a wall of cynical blocks that shielded him from the world before it could hurt him again.

"Did you get married in a church?" Tío Ricardo asked suddenly.

"We did," I said. "With a chaplain."

My uncle smiled. "It isn't legal yet, Inez."

"I sent a telegram to my brother," Whit said. "He'll file accordingly, and the banns will be read. It's all over England by now. Lord Somerset broke his betrothal agreement and is officially off the marriage market."

I shot him a questioning glance. I hadn't seen him send anything of the sort. But then, we hadn't been together the whole time. He could have sent it in the morning after he had woken me up. Whit didn't meet my eye, and realization dawned. Perhaps he was lying? Yes, it had to be a ruse meant for my uncle.

Tío Ricardo seemed at a loss with this information, and I silently cheered Whit's quick thinking. Then my uncle swayed forward, and I automatically gripped his elbow, steadying him. He still looked much too pale, and his clothes hung off his slighter frame. He'd lost weight since he'd been struck by that bullet. I knew that he'd been given excellent care, along with some maple syrup that had a touch of an old healing spell attached to it. The physician had shown me the bottle himself.

"I'll never forgive you," he said.

I was about to ask if he had spoken to me or Whit, but I held my tongue. It didn't matter who. "I know this was a shock, but I made my decision. My inheritance is my own, and you are released from all guardian responsibilities. I'm free to stay in Egypt, and I'll hear not another word about it, or my marriage to Whit. It's done."

Someone knocked on the main door of the suite, and the noise momentarily threw me. We had seemed out to sea, cut off from land, the three of us trying to stay afloat when there was a hole the size of a crater in our raft.

Whit left the room and came back a moment later carrying something in his hand. He brought it to Tío Ricardo. "It's a telegram for you."

My uncle ripped it open and pulled out the sheet, reading the curt lines quickly and bellowing a loud curse. He flung it away, and it landed on the bed.

The note read,

I NEED YOU IN PHILAE STOP DISASTER
COME QUICK STOP BRING A DOCTOR STOP
ABDULLAH

"I don't understand," I cried. "Is he ill? What could have happened?"

"He would never send such a message if it wasn't serious." Tío Ricardo stomped to his trunk and flung his shirts inside. He bent to retrieve his boots, but he let out a sharp groan, immediately touching his injured arm. I rushed forward to help him, folding his shirts to prevent additional wrinkles. Whit's arm appeared across my vision as I packed, and I startled, lifting my gaze. Whit was handing me my uncle's jacket, a pair of pants, and several pairs of socks.

"I can take care of my own things," my uncle grunted. "I'm *not* helpless."

Whit and I ignored him, working together to finish the task. He threw in two pocketknives, matches, several Egyptian notes, my uncle's reading glasses. I folded in his toothbrush and powder, along with clean bandage rolls.

"I think you ought to reconsider going," I said. "You're still recovering. Why don't Whit and I go? I'm sure that we—"

"No," my uncle interrupted. "Whit and I will go, and you'll stay here."

My uncle's ability to annoy me knew no bounds. His repeated attempts to leave me behind or send me away grated, as if he'd tried using a blunt knife against my skin.

"Where Whit goes, I go."

My husband nodded imperceptibly. "Don't forget his medicine, pocket watch, and that bottle of maple syrup. You ought to pack an extra blanket for the chilly evenings. He's weaker from the wound."

"Practical," I said.

"Prepared," he countered.

"Same thing."

My uncle raised his voice, clearly tired of being left out of the conversation. "This won't be a leisurely voyage up the Nile on a dahabeeyah, Inez."

"We go together," I said stubbornly.

Tío Ricardo grimaced and addressed my husband. "We need to get there quickly, so we'll travel partway by train and the rest by camel." He clenched his fist. "Remember what you owe me."

Whit let out an annoyed huff and then motioned for me to follow him out of my uncle's bedroom. I did so, dread pooling in my stomach.

I shut the door behind us for privacy.

Whit faced me, his hands deep in his pockets. "He's right. You'll slow us down, and the most important thing is we get to Abdullah in time."

His words didn't register at first. He wouldn't say such nonsense to me, he couldn't. I stared at him incredulously. "I'll *slow* you down? I practically run everywhere."

"You know what I meant."

I stiffened. "I'm afraid I don't. I have two legs same as you, don't I?" Frustration made my eyes burn with tears.

He didn't notice or he pretended not to see. Either way, he continued speaking, but the words seemed to blur together. "You've never ridden a camel," he said. "The train ride is miserable and hot, and that's just on the way to Aswan. Then we must trek through the desert, sleeping in tents. No, wait—one tent. Singular. We can't carry too much."

My lips parted. Whit was going to leave me behind, alone.

"You're not serious."

He stared at me gravely and raised his eyebrows suggestively. "I am."

"You actually want me to stay behind."

Whit nodded. "Correct."

My uncle was right. I didn't know my new husband at all. "You're going to do what you want no matter what I say, aren't you?" I said with an airy swipe of my hand. "As if I hadn't proved my capabilities or worked hard enough—"

"Inez." Whit glanced meaningfully toward my uncle's door, his brows rising suggestively again. "It's not about that. Ricardo needs time, and I think the distance will help. I'll work on him, talk to him, and when I return, I think he'll have gotten used to the idea of our marriage."

What logical reasoning. Everything he said made sense, but I still hated every word of it. "But—"

"I'm not going to change my mind," Whit said abruptly. "I don't think I'm being unreasonable."

"When we got married, I hoped that we would be on the same side."

"We are."

I met his gaze levelly. "No, you just made a decision without me. That's not what a teammate does." I swallowed hard, giving him time to respond. When he didn't, I walked to the door leading out of my uncle's suite, my back straight. "Have a safe trip, Whit," I muttered, exiting the room before he could see the extent of my hurt. I stomped down the hallway, folding my arms across my chest, absolutely raging. If he didn't know how much I hated not to be included, to be ordered around as if I had no opinion or voice or—

Quick footsteps behind me.

"*Inez.*"

Oh no—I was not ready to hear more directives from him. I marched on, faster now, but Whit hooked his hand around my elbow and swung me to face him.

"We have got to work on our communication," he said, exasperated.

"Oh, I heard what you said," I fumed. "*I'm not going to change my mind.* No confusion there, Mr. Hayes. I'll have you know that I don't appreciate the pompous—"

"Usually you catch on quickly," Whit was saying. "How many times did I have to look over at your uncle's door—"

"—behavior with no thought to what I feel—"

"—where he was obviously listening—"

We both broke off at the same time.

"What?" Whit asked. "Pompous behavior?"

I blinked. "Catch on quickly? My uncle was listening at the door?"

We stared at each other in bafflement.

"What the bloody hell are you talking about?" Whit asked.

"What are you?"

He began laughing, gasping loudly, shoulders shaking. He bent over, taking deep breaths to compose himself. Except I was still frowning, and when he got another look at my face, he doubled over again, laughing. Whit released my arm and wiped his eyes, needing the corridor wall to help keep him on his feet. "Did you call me pompous?" he asked between breaths.

"You were acting like it," I said.

"I was only saying what your uncle wanted to hear," Whit said, still grinning, "because I could hear him shuffling around near the door. My God, you're no better than he is."

"Oh," I said, finally understanding, my mood brightening considerably. Whit didn't want to be parted from me just yet. "You do want me to join."

He slowly shook his head, and my sudden elation deserted me. But he stepped forward and placed his hands on my shoulders, and his next words made everything better.

"Actually, what do you think about going through his room while we're gone?"

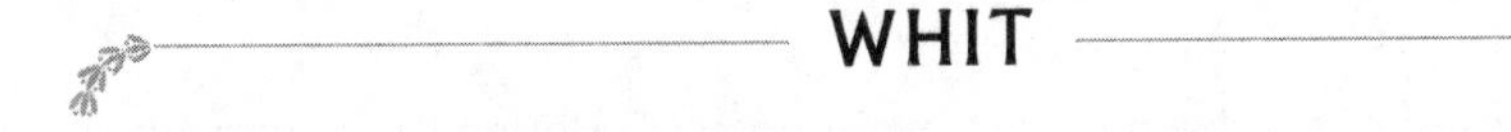

WHIT

We took the train as far as Aswan, Ricardo only speaking to me when absolutely necessary. To be fair, he appeared ill the whole of the journey; every jolt of the carriage left him reeling and sweating. But no matter how sick he felt, he somehow managed to glare at me at regular intervals. If he'd had a gun on him, he would have shot me—I was sure of it. I saw so much of Inez in him I couldn't quite meet his accusing eyes.

I knew one day she'd look at me the same if my plan failed.

Ricardo slumped over the side of the boat that carried us to Philae. The river lapped against us in gentle waves, but even so, he regularly threw up into the river. The sun's glare was relentless, and sweat dripped down my back. It was hotter during the day in Aswan than in Cairo, despite it being winter.

"Maybe I should have come alone," I said as I rowed.

Ricardo wiped his mouth with his sleeve. "Estoy bien."

I fell silent, hearing the dismissive tone. But I had told Inez I'd speak with him, so I stopped rowing, dragged the oars onto my lap. "You can't pretend it didn't happen."

He sighed, rubbed his eyes as if he wanted to rid them of the sight of me. I never thought he'd embrace the idea of the two of us, but I hadn't believed he'd thought so low of me.

A drunk and a womanizer and a liar. Out for a good time and nothing else. Sneaky and secretive. It was something my father used to say. Probably still would if we were ever in the same room again.

"I'm disappointed in you, Whit," Ricardo said. "You took advantage of her."

There was no way around that, so I kept silent. I got the sense that he knew the truth, and I forced my face into a nonchalant expression. Maybe he'd think I was hoping to avoid an argument. Part of me was, but the other railed at his dismal opinion. His disappointment made me want to howl, made me want the bottle.

"I see you won't deny it."

"Everything will work out," I said through gritted teeth.

Ricardo regarded me stonily. "Now that you have access to her fortune, you mean."

For fuck's sake. I shifted on the wooden seat. Philae came into view, the temple rising high above the water. It never failed to pull a gasp from me. Ricardo flicked a glance over his shoulder, but then he faced me once again. He wouldn't let me ignore him.

"I know what I'm doing," I said finally. "I have a plan."

"Which is?"

"None of your business."

"She's *my* niece."

"I know," I said. "And she's *my* wife."

A muscle ticked in Ricardo's jaw. "If you hurt her . . ."

He didn't need to finish. I understood perfectly. Ricardo would make me rue the day I ever laid eyes on Inez Emilia Olivera.

As if I didn't already.

I dipped both oars into the water and rowed us to the island shore. Ricardo stumbled over the side and began dragging the boat up the bank. I'd never met anyone so stubborn in my life, except, of course, for my wife. But I kept my mouth shut and helped him with the task. That done, I went up the gentle slope, careful to avoid the jutting rocks rising from the packed earth, Ricardo trailing after me, breathing heavily. We passed the spot where I told Inez I was leaving for England. The look on her face, the utter resignation.

Bloody hell.

The mess I was in.

"Abdullah!" Ricardo yelled as he reached the seemingly abandoned campsite. Sand nearly covered the fire pit, and even from where I stood, I caught sight of the ransacked headquarters, crates overturned, empty bottles half-buried, the crate of magic-touched objects pillaged. "What the hell is going on here?"

I squinted, using my hand to shade my eyes from the fierce glare of the sun. The hot sand scalded the leather of my boots, but I barely noticed. Where there ought to have been dozens of workers digging or enjoying the noon meal, there were none. The tents had all been torn apart, and there were stretches of sand stained with blood.

"Shit," I muttered.

"Don't just stand there; help me look for them," Ricardo said, stumbling off in the direction of the temple.

I searched Trajan's Kiosk, a temple dating back to Emperor Trajan, maybe even as far back to Emperor Augustus, but there was no one underground, no one shoveling or picking their way through the tunnel. I climbed up the hidden stairs and walked back to the campsite. Perhaps someone had left a note. But there was nothing. Only the hallmarks of a fight—equipment stolen, blood on the sand. Without warning, memories flooded my senses. Anguished screaming, the sound of horses shrieking in pain, the clang of steel against steel. My breath turned cold in my chest, and I rubbed my arms.

Hold it together.

A soft groan came from the stone structure we'd used as makeshift rooms. I spun, veering toward it as a figure stumbled out of one of them. His eyes were red-rimmed, cheeks hollowed out.

"Thank God," Abdullah said in Arabic. "I hoped you'd be here days ago."

"We came as soon as your telegraph arrived." I peered at him, anxious. His clothing had seen better days—his shirt and right jacket sleeve were ripped. A bruise on his cheek bloomed an angry dark purple. "You look awful."

"I'm fine."

"You are clearly *not* fine," I said. "Have you been sleeping here? Alone?"

"I know, I know." Abdullah wiped his sweating brow. "If Farida knew, she'd be furious with me."

"Abdullah!" Footsteps thundered as Ricardo stomped toward us. His cotton shirt clung to him like second skin, soaked in sweat. "Her tomb! It's all . . . it's all—" He broke off with a hoarse cry, his gaze latching on to his brother-in-law's battered state. "Dios mío, ¿qué te pasó?"

Abdullah frowned. "Why are you bleeding?"

"I was shot," Ricardo said, pale and sweating, holding his arm. It was clear I needed to take control of the situation. I immediately went to his side and inspected his shirt. His bandage was soiled again. I rubbed my eyes, muttering curses to myself. Ricardo didn't notice, his attention still fixed on Abdullah. "Where is everyone?"

"They left after the attack on the campsite," he said, tugging at his graying beard. "So many were injured."

"Let me help you," Ricardo panted. "You need medical attention."

"Sit down before you fall over," I snapped at him. "You have to help yourself, too. Let's go to the boat. I brought supplies and your medicine that will help you both, and Abdullah will tell us what the fuck happened."

"Why haven't you gone to a doctor, Abdullah?" Ricardo demanded.

Pot, meet kettle. I barely restrained my eye roll.

"I couldn't leave camp until you got here," Abdullah said. He had the good sense to sound sheepish, before turning grim. "Even if it's all gone."

"*What?*" I asked sharply, trying to herd them both toward the river. They were worse than cats. "What did you say?"

"Cleopatra's tomb was ransacked. Everything has been stolen," Ricardo confirmed dully. "The sarcophagus, all the statues, the jewelry. Gone."

"Christ." My gaze swung to Abdullah. "Who attacked the camp?"

Abdullah licked his dry lips. "It was Mr. Fincastle."

Then his eyes rolled heavenward, and he keeled over. Ricardo lunged for him as I turned away and sprinted to the boat, my heels kicking up sand. Behind me, Ricardo shouted at his brother-in-law, demanding that he wake up and not frighten the hell out of him.

I swear to God the pair of them would send me to an early grave.

By the time I'd gotten both of them settled, given them medicine, and rewrapped Ricardo's wound in fresh bandages, they were both stable enough to move. Abdullah had woken a few times and now fitfully slept as I rowed us away from Philae.

Ricardo's normally tanned face was pale and wan and half turned away from me as we left the island. Despair worked itself across his lined brow, deepening the grooves. "He'll be all right," he said.

I would have replied, but I didn't think he was speaking to me. His voice was a murmur, barely loud enough to hear over the sound of the river pulsing around us. Ricardo abruptly turned away from the sight of the temple, rubbing his eyes.

"He took everything," he said. "Hundreds of artifacts and every single roll of parchment. I never got the chance to read any of them." His shoulders slumped. "He has the Chrysopoeia of Cleopatra—I'm sure of it."

Without thinking, I shook my head and said, "He doesn't."

Ricardo slowly straightened, pierced me with an intense glare. "¿Cómo sabes?"

The devil damn me. If I weren't so tired, so worried about the pair of them, I would have stayed silent. But there would be no putting Ricardo off. "Because I went looking for it first."

"Why?" His voice was frigid. Not even the sun at noon would be able to melt the icy edges.

I rowed harder, hating his disappointment, his censure. "Besides the obvious?"

Ricardo eyed me shrewdly. "That's why you wouldn't go home when the first letter from your parents came?"

I hesitated. "One of the reasons."

"If the alchemical sheet isn't here, then where is it?" Ricardo mused.

That was the question that had been plaguing me every waking hour.

And I would do *anything* to know the answer.

CAPÍTULO SEIS

I tossed the smelliest of my uncle's socks over my shoulder and moved farther under his bed. My full skirt made the movement less than graceful, and I tugged hard at the material. I found abandoned ties and sand-coated boots, but nothing else of significance. I hissed out a breath and clumsily slid out before standing, brushing the sleeves of my jacket to rid them of the worst of the dust balls. I had already gone through all of his books and looked through the desk in his suite. I'd found nothing that would tell me more about my mother.

Hands on my hips, I glanced around his bedroom with narrowed eyes. Surely there was something here that my uncle didn't want me to know. When Whit explained that he didn't trust my uncle to share everything he knew or remembered about my mother's double life, I understood what he wouldn't say to my face. He had been nonchalant, but I could read him better now.

Because of *me*, Tío Ricardo now didn't trust *him*.

Our marriage was a betrayal and one my uncle wouldn't forgive so easily, if ever. He wouldn't confide or plan or scheme with Whit anymore. My uncle had lost an ally, someone who would do what was demanded of him, no questions asked. Their relationship broke, and Whit would pay for it with my uncle's cold and aloof behavior.

What I didn't know was how exactly Whit felt about it.

If I asked, he'd probably tell me some variation of the truth, but my instincts told me that he'd want to spare my feelings. I wished that he wouldn't, but that was a conversation for later.

I sat on the bed, fingers curling around the sheets until they brushed up against a sharp corner. Frowning, I looked down, realizing that my hand had found a pillowcase.

A pillowcase filled with something other than feathers.

"Hello, secret something," I breathed, dumping the contents onto the bed.

But there was only one thing hidden inside. A journal, its cover decorated with painted peonies. It belonged to my mother, and I had read it before when the *Elephantine* had been struck by a sandstorm. Now I knew Mamá had filled every page with lies about my uncle. He was violent and abusive, up to his arms in criminal activities, and intent on stealing precious artifacts.

None of it was true. Why, then, did my uncle insist on hiding my mother's journal?

And even more curious, why would he keep it at all?

After I moved all my belongings from my parents' suite—gracias a Dios I had already packed most of it—into Whit's much smaller room, I turned to the next item on my list.

More packing.

I had put off sorting through all of my parents' things long enough, and now that I didn't have their room, I could no longer put it off. All their clothes went back into their trunks, along with a myriad of other things, and I called up one of the hotel attendants to carry them into Whit's room, which was quickly becoming crowded with stacks of books and several purchases my parents had acquired. They had bought rugs and lanterns, alabaster statues of the pyramids and cats, and several jars of essential oils. There was barely any room to walk between the narrow bed and nightstand and the old wooden dresser. Whit's once-tidy room now looked like an attic where things went to be forgotten. He'd *hate* the clutter.

What we needed was a bigger room, and I would have gone straight to the bank to withdraw money, but I couldn't without Whit—my husband now had total control over my inheritance as permitted by law.

I scowled as I sorted through the mess, dividing everything into two piles: one meant for Argentina and the other for donation. It ought to have come as no surprise to anyone that one pile was larger than the other. I just couldn't bring myself to part with Papá's books, or his collection of Shakespeare's plays, or his suits. Maybe Whit could wear them? No, that wouldn't work. Whit stood six inches taller than my father.

I'd have to give it all away.

By the third day, I was so emotionally drained by the task that I became more ruthless with where everything would end up. I was giving away every last thing of my mother's, and I didn't feel any grief over it. Elvira would applaud my decision with a witty quip about Mamá's poor taste. She'd be making me laugh or annoying me by trying on my mother's dresses. She never thought of herself as particularly funny, but she'd made me chuckle easily. It was her outlook, a way to see the quirks of the world. Grief settled over me, blanketing everything I saw and touched with a sense of gloom that I couldn't shake. Elvira ought to be here in the room with me.

I sat down on the plush bed and pulled my mother's journal into my lap, staring down at it morosely. I'd found nothing useful since Whit had left, and I hated not having any sense of where my mother could have gone. The only thing I felt certain of was that she wouldn't have left Egypt—not with the artifacts she stole. It was too risky for her to move such quantities without drawing notice.

Although . . . Mamá clearly had many connections in Cairo. Someone could be assisting her—her *and* the trunks filled with Cleopatra's belongings.

With a sigh, I flipped through the pages of her journal, reading bits at a time as I went. There were many entries of her day-to-day life, things she did or saw, places she visited, and people she met. I took notice of a pattern emerging with every turn of the page. At first, my mother wrote in the journal almost daily, but then the entries were spaced out by months and then, curiously, years.

The most recent pages switched back to daily writings that were filled with her worries about my uncle. Which I knew to be lies. At some point, this diary had turned into a deliberate and curated way to damn my uncle. An asset she could use against him.

It was clever and so calculating it made my stomach turn. How could she have planned to ruin her own brother's life?

My brow furrowed as I flipped back to the earlier entries, dated seventeen years ago, and picked a page at random to read.

Back again in Egypt so soon after our last visit, at Cayo's insistence. And now he tells me that he wants to stay even longer. Possibly over a year. Cayo insists Inez will never feel our absence throughout her infancy, but I'm not so sure. It's as chaotic as always, the hotel filled with people from all over. I've run into old friends, at least, which has kept my days full of conversation that doesn't revolve around excavating, thank goodness.

Cayo is demanding we leave for the site earlier than planned, and I'm dreading it. Once he has an idea in his mind, there's no changing it. But I'd rather enjoy the comforts of the hotel and the little rituals that make the time spent here bearable.

I wonder if it would be so terrible if Cayo went on without me?

That way, I wouldn't slow him down, or bother him with my boredom and complaints. Even Abdullah sees how miserable I am out in the desert.

Perhaps I'll ask him. It would be better for everyone if I stayed behind. I could draw and paint, visit with the various ladies and gentlemen I've befriended. Read to my heart's content. The hotel has scores of books and material that I might enjoy.

Mamá's words and the depth of feeling she hid between the lines fully struck me. She had been miserable returning to Egypt. She had searched for ways to occupy her time, anything to make her days bearable. Meanwhile, Papá's enthusiasm was abundantly clear, and perhaps he was oblivious to my mother's apparent misery. I had no idea they had abandoned me for longer stretches of time when I was baby. Why didn't they care to be with me? I inhaled, my breath shaky, and fought to keep the rising emotion I felt under control. It hurt too much, and it made it impossible to think.

I turned the page and encountered the first of her many sketches. It was dated the next morning after the entry I had just read, and a chill skittered down my spine when I recognized her magic-touched scarf. She'd found it right here at Shepheard's.

A rap on the door interrupted my thoughts. I stood, my knees popping—I hadn't realized that much time had gone by—and hobbled to the door. I must have ordered tea and forgotten all about it. But when I opened it, a tea tray wasn't on the other side.

A young woman stared back at me, her honey-colored hair pinned at the crown of her head, thick curls framing a hollowed-out face. Her skin looked pale, ghostlike, as she stood in the candlelit corridor, and her blue walking dress first appeared respectable for company, but on a second look, I noticed the dirty hem.

I almost didn't recognize her.

"Isadora!" We'd met weeks ago when I had snuck about my uncle's dahabeeyah. I hadn't known what to think of her at first. She was well brought up with pretty manners, but I sensed there was much she tucked away out of reach. But then, within days of meeting her, she had helped in saving my life, deftly handling a sleek pistol while she shot at a crocodile.

My admiration and respect for her soared.

Isadora lifted her chin, and despite the deep cavern under her eyes, she held herself regally, back straight, hands demurely clutching a cotton traveling bag. It, too, looked the worse for wear, covered in dust, the leather handle bent out of shape.

"Are you all right?" I demanded. "You look . . . like you've been through an ordeal."

"Do you still consider me a friend?" Isadora asked without preamble.

"Of course," I replied instantly. "Why wouldn't I?"

Her stiff expression relaxed into a tentative, relieved smile. "Then will you let me come in?"

I stepped aside quickly and repeated, "Of course."

Isadora brushed past and abruptly stopped, almost crashing into the tower of wooden crates, but steadied herself in time. She looked over her shoulder, raising a delicate brow, before skirting around the boxes and examining the rest of Whit's—*our*—room. "What on earth?"

"I've been trying to tackle it for three days," I said. "But it only seems to be getting worse."

She let out a low whistle. "There's more in the bathroom! Where did all of these things come from?"

I sighed, shut the door, and followed the sound of her voice as she looked through the tall rolled-up rugs propped against the wall. "Everything belongs to my parents. Well, mostly everything. I have my own trunks in here somewhere."

Isadora glanced around, her blue eyes flickering over every corner. "I imagined your room would be bigger."

"How did you know which one was mine?"

"The front desk," she replied absently. "Good God, this is really small."

"It'll do for now."

Isadora nodded, her face partly turned away from mine, and I finally caught what she was trying so desperately to hide. Her hands shook, and her breathing came out in soft, shallow huffs. She swayed, and alarm flared in my chest. I motioned for her to sit on the bed.

"Are you all right?" I asked again.

She sat, still coolly composed. "I'm fine. Only a little light-headed."

Once again, I observed the state of her wardrobe, the tired lines across her brow. Her posture was perfect, but she seemed to be struggling to keep her eyes open.

"When was the last time you drank anything?" I demanded. "Have you eaten? Where is your father?"

Isadora blinked. "I managed to have a cup of tea this morning. I haven't eaten in a couple of days. And as for my father . . ." Her voice trailed off, and her composure cracked. "I have no idea."

I sank down next to her. "I don't understand."

"I've had a trying few days," she admitted softly. "I came here because . . . well, because I need your assistance."

"You need my help?" I asked, raising my brows.

She winced, looking away, attempting to compose herself. "Sorry, this is hard to talk about."

The polite thing to do would be not to press her for more information. I knew that, except that familiar flare of curiosity burned in my throat. Questions bubbled to the surface. Isadora never complained in the days we spent underground, working together to record the wondrous artifacts we'd found in Cleopatra's tomb. She bore the heat and toil and her father's constant supervision with a steady hand and a calm precision. If she was telling me she had had a trying few days, then it really meant that she'd been through hell and back.

I would have to be blunt. "You look ill and exhausted. What has happened?"

She shifted, met my eyes squarely. "Can I trust you?"

I blinked, taken aback. "In what sense? With a secret? Yes. If you're asking me to help you cover up a murder, then no. I don't know you well enough for that, and I hope you'll agree." I blanched. "Not that I'd ever help cover up a murder, but I do hope you know what I meant, don't you?"

She laughed, and the hot tension she carried on her shoulders cooled by several degrees. "I think I feel a bit better. An hour ago, I would have thought it impossible."

"Wonderful," I said. "Meanwhile, I'm slowly going mad with curiosity."

I had thought to make her laugh again, but all the mirth bled from her face. "Once I say this aloud, it's done. It's real. I won't be able to unsay it. There's no coming back from it." Her bottom lip wobbled, and I almost leapt to my feet from the shock of seeing her so discomposed. But I forced myself still, forced myself to remain calm even as my body waged war. I wanted to shake her senseless.

"It will be all right," I said. "Tell me. Are you in some kind of trouble?"

Isadora inhaled, clearly trying to calm herself. "You'll think differently of me."

We were friends, but only recently. I couldn't imagine why it would matter to her what I thought of her. Isadora watched me with a shrewd expression on her face.

"I do care what you believe of me," she whispered. "Which is why I don't want to tell you that my father is a thief of the worst kind. He's not the man I thought him to be."

"A thief," I repeated.

I barely heard her hushed reply. "Yes."

A sense of unease rose within, like weeds poking through an orderly garden. Dread curled deep in my belly. I was afraid to ask, somehow already anticipating the answer. The last time I'd seen Mr. Fincastle, her father, I was leaving him behind on Philae—where we'd found Cleopatra's tomb. Surely she wasn't speaking of . . . of . . .

But she confirmed the fear building inside me.

"Yes," she said softly, reaching for me. "You understand me perfectly, I see." She inhaled one long, shuddering breath. "He and a party of six men, maybe seven, attacked the camp and took everything on Philae."

The room spun. I pulled free from her grasp and wrapped my arms around my stomach, desperately trying to keep myself from falling apart. I covered my face with my hands and let out a muffled shriek. This was why Abdullah had sent his urgent telegram to Tío Ricardo. By now, they would have made it to Philae and discovered Mr. Fincastle's treachery. Isadora's words penetrated my wild panic and the sense of despair crawling across my skin. Her father had *attacked the camp*. Used his guns to overtake the team. *Dios mío.*

I prayed no one had been hurt.

I ought to be there, and I raged against the miles between Cairo and Philae. I'd never felt so helpless.

"Anything valuable, anything made of gold was hauled away. Even . . . even—" Isadora broke off.

I wished she would stop talking, even as her words came from far away. As if they'd been buried under sand. I had to dig deep to finally understand her meaning.

"Even *what*?"

"Her mummy. My father took her, too."

Horror gripped me. "You mean . . ."

Isadora nodded, acute misery twisting her features.

Mr. Fincastle had stolen Cleopatra.

"This trip was supposed to be about our relationship," she said, her voice louder, more like herself. "It was meant to bring us back together after what happened."

"What happened?" I asked through numb lips.

"Here it is," Isadora whispered. "The reason why I care so much about what you think of me." And then she took my hand and held on, as if for dear life. "My parents had been lying to me for most of my life, until I found out the truth. Father had an affair with a married woman." She inhaled deeply, visibly fighting tears. "It explained so much—why my mother was gone for half the year, every year, for some mysterious job in South America."

"South America?" I repeated dumbly.

"In Argentina."

I squeezed my eyes shut, the darkness a pit yawning wide, and I wanted to throw myself into its depths. Again, I knew what she was going to say before she said it. I bowled over, having to put my head between my knees.

She reached for my hand, held on tight. I barely felt her touch. Instead, I braced myself for what was coming next. But there was no preparing for the depth of my mother's deception and how badly she had betrayed Papá and me. And when Isadora spoke again, I felt her words like a kick to the teeth.

"I'm your sister."

CAPÍTULO SIETE

I splashed cold water on my face and avoided looking in the mirror. The wake of damage my mother had left behind overwhelmed me. This entire time, I had thought my mother had her affair with Mr. Burton—a man she later betrayed. But no. She had cheated on my father with Mr. Fincastle.

Mr. Fincastle, whose first name I never learned.

The brawny, rude, and domineering Englishman with a penchant for guns, who had managed every minute of Isadora's day. The one who spoke down to the rest of the digging crew, who looked at everyone and everything with suspicion and disapproval.

I couldn't *believe* my mother had been with such a man.

Surely she had better sense. Surely she had better taste. My father had been two decades older than her, but he had been kind and thoughtful and clearly supportive, he hadn't minded her lifestyle while in Egypt, so different than his own. She had left his side for months at a time, when I believed them to be together. A sharp ache bloomed in my heart, and I knew that it'd never heal, no matter how much time went by, no matter the distance.

My mother had broken us.

And she knew the truth about my father. I knew Whit and Tío Ricardo believed him dead, and the longer Papá remained unaccounted for, the more I believed it, too. I leaned against the washbasin of the small water closet adjoining Whit's room. My face felt warm still, despite the number of times I'd pressed a cool washcloth to my cheeks. I didn't know how long I'd been inside, with Isadora still waiting on the bed where I'd left her.

My sister.

Hermana.

My emotions were all over the place: disbelief and confusion and heartache. And a surprising happiness that covered everything else. When Elvira had died, I'd lost someone fundamental, and the days since, I'd felt discordant and unsettled.

But now I had a sister.

Then it hit me. Isadora shared many of the same qualities Mamá had. Back in Philae, I had witnessed her moments of manipulation and cunning, her tendency to weigh her needs above others', and a penchant for getting into trouble.

She and I had all those attributes in common.

I gripped the edge of the wooden counter, still unable to look in the mirror. Were we both doomed to become like our mother? Repeat her same mistakes? Hurt people without thought or consideration? The idea terrified me. Because I knew if I looked into the mirror, it wouldn't be my face reflected back at me.

I'd see Elvira.

The door opened, and I glanced up from the porcelain bowl, gaze finally on the accursed mirror. My eyes crashed with Whit's, his tall presence behind me. I spun around and threw myself into his arms. He made a noise of surprise and kicked the door shut behind him as his arms wrapped around my waist. His scent enveloped me, fresh air and the hint of sun-warmed citrus. He smelled like a long traveling day.

"You're back," I murmured against the soft linen of his shirt. Another blue hue that complemented his eyes.

"I'm back," he confirmed. "Was that ever in question?"

"You didn't write."

"There wasn't time," he murmured. Whit pulled far enough away so that he could look down into my face, his own expression clouded. He studied me intently. "You've been crying."

"A little."

Tension gathered across his brow. "Right. I can handle this."

I blinked, confused, but he'd stepped away and yanked open the door. Because he had only just returned from Philae, I knew what he must have discovered and how it had impacted not only him but Abdullah and my uncle. Still, when Whit raised his voice, I let out a startled gasp.

"What the *hell* are you doing here?"

I rushed out of the water closet, gaping and carefully avoiding the tall stack of trunks. I'd never heard that tone from him. This wasn't anger; it wasn't cold—this was scathing contempt at its most profound capacity. I didn't think him capable of it.

"Whitford Simon Hayes."

My husband swung his head around to look at me. He appeared astonished to hear his full name out of my mouth. But when Isadora loudly cleared her throat, he fixed a glare at her. "I asked you a question. What the *bloody* hell are you doing here?"

"What are you?" Isadora countered, her cool composure intact, but her words sounded threadbare. As if she'd been crying while I hid in the water closet. My heart gave a strong tug, as if she'd pulled on it herself. My protective instincts flared.

"This is *my* room," Whit said.

"No, Inez sleeps here."

There was a long silence. I could guess at Whit's thoughts. The rueful twist of his lips gave him away. Neither of us had publicly announced our marriage to the people we knew here, and I hadn't prepared myself to answer the complicated questions that came with the revelation. But the truth was bound to come out, even some of the staff at the hotel would have guessed. Many of them had helped me transfer rooms.

"She's my wife."

Isadora gasped. "Since when?"

"We married a few days ago," I said. "Surprise."

"Not that it's any of your business," Whit said, leaning against one of the towers of crates. "I'm still waiting for that answer, though."

Isadora drew her shoulders back. "I came to Inez for help."

"Look elsewhere," Whit said through gritted teeth. "Maybe you can join your father wherever he is. No doubt sorting through all the stolen artifacts from Philae, the bastard."

"She had nothing to do with it," I said sharply.

"Of course she did," Whit said.

"No," I said calmly and then turned away from him. Isadora held herself stiffly, as if she didn't quite believe that I'd take her side. "I've thought about it—you may stay with us," I reassured her. I gestured to the small space. "It will be cramped, but we can make it work. Perhaps we can get—"

"Inez," Whit growled.

"—a cot," I finished loudly. I glanced at him. "You look tired."

"I am," Whit said. Then he pointed his index finger at Isadora. "She can't stay here. In fact, I'm taking her to the consulate where she can be thrown into the dungeon."

"The dungeon?" I gasped.

"Where she belongs."

Isadora inhaled sharply. "How dare you condemn me. You were a soldier in the British military. Your hands aren't clean."

Whit clenched his fists, the blood draining from his face. His years as a lieutenant had left scars. He seemed to take up the space of the whole room. He looked worn down, shoulders hunched, eyes withdrawn and brooding. I tried to imagine what it must have been like, to arrive on Philae and see the total destruction, to see Cleopatra's final resting place ransacked and looted. A horror I hadn't experienced but had felt from a distance. It was enough to bring me to my knees.

Years of Abdullah's and Tío Ricardo's life had been taken away from them.

"And where were you?" he asked her icily. "While your father was attacking the camp?"

"He kept me locked up in one of the chambers in the temple when it became clear I wouldn't support his decision," she said. "I tricked one of his men and made my escape."

"From an island on the Nile?" Whit didn't hide his disbelief. "Did you fly? Ride on the back of a crocodile?"

Isadora straightened her spine, color flooding her cheeks. "Just because

I'm a girl doesn't mean that I'm helpless. I had my purse, and I can make do with the language."

"Your being a girl has nothing to do with anything," Whit said through gritted teeth. "Look at my wife—if she wanted, she could make it to Paris on the back of turtle." He clenched his jaw. "Admit it—you were a part of your father's schemes."

"I believe her," I said. If I were in her position, I would hate for anyone to paint me with the same brush as my thieving mother.

Whit fell silent, strung tight as a bow. "She's trying to manipulate you."

"Maybe that's what it looks like to you right now." I went to stand by her side, our shoulders brushing. "It's *you* who doesn't have all the information."

Whit regarded me stonily.

"My mother had an affair with Mr. Fincastle. It's been going on for nearly two decades, apparently." I inhaled deeply, nervous energy making my fingers tingle. His clear dislike and mistrust of Isadora unsettled me. Not because he didn't have due cause, but because he was married to me. In a matter of seconds, he'd learn that we were all family. "She's my sister, Whit."

If I'd told him that I planned to join the circus, he would not have been more surprised. "Bollocks."

"It's not," Isadora said, her tone even and calm. "And I can prove it." She wheeled around to face me. "I knew her as Mamá, but her close friends called her Lulis. She liked to stay up late and sleep away the morning. Mamá hated coffee but inexplicably liked dark chocolate. She preferred cats to dogs, sweets to salty foods, and liked her tea with milk, not lemon."

Whit scoffed. "You could have learned this by asking around. Her old maid, perhaps."

Isadora ignored him, her sole attention fixed on me. "She had a birthmark on her stomach, near her belly button."

"Again, a maid could have told you that."

"She was coloring her hair, because she hated the gray strands growing at her temples. But I always thought she looked beautiful." Whit opened his mouth, but Isadora's words came out rushed, her attention now on my husband. "When she was sixteen, she fell in love with the boy who brought the newspaper to the door. Feliciano was his name."

Whit fell silent.

There was no way Isadora would know that unless Mamá had told her. I'd only learned by accident, listening in on one of the rare fights my parents had behind closed doors and when they thought I was sleeping. Father had accused her of keeping in touch with Feliciano, but she categorically denied it. And Mamá had kept a bottle of the dye in the nightstand next to her bed in our home in Argentina. For years, I watched her rid the evidence that she was aging.

"She loved perfume from Italy." Isadora clasped her hands tight in front of her. A girl waiting to be sentenced and doomed. "She thought it smelled roman—"

"Romantic," I cut in softly.

She met my eyes, her back straight, hands still clenched, pride demanding that she not lower her chin an inch. She waited for me to decide, but there was never any question. I would not cast her out. I reached forward and took a hold of her hand and gently tugged. We were the same height, had the same build. We were close in age. Emotion clogged my throat as I hugged her. I peered at Whit from over her shoulder, knowing I'd find disappointment.

Whit pressed his lips into a thin slash, his arms folded across his chest. But he remained silent.

"She stays," I said to him.

He looked away. Well, he hadn't said no. A small step in the right direction, at least.

Isadora pulled away from me, her chin trembling slightly. "Thank you. I don't know what I would have done if you hadn't believed me."

"Somehow, I think you would have figured something out." We had that in common, too. I smoothed her hair from off her face. "Will you go down and order us a tea tray? I think we'll need it. And perhaps a cot?"

She nodded and left the room, taking care to give Whit a wide birth.

His frustration radiated off him in widening circles. For the first time in three days, I was alone with my husband.

"I don't trust her," Whit said, moving away from me.

"You've made that clear."

He held himself at the other side of the bed, his gaze still averted from mine. Our first real disagreement as a married couple. I wondered how we'd weather it. My parents had rarely fought, had rarely even disagreed. I didn't know how to navigate this territory. But I knew I cared enough to see it through to the end.

"Come here, Whit."

His head jerked up. He came closer, warily, as if he thought I'd run if I had the chance. When he stood in front of me, I pressed the flats of my hands on his chest.

"I don't have a lot of family," I said softly. "And I believe Isadora, Whit."

He covered one of my hands with his own, and his expression turned contemplative. He didn't seem to agree with me, and I bristled. I tried pulling away, but he held on.

"I know I haven't shown great judgment," I said. "But it would mean a lot to me if you gave her a chance."

"Are you talking about your mother?" Whit asked, squeezing my hand. "Are you still feeling guilty about what happened on Philae?"

"No matter how I look at it, it still feels like my fault. It was my naivete that ensured my mother's success."

"She was manipulating you," Whit said. "And using your emotions and love for her against you. In no way should you blame yourself for wanting to believe your mother had your best interests at heart."

I nodded slowly. "Fine, but then you can't have it both ways." I stepped forward, tilted my chin up to better meet his eyes. "Isadora was surprised and caught off guard. Just like I was. Her father's actions don't automatically make her complicit."

"I *knew* you were going to say that," Whit muttered. "Here, I was thinking I was comforting my wife while you were preparing an argument against me."

"I'm not against you," I said. "I'm only asking that you give her a chance."

Whit stiffened, the line of his shoulders tightening. He let out a long, annoyed sigh.

I reached up and, with the tips of my fingers, brushed along his jaw. "She's alone and needs help—"

"I don't want to talk about Isadora," he cut in. "I don't want to talk at all."

Then he dropped his hand to my waist and tugged me closer. I slipped my arms around his neck and I rose onto my tiptoes and kissed him. He groaned against my mouth. He swept his tongue across mine, and I shivered, my fingers playing with the hair at his nape. Whit lifted me off my feet and slanted his mouth, deepening the kiss. When we parted, both our breaths came out in ragged huffs.

Whit pressed his forehead against mine. "Did you think of me while I was gone?"

I breathed in his scent and nodded. "Did you?"

"You crossed my mind."

I tugged hard on his hair, and he laughed before releasing me. He led me to the bed, the only place to sit, and we settled onto it, side by side. My feet barely reached the floor, while his long legs stretched out. His thighs were muscular, and I gulped, remembering how he'd looked hovering above me, soft shadows flickering across his face.

"Why are you blushing?" he asked, peering at me with a faint smile.

"No reason," I said quickly.

"Tell me," he coaxed, leaning forward, a warm glint shining from his blue eyes.

"I can't believe you haven't asked me what I found in my uncle's room."

Whit arched a brow. "What have you found?"

I jumped up, and his soft chuckle made me blush harder. But his smile faded when I handed him my mother's journal.

"I've seen this before," he murmured. "This belonged to Lourdes. I caught her writing in it right before they disappeared." He flipped through the pages.

"It's mostly all lies," I said. "But curiously, my uncle kept it hidden in his pillowcase."

Whit shrugged. "This journal could be damning in the wrong hands."

"Then why keep it?" I persisted. "Why not burn it? Throw it in the Nile?"

"Because he's not a fan of littering?"

"Be serious, Whitford."

His lips twitched. "Well, what do *you* think?"

I took the journal and flipped the pages, desperate to find anything that might help us locate her.

Whit's hand snapped forward. "Wait. What's that?"

I looked toward where he pointed. My mother had filled up a page with drawings and scribbles.

It looked indecipherable. Random sketches next to drawings and tidbits about ancient Egyptians. I could just picture my mother, reading in Shepheard's library, trying to understand my father's fascination. Learning what she could, trying to keep up while in conversation with him. I flipped the page, and noticed another entry.

I received a letter from Cayo, another delay in returning from the excavation site. Most of my friends have moved on to see the sights. Perhaps I should have gone with them, but I had been expecting Cayo any day. That had been a mistake. Still, the library in the hotel has many interesting materials to read through. I found a few books about the last pharaoh of Egypt—Cleopatra the seventh. A fascinating woman by all accounts, with an even more interesting ancestry.

He took the journal from me, turning the page back again, and examined the doodles. I stared at him in bemusement. "What is it?"

"It might be nothing," he admitted.

"*What* might be nothing?"

He held up the page. "Does this look like a snake to you?"

"Maybe a little. It has an odd, wiggly edge."

"Made by a snake." Whit nodded. "This mark might be an eye."

I squinted, trying to see it. Perhaps it was a snake, but it could also just have been a random mark.

"It looks like an Ouroboros."

"So . . . ?"

Whit tapped his bottom lip absently. "Remember how your mother was looking for something in particular on Philae?"

I nodded. "Go on."

"In the ancient world, there were four women who were rumored to be able to produce the philosopher's stone."

I tilted my head, frowning slightly. "I've heard of it—one of the ancient spells that's been lost." The philosopher's stone—where had I read about that before? It sounded incredibly familiar to me. It was an object of some significance.

"Right. These women were alchemists and Spellcasters. And one of them was named Cleopatra—remember I told you about her?" When I nodded, he continued, saying, "An ancestor of *our* Cleopatra who was buried secretly on Philae." He tapped his finger against my mother's entry. "Look here—she even talks about reading up on her ancestry."

Excitement pulsed in my throat.

"Cleopatra the alchemist is rumored to have written down how to make the stone on a single sheet of parchment. This legendary sheet is called Chrysopoeia of Cleopatra, and on it, she had drawn an Ouroboros."

I looked down at my mother's drawing. "And it looked something like this?"

Whit nodded, grimacing slightly. "I know it's a stretch. But if your mother didn't find what she was hoping for on Philae, then she could still be looking."

"Look at the date on the other page," I said. "This is from years ago. It seems incredible that she stumbled upon a book, saw a drawing, and then randomly reproduced it in her journal. Then, over a decade later, she decides to search for the Chrysopoeia of Cleopatra?"

"It *is* rumored to have been buried with her descendant," Whit said. "Do you understand what the philosopher's stone is, Inez?"

I shook my head. "I've heard of it but can't quite recall—"

"The Chrysopoeia of Cleopatra has instructions on how to turn *lead into gold*."

When my father used to tell my mother stories about magic, it would always leave her breathless. With the gradual disappearance of magic-touched objects in Buenos Aires, it was easy to forget that it was once commonplace. That spells and the use of them were woven into the fabric of everyday life. Whenever I came across something that still held the heartbeat of a long-ago cast spell, it would hit me all over again, how we let something so extraordinary become endangered.

And one day in the near future, magic would cease to exist altogether, fading to the background and becoming a footnote in history.

I understood why anyone would hunt and kill for the Chrysopoeia.

"Whoever finds the sheet could sell it for an exorbitant sum," I said.

Whit shook his head. "Think bigger. Imagine if the person understood alchemy and could create the stone. For centuries, people have been searching for this document. Like the Holy Grail," he said. "Noah's ark. The final resting place of Alexander the Great."

"Or Cleopatra's tomb."

Whit nodded. "Exactly."

A memory niggled at the back of my mind. I fought to hold on to the feeling, and a second later, I recalled a moment with my mother. We were inside my makeshift tent on Philae, and she asked me if I had encountered a single sheet of parchment.

"You're right," I said. "My mother asked me about a sheet of parchment—she *is* searching for the Chrysopoeia." I tapped my finger against the page of the journal. "We have the proof written in ink that she knew of its existence over a decade ago."

"Well, she wasn't successful in finding it." He twisted his lips. "I wish it made me feel slightly better."

"My mother won't give up," I said. "She's crossed too many lines. Now we all know her for who she is, and what she's done. There's no coming back from that. So where would she look for the sheet next?"

"I have multiple locations in mind," he said. "She could be anywhere in Egypt that was of some importance to Cleopatra the alchemist—or her descendant, who was also rumored to be adept at magic."

"She was," I said, remembering the potent visions I'd stumbled across—the last pharaoh of Egypt hunched over a long table, herbs and elixirs at her elbow as she mixed and measured. "A potion maker, maybe even a Spellcaster herself."

Whit lowered his chin. "How do you know?"

"The magic from the golden ring," I said. "It linked me to some of Cleopatra's memories. I saw her at work, muddling ingredients, recalibrating tools."

"Well, that narrows down the places where your mother might be to a dozen temples, give or take."

I groaned, burying my head in my hands. My voice came out muffled. "One too many." A thought occurred to me, and I looked up. "Wait . . . Weren't you searching for the same thing?"

Whit shifted, the corners of his lips turning downward. "Yes, and I made the mistake of telling your mother. Our conversation might have rekindled her interest. She might have remembered stumbling across this book she references in the journal entry."

"And how did you discover it?"

He hesitated. "I learned about Cleopatra the alchemist from one of my books on chemistry."

"Alchemy and chemistry are related subjects? Isn't one predominately magical, the other scientific?"

"In some schools of thought, those two are one and the same. Alchemy was the precursor to chemistry. Invented right here in Egypt."

"I had no idea." My shoulders slumped. "I feel as if I'm still catching up, still falling behind my mother and what she knows. How can I find her when there are too many gaps in my education?"

Whit tucked a strand of my hair behind my ear. "Don't fret, Inez. We made progress, even if it was a tiny step."

I smiled small. "Are you ready to talk about Isadora, yet?"

Whit groaned. "Absolutely not."

"She asked for my help and I can't turn her away."

"There's something off about her," he said, playing with the ruffles on my skirt. "Isadora and her father were inseparable back in Philae. Have you forgotten?"

"She explained that. They were in the process of reconciling. From what she told me, her parents argued constantly, and they hated traveling around together. It doesn't sound like she had a happy childhood, and the trip to Philae was her father's attempt at making amends."

Whit nudged a stack of books with the toe of his boot and stood up to pace the room, walking around the boxes and trunks and random objects strewn about. "How convenient."

"All right," I said, my eyes trailing after him. "Say she has a nefarious plan. What is it? Maybe she's trying to overthrow the British monarchy."

He glared at me. "Try to take this seriously."

"I'm not used to seeing *you* so serious."

"Me neither; it's quite tiring." Whit sighed, glancing away, brows rising. "What have you done with my bedroom?"

"I think you mean *our* bedroom."

Whit opened his mouth but abruptly closed it when Isadora returned with the tea tray. We busied ourselves with the making of it. I wasn't particularly hungry, and it seemed no one else was, either, but there was comfort in performing a ritual, even one as ordinary as pouring tea.

When the cot arrived, Whit moved as much of the mess around as he could to clear enough space for it. He piled the crates higher and higher until they formed a half wall around our bed. I hid my smile at his attempt to create privacy in such a small space. Isadora automatically went to the narrow bed instead of the cot, settling onto it. "I think there's just enough room for the both of us, Inez."

Whit froze in the act of tossing the extra blanket onto the cot. He shot me an exasperated look, and he pointedly cleared his throat. But Isadora was vulnerable, and if this was what she needed, then I'd give it to her.

"It's only for a night or two," I whispered. "Until we can get larger accommodations."

He grunted and threw Isadora a scowl as he settled onto the cot he'd set up in the corner of the bedroom. Like I'd thought, it was a tight fit, but I couldn't see what could be done about it. We hadn't gone to the central bank in Cairo to retrieve funds from my account. For one thing, there hadn't been enough time, and for another, I wasn't sure if my uncle still maintained control of my fortune, despite my marrying Whit. But we clearly needed my funds, if only to request a larger room.

I settled onto the narrow bed next to my sister—when would I get used to the revelation?—and she automatically curled around me, her hair partially concealing her face. She looked impossibly young and vulnerable. A protective instinct rose, and it was so similar to the one I'd felt for Elvira that unshed tears burned at the backs of my eyes. I would do whatever I could to help her. I would do whatever I could to stop my mother and her deplorable lover, Mr. Fincastle.

But first things first.

Tomorrow, I would make Whit take me to the bank.

WHIT

I woke up early, the room dark and silent, save for the two women sleeping, their soft breaths mingling. The cot made a miserable bed, and I let out a foul curse under my breath as I stretched, trying to unknot my sore back.

God, take me now. This was not how I imagined my reunion with Inez. But this was the last night I'd spend on this poor excuse for a bed, even if I had to drag Isadora out of the room kicking and screaming. I sat up and glanced in her direction. She was wrapped around my wife like a barnacle. I wanted to pry her arms loose, shake her awake, and demand the truth from her.

Because the chit was *lying.*

I had no proof—only instinct. It was what kept me alive in the war; it was what prompted me to go back for General Gordon, even when it was forbidden. I wouldn't ignore it now, whatever Inez believed. She had a soft spot for Isadora—that much was clear—while everything inside me screamed her sister was a viper.

Suspicion curled tight in my chest.

Isadora's father had kept a close watch on her during our time in Philae. I remembered them pairing off, engaged in private conversation. He had been affectionate with her when he thought no one was looking. But I was always watching. It seemed inconceivable to me that he would have locked up his only child in the temple, that he would have put her in harm's way at all. Abdullah had recounted all the violence that had happened—some of our crew were shot when they tried to resist; others were bound and left to die out in the desert. Mr. Fincastle had either sent his daughter away before he'd acted *or* Isadora was a part of the plan.

It had never occurred to me to ask Abdullah which one it was. But he was now in the hospital hundreds of miles away, recovering. I'd have to send a letter or telegram and hope that he felt well enough to answer sooner rather than later.

I slid off the cot and padded to the small water closet, performing my ablutions efficiently and quietly. A talent courtesy of the army. I was conscious of the mirror hanging above the washbasin, but I carefully avoided it. I hadn't been able to look at myself in the mirror since I'd married Inez. I clutched the edge of the porcelain basin, my knuckles turning white. It took me several minutes to gather myself.

I had time. Plenty of time.

But even with the reminder, I still couldn't look at myself in the mirror.

Morning light had finally dawned in the small room, illuminating my wife, curled on her side, her wild hair blooming around her like spilled ink. I left without another look in her direction. The corridor was empty, which I preferred. Mornings were my favorite part of the day. For a long time, I didn't let myself enjoy them. Too much drink made sure of that.

The dawn had been tainted from my stint in the militia.

The terrace had many open tables, and I picked one closest to the balcony overlooking the gardens, my back to the wall. It was a cool morning, and when the server came to take my order, I requested my usual pot of coffee. While I waited, I meditated on the problem of Isadora and what the hell I was going to do about it. Abdullah would have to be questioned again. Ricardo wouldn't trust Isadora, either, but I debated the wisdom in including him. Inez might feel ambushed and less inclined to trust my instincts if I was aligned with her uncle. Their relationship was already complicated enough.

To say nothing of what he thought of me.

The coffee came, and I took the first heavenly sip. Dark, nutty, no cream.

But then someone sat onto the wicker chair opposite mine, surprising me, and I was never surprised. He wore his clothing stiffly, as if he would have preferred something other than starchy cotton and pressed trousers. He smiled at me in greeting, and even though it had been years since I'd seen him, my words came out angry and accusing.

"What the bloody hell are you doing here?"

Porter raised his hand, signaling to the waiter. "Are you hungry?"

I folded my arms across my chest, panic licking at my edges. But I refused to let him see. I shook my head. The server came and Porter ordered his breakfast: boiled eggs and two slices of toast. Plain, no butter. He never allowed himself any indulgences. Like Father.

Except when it came to playing cards. Father wasn't so sanctimonious then.

"I'm here to collect," Porter said in his damnably calm voice when we were once again alone.

"Collect—" I repeated.

Jesus. When I'd sent the telegram, I hadn't thought my brother would act that quickly, or that he'd come to Cairo himself.

"You explained your new situation in the telegram before your last."

"Yes," I said, my voice hard. "But that wasn't an invitation to come visit. I'm still working on it. The matter is quite delicate, and if I fuck up, we'll be worse off. I've only just—"

"It has to be today."

His words rushed around me, a furious bee storm.

"It can't be today. It can't be tomorrow. It can't be this month, Porter." I clenched my jaw. "They've lived in that crumbling house for years. Another year won't kill them."

"Another *year*," Porter repeated faintly.

"Tell them to sell my piano if they need the cash."

"Already sold."

Years of training kept me from flinching. "Fancy that."

"Along with the rest of the paintings and copper cookware and brass candlesticks," Porter said. "Before you ask, there's no more money I can give them."

I *had* been about to ask. Porter had been married off years earlier to an heiress when he was barely eighteen. He and his wife were estranged and living entirely separate lives. To my knowledge, Sophia didn't even live in England.

Which I knew Porter preferred, even if our father had tried to cut him out of their life from the ensuing scandal.

"And need I remind you who else lives in that crumbling house?"

I flattened my mouth. "She'll survive another year. She'll have to."

"The roof is leaking," Porter went on. "They've let go of the staff. Only the cook remains."

I had a plan, and I meant to stick to it. I tried to block out his words, but they seeped through.

"All the jewelry is gone," Porter said. "Anything valuable. They reached the end of the road. They *all* have. It's why I'm here."

"This may come as a shock to you, but I do have a strategy." I dragged a hand down the length of my face. Then I tossed some bills onto the table and stood up, my brother stumbling after me, awkwardly pushing back his chair. I was moving before I knew where I wanted to go. I only knew that I had to get inside.

"Well, what is it?" he called from behind me.

"Everyone will get what they want." I shook my head, my blood rushing to my ears. "Porter, I need more time."

He caught up and regarded me with his head tilted to the side. We were similar in appearance, like looking in the mirror. Same color hair, same pale eyes. But somehow, I took after my mother, and he took after my father. Porter had more hard lines to him than I did, and he was thinner.

"What have you been scheming?" Porter asked again.

I watched as all the pieces I'd lined up were moved around. My frustration mounted as I rearranged the puzzle and tried to come up with something that worked. But with my brother staring at me disapprovingly, the answer became hard to reach. We swept past the lobby, and I took the stairs two at a time, desperation making me pump my legs faster and faster.

"Tell me about your wife," he said, panting. "I've been curious."

"She cares for me," I said hollowly.

"That's unfortunate."

When I made it onto our floor, I breathed easier. His words bounced around in my mind, giving me a headache. I was standing in front of our room before I had entirely realized what I was doing. I didn't know why I'd come up, but even so, I pulled the key from out of my pocket and unlocked the door, pushed it open. "Wait here," I said curtly.

"Whitford, what are you doing?"

I barely heard him. The room was empty. I thought she would still be sleeping.

Porter poked his head inside. "Is this a bedroom or a storage closet?"

Where could she have gone so early? She and her infernal sister. My brother stepped into the room, and I felt, rather than saw, how he assessed every inch.

"Good gad! Do you sleep on this cot?" Porter exclaimed. "It looks uncomfortable."

"Let's go," I said, thinking hard. Inez could be out for a walk on the terrace. Wouldn't I have seen her, though? She was hard to miss, with her wild hair and quick stride.

"You care for this girl," my brother said in a marveling tone. "Your wife."

"If I did," I said, "I wouldn't have married her."

He studied me from the corner of his eye. I felt his judgment, his desperation. I understood why he came all this way. But I wouldn't yield.

"Whitford."

"I'm going to follow through with my promise," I snapped. "I'm going to do my duty as their heir. Surely more time isn't too much to ask?"

Porter's stoic veneer cracked, and I took a step forward in alarm. "Arabella doesn't have time. They're signing the marriage contract at the end of the week. She'll be married in *two weeks*—to Lord Fartherington."

I froze, the full meaning of his words cutting through my defense. I'd held up a shield to counter him guilting me into action. One of his favorite tactics—that and telling me I had to fall in line because I was the younger son. But I had no armor against Arabella. I knew my parents were at their wits' end. I knew Father's collectors would come calling. I'd also known, for years, that my father was deplorable at poker. But I'd forgotten how desperation made monsters of men. "*Fartherington?* He's ancient. At least two decades older than Father."

"Now that you understand the gravity of the situation, you have a choice to make." Porter met my eyes. Instead of his usual poise, he let me see his raw fear for our sister.

There were many things I'd had to learn how to handle.

My parents' disappointment.

An arranged marriage.

A career, bought and paid for.

A gun.

But when my older brother, as infuriating as he was, allowed me to see beneath his impenetrable veneer, I paid attention. It always meant that he was afraid. And *never* for himself.

It was this look on his face that made me think: time for a new plan. I pulled at my hair, my heart slamming against my ribs. I wanted a drink. I wanted oblivion. I didn't want any of this to happen. "I hate you."

Porter waited, one eyebrow raised. "Choose, brother."

CAPÍTULO OCHO

I could tell Isadora liked the dining room. Her attention flickered from the glossy flatware to the plush rugs, the sparkling glasses and satiny tablecloth. She faced me from across the table, her posture straight and not touching the back of the chair. For years, my mother had tried to ensure I'd do the same. There were other little things that telegraphed we were both raised by the same woman. Isadora wore her hair in the style my mother liked, braided and coiled at the crown of the head, a few delicate strands grazing her cheekbones. She kept her elbows off the table and both feet planted on the ground. My mother and Isadora knew how to sit still while I never did, constantly fidgeting, playing with my wineglass, tapping my toes against the floor.

Isadora knew all the rules of perfect etiquette—but she had been allowed to explore and shoot guns and excavate. She had been allowed to be herself. While I'd had to resort to trickery and secrecy and lying. It dawned on me how my mother had to do the same in order to lead the life she wanted.

With a whole new family.

The plate of food in front of Isadora sat untouched. The warmed pita had long since cooled, along with the ful mudammas, a savory fava bean porridge flavored with cumin, fresh herbs, and a lemon-garlic sauce and then slow-cooked overnight. I'd watched Kareem make it while on board the *Elephantine*, and the dish was a personal favorite of mine.

"Have you tried the tomato-and-cucumber salad?" I asked. "It's delicious dipped in the—"

"I'm not hungry," Isadora said.

Frustration and concern pulled me forward in my seat, and I leaned across the table to push the pot of tea toward her. We were in the dining room, surrounded by tourists and waiters, the noise level bustling and loud.

"Eat a little something."

Isadora's lips twitched. "You are so . . . *sisterly*."

"Am I?"

"Need I remind you that I know how to take care of myself?"

"And need I remind you that you've barely had anything to eat in the last couple of days? That you're under enormous stress?"

She smiled.

"Why are you smiling?"

"It amuses me that you're concerned about my nutritional intake."

"I'm only being practical," I muttered, leaning back against my chair, breaking one of Mamá's rules. "What would happen if you fainted in the middle of the street?"

"That has literally never happened to me."

"Papá always said he felt better when he'd eaten something after going through a trying day." He used to leave alfajores for me before voyaging to Egypt. The sandwich cookies were coated in powdered sugar and filled with layers of dulce de leche. Because of him, I'd developed quite a sweet tooth.

"What was he like?"

I looked at her sharply. "Did my mother ever talk to you about him?"

Isadora pushed the plate away. "She didn't. I think she wanted to keep that part of her life separate."

"Did you know our mother had another daughter?"

Isadora gazed at me unflinchingly. "No. Not until after you, Ricardo, and Whit left Philae. My father told me then who you were." Her eyes flicked down. "In a way, I wasn't surprised. I'd been drawn to you ever since you were pulled out of the river."

"But my mother kept me a secret," I said, bitterness stealing over me.

"I think she's an unhappy person who tried to make a new life for herself."

A new life that had set fire to our family. A new life that had turned her into a criminal. I couldn't believe Isadora was defending her. It seemed incredible that she didn't know who Mamá really was.

"You know," I began slowly, "that our mother is just as guilty as your father."

Isadora's jaw dropped. I startled, realizing that it was the first real expression I'd seen on her face. She leaned forward, her breath coming out in quick huffs. "What? What are you talking about?"

"Where do you think she is right now?"

Isadora frowned. "Back home, of course."

"Where is *home*?"

"London," she said. "We divided our time between England and Alexandria. We have an apartment there, and a house in Grosvenor Square."

It hardly seemed believable, the lengths my mother went to to secure a new existence for herself. She must have hated my father. Had she been planning on leaving Papá and me altogether? "Isadora, our mother trades in the black market here in Cairo."

She stood up, tucked her chair neatly under the table. "You're lying to me."

"Please sit down."

"Why are you doing this?" she asked. No emotion warbled her voice, and she held herself tall, chin tilted upward. She was frighteningly composed while I wished I knew how to keep myself from shattering. Talking about my mother always unsettled me—I was either angry or hurt or terrified.

"It's the truth," I said. "Please sit down."

She gazed toward the exit and I waited, breath caught in my chest. I didn't know what I'd do if she walked out of this room and out of my life.

"Where will you go?" I asked.

Isadora slowly turned her head. Her face remained expressionless, but her hands were shaking. "I have friends in the city."

I nodded, heart sinking. At least she wouldn't be alone. "I'm glad. Please keep in touch."

She remained standing, but she didn't make a move toward the dining room entrance. She must have expected me to argue with her, but I'd had plenty of experience in begging people to stay. It never went well. My parents always left, even when they knew I would have given anything for them to take me along or for them to stay home with me.

"Do you have proof of Mother's involvement?"

"I do," I whispered.

Isadora pulled out her chair, and slowly sat down, watching me warily. Then she drew her plate closer and took a delicate bite of the cold pita.

"We've both gone through a shock—"

"Like realizing one's father is a criminal?"

I played with the fork on my empty plate. "Yes—that would certainly constitute a trying time. Did you really have no idea?"

Isadora pulled at her lip, remaining quiet for so long I thought she wouldn't answer. When she did speak, her words came out haltingly.

"I've gone over and over it in my head . . . and the truth is there was always . . . some question I had at the back of my mind."

"Go on," I prodded.

Isadora took a sip from her teacup. "I suppose a part of me thought it *was* strange that they'd be gone all hours of the night several times a week. And I never questioned them when they hosted scores of people in the drawing room, even if they appeared to be . . . suspicious."

"Suspicious how?"

Her lips twisted in a grimace. On her, it looked like she'd just sucked on a lemon. "They weren't part of gentle society. Mother never served them anything to drink or eat. Some of them looked quite rough, and they stayed over long into the night."

I didn't know how much to tell her of the truth. My instincts were to shield her. It was likely the people Lourdes and Mr. Fincastle were meeting dealt with the illegal-artifact trade, too. But if it were me in her position, I wouldn't want to be coddled.

"What is it?"

I grimaced. Isadora was perceptive, and hiding something from her would take considerable effort. I deliberated, and for some reason, Elvira's face clouded in my mind. I had tried to shield her, too, often giving her only half truths. And look where that had gotten her.

"Have you heard of Tradesman's Gate?"

"No," Isadora said. "It sounds like something Wilkie Collins might have written."

I furrowed my brow.

"He writes mystery novels," Isadora explained.

"Ah," I said. "Well, I'm afraid this organization is real, and they steal priceless artifacts and fence them to buyers across several markets, predominately in Europe. Museums, private collectors, and the like. Our mother is just such a thief, and she's used the market to make a fortune. It seems like Mr. Fincastle is not only involved, but they are partners as well. They clearly planned what happened on Philae together."

Isadora made an unladylike groan, sounding so much like me it made the hair on my arms stand on end. Now that I was paying attention, her mannerisms continued to remind me of my mother. The way she tucked her hair behind her ear, how she fiddled with the collar of her dress, making sure it was perfectly flat. The straight line of her shoulders, her perfect posture. Isadora really was the young lady my mother always hoped to raise.

But then I remembered how Isadora had pulled out her sleek handgun, firing at the crocodile. It had been a bold and confident move. She knew how to behave, but that didn't mean she was stuffy and prim.

It meant she knew how to play the game to her advantage.

"That makes sense," Isadora said. "I'm only sorry I was a part of it, even peripherally. I don't know what to do now. How to move forward from all this."

"There are many particulars we need to discuss," I acknowledged. "But for now, please know that you will always have a place with Whit and me. It's perfectly acceptable for you to live with us, and I have the means to care for you."

"Speaking of, where is your husband this morning?"

"I don't know," I said, the corners of my mouth turning downward. "Running an errand most likely."

It annoyed me that he had taken off without so much as a goodbye. If I had done such a thing, he wouldn't have appreciated it. In fact, that was exactly what I was going to do. I knew that I would most likely need Whit at my side for what I wanted to accomplish, but I needed to do something, and perhaps I'd learn exactly what I would need to do in order to have access to my fortune. Perhaps I only needed a note from Whit or my uncle, or to show proof of our marriage in the form of a license. Regardless, I could go and ask my questions in person.

I was so sick of doing nothing.

Isadora eyed me shrewdly. "What were you thinking just now?"

"How would you like to accompany me to the bank?"

"I'm not sure," she said dryly. "I'm quite busy these days."

I laughed and polished off my coffee.

I left Isadora waiting in the lobby of the Anglo-Egyptian Bank, settled comfortably on a wooden bench laden with brightly woven pillows. The building had a blend of European and Arabic decor, and while it was designed to look like something from a Parisian street, the windows had the gorgeous latticework popular in Egypt. Outside, the Ezbekieh Gardens could be seen in all of their lush greenery, and beyond the tall palm trees, the stately Khedivial Opera House stood, flanked by two reservation kiosks.

Perhaps I'd walk there afterward and buy tickets to whatever musical was in season. Maybe a night out was what the three of us needed. Isadora and Whit needed time together to become better acquainted. I wasn't lying when I told Isadora that she had a place with us if she wanted.

"Right this way, Mrs. Hayes," a bank teller named Ahmed said, motioning for me to step into his office.

I blinked in surprise—I still wasn't used to my new name, and a pleasant thrill skipped down my spine. For the rest of my life, I would be Inez Emilia Hayes. We could be a real family. Legally, I supposed we were one. It was a fresh start, a chance to do things our own way. Warmth pooled in my belly, and I beamed at the bank attendant. He seemed surprised by my expression, but I couldn't very well tell him that he was the first person to address me as *Mrs. Hayes.*

I took the seat Ahmed offered, and settled across from him as he made himself comfortable in a high-backed chair. He wore a dark business suit, all clean lines and precise hems.

"I'm sure it's highly unusual for you to host a woman," I began. "But I've recently married, and I would like to begin the process of transferring ownership of my funds from my guardian over to my husband."

Ahmed opened his mouth, but I pressed on before he could tell me no.

"I can assure you that my husband would approve," I said. "In fact, will you tell me what I would need in order to set him up as the—"

"But he's already been here," Ahmed cut in. "He showed proper documentation, and your uncle is no longer the name on the account. The honor belongs to your husband."

My mouth dropped. So that was Whit's errand. He must have been wanting to surprise me. Well, that made things quite easy. "Excellent," I said, grinning. "I'd like to withdraw funds—"

Ahmed frowned. "Withdraw?"

"Yes. Please."

"But you cannot."

A flare of annoyance rose to the surface, and I squashed it with a determined smile. "My husband wouldn't object. In fact, I'm sure he gave you permission to allow me access to the money?"

Ahmed shifted in his seat and steepled his fingers. He seemed uneasy, and my annoyance turned into impatience.

"I'm sure that he would have," Ahmed said slowly, "if he hadn't withdrawn every last shilling in your account."

"He withdrew the money?"

Ahmed nodded.

A roar sounded in my ears, and I shook my head, trying to escape from the sound. It persisted, growing louder and louder. Tension gathered at my temples. I wished for a glass of water—my mouth was suddenly dry. I began reasoning with myself. There was a suitable explanation, I was sure of it. "Did he open a new account?"

"Not with us, no."

"I don't understand. I'd like my money."

"There is none left in the account your uncle previously managed."

I felt the blood drain from my face. I leaned forward, sure I had misheard. It sounded like he'd said that Whit had taken all of my money. Without speaking to me first. Without telling me his plans. That couldn't be right.

I swayed in my seat. "But—"

"Are you well, madam? You've gone pale. May I fetch your companion?"

"There's been a mistake," I said, hardly recognizing the dry rasp of my voice.

Ahmed shook his head. "No mistake. He left not five minutes before you arrived, madam. He showed me the proper registration and license of your marriage, and he asked me to place a call to a bank in London, where your uncle ran your account."

"So he moved—"

"He wired it to another bank in London."

"Can I access it?"

"Not from our establishment," Ahmed said gently. "You'd have to reach out to that particular bank in England." He hesitated. "Or ask your husband."

"There must be a perfectly reasonable explanation as to why my husband would move my money before I could access it for myself."

The bank teller stared at me silently with a faintly pitying expression on his face. He didn't have to speak in order for me to comprehend his thoughts. My husband was in control of my fortune, and at the first opportunity, he had wired it to a bank account I couldn't access.

Without talking to me first.

"No," I said faintly. "*No.*"

"It was all rather straightforward," Ahmed said.

Anguish crept up my throat, tasting like acid. This couldn't be. Whit wouldn't betray me; he wouldn't steal—

"Is there anything else you need from me?" Ahmed asked.

It would have been better for someone to have stabbed me in the gut.

It would have hurt far less. I stood on shaking legs, my head swimming. I was strangely light-headed and nauseated, as if desperately ill.

Ahmed came around the desk, concern in his dark eyes. "Mrs. Hayes, are you all right?"

I licked my dry lips. "Don't call me that."

Somehow, I made it to the lobby, where Isadora immediately came to stand by my side. She seemed to know something had gone terribly, disastrously wrong. Later, I would call it sisterly intuition. But right then, I wouldn't know my own name if someone asked me.

"I don't understand what happened," I said to her dumbly. My hands were shaking, my heartbeat thundering in my ears, the only noise I heard, the only thing I could hold on to that didn't make me feel as if I were adrift.

"Inez, what is it?" she said, peering into my face. "You look like you've seen a phantom."

Yes, it did feel like that. I would be haunted by this moment for the rest of my life.

"Please," I said. "Let's leave at once."

We went out into the blistering sunlight, and it seemed wrong. There ought to have been a torrential downpour and angry-looking clouds. Everything ought to have been backward or upside-down to match the turmoil flooding my body. I stood off to the side as Isadora whistled for a cab. It was long and piercing, and I had the fleeting thought of asking her to teach me how to do that.

A bubble of hysterical laughter escaped me.

Isadora glanced at me in alarm.

"I think I've been robbed."

"Come," she said, frowning at the street. "Let's walk over one block. I can't seem to find any available drivers."

I followed her in a trance, the swish of my skirt barely brushing against the path. Once again, she let out her sharp whistle, and this time a pair of horses ambled toward us, the driver flicking the reins lazily. My conversation with Ahmed repeated in my mind, and slowly I began to understand that my life had changed in an instant.

And that I had been a fool.

"*Inez?*"

Horror gripped me. That voice. I'd know it anywhere. I'd heard it nearly every day since I first arrived in Egypt. Slowly, I turned to find Whit striding toward me, dressed in an English suit: dark trousers, crisp shirt buttoned all the way to the chin. His jacket was all sharp lines and expertly tailored. A tall man trailed after him. He looked remarkably like my thieving husband. Same auburn hair. Same pale blue eyes. I knew who he must have been.

"Hola, Porter," I said. I was amazed at how calm I sounded when all I wanted was to scream until my voice left me altogether.

Whit's brother didn't offer a greeting or a smile, only shooting an uneasy glance at my husband.

My lying husband. My manipulative husband.

"Inez," Whit said, his expression revealing a hint of unease. "What are you doing here? I thought you'd still be at Shepheard's."

I couldn't frame the words, even as the truth settled deep in my heart, fracturing it into sharp pieces. I felt as if I were staring down an oncoming locomotive, and I could do nothing to save myself from being plowed over.

"Look at me," he said softly. "Are you all right?"

I needed a moment to compose myself, and so I averted my gaze, staring blankly at a long row of carriages ambling to their destinations. After a few moments of breathing deeply, fighting to remain calm, steadying my rioting heartbeat, I wrenched my gaze from the street, meeting his blue eyes.

My stomach somersaulted, and I flinched.

I had been fooled on every level by Whitford Hayes, starting with any warmth and tenderness I had imagined in his gaze. I relived every moment that I'd had with him. Every kindness, every soft word, every promise.

All *lies*.

"What are you doing here, so far from the hotel?" Whit repeated. "You ought to have—"

"What are you going to spend my money on, Whit?"

He froze, and all emotion bled from his face. He was a door snapped shut, the lock sliding into place with an almost audible click; all that remained was his English suit. His impassiveness only made me angrier. The longer he stood silent and remote, the worse I felt. As if by some mutual agreement, Isadora and Porter drew away, giving us some privacy on the busy Cairo street. Everything went on as normal, but I felt as if I were in another world, lost in parts unknown.

And it scared me.

"I just spoke to Ahmed," I said at his continued and infuriating silence. "And he told me that you've stolen all my money from me. Unless, of course, he's mistaken?"

Whit shook his head.

My heart fractured. A part of me had held hope it wasn't true. "You've stolen everything, then?" I asked again, even as I cursed the fragile hope still clinging to my edges.

"Correct."

"Well, thank you for being honest," I replied sarcastically.

His jaw locked, but he nodded. Perhaps he would never speak to me again. Perhaps this was the end of everything between us. Fury rose, blinding and obliterating.

"Do you have anything to say?" I demanded.

Still he said nothing—but I knew his mind was working. He was hiding behind that aristocratic English mask that I hated so much, faintly polite and bored. But his heart visibly pulsed hard on the side of his throat, a quick rhythm that revealed he wasn't as unaffected by me as much as he would have liked to have been.

And that *infuriated* me.

I acted without thinking, on instinct, my hand rising as if by its own accord. The slap turned his face, the sound ringing in my ear. Irritated skin turned red from my hand's imprint.

Whit shut his eyes, and I expected him to become cold and angry, but then he turned back to me, opening his eyes, and lifting his chin. His blank expression stole my breath. His face had lost all color, all warmth. He had retreated so far from me he might as well have been on another continent.

"You married me for my money." If I had to speak the words underwater, it would have been easier. In my whole life, I never thought I'd be in this situation. "You *used* me."

I shoved him, both palms against his immovable chest.

He bore it without a ripple of emotion, only staring back at me stonily.

"You're a liar," I said sharply, my voice rising with every word. "Everything between us was a lie. Every word, every vow."

A muscle jumped in his jaw. The only indication he had heard me at all.

"Say *something*."

Color returned to his cheeks, twin patches of red blooming bright. "Not everything," he said through clenched teeth. "Our friendship was—*is*—real to me."

"It was never a friendship," I said in disgust. I regretted pushing him to talk to me. "And you *knew* that."

He flinched. Opened his mouth—

"You want to say more words to me, Whit?" I asked incredulously. "Really?"

Whit closed his mouth.

I couldn't stand to see this version of him, remote, locked up tight. I was unraveling, fracturing into a million pieces, while he became more stiff, more rigid, more isolated. "Your words are cheap. They mean nothing."

He didn't bat an eye at this. That should have been the end, but my feet remained rooted to the ground. Curiosity burned in my chest, a sharp ache. I wanted to know why he'd betrayed me. I wanted to know what was worth our marriage. Our relationship, and whatever it might have been.

My damned heart.

I was torn, wanting to run as far away from him as possible, to create enough distance that it'd take him years to find me. But I wanted answers, too.

"I have a right to know where the money went," I said.

He clenched and unclenched his jaw. "I sent it to my family," he said, after a long, torturous beat. "They're in debt and they were about to marry off Arabella to a man forty years her senior. I wanted to protect my sister from that fate."

My heart foolishly leapt. He'd taken the money for love of his sister.

But he was being cruel—he'd made a choice, and it wasn't me. He married me and then robbed me blind. Did he expect me to be sympathetic? Was I supposed to be moved? Everything he was saying might be more manipulation.

More words that cost nothing.

I wasn't sure if I could take anything else from him, but the question ripped out of me. "Why didn't you ask me for it?"

Whit stared at me unflinchingly, his expression hard. "Are you honestly telling me that if I were to have told you that I needed all of your money, you would have given it to me?"

Everyone had warned me off from anyone who was even in clamoring distance of a fortune hunter. It was why all my suitors had come from families with means. Men who had no need of my fortune. Who might come to care for me, without the allure of piles of gold in an account.

If Whit would have asked me for the money, I certainly wouldn't have given him all of it, but I might have given him some. I stared past his shoulder, considering. But I would have always wondered if he had married *me* or my inheritance. Except, he had clearly planned all of this from the beginning. He had known about my parents' money even before I had met him, would have seen where their cash had gone in funding Abdullah and Ricardo's excavation seasons.

Whit's expression turned shrewd. "Would you have thought of me as a fortune hunter?" He let out a mirthless laugh. "You would have, Inez. And I couldn't risk asking you. My sister's life was at stake."

Well, I'd heard his explanation. He had married me to save someone else. I was the one who had been lied to, the one not picked. The one rejected. Again. Tears clouded my vision. With a start, I realized that I didn't care that the money was gone. The fortune belonged to my parents. Then it became my uncle's. It was always out of my reach. No, what I cared more about was the fact that I had married a man I loved, hoping to call him family.

But he had never planned to have a life with me.

I let out a shuddering breath. Anger burned, icy and hot in my veins. My voice shook with it. "This whole time, I was just a pawn to you. You're a con artist, and you know how to play the game. Isn't that basically your job description for my uncle?"

Whit rocked back on his heels, staring at me as if I were a stranger. It broke my heart, because we were slipping away from each other, and even if a small part of me wanted to hold on to him for dear life, I had to let go.

Something fractured between us. Or maybe it had always been broken.

"I trusted you," I whispered haltingly.

Isadora came to stand next to me and pulled me gently backward. "Let's return to the hotel, Inez."

I nodded, still shaken, climbing into the cab as if in a hazy dream, barely noticing as my sister rearranged my bustle. When I glanced back at Whit, the reality of our situation crashed into me. Time seemed to freeze, oddly suspended as our gazes met. Mine roiling in despair, his guarded and remote. An intense and obliterating tension flashed between us.

His brother approached him, whispering something into his ear. Whit glanced away from me, as easily as if I were a mere stranger, and stared blankly in the distance.

We were over. We had to be.

The hackney cab lurched forward, and we left Whit and his brother staring after us in the dust swirling in our wake. My heart locked itself away, tight in my chest, and I vowed I would never be so stupid as to reveal any part of it to Mr. Hayes ever again.

PART TWO

THE GATE THAT MOVES

WHIT

Porter dropped his hand onto my shoulder and tugged me to his side. The gesture lasted for only a second, but I knew what it meant. Like my father, my brother wasn't affectionate. Except when it was absolutely necessary.

Evidently stealing from one's wife warranted a hug.

"You saved Arabella," Porter said.

"There's that, at least," I muttered.

My brother arched a brow. He always did that better than me. I looked cheeky; he looked impervious. "Do you regret it, Whitford?"

My insides felt as if I'd lit a stick of dynamite, and now I was charred and hollowed out.

I glared at him. He was taller than me and thinner, but I could never intimidate him. "Father can't go back to the gaming halls, Porter."

My father and his obsession with cards. For years, he'd come home drunk, reeking of cigarettes and cheap perfume, his cravat undone, his head bare. He always lost his hat, and he'd have to buy another. When I was little, I used to wonder if all of his hats were together somewhere, waiting to be rescued. Most of my memories of him were of sitting at the top of the stairs to wait for him, my eyes trained on the front door, at the sliver of light that would appear when our butler—when we still had one—let my father in. I didn't care what time he came home; I worried he wouldn't come home at all.

But eventually he would, and the next day, he was the proper gentleman, strict and unfeeling, his stiff upper lip never wavering. Disapproving of what I said or how I behaved. And the only way I knew how to bear his recriminations was to pull myself far enough away so that I didn't feel anything at all. But on the nights he won, the next day he was joyful, downright radiant.

He'd take his sons for a ride, his daughter for a promenade in Hyde Park, our mother to the theater.

But his luck didn't last. I learned to keep a part of myself hidden during the rain, but especially when the sunlight shone.

"I'll make sure of it," Porter said. "I won't give them the money unless I have it in writing that he won't gamble. I'll tear up the marriage contract and set Arabella up with a dowry neither of them can touch. I'll manage the repairs on the house so the roof doesn't fall down on our sister's head."

I shuddered. In my family, my siblings were the only people I could trust. If Porter said he'd take care of something, he would. He ought to be my father's heir. It was ridiculous he wasn't, all because of a marriage they'd forced him into.

"I'm leaving today," Porter said. "Come with me."

My expression shifted, and my brother stiffened. Anger bled out of me. I'd made a commitment to Inez; I'd given my word. I wouldn't desert her, not after marrying her. I meant every word of my vows until she said otherwise.

"There's nothing for you here."

"How about *my wife*?"

"Do you still have one?"

Her look of devastation had seared itself into my brain. I ruthlessly shoved it aside and considered my brother's question. If I were her, I would run as far from me as I could. But unfortunately for Inez, I could help her in a way no one else could. Whatever skills I had, I'd use them for her. At the present moment, our interests were aligned.

We were both looking for the same person.

My attention returned to the street. A sense of urgency built in my chest. I let out a piercing whistle. "She's going to go after her mother, and I'm going to be there when she finds her."

And if I stayed with Olivera, my chances of finding the alchemical sheet greatly increased. Resolve hardened inside me. I would not leave Egypt without finding it.

Porter opened his mouth, but I stepped away from him as a hackney approached. The driver clicked his teeth, drawing up on the reins. The horse flicked its ears, annoyed. Wordlessly, I climbed inside, my mind whirring.

I turned around to meet Porter's eyes, identical to mine. "Goodbye, brother. Don't let it have been for nothing."

CAPÍTULO NUEVE

It infuriated me that the only place I could return to belonged to Whit. It was his hotel room, because I had no money to acquire another. No money, thanks to my scoundrel of a husband. My uncle's face crept to the surface, and I flung the image away. He would be intolerable once he found out what had happened. Not because he'd be cruel, but because he *wouldn't* be. He loved me—I knew that deep down—and seeing me brokenhearted would tear at him. And his kindness would ruin me because I had no one to blame but myself. Not only had I been wrong about Whit, but I'd been incredibly stupid.

How many times had he warned me not to trust him?

I hated that a small part of me understood his motives. It would have been easier to hate him outright if he'd taken the money for himself like a proper villain. My own heart would have slammed the door, given up fully. Instead, I felt as if it had been rent into two halves.

Two sides that warred against each other.

He had saved someone he loved, one half said.

That person had not been me, said the other.

"What about an annulment?" Isadora asked, breaking the tense quiet.

The cab lurched, and my hand immediately shot up to brace myself against the sudden movement. "It's too late for that." If I thought about that night, I'd shatter. It had meant something to me, but to him it was all an act. The next step in his plan. A way to secure my fortune for his use.

"Ah," Isadora said without a trace of a blush. "Then what about a divorce?"

Frustration laced my blood. "I'd be worse off. Not married, no money, and my uncle would then have grounds to become my guardian again. Especially since I was robbed within days of my marriage."

"Technically speaking, your fortune became Whit's once the marriage contract was signed. He was within his rights to do whatever he wanted with *his* money."

I glared at her.

"I'm not saying I agree with the law," Isadora said hastily.

"I don't want to talk about the law and how biased it is against women," I snapped.

Isadora nodded. "Fine. Is there no other family you could ask for assistance?"

My lip curled. "I have an aunt, but she wouldn't help me through this, either. She'd force me back on that boat to Argentina." Horror gripped me. "In fact, it wouldn't surprise me if she was on her way to me now."

My sister sighed. "Mr. Hayes might return to England."

If only he would. I never wanted to see his face again. It was too painful, too raw. He made me feel foolish. A young girl playing at adulthood. "Now that he has money, he very well might."

"So you're penniless," Isadora mused.

"It would seem so."

"And your uncle won't help?"

I shook my head. "My uncle wants me safe. And to him, that means far from the life he leads here in Egypt."

"And what do *you* want?" Isadora shifted in the seat, tucking her full skirt demurely around her. I was amazed at her ability to appear unruffled when the slightest gust of wind would ravage my own appearance. Despite the steady rocking of the cab as it crossed the street, veering away from the numerous donkeys and horses and carriages crowding the path, Isadora didn't have a hair out of place. There was magic involved—there had to be. I marveled at her. As a girl of nearly eighteen, she was remarkable; as a young lady she would be formidable. If I could keep her safe long enough from her horrifying parents, that was. The idea of failing her sobered me immediately.

"Elvira died because of Mamá," I said. "I want her in prison. She knows what happened to my father. He might still be *alive*. I want her to tell me the truth."

Isadora studied me for a long moment. "I have another idea. What if you went home?"

I opened my mouth to protest, but she laid a hand on my arm.

"Listen to me before you dismiss the idea outright. Removing yourself from the situation might help matters. Your uncle might calm down, and distance from Whit might give you perspective. Without means, how effective will you be against our mother?"

My conversation with Whit came back to me. Spoken softly in a moment of vulnerability. I'd never put myself in that position with him ever again. But I held on to what he had communicated—I didn't need money to move against my mother. To track her down and force her to confront me.

I only needed to know the right people.

"I have first-class tickets," I said slowly. At Isadora's confused expression, I elaborated. "One is a train ticket, the other a passage to Argentina on a luxury liner," I explained.

"I'm not following," Isadora said.

"I can return both tickets," I said. "And I'll still have some money left over. Enough for food and perhaps a couple of nights of accommodations." The driver pulled up at Shepheard's entrance, the terrace overflowing with tables and chairs filled with hotel guests, surrounded by potted plants and large trees. "Though, perhaps not *here*."

"All right," she said in her cool voice. "And then what?"

"I have no idea," I admitted, my mind spinning as I tossed one idea over another. "But there must be some trace of her. Someone must know where she lived, who she spoke with, where she frequented. Mamá isn't a phantom. She had contacts, friends. She traded artifacts. There has to be—" An idea slammed into me. "Isadora! *The artifacts*. We need to think about the items she stole."

Isadora stared, her lips parting in surprise. "I beg your pardon?"

"Mamá can't hold on to them for too long—it isn't safe, and word will only spread that Cleopatra and her cache have been located. People will find out. It's the discovery of the century."

"This is sheer idiocy," Isadora protested. "If we don't know where Mother is, then it follows we have no idea where the relics are, or where to look for them."

A square card printed with the image of a gate leapt into my mind. That card was an invitation to Tradesman's Gate. "She'd fence the items." I nodded, buzzing with excitement as a plan formed in my mind. Finally, a way forward. "And she'd do that by attending the next auction."

"And do you know when that will be?"

"No," I muttered in frustration. "But someone has to. Maybe we can sneak into one of the clubs in Cairo?"

Isadora narrowed her eyes at me. "You like to rush headlong into situations before really thinking them through, don't you?"

"I'm told it's one of my more exasperating traits," I admitted.

"And you have a habit of doing things on your own." Isadora studied me frankly, her eyes seeming to miss nothing. They didn't match the softness of her face. They were too old for someone who was so young. "I was their child, too."

A part of me had known she would offer to help me, and I recoiled at the thought. It was Isadora who stared at me expectantly, but all I saw was Elvira's destroyed face.

There'd been so much blood.

"We ought to work together," Isadora insisted.

"You'd see your father in prison?"

She pulled at her lip, and for the briefest moment, her eyes watered with genuine regret. "I can't believe he'd do such a thing." She shook her head, as if to clear it from any doubts. "He'll end up dead if he continues on this road—I'm sure of it. I'd rather visit him in prison than at his grave."

I opened my mouth to tell her that I'd manage this alone. It was too dangerous, and I'd only just found her. I had every reason to forbid her from doing this with me—but the words stayed put. Past conversations with Tío Ricardo swept through my mind. He, too, had tried to tell me what to do, to send me away, to not participate. It struck me how much I'd sound like my uncle or Whit, and everyone else who wanted me to leave Egypt, if I told her to stay away.

I couldn't do that to Isadora.

In one act, her father had upended her life and made her an accomplice to his criminal activities. At least, that's what everyone would think. I only had to think of Whit—that was his first conclusion, too. Could Isadora's reputation survive the gossip? The implied accusations?

I didn't think so.

"What are you thinking?"

"I'm having second thoughts on how to proceed," I said slowly. "It's not like me to feel so undecided. Usually, I can make up my mind quickly—but there are too many unknowns. I'm not a soldier; I can barely shoot. I've slapped someone exactly one time. Even if I were to discover the location of the next auction, what can I do to defend myself against any of these people?"

"I know how to shoot," she said.

A protective feeling swelled in my chest. Elvira was irreplaceable, a human being I had adored with all my heart. And now here was Isadora, a sister that I'd always wanted. The family I could hold on to for the rest of my life.

If something were to happen to her . . .

"I have been taking care of myself for a long time," she said, eyeing me shrewdly, accurately reading my thoughts. "It seems to me that you have two options. Stay in Egypt with hardly any funds and complete the daunting task of locating our mother and work with the authorities in charging her for her crimes with the ultimate goal of her landing in prison. Or you can return home and regroup. Perhaps there are ways for you to acquire more funding. I'm assuming you own property, yes? Well, then. Hope is not lost."

"If I go, what happens to you?"

"Well," she said slowly. "I've always wanted to visit South America."

I raised my brows, struck by the idea. I'd fought for so long to stay in Egypt—I'd gotten married to ensure that—and it hurt my brain to consider another option. But I wouldn't be going home alone. I'd have a sister who could help me reassess and calculate a better plan.

"Think about it," she said. "I'll support you in whatever you decide. For now, return the tickets and give yourself time to think about what *you* want to do."

"If I stay, I'd be risking *both* of our lives."

She reached over and clasped my hand. Her voice was warm, rich like honey and just as comforting. "I know. But it's my decision."

I met her eyes. Hazel to her blue. "Yes, it is."

I hoped she wouldn't come to regret it.

"Here's your change, Señorita Olivera," Salaam, the hotel manager, said, handing me an envelope near bursting at the seams. "The concierge was able to return your train tickets, and your passage to Argentina was refunded in its entirety." He smiled. "I'm pleased you've extended your stay in Egypt."

I nodded, unable to match his pleasant tone. "Shokran."

As I turned away, a tall figure leaning against a granite pillar caught my attention. His arms were folded tight across his chest, as if he had to physically restrain himself from drawing near. I pivoted and marched toward the stairs, but moments later, his footsteps thundered after me. I looked over my shoulder as he took hold of my arm and swung me into one of the alcoves off the main lobby.

"Please sit," he said.

I remained standing. "I thought I told you I don't want to speak to you. I don't want to be near you. I don't want—"

"You've been very clear," he said in an even tone.

"Apparently not," I muttered.

"I can chase you," he said in a chillingly soft voice, "or you can take a minute and listen to what I have to say and then decide never to speak with me again."

"Say what you have to say, then," I said, pulling free from his grasp. I sat on the low-backed chair and drew my legs as far from the opposite chair as possible.

Whit settled across from me. "You want to find your mother."

It wasn't a question, so I remained silent.

"I have some ideas where she might be."

My lips parted. "Where?"

"She has a cache of artifacts," he began. "It's too risky to hold on to them for too long, and so she'll have to—"

"Sell them at Tradesman's Gate," I broke in smugly. "I'm aware."

Whit pinched his lips, the only sign I'd annoyed him. But I didn't care. He wasn't relaying anything I hadn't figured out for myself. "If that's all," I said, rising. Once, I would have talked to him about the choice I had to make. Back then, I would have trusted him to give me his honest opinion and advice. But he had ruined that for the both of us. There was no way that I could tell him I was considering leaving. I couldn't bear to see the relief on his face.

"*Sit down*."

I dropped back into the chair, startled.

Whit leaned forward, elbows propped on his knees. "The gate always moves, from one location to another. I can find out where it will be next."

I narrowed my gaze. "How will you come by this information?"

He only looked at me blandly. "Recall what I do for a living."

"You still work for my uncle?" I said in surprise. "I thought he was too furious at our—" I faltered, unable to continue. We had tricked Tío Ricardo, and then Whit had tricked me. All I'd done since arriving in Egypt was to plot and scheme until I had gotten my way. I'd disguised myself, stowed away in my uncle's dahabeeyah, lied to everyone—including Whit—when I snuck the artifacts from Cleopatra's tomb and into my mother's hands. I had allowed Elvira to dance at a ball, when I knew it was dangerous.

What hadn't I done to get my way?

A sickening pit yawned deep in my belly. Whit and I were the same kind of human. People who maneuvered chess pieces on a board, aiming to win. Whit stared at me broodingly, seeming to understand every nuance to my expression. He looked primed for action, his shoulders tense, readying to chase after me if I so much as moved. His being here at all confused me. He'd taken my money. What else did he want?

"Why are you still here?"

"I know it's hard to believe," he said softly, "but I meant every word of my vows."

"Did you?" I said, in what I hoped was a biting tone. To my ear, I sounded breathless. I forced myself to lean away from him.

"Yes, I did."

I thought back to the promise he'd made me, said in his confident and arresting voice—the one that made others sit up and listen or get out of his way. That night, he'd spoken vows of *protecting* me. That had been the gist. Disappointment clouded my vision, and I turned my face away so he wouldn't see my watery eyes. At no point did he promise to love me. He had been warning me, even then.

I was too much of a besotted fool to hear the words he didn't say.

Papá used to say that whenever I felt lost, it was because I wasn't telling myself the truth. He explained, in his soft, breathy voice suitable for libraries and churches, that people were often afraid to tell themselves the truth. They would rather lie, would rather deny, would rather ignore what was right in front of them.

I vowed to myself that I would always deal in truth. No matter how much it cost me, or weakened me, or even if it killed me.

One, I couldn't count our wedding night as some kind of declaration on his part. It had been my choice. He would have waited, but I was the one who convinced him it had to be done.

Total ruination. That had been my intent.

Two, he had needed money and I was there for the taking. That, *and* he knew how badly I wanted to stay in Egypt. In proposing marriage, he was offering a solution—one that benefited him, but a solution nevertheless.

Three, he had told me never to believe a word he said.

A small voice whispered against my skin, a *lie* pulling me toward that moment in the tomb when he had kissed me in the dark. I thought we were finally laying bare our feelings, our souls. We were dying—slowly but surely—and I had stupidly thought the time for honesty had finally come.

Here was truth number four: Whitford Hayes would have kissed anyone.

And the last, most devastating truth: Whit was still in Egypt, not because he was honoring his vows, not because he wanted to help me, but because he wanted to find Cleopatra's Chrysopoeia. He *might* have some misguided sense of obligation toward me, some sense of the responsibility that lay on his shoulders. He might even *pity* me. Either way, that was what was motivating him now.

I shuddered.

I couldn't stand the idea of him feeling that way about me when I had been prepared to give him my life. He was here because our goals ran parallel to each other's, and it gave him an opportunity to atone for what he had done. No—atoning for something meant that there was regret, there was remorse.

Whit felt neither of those things.

"Do you know that you never apologized?" I whispered.

"I'm aware," Whit said in a flat voice. "And I never will."

I could only gape at his ruthlessness. I couldn't believe how much I'd misjudged him.

"I am sorry for the way it happened," he amended. "That wasn't what I had planned. But I can't apologize for saving my sister, because I would make the same decision all over again," he said quietly. "Arabella means a great deal to me."

And I did not.

The implication hurt, but I refused to let it show.

It would be profoundly foolish not to accept his . . . expertise. But we had gotten off topic, and the sooner we discussed the parameters of our partnership, the sooner I could walk away from him. There was only so much of this I could handle. My heart was the one that was broken. Not his.

"I'm not accepting your help without conditions."

He nodded in resignation. "I thought so."

"No more lies," I said. "No more scheming, no more half-truths and omissions."

He made a noise at the back of his throat. "I'm not going to volunteer information that you don't ask for— *Will you let me finish, Inez?*"

I snapped my mouth shut and glared at him.

"But if it pertains to you, I'll share what I know."

"Fine," I said icily. "Tell me the real reason why you're still here. Is it to find the Chrysopoeia of Cleopatra?"

Whit's jaw tightened. "It's part of the reason."

"And the other?"

"What are your other conditions?" he countered. "I know you have more."

"No more leaving me behind. Wherever you go, I go."

His brow darkened. "I'm not risking your life. Next."

I went to stand and he flung out his arm, snarling. "*Fine*. What else?"

"We are through," I said, fighting to keep the tears at bay. "You can't kiss me."

Whit regarded me stonily and dipped his chin.

I stood, and this time he didn't stop me. I walked three paces, when another condition pressed hard against my chest, robbing me of breath. Isadora had suggested it, but I'd dismissed the idea outright. Except she was right, it was the best course of action to take. For *my* peace of mind. For my heart. Once I said it aloud, there was no going back. But it had to be done—I would grieve afterward when I was far away from this place. Slowly, I turned, my heart racing. "And Whit?"

He regarded me warily. "What else?"

My lips trembled, but I was reasonably proud when my voice didn't crack. "When this is all over, you will let me quietly divorce you."

His eyes burned into mine. A muscle in his jaw jumped. "Understood."

WHIT

Hours later, I was already lying to her.

The streets were quiet this time of night, but even so, I was not going to bring Inez to an opium den. I could only imagine her expression the moment she crossed the threshold, swirls of smoke covering every inch of her, her face turned toward mine, alchemical eyes burning gold in disapproval.

No, thank you.

I kept my feet light on the dirt street, having turned off the main thoroughfare and away from the fancy buildings with their Parisian arches and elegant doorways. The road narrowed, and overhead, shutters were closed. Only the soft sounds of others milling in darkened alleys disturbed the sharp quiet. My revolver was a sure weight against my hip as I glanced behind me once, twice, three times.

Someone followed.

I couldn't hear them, but my intuition sparked under my skin, raising the hair at the back of my neck. Whoever trailed after me was silent and no stranger to the streets. They knew where to step; they knew what shadows to embrace. I could guess who they were—I'd killed a contact since arriving in Cairo, and word would have spread.

Peter's associates would be none too pleased with me.

At last, the nondescript entrance to the opium den I sought loomed ahead, a narrow doorway flanked by men lounging on the front steps. I passed through without comment, knowing they'd recognize my face under the harsh moonlight. Inside, low couches were filled with officers, diplomats, effendis, and beys, all enjoying the dancing women and drink, and the potent siren of the crushed poppy seed. I found a stretch of the wall unoccupied and leaned against it, tucked into the shadows and behind a half-drawn curtain separating one small room from the next. The low chatter of conversation became a constant thrum as I waited to see who would walk in after me.

I expected it to be my stalker, but a group entered—three, no four, people dressed in dark clothing, laughing quietly, already at their second or third establishment of the night. Frustration pricked—I didn't have all night to see which of Peter's friends was after me. I wanted to know where the gate would move next. My attention flicked to the adjoining room, and I slid inside, immediately noticing the man I needed to see. He was an antiquities officer by day and a curator for Tradesman's Gate by night. He'd know where the next auction would take place. And fortunately for me, he knew who I was.

I sat down next to him, and he looked at me through bloodshot eyes.

"Bonne soirée, mon ami," he said in a thick French accent. "That is, if we still are."

"À vous aussi," I said, accepting a drink from one of the women carrying a tray. "And we are. Why wouldn't we be, Yves?"

He arched a blond brow. "I know at least one *friend* whom you have killed."

I held up both hands, smiling. "I was provoked."

"Hmmm." Yves placed a cigarette between his lips and struck a match. He inhaled once and then held out the lit cigarette to me, which I took. "It's been a long time since I've seen you around."

"You know how it goes," I said after a long inhale. "Different jobs, different cities."

"What brings you tonight?"

I dropped my voice, acutely aware of the people surrounding us, sitting at adjacent low couches, standing along the wall, walking through the small room. The conversations mixed together, like several ingredients in a beaker, impossible to parse through who spoke what and from where. "I'm representing a buyer." I exhaled through my nose, and I watched the plume drift upward, swirling in his face. "He's heard of a cache from upper Egypt that will become available at the next auction."

Yves flagged for another drink, his present one only had one or two sips left. "Dis m'en plus."

I hesitated and then shrugged. Lourdes would have moved fast, and doubtless Yves already knew. "Cleopatra."

He froze, his hand holding the glass halfway to his mouth. His eyes flickered over the room. "I wasn't aware many people knew of the discovery. Très intéressant."

"Quite," I murmured. "Where will it be? The buyer is keen on attending."

"Why wasn't he sent an invitation?" Yves narrowed his gaze. "You haven't gone clean, have you, *mon ami*?"

"I just killed a friend." I flicked the cigarette against a silver tray on the low coffee table. "Does that sound clean to you?"

Yves studied me. "Answer my question."

"He's new." I finished the last of the cigarette and craved another. "Wealthy American."

My companion rolled his eyes, but his shoulders loosened. "He needs to be vetted."

"In process," I said. "But he doesn't want to miss the next one until then."

"Hmmm," Yves said. "I suppose I can't deny you, can I? Or you might follow me down an alley and force it out of me." He looked at me for confirmation, but I gave him nothing. Then he shrugged. "I'd rather have a pleasant evening. It's the old government building this time. Le savez-vous?"

I nodded. "I know it. What day and time, s'il vous plaît?"

"You know, I heard the strangest rumor about you."

I tensed. "Date and time, Yves. I don't care for gossip, especially about myself."

"I think you'd care about this one," Yves said. "I heard you married."

Nothing in my expression changed, but ice crept over my skin, creating goose bumps.

"In secret," he continued. "Quite the story, don't you think?"

"I pity the broad, whoever she is," I said with a laugh. "I thought you wanted a pleasant evening? I'm not going to ask you for the details again."

"I gave the location for free," he said. "If you want more, it will cost you."

"How much?"

Yves's eyes dropped to the gun, nearly concealed by my jacket. "I've always liked it."

The revolver had not left my sight since General Gordon's death. It was the only thing I owned that belonged to the general. The only physical link I had. I reached for it daily, unconsciously, as if it were an extension of myself. I hesitated, knowing there'd be no way I could get it back. But I had nothing else to offer in exchange, and while I could force him to tell me what he knew, I would not kill him for the information. He was, unfortunately, a useful contact. I let out a hiss and handed it over, taking care not to look at the initials carved in the handle. "Bastard."

"Nothing comes free," he said mildly. "As you've told me many times before."

I waited, practically having to sit on my hands to keep myself from snatching the weapon back. Yves tucked it away, and I knew I'd never see the gun again.

"The day after tomorrow, four in the morning." He drank his whiskey down to the last drop, set the glass on the table. "I hope your buyer gets what he wants."

Then with a small salute, he stood and left the room.

A server immediately appeared, a man dressed in a floor-length tunic, and told me what I owed—for my drink and the incredible amount Yves had consumed. "Fucker," I muttered as I rummaged through my pockets, searching for the last of my bills. Maybe I *would* follow him down an alley. From the corner of my eye, I sensed a figure brush past, dropping coins as they went. The money clattered against the wood of the coffee table, and I glanced up sharply in time to see the shadow of someone slinking out of the room, nearly made invisible by the curls of smoke and patrons crowding the entrance.

I jumped to my feet, quickly counting the amount, realizing a moment later it was exactly what I owed. Without another glance at the server, I rushed forward, leaving that room and then the next, bounding out into the night. I reached for my gun before remembering I'd traded it for information.

"*Shit*," I hissed.

Both ends of the street were unnaturally empty. Nothing and no one moved. I backed up a few steps, my heart thundering wildly, until my shoulders hit a stone wall. I waited, sure my stalker would appear any second from their hiding place. Whoever they were, they had been close enough to hear my conversation with Yves—every word. Why else would they drop the exact amount of money we owed?

Onto the damn coffee table.

Right in front of me.

Ten minutes passed, then fifteen. My breathing was even and soft, and I thought of reaching for the knife hidden in my boot. I sensed they were watching for any movement, waiting to hear the brush of clothing. Another ten minutes passed, and I remained coiled tight, ready to spring at the slightest provocation.

But no one materialized in the dark.

The room was quiet when I returned, both women sleeping on the bed, ensconced in the mosquito netting. I barely managed to keep from knocking into one of the stacked boxes surrounding the narrow cot. Quietly, I sank onto the bed, peeling off my jacket, unlacing my boots, before slumping backward, forgetting that my makeshift sleeping arrangements didn't include a pillow. The back of my head hit a spring.

"Ow," I muttered.

I tried to sleep, but the glimpse of my stalker stayed with me. I'd felt, rather than seen, them walk past the table. By the time I'd looked up, they were walking out of the room—a black coat, hat. I replayed the moment over and over, but no other details came.

The lack of them kept me up for the rest of the night.

CAPÍTULO DIEZ

There are only a few sounds in the world that make me quake in fear. The scrape of rock against the entrance of a tomb. The hiss of gunpowder before the inevitable explosion. A bullet fired, followed by the telltale whistling noise of impending death.

And one other.

Tía Lorena's voice.

I heard it distinctly, and I sat up straight in the wicker chair out front on the terrace of Shepheard's, where my sister and I were having our morning tea. Isadora glanced at me, her brow crinkled in puzzlement. Loud footsteps approached from behind, the echo of my aunt's exclamations roaring in my ear. I turned in my seat with trepidation to find a familiar face gazing down at me.

My aunt.

And behind her, the cold face of my cousin Amaranta.

I jumped to my feet, swaying sharply, tears clouding my vision. I knew this day would arrive eventually—the inevitable confrontation with Elvira's grief-stricken mother and sister—but I hadn't expected it so soon. But of course they would come.

Come to collect Elvira's body.

"Inez," Tía Lorena murmured. She gazed at me in confusion, hands trembling as she reached for me. "You look so different."

Words left me, stolen by the sense of despair rising in me. I could only stand in front of them both and wait for their judgment—I deserved nothing less than total condemnation.

"I'm so sorry," I gasped. "Lo siento—"

My aunt stumbled forward and embraced me, arms tight around my waist, her wet cheek pressed to my own. She sobbed quietly, her body shaking. I couldn't stop my own tears, and together we clung on to each other for dear life, right there in the middle of the terrace, with dozens of people staring at the scene in confused astonishment.

I hardly cared, but it was when my vision cleared enough to catch sight of Amaranta that I finally tried to get a hold of my overwrought emotions. She wouldn't appreciate my tears. She hadn't come for that.

If I knew my cousin at all, then she had traveled all this way for retribution.

It was Isadora who managed to herd us indoors from the prying eyes of the other hotel guests. Somehow, she'd figured out my aunt's room number and led us all to the second floor. Amaranta took charge then, using a brass key to unlock the door to their suite. My aunt was inconsolable, stumbling as we all helped her inside. I barely took in the surroundings, dimly registering the suite resembled the one I'd just vacated. It, too, had a comfortable seating area that led into two bedrooms.

"Please tell us what happened," Tía Lorena said in a watery voice, mopping up her streaming eyes. "I haven't been able to sleep or eat since I found out."

I glanced at Amaranta, who had remained coldly silent, arms folded tightly across her chest. I knew her well enough to know that anger made her quiet. From her pale face and lips, her drawn eyes, and the black she wore from head to foot, I knew she was raging on the inside.

Isadora reached for my hand and squeezed and then murmured, "I'll be right outside." Without another word, she left, closing the door behind her.

I licked my lips, unsure. I couldn't tell them what I dreamt of every night—Elvira's blown-up face, the blood staining the gold sand underneath her head. "She was murdered," I whispered finally. "By one of my mother's associates."

My aunt—who hated wrinkles in her clothing and untidy hair, and who always carried a handkerchief—slumped to the carpeted floor in a heap of black cotton. I didn't know how to help her, what I could say to lessen her grief, and when I took a step forward, Amaranta snatched my arm, tight, her fingernails digging into the sleeves of my shirt.

"Don't," she seethed. "Don't you touch her again." She released me, recoiling sharply, and then swooped down to help her mother stand. In a hushed voice, she coaxed her mother into one of the bedrooms. My cousin reappeared a moment later and sat in one of the high-backed chairs, her hands tightly laced in her lap.

"Sit down, Inez," she said through gritted teeth. "And tell me everything."

So I did, in fits and starts. Amaranta never interrupted me, listening intently, a frown pulling her dark brows into a straight line across her forehead. Her expression only changed when I came to the part about Elvira's kidnapping. All the blood drained from her face.

"Your mother sacrificed my sister?" she asked in a flat voice. "To save your life?"

Mutely, I nodded.

Her voice remained emotionless. "Continue."

I got through the rest, a hard knot at the back of my throat. Once again, I sensed that she wouldn't appreciate any display of emotion. When I finished, Amaranta was silent for a long time. Then she speared me with her dark eyes, a sharp contrast to her pale, drawn face.

"Your mother needs to die."

My lips parted in surprise.

"She has to pay for what she's done." Amaranta leaned forward, the iron line of her spine finally bending. "Do you hear me, Inez? What are you going to do to make this right?"

I flinched, my guilt creating a yawning pit deep in my belly. "I'm going to find her."

"And then?"

"You and I want the same thing," I whispered. "I want my mother gone."

Amaranta studied me, running a critical eye over every line and curve of my face. "This is your fault, and I will never forgive you. But if you do this, my mother might be able to tolerate the sight of you one day." She stood up. "I want you to leave now."

Shakily, I got to my feet, leaving without looking in her direction. I understood then that I could never go back to Argentina until I made things right. My aunt wouldn't want to see me, and Amaranta would make it very clear that I was unwelcome in my own home.

I couldn't blame her.

Isadora waited for me in the corridor, rigidly composed. She had been looking better in my care, but now she resembled the withdrawn figure from a few days ago. I *hated* that.

"They aren't happy with me," I said. "With good reason. Amaranta wants—"

"Our mother dead," she said. "I know."

Her face rippled with an expression I couldn't read. We stared at each other silently, and I wished I knew her well enough to ask how she felt. My cousin's words had shocked me, and I could only imagine Isadora having mixed feelings as well. Her words from an earlier conversation swept through my mind—and I realized that she'd rather her mother be in prison than buried underground.

The feeling was mutual.

I hated my mother, but I didn't want her to die. She loved me, in her twisted way, and I couldn't stand how that meant something to me when it shouldn't matter at all. But it did, and so I wouldn't kill my mother.

I wasn't a murderer like she was.

"What are you going to do now?" Isadora asked.

"Finalize our plans."

Tío Ricardo shoved away the steaming cup filled with black tea. "No more. I need something stronger."

I sighed, sitting down in the chair next to his unmade bed. "I suppose I shouldn't bother telling you to rest?"

"You ought to be groveling. Begging for my forgiveness is what you ought to be doing," my uncle snapped as he settled against the pillows. "Where is your bastard of a husband, anyway? He hasn't checked in with me since we came back from Philae."

"He's out running errands," I lied. I hadn't seen him, either. This morning, I'd woken to find him gone. I doubt he knew my aunt and cousin were also staying at the hotel. Not that I cared what he did. But since he wanted to supposedly help me, I would have thought he'd make himself more available.

"Whit still works for me," he said. "He knows better than to disappear without telling me."

I frowned. "Are you worried about him?"

My uncle scowled. "Wherever Whit goes, trouble seems to find him."

That was certainly true, though the same could be said of me. "What do you need him to do? Perhaps I can do it instead?"

"I suppose you could," my uncle said thoughtfully. "Abdullah checked in at the hotel, and a physician has been tending to him. Perhaps you can pay him a visit? I believe he's on the same floor."

"Certainly," I said. I couldn't imagine what he was going through. The find of the century and it had been taken away from him. "How is he?"

"No lo sé," Tío Ricardo said testily. "Hence why I'd like you to pay him a visit."

"You are grouchy this morning," I observed.

"My ward got married in secret to a man with questionable ethics and morals," he said. "The work I'd done at Philae, alongside my brother-in-law, has been destroyed. Cleopatra's mummy will be pulverized and used for wealthy aristocrats to heal, I don't know, a mild headache. Her life's possessions will be sold off to the highest bidder in an illegal market, which my sister is a known member of. Your aunt, a woman I cannot stand, has lost one of her daughters thanks to me and is now hysterical two bedrooms over—shall I keep going? I have cause to be grouchy."

Privately, I added, *Isadora is my sister and the daughter of the man who pillaged Philae. Oh, and Whit stole my inheritance.*

But perhaps I ought to save that bit of news for another time.

"Let me know how my friend is doing," Tío Ricardo said. "Perhaps you should make him drink this awful tea."

"I will, as soon as you finish your break—"

Loud and insistent knocking broke through our conversation. My uncle sat upright, intent on getting out of bed, but I held up a hand and said sharply, "I'll answer."

My uncle glared at me, but I was already on my feet and opening the bedroom door, fully expecting to find my errant husband on the other side. Instead, a short, balding man stood before me, flanked by somber-looking men dressed in dour clothing and displaying equally dour expressions.

"Mademoiselle," Monsieur Maspero said in surprise. "I didn't expect to find you here."

"Is that Maspero?" my uncle called out. "Hold on a minute, and I'll get dressed."

"*Please* don't get out of bed," I shouted in return. "I'm sorry, monsieur, but I fear your business will have to wait. My uncle is ill and recovering from a gunshot wound. He recently pushed himself too far—"

A strangled oath reverberated in the sitting room. My uncle appeared, hair unkempt, his beard overtaking more than half of his face. He tucked in his shirt and looked around for his shoes.

"You'll tire yourself," I protested.

"I believe I gave you something to do, didn't I, sobrina?" He dropped onto the chair and began lacing up his work boots.

I let out a long sigh and turned to Monsieur Maspero. "I don't have any refreshments to offer, but if you'd like, I'd be happy to send for tea."

"No, thank you," Monsieur Maspero replied, stepping aside to give the other two men space to enter my uncle's hotel room. "These men have come to arrest your uncle and his business partner, Abdullah."

"*What?*" I gasped.

My uncle jumped to his feet, his face turning a mottled red. "On what grounds?"

"For the discovery of Cleopatra, which you never reported, and whose mummy and artifacts are now missing." He inhaled sharply, eyes narrowing in distaste. "We are holding you and your associate responsible for losing Egypt a national treasure."

"Now, wait a minute." My uncle took a step away from the two men intent on grabbing a hold of him. "I can explain our intention."

"What's clear to me is that neither of you *intended* on registering the discovery," Monsieur Maspero exclaimed. "And now I must deal with hunting Cleopatra down in the black market. I have been far too accommodating with you in the past, Ricardo, and it ends now. You and Abdullah have much to answer for."

"You can't take them," I cried, throwing myself in front of Tío Ricardo. "Please, sir, you don't have all the information."

"*Inez.*"

"Calm yourself, mademoiselle," Monsieur Maspero said. He used his chin to point in my direction, and one of his comrades took a hold of my arm and shoved me toward the couch. He pushed on my shoulders, forcing me to drop onto the cushion. "You're becoming hysterical."

"Don't touch her," Tío Ricardo growled.

Monsieur Maspero snapped his fingers. "Arrest him."

"It wasn't their fault," I yelled over my uncle's roar of outrage, jumping to my feet. "It was my mother who stole everything. Her and Mr. Fincastle!"

The room fell silent as everyone's faces snapped in my direction. Monsieur Maspero's impervious expression softened to one of profound pity. As if I were spouting nonsense, as if I'd just declared I lived in a castle on the moon.

"Mademoiselle," Monsieur Maspero said gently. "Your mother is deceased. She is no more."

"No, she's *alive*. She's—"

"Come now," Monsieur Maspero said in a brisker tone. "I will not hear such talk. Your uncle and his business associate must be held accountable for their actions."

"But—"

One of the men tried to snatch my uncle's wrist, but he pivoted out of reach, snarling. The other man, short with long sideburns, managed to grip Tío Ricardo's shoulder.

My uncle threw a punch and then groaned, clutching at his arm. Blood seeped through his shirt.

"The stitches," I exclaimed.

"Don't make things worse for yourself," Monsieur Maspero told my uncle coldly.

"You turn a blind eye to other archaeologists and their findings," Tío Ricardo fumed. "Don't pretend to run a clean enterprise. Your hands are just as dirty as the rest of theirs. Think, Maspero! There are no systems or practices in place to protect any discovery from greedy collectors and dealers. This is to say *nothing* of the subversive agents running rampant in the antiquities department. Don't look at me like that—you know it's true! Abdullah wanted to record our findings so that when someone else found Cleopatra—and inevitably destroyed the site of her tomb—there would still be some record of what it originally looked like!"

"How dare you," Monsieur Maspero seethed. "You'll be held in the Cairo prison throughout your questioning. And trust me when I tell you that I will be thorough." He looked in my direction. "Good day, mademoiselle."

I gaped at him as the two men dragged my uncle out of the room. I flew after them, wishing I had the power to stop them from arresting Tío Ricardo. But what power did I have in this situation? I had no influence, no helpful connections. My voice was a whisper against theirs. Frustration burned a path straight to my hands, and I curled them into fists, my mind racing.

What could I do? Who could I—

"*Inez!* Find Whitford and tell him what's happened," Tío Ricardo shouted as they hauled him down the corridor. "He'll know what to do!"

Another door opened, and two men walked through, leading a tired-looking Abdullah, his skin gray. He was still so unwell, and fury detonated in my chest. My uncle let out a stream of curses at the sight of his friend, whose shoulders were slumped, his feet dragging.

I trailed after them, my heart thundering hard against my ribs. Other hotel guests opened their own doors, jaws dropping, as they stared at the parade of people walking past. My uncle didn't let up his enraged shouting, while Abdullah stayed silent.

We reached the stairs, and they hauled both of them through the lobby, in front of scores of people milling about, enjoying the hotel amenities, booking rooms. It was then that I saw Whit near Shepheard's entrance, standing close to a familiar figure. His arms were crossed tight against his chest, as if he was having to physically restrain himself from attacking Maspero's men. The figure next to him threw up her hands, and I squinted as I approached, still in a furious daze.

"Can't you do something?" the young woman cried. "Anything at all?"

I finally recognized Abdullah's granddaughter, Farida. Her lips twisted in a grimace as Monsieur Maspero's men forced Abdullah and my uncle into a waiting hackney cab.

Whit watched the scene with a narrowed gaze. His anger radiated off him, a fire crackling, spewing embers. "We can't make a scene here," he said grimly. "It's exactly what they'd hope for."

"But what can be done?" Farida repeated, despair edging into her voice.

Whit turned his head and met my gaze. I read his expression clearly, heard his voice as if he'd spoken out loud.

Only finding my mother would save them now.

CAPÍTULO ONCE

"I'll follow them," Whit said grimly. "Perhaps I can talk some sense into Maspero. It was only a matter of time before the department learned of the discovery, and now he looks foolish. Everything he does next will be to regain control of the situation. I might be able to reason with him—" He broke off, shaking his head slightly, as if realizing the improbability of such a feat. Then he glanced at me. "I'll be back as soon as I'm able."

I averted my gaze. I found it hard to look at him without feeling a razor-sharp spike of anger ignite my blood, without remembering the night when he'd held me in his arms and lied to my face.

"With answers," Farida said. "Please."

From the corner of my eye, I caught him nodding, but not to Farida, to me. I could feel the weight of his stare. Then he strode out the door, and I finally lifted my eyes in his direction. He broke into a run the second he'd descended the front steps. The last time he ran that fast, he was chasing after my carriage as if his life depended on it. Farida and I stared into the street long after Whit was out of sight, where other guests were enjoying lemon squash and cups of coffee. "What if I never see him again?" came Farida's anguished whisper.

Before I could reply, a familiar voice rang from behind us, coming from the packed lobby.

"What on earth has happened?" Isadora demanded, pale blue skirt swirling around her ankles. "Everyone is in a flutter, talking about the authorities coming to the hotel."

"They were here to make arrests," I said.

"*What?*"

I motioned toward Abdullah's granddaughter. "Isadora, I'd like to present Farida, Abdullah's granddaughter, to you. I believe you didn't have the chance to meet her in Aswan. Farida, this is my . . . my sister, Isadora."

Farida startled and looked at me questioningly. "I wasn't aware you had a sibling. Your parents never mentioned another child."

A faint tremor rippled through Isadora so quick I might have imagined it. When she spoke, her voice had its usual direct quality to it that I'd come to admire. "A pleasure to meet you. I gather this morning's interlude had something to do with the two of you?"

"Unfortunately, yes," I hissed. "Let's go up to the room to talk."

We made a somber party, squished on the narrow bed, the tall stacks of boxes surrounding us like fortress towers. I really needed to figure out what to do with my parents' possessions. Farida settled against the wood headboard, fingers twisting around the bedding. Her dark hair was pulled into an elaborate roll, and the long stretch of her skirt flounced around her like the cap of a mushroom.

Isadora sat at the foot of the bed, watching us uneasily.

"When did you arrive?" I asked Farida.

"Yesterday evening," she said, rubbing her eyes. "I came as soon as I heard what happened. My poor grandfather—he feels so defeated, and now for this to happen? I wanted to care for him, and now I won't be able to."

"I don't mean to interrupt," Isadora said. "But can someone please tell me *what happened*?"

"Monsieur Maspero had my uncle and Abdullah arrested," I said. "For failing to report their discovery and the subsequent thievery of Cleopatra's cache, and of course, her mummy is missing also."

Isadora raised her brows. "What will happen to them?"

"Ricardo will most likely face trial in the mixed courts," Farida answered. "As for my grandfather . . . I doubt he'll be dealt with fairly in any court." Her bottom lip trembled, and her hands tightened into a death grip. "When he wrote me, he only mentioned his injuries, but he was vague about the actual theft."

I glanced at my sister. "She deserves to know the truth."

Isadora pinched her lips, as if expecting my response. "It was my father," she said in a hushed voice. "He was hired by Ricardo as security, but he used his position to access the dig site."

"And I believe our mother had a hand in this plan," I said. "It's no accident her lover ended up in that role on Philae. Mamá must have known Ricardo was looking for someone to guard the island."

Farida's eyes had gone wide, flickering between us. "I'm sorry, I seem to have missed crucial information. Lourdes and—" Farida gestured toward Isadora. "And your father?"

Isadora and I nodded in unison.

"And Lourdes was involved in the theft?"

I grimaced. "I accidentally helped her."

"She manipulated you," Isadora said, and I threw her a grateful smile. It was hard not to feel responsible, and no matter how many times I told myself that any other person might have done the same thing for their own mother—who they'd believed had died—it still didn't signify. My guilt knew no reason.

"I can't believe this of Lourdes," Farida murmured. "She seemed so lovely, so considerate." She sat up straighter, unclasping her hands. "I just remembered—I brought something for you."

"For me?" I asked in surprise.

Farida nodded, scooting off the bed. "I'll be right back."

When the door shut, Isadora half turned in my direction. Only her expression revealed the merest hint of her distress. Her brows knitted together in a frown as she said, "And so, if we don't find my parents, two people will be charged with a crime they didn't commit. Though, both ought to have reported their discovery as is mandated by the department of antiquities."

"It's complicated," I said, my hackles up in defense of Tío Ricardo and Abdullah. She didn't know of their lifelong mission, how they meticulously recorded their findings and did their best to leave their discoveries as undisturbed as possible. I made a promise never to reveal their practices, and I meant to keep my word. "If you had the full picture, you might think differently."

"What is the full picture, then?" she demanded.

"I cannot say."

She rolled her eyes. "Well then, my judgment stands."

"They had their reasons," I insisted. "And I believe they are doing the best they can in a tough situation."

"But had they been forthright, had they worked with the department," Isadora countered, raising her voice slightly, "then Maspero could instead concentrate on finding the actual culprits. But all of his energies will involve interrogating the wrong people while attempting to locate the stolen artifacts. Not to mention Cleopatra herself."

"What if *we* found the actual culprits?" Farida asked. She stood within the doorframe, holding a small bundle of photographs in one hand, her portable camera in the other. Isadora and I both jumped; we hadn't noticed her return. Farida closed the door behind her and resumed her place on the bed, spreading everything on the dark green coverlet. "I've been practicing taking pictures, and I have several of your parents, Inez, from my time in Philae." She lifted the bundle. "These were taken before they disappeared."

I looked down, unable to speak.

Farida reached forward and lightly placed her hand on my arm. "I brought them because, well, I thought you might like keepsakes of your parents. But now I'm wondering if I ought to look through every photo I've taken while on Philae. Perhaps there might be something that could help us build a case against your mother?" She fanned the photographs on the bed. "I've taken hundreds, and I'm still waiting for Kodak to develop the rest. They should arrive any day now from their facility."

"That's very clever, Farida," Isadora said approvingly.

My eyes burned and I looked away, inhaling sharply to fight the tears threatening to spill. When I felt in control of my emotions, I gazed at the pictures. There were at least a dozen images of the campsite, the temple, and in each one, Mamá and Papá could be found within the frame. Sometimes it was the two of them, sometimes they were each alone. None of the photographs were posed—all of them seemed to be taken when my parents were in a flurry of motion. Their edges were soft and blurry, their faces looking smeared, as if someone had skimmed over their features with a large paint brush.

But it was easy to identify them. Mamá's neat dark hair, high-collared shirts, and long skirt, Papá in his button-down shirt and gray trousers, his slim build hunched at the shoulders, as if readying to read a book. His spectacles caught the sunshine, and a bright flare covered his face in nearly all of the photos.

There was one photo in particular that drew my eye. It seemed to be of a room, but the lighting made the image hard to grasp. The picture wasn't blurry, but something about it was odd. It was clearly someone's bedroom on Philae, one that looked incredibly familiar to my eye. I leaned in closer. In fact, I had seen this room before.

"It is your parents' accommodations while at the campsite," Farida said quietly.

Isadora turned the photo upside down and then right again. "I don't understand. Where is the wall? It looks blown through, but when I was there, the rooms were all intact."

Farida inhaled deeply and pulled out her Kodak from a leather carrying case. "After I bought my camera, I made an incredible discovery of my own."

I'd seen it before when I had first met her in Aswan. It was ordinary looking, a wooden box with a brass wind-up key at the top, a round hole for viewing, and a small button placed on the side.

"This camera is magic touched."

I let out a low whistle, while Isadora bent her head to examine it more closely.

"There's something that was used in the making of this camera that allows me to take photos that reveal what's on the other side of a wall. An unusual but useful spell. My hunch is that it's the brass key at the top that's used to roll the film to the next slide. The magic doesn't work on clothing or metal or anything like that. Only certain kinds of walls. Stone, rock, clay, granite, limestone." She pursed her lips thoughtfully. "Anything that might have been used in antiquity, I suppose."

"Interesting," Isadora said. "So we're essentially seeing our mother's room and all of her things." She held up the picture. "Everything looks ordinary. Plenty of books and linens, her trunk and extra candles, matches. One mirror."

"Mamá carried around her journal frequently," I said, studying another photograph. I recalled the curious doodles Whit had pointed out. His face appeared in my mind, and I winced slightly, forcing him far from my thoughts. I *hated* how often he cropped up in my head. Especially in the quiet moments when I was still, my thoughts unguarded.

I gave myself a mental shake, and reached into my canvas bag for my journal and charcoal pencils. Flipping to a blank page, I searched for something to sketch. Drawing always brought me back into focus, smoothed away my worries. It helped me redirect my thoughts in a proper direction.

My gaze landed on Farida's camera, and as if by their own accord, my fingers tightened their hold on the pencil and began to move.

"She also was tasked with recording any findings," Farida said. "There's one where she's writing in a thick leather book." She rummaged through the photos. "Here it is—look. I remember taking this one, actually. She used to have a little wooden desk that she carried everywhere so she could write. This photo is when she had placed the desk overlooking the river. It was in a more secluded area, and I thought she looked, well, picturesque."

I squinted at the photo. Isadora leaned closer to look over my shoulder. Mamá sat in a wooden chair, her back straight, her slim neck bent as she wrote in the book. In her other hand was a small square-shaped card. I drew in a quick breath.

"What is it?" Isadora asked.

I blinked, my eyes watering from the strain of trying to see what my mother held in her hand. "I might have this wrong, but I think that card could be an invitation to the illegal mar—"

"Wait a moment, Inez," Isadora said sharply.

I glanced at her in surprise. She jumped to her feet nimbly, resembling a graceful cat. "Excuse me?"

"May I speak with you a moment? Out in the corridor?"

Hurt flashed across Farida's face.

"Isadora, is that really necess—"

"Yes," she said and then went to the door and held it open until I followed after her. Farida had her face turned resolutely from me, and a flicker of annoyance at my sister bubbled to the surface. I walked through the door, and she closed it softly.

"What *is* it?" I demanded, one hand on my hip.

Isadora rubbed her temples, her eyes squeezed shut. "You are so trusting."

I lowered my chin at her, lips parting in outrage. "Maybe so, but it's *Farida*."

She rolled her eyes and led me down a few steps from my hotel room. "How well do you know her? I'm not saying she isn't a lovely person, but I just met her, and I think we ought to be cautious."

"Well, I disagree. She's as involved as we are and highly motivated to help her grandfather. Our interests are aligned, and I happen to like her.

I think she'll be very helpful—you said so yourself. You called her clever, remember?"

Isadora waved her hand dismissively. "It's one thing for her to collect photographs, quite another for us to include her in our plans to attend an *illegal auction*. Think of the risk we'd be asking of her! We must move quietly, and the more people we involve, the more attention we draw to ourselves."

"One more person won't shatter our plans," I said.

"Really?" Isadora said, one honey-hued brow arching. "Three women, without a chaperone, sneaking into one of the most illicit activities Cairo has to offer? In the dead of night?"

"I'm a married woman," I said, crossing my arms. "Obviously, I'd be the chaperone, but are you really concerned with the proprieties at this point? Because I'm not in the slightest."

She bit her lip, considering. "I suppose you're right. But should anything happen to her, it's on your conscience."

Her words bit into my skin. I didn't want to be responsible for another person. I didn't want to fail another human being I cared about. "It'd be her choice, of course," I replied stiffly, but even to my own ears, I sounded unsure.

Isadora nodded and together we returned to Farida. She had stood, gathering all of the photos, picking up her camera.

"Oh, please don't leave yet," I said hurriedly. "Isadora and I have been working on a plan—but it involves a degree of risk that we had to discuss."

Farida stilled, warily looking between us. "Your plan is dangerous."

"It could be," Isadora said. "I have something to share with both of you, but once I do, we need to carefully consider all potential outcomes. It might not be worth it."

"I know a story about Monsieur Maspero," Farida said quietly. "Regarding the arrest of three brothers from a small village. This family had made a monumental discovery, and for years, they illicitly sold and traded countless artifacts. It was only a matter of time until Monsieur Maspero caught wind of their dealings. While in his custody, the three brothers were tortured until they revealed the location of the cache."

"Tortured," I choked out.

"I heard about this," Isadora said in a horrified whisper. "One brother died, and another turned."

Tears swam in Farida's dark eyes. "There's nothing I wouldn't risk to help my grandfather. Please tell me your plan."

"When I left Philae, I mailed a few letters to some of my father's friends, letting them know what happened and to ask for help in locating him." Isadora's lips twisted in distaste. "I even wrote to a scoundrel my father sometimes hired when working bigger jobs. Well, this man wrote me back and offered information about one place my father might turn up."

"Tell me," I breathed. "Is it . . . ?"

Isadora nodded slowly. "I know when and where the gate will move."

"And?" I demanded.

"Tonight," she said. "Four in the morning."

Farida frowned. "What is a gate that moves?"

"It's *the* illegal black market in Egypt, called Tradesman's Gate," I said. A sudden idea struck me, and I smiled shyly at Farida. "How would you feel about bringing your camera with you?"

"To the black market?" she asked. "Won't that draw suspicion?"

My smile widened as I pulled at the scarf at my neck. The silk caressed my skin as I twirled the ends around my finger, loosening the knot. "I have something that will help with that." In one fluid motion, I dropped the scarf over the handheld camera. The fabric rippled as it fell softly against the bed.

Farida gasped. "Where did it go?"

I lifted the scarf and found the shrunken camera and held it in the palm of my hand. "Little less suspicious, don't you think?"

"Mother's scarf," Isadora said softly. "I've always loved it."

"I never gave it back." I glanced at my sister, at the sudden bleakness pooling in her blue eyes. I knew she was thinking of how this seemingly harmless stretch of silk had caused so much trouble. "And tonight we'll use it to take as many photos as we can. The artifacts, the location, and all the people attending the illegal auction."

WHIT

Sir Evelyn had made me wait hours to see him. I spent the majority of my time restraining myself from kicking down his door. The rational part of my brain kept reminding me that wouldn't help my case.

In the end, controlling my temper hadn't helped me.

The sanctimonious twit forbade me from speaking with either Ricardo or Abdullah. He was the most powerful man in Egypt, the one who could have opposed Maspero's order to detain them in prison, but did he use his power and influence for *any* good? Of course not. His dislike of the pair overruled common decency or sense. From Sir Evelyn's office, I rushed to the antiquities department to speak with Maspero, which had turned into a shouting match. He refused to listen to my arguments, no matter how loud I yelled them, and ignored my demands that the two men be kept out of the prison.

An absolute mess of a day.

I yearned for my flask.

But it was keeping company with crocodiles at the bottom of the Nile. I dragged a hand down my face, blinking wearily. Shepheard's lobby, while extravagant, wasn't exactly the best place for sleeping. The alcove, at least, had several chairs. I pushed two together and tried to make myself comfortable.

Wasted effort. My legs were too long.

With a sigh, I tipped my head back and stared up at the ceiling, wishing I were anywhere else. I'd give myself three minutes. Three minutes to let myself feel the weight of my exhaustion, to let the soothing dark of the alcove quiet my racing thoughts. It had been the darkest place I could find with easy access to the hotel entrance. My eyes drifted shut.

One more minute.

But my mind wouldn't rest. I had a feeling it wouldn't until this was over. For a second, I debated going upstairs to lie down on that miserable cot in our room, but I didn't want to risk waking my wife, who hated me, and her sister, whom I didn't trust. There was no point, anyway, since I'd be leaving for the auction soon.

Slowly, unwillingly, I opened my eyes and fixed my attention on the grand wooden clock at the end of the room lording over the space like a sentry on watch, the minutes dragging to four in the morning.

No one stirred in the lobby, and even the hotel attendant behind the counter had propped his stool near the wall so that he might sleep. I could have another few minutes. There was still time. I tipped my head again, resting it against the curve of the back of the chair, and stretched my legs out in front of me. My eyes drifted closed by their own accord.

And still, sleep evaded me.

Alchemical symbols swam across my mind, golden and glittering against a dark backdrop. My fingers itched to turn the pages of my textbooks where I might find another clue. More than ever, I needed to find that sheet. I would not allow Lourdes to beat me to it.

I needed it with a desperation that burned me all the way through.

The sound of people coming down the stairs jolted me upright. I squinted across the shadowed lobby, wondering who in their right mind would be awake at this hour. Three slight figures descended, covered in long coats, desperately trying to be silent. They crossed the lobby on tiptoes, furtively glancing over their shoulders at the hotel worker, who was blithely unaware that some of Shepheard's guests were leaving at an ungodly hour.

But it didn't matter how sneaky they thought they were being, or how quiet.

I had recognized one of them.

My crafty wife.

I stood up as I slung my jacket on. Out of habit, I checked to make sure my knife was safely embedded in my boot, and then I followed after them, my temper rising like steam.

Inez, darling, *where are you off to?*

CAPÍTULO DOCE

I eyed our surroundings in distress. We were in an alley, several blocks away from the hotel, the moon blocked by tall stone walls enclosing the narrow path. I hadn't thought to bring a candle, and anyway, something told me Isadora would have protested.

We were, after all, attempting to be stealthy.

"Are you *sure* you know where we are?" Farida asked with another quick glance over her shoulder. She was dressed in a dark skirt she had borrowed from Isadora, and my mother's scarf was wrapped twice around her neck.

Isadora didn't break her stride, easily navigating muddy puddles, her dress somehow repelling all manner of dust and dirt. *Magic*, I thought again. "Yes, for the tenth time," she said. "Hurry—we don't want to be late."

My corset was an iron cage around my ribs, and I profoundly regretted not shedding the awful contraption before we had set out. I thought we still had plenty of time before the auction began, but Isadora kept us moving at a brisk pace. An awful stitch worked its way deep in my side, and I let out an exasperated huff.

"It's not like the market is going to suddenly change its mind and move again," I said between breaths.

"No, but I don't want our arrival to distract from the proceedings," Isadora explained. "Here—I think it's down this way."

"You *think*?" Farida asked, aghast.

"Strongly believe," Isadora amended. She made a hairpin turn, and the street widened, providing enough space for me and Farida to flank Isadora, the three of us walking alongside one another. At a distance, the sound of music playing and the odd yip of a stray dog joined the clamor of our steps against the packed dirt. This particular stretch of street remained dark, no sight of lamps anywhere, and a heavy gloam seemed to coat every surface. We were in a part of town where it didn't pay to be negligent.

"Where is this place?" Farida asked, clutching her side. "A warehouse?"

"No, it's a—" Isadora broke off sharply. Her eyes narrowed at the sudden movement at the end of the street.

I followed the line of her gaze as three shadowed figures materialized. An uneasy feeling scraped against my skin. The scent of sweat and alcohol wafted into my nose as they drew close. There was just enough moonlight to make out their features. They were pale skinned and mustached; one had a pockmarked face, another was balding, and the last was short and built like a barrel.

Isadora stopped, holding out her hands. "Step behind me."

Neither Farida nor I moved. I was in too much shock, my mind only beginning to understand the extent of the danger we were in. It was only when I caught the glinting edge of a knife that I gasped. The barrel-shaped man grinned at me, waving his weapon as if demonstrating that he knew how to use it.

"Not one pace closer," Isadora warned.

In a blink, her sleek little handgun was in her palm, aimed at the apparent leader of the group. He stood a foot ahead of the others, his head angled down, thick brows curving in amusement as he inched forward.

"What are you going to do with that?" he said in an American accent.

"Take another step forward, and you'll find out," Isadora said sweetly.

The short man laughed. "I bet it's not even loaded," he said, taking one exaggerated step.

Without a single tremor, my sister fired.

The noise exploded everyone into action. Isadora's target dove out of the way while Farida scooped up a rock and threw it at one of the assailants racing toward us. She hit one of the bald men square in the chest, and he floundered.

"Bitch," the pockmarked man spat.

Another American. They must have come to Egypt by the boatload. He'd spoken only once, but that word alone told me he'd enjoyed several rounds of drink. My heart escalated as he swerved in my direction. I let out a gasp and stumbled back a few steps. From the corner of my eye, I saw Isadora sidestep one of the taller attackers, whose blond curls gleamed in the moonlight.

"Shoot him," Farida yelled. She had found another rock, which she clutched in one hand, and the other hand was tucked into the pocket of her skirt. I knew she was feeling to make sure her shrunken camera hadn't gotten lost in the scuffle.

Isadora took aim as my assailant went for my throat.

The sound of someone running filled the alley, footsteps thundering like a battering ram. My sister spun around, eyes widening at the sight of a young man running at full tilt toward us. My gaze chased the blur of movement rushing past. A cannonball intent on destruction.

Whit.

But not the roguish Whit, who could charm a smile from even the most dour of personalities, but Whit the brawler, unrefined and furious. He bent and struck the man in his belly and somehow managed to flip him up and over, until the pockmarked man roughly hit the ground with a reverberating smack. Isadora fired her gun again, this time narrowly missing Whit, who took a second to flick a contemptuous glance in her direction before ducking the fist of the mustached man.

My sister loaded her gun and aimed—

"For the love of Christ," Whit shouted. "*Stop shooting.*"

Farida edged closer to me, her eyes wide. My erratic heartbeat had slowed, and I found that my earlier fear had all but vanished. "Isadora, come watch the parlay from over here," I said in a pleasant voice.

Whit threw *me* a dirty look and then narrowly avoided the jab of a knife aimed at his midsection. The barrel-shaped man had his arm outstretched, and Whit latched on to it, using the man's momentum to yank him forward, knocking him off-balance. With his elbow, Whit slammed down into his back, and the man slumped onto the ground.

Farida nodded in approval. "Well done."

Whit spun around, blue eyes blazing. "We had an agreement, Olivera."

I raised a brow. "I haven't broken it."

He gestured to the three men moaning on the ground. "Oh? Care to explain this to me?"

Farida pointed to one of them. "That one is trying to stand, Whit."

My insufferable husband turned and aimed a kick at the mustached man—who groaned and fell silent. Whit bent into a squat, one muscled forearm draped across his knee, and said cheerfully, "If anyone *thinks* about moving, I will feed the lot of you to a crocodile, bit by bit."

The three assailants stilled.

Then Whit stood, hands on his hips, and waited with an air of impatience. When I stayed quiet, he muttered a curse under his breath and said, "What does saving your life get me?"

"Excuse me?"

"I think I'm entitled an answer to three of my questions."

I narrowed my gaze. "One."

"Two."

"Fine."

Whit crooked a finger at me, and I rolled my eyes as I walked to him. I would have ignored the gesture, but my companions were openly staring in bemused fascination at our interaction. Since I didn't want to answer any of *their* questions, I allowed Whit to lead me off to the side.

"We really must move on," Isadora called out in warning.

"This will only take a minute," I said.

Whit scowled. "I only get a minute?"

I feigned looking at a pocket watch. "Less now."

"You are the most . . ." Whit's voice trailed off. "Never mind."

"This is why you wanted to talk to me?" I asked coolly. "To insult me?"

"I wasn't thinking of an insult," Whit said softly.

I ignored the way his voice sent a shiver down my spine. For the hundredth time, I reminded myself that he had betrayed me. That I didn't care about his sister, a woman I'd never met, that he ought to have been honest with me from the start. I repeated this over and over until I was able to return his stare without flinching, without blushing, without feeling anything at all.

"What are your questions?"

"Where are the three of you going?"

"You could have asked them."

Whit dipped his chin, the moonlight casting silvery shadows across his face. He stood not even a foot away from me, looming tall and broad shouldered. He wasn't even panting from the exertion of pummeling three people to the ground. "I'm asking *my wife*."

The only reason why I bothered to reply at all was because he had saved my life. At least, that was what I told myself in the constant argument I had in my mind to stay firm, to not give in to any admiration for the way he had rescued us. "Isadora was able to discover the location of the gate."

"Why didn't you tell me?"

"Is that your second question?"

He nodded.

"If I can do something without you," I said simply, "I will."

His face turned to stone, his expression inscrutable, and I gave up trying to read someone who had no compunction about robbing me.

"Fine. And what were you going to do when you arrived?"

"Farida's camera is magic touched," I said, then explained the rest of our plan quickly.

"The developed photographs will show what's behind walls?" he asked. "That's astounding. And useful."

"I know," I said dryly. "Hence the plan."

Whit watched me narrowly. "Well, I also discovered the location of the gate," he said in a testy voice. "And it's in another part of the city. Were you thinking to get there by tomorrow?"

"Oh," I said. "Were we *lost*?"

"Damn it, Inez."

I stiffened. "Isadora must have gotten confused. She can be quite stubborn once she gets an idea in her head."

"Can she." His implacable look returned. "Well, I'm on my way there. Would you like to come with me?"

I managed to hide my surprise, but only just. "Lead the way, Mr. Hayes."

It was at that moment when one of the men lurched to his feet—the bald one—and lunged toward us. A shot rang out, and his body fell in a downward arc, blood splattering across my feet. He was utterly still, a dark puddle growing under his chest. One of his arms was reaching toward me, his index finger brushing against the toe of my left boot.

Whit dropped, peering into the man's face. His eyes were open. Somehow, he still looked angry. "Dead."

Isadora lowered her smoking gun. "One less for the crocodile."

Whit led us to a dilapidated building he explained was rather close to the hotel. Not even half a mile away from Shepheard's entrance. Isadora blushed and apologized profusely, again and again, for her error. I got the sense that she hated to be mistaken—about anything.

"It's all right," I said for the fifth time. "I would have gotten turned around, too."

She walked alongside me, Farida accompanying Whit farther up ahead. Every now and again, he looked over his shoulder to make sure I was still trudging after him like a well-behaved dog. I ignored his glances, focusing instead on learning where *not* to go in Cairo.

Isadora winced and shook her head. Her honey-gold hair gleamed under the soft light of the moon. "It's only that I wanted to be helpful," she explained. "I thought I knew most of the streets of Cairo, and I didn't want you to need Whit or spend more time with him than what's absolutely necessary."

"Sister," I said. "Can I call you sister?"

She smiled gratefully. "Of course, but only if I can call you hermana in return."

Warmth spread outward from my heart. "You shot a man and saved my life. I think you more than made up for it."

"It shouldn't have come to that," she said. "I ought to have known we were lost."

I studied her. "You're being awfully hard on yourself."

She slanted an arched look in my direction. "Must be a family trait."

I shrugged, averting my gaze. It was second nature to berate myself into thinking I could have done more, been better, acted faster. Sometimes nothing I did felt like it was enough. And other times, the things I did do were often wrong. Perhaps it was a family trait, and I was too much like Mamá. We'd come up to Whit and Farida by then, and I chose not to respond to Isadora's observation, but her words stuck with me, unnerving me.

This was the most amount of consecutive time I'd spent with her, and it was galling to learn how easily she could read me, especially when I was still trying to figure myself out, considering what my mother did to me.

To my father. To Isadora, even.

But I was beginning to understand how yearning for my parents, wanting their attention, and missing them terribly when they were gone half the year while traveling in Egypt had shaped me into the person that I was now. It was why I craved a family, a sense of belonging.

To fit somewhere.

And I often blamed myself, or was *too hard on myself,* because maybe there was a small part of me that believed there had been something wrong with me, and that was the reason why my parents left me behind.

Every year. For months.

I felt the weight of Whit's gaze, and I wondered if he could feel the tension radiating off me, the sudden grief coating my skin, but I kept my gaze straight ahead. The abandoned building, evidently once used by the government, was flanked by handsomely constructed homes with arched windows and paneled glass. We stood off to the side, half-hidden by lush greenery and prickly palms that overflowed onto the street. Whit studied the exterior of our destination, and then looked over to the three of us quietly waiting. I wasn't sure *why* we were waiting. The entrance was clearly a large door that had once been painted chartreuse but had long since faded and chipped down to something resembling wilted lettuce.

"None of us have an invitation," Isadora said suddenly. "How will we get inside?"

"There's a side door," I said. "Perhaps we can sneak in that way?"

"Let's go," Whit said. "Everyone behind me."

We hustled after him as he crossed the street, glancing both ways. The side door was little more than a narrow entry, something designed for servants. Whit pushed and stuck his head around the edge; half a second later, he jerked backward and flattened his palms on the wood. He gave a violent shove, and a loud smack came from the other side. Something slumped to the ground with a loud thud, and Whit once again pushed the door, shoving until he could open it fully.

He walked inside, motioning for us to follow. When I went through, I made the mistake of glancing down at the man sprawled across our path.

Whit had hit a guard hard enough to render him unconscious.

There wasn't time to check on him. Whit was already rounding the corner at the end of the corridor, which opened to a dusty kitchen, cobwebs in every corner, rusty iron pots and pans hanging along the wall, and shelves laden with jars filled with flour and the like. The sounds of raucous shouting drifted into the confined space, people yelling—though not in anger, but rather in palpable excitement. I glanced up to the ceiling, noting the direction of where the noise was coming from. The auction must be taking place upstairs.

We needed to locate the staircase.

The problem was the two men playing cards at the rickety wooden dining table. They turned in their chairs, gaping, one of them already reaching for the revolver at his elbow.

Whit threw one of the pans, and it spun, handle over handle, until it slammed into his face, catapulting him off his seat. His bloody tooth flew in my direction, and I scuttled out of the way with a muffled shriek. The other man reached for his gun, but by then Whit had taken the now-empty chair and swung it hard at the man's head. He crumpled onto the table.

It was over and done within a matter of seconds.

Isadora picked up the gun and tucked it into her belt. "You are so violent."

It sounded like a compliment.

Farida shook her head, half-amazed, half-shocked. "I've never seen this side of you."

Whit went to the stove and sniffed inside a steaming pot. He smiled to himself and retrieved a cup, which he blew into to rid it of dust. "Thank God."

"Are you having tea?" I exclaimed.

"Coffee," he said reverently, pouring a generous serving into the mug. "Would you like some?"

I stared at him. The noise above us grew louder; sounds of chairs scraping against the floor over and over again infiltrated the kitchen.

"We ought to—" I began.

Whit downed his coffee and then turned to shove the guard slumped over the table with his boot, and the man fell hard onto the floor. Then Whit calmly picked up both chairs and walked to the door. "Let's go."

CAPÍTULO TRECE

The stairs were rickety, groaning under our weight as we climbed to the floor above. They must have been intended for the staff, as the space was cramped and narrow, opening to a small hallway lined by shut doors. Ahead, the noise of people settling down drifted toward us as we tiptoed closer.

Whit silently peered around the corner at the end of the corridor. "Stay here."

"Where are you going?" I whispered.

"I'm going to add these chairs to the back row," he whispered back.

He crept forward, returning after a moment, the line of his jaw tight. I skirted around him to have a look myself and nearly gasped. The auction was about to take place in a large room, rectangular in shape, with peeling wallpaper and a dusty candle chandelier that swung precariously above rows and rows of seats. Every single one of them, except the two Whit had just added, were filled. I tipped my head back to note how the third floor overlooked the second, as if it were an open courtyard. From the outside, the building hadn't appeared that large, but now I realized that it went back farther from the street.

How were we going to explore every inch? It would take hours.

Although, I supposed we didn't have to do the actual exploring right now. Not if Farida was able to take pictures of the walled rooms. We could always examine them later—but then I recalled her mentioning that she was still waiting for her other photographs to be developed and mailed back to her. We would have to search as much as we could during the length of the auction.

"Here's what we should do," he began in a hush.

"No," I said firmly and just as quietly. "Here's the plan."

He lifted a single brow, and waited for me to continue.

"One of us needs to sit in during the auction to see if any of the Cleopatra cache is actually here," I said. "Isadora and I will do that, as we are familiar with what to look for. Farida, you and Whit ought to go and see if you can locate any of the items that are going to be displayed. Take as many pictures as you can."

"What happens afterward?" Isadora asked.

Whit gestured toward me with a faint smile. "My wife is the one with the plan."

I ignored the label. "We meet down the street after the auction," I said. "If that's impossible, then the lobby of the hotel."

"Wait a moment. She's your *wife*?" Farida asked, her rich brown eyes widening. "Since when? And why didn't you invite me to the wedding?"

The corners of Whit's lips tightened.

"We would have," I said hurriedly. "But it happened quickly. Besides, it's only a business arrangement."

"Oh," Farida said uncertainly, looking between us. I felt Whit's quick stare; there was a faint air of outraged disbelief radiating from him, but I refused to look in his direction.

"Shhhh," Isadora hissed. "Do you want them to hear you?"

Farida rubbed at her temples. "I'm trying to keep everything straight in my mind. This is new information I have to process."

"Later," Isadora said. "You have photographs to take." Then she swept past, walking into the room as if she belonged there, and sat in the chair Whit had placed. Farida looked down the hall from where we had just come and then unwrapped my mother's scarf from around her neck. She dug up her camera from deep within her skirt pocket, cradling it in the palm of her hand. I took the scarf and dropped it over her hand. A second later, her camera grew back into its normal shape.

"Magic is a beautiful thing," I whispered. "It's a shame it's becoming extinct."

"Everything comes to an end at some point," Whit said, with the slightest inflection on *everything*.

I knew his words were in reference to my decision for a divorce. I tried not to read into his tone and how it sounded the littlest bit bleak. Or maybe that's how I wanted him to sound. I was having a hard time keeping my heart in line with my mind.

Silly, foolish thing.

"I'm going to take pictures of the rooms on this floor," Farida said. "Whit, I'm sure there are more above us?"

He nodded. "We'll have to move fast to go through them all. Get started; I'll be right behind you."

My gaze skipped around the room to familiarize myself with the layout, in case we needed to leave quickly. There was another exit on the opposite end from us, next to a grand staircase.

"You'll be fine on your own?" he asked her.

Farida nodded, already fiddling with her camera as she walked back the way we came. She tried the knob at the first door and found it locked, but she centered herself in front of it and snapped a picture. Then she moved a few paces to the right, angling herself in a different direction, and snapped another picture, this time of the wall. Her expression was determined, thoughtful, and I hoped that room was filled with enough evidence to damn the whole black market enterprise. Farida tried the next door, found it unlocked and presumably empty, then she flashed a quick, triumphant grin before disappearing inside.

We were alone, the tension crackling between us.

"Isadora is waiting," I said, turning.

Whit reached for me but then seemed to change his mind. His hand dropped to his side. "Be careful."

I bristled. After what he had done to me, I hardly believed he had any concern over my welfare. "Don't pretend to care."

"But I do," he said quietly. "If you're caught, the rest of us will have a harder time making it out of this building."

It made perfect sense; the people who ran the auction would search the place from top to bottom, looking for anyone who had come with me. I ignored my sudden feeling of disappointment that he wasn't, in fact, worried about *me* personally.

"I'll be careful," I muttered. Before he could say anything else, I went to the empty seat adjacent to Isadora. She stared fixedly to the front of the darkened room where a wooden stage stood. An older gentleman with graying hair and a wide smile stood behind a creaky podium. He leaned against it casually, one elbow bent as his eyes moved over the room. To his right was a stand illuminated by dozens of squat candles that hovered in the air, as if on strings.

At first, I marveled at the magic. And then my attention shifted to the object resting on the platform. I squinted, trying to identify what it could be. It looked to be a golden amulet in the shape of a scarab with a long chain, and when the auctioneer carefully picked it up, he showed the underside to the crowd.

"Just a little preview of the item before we begin," he said with a grin. His cheeks creased, reminding me of a wrinkled sheet of paper. "I'm very excited for this evening's lot."

There were probably close to fifty people in this room alone. The majority of people, gentlemen and ladies both, were notably from Europe, with hair color ranging from pale blond and gray to sable. Several were dressed in fashionable, well-tailored clothing, outshining the drab surroundings. They were all wearing black satin masks, simple and austere, which covered the majority of their faces. Everyone sat in the same wooden chairs, and most had a paddle gripped in one hand.

"We don't have one," I said, nudging Isadora's side.

She looked at me in alarm. "Were you planning on buying something?"

"Of course not," I said. "But we'd fit in more if we had one as well."

"No one is looking at us," Isadora said with a dainty shrug.

"Ladies and gentlemen, welcome to Tradesman's Gate," the older gentleman suddenly called out. "I'm Phillip Barnes, and I'll be your host for the evening. I'd like to thank our founder," he said, gesturing to a man sitting in the front row, "who, for obvious reasons, will remain nameless."

The founder stood and turned around, inclining his head. So, this was the man who was responsible for so much damage and destruction up and down the Nile River. His callous attitude toward Egypt and its people, its history, struck a raw nerve.

Part of me wanted to jump to my feet, just so I could scream at him, for my anger to fill up the entire room so that he might feel it in his bones. But I clutched the edge of my seat to keep myself in line and focused on cataloguing his appearance instead. My description could be useful for Monsieur Maspero, and I tried to remember as many details as possible: He had a round belly, and while his head was covered by a hat, his face covered by a mask, I could see that he had dark hair. His clothing was nondescript: black trousers, crisp light shirt, and the customary vest under a dark jacket. The founder shifted to resume his seat, but his face turned in our direction, and he paused, half-seated, half-standing. He righted himself and then motioned to someone standing off to the side.

The man nodded, looking in our direction.

Isadora inhaled sharply. "What do we do?"

Cold sweat beaded at the back of my neck. I forced myself not to fidget, not to run from the room. "Don't panic and stay still," I whispered. "It might be nothing."

"I *never* panic," Isadora said, frowning. "An utter waste of time. They could have noticed that we aren't wearing masks," she said. "We ought to go now, before—"

But it was too late. The man was already walking toward us, and my stomach swooped. I drew my feet closer together, readying to jump. If need be, I'd scream for Whit. He'd come running. Guilt was a powerful motivator.

"Don't shoot him," I said out of the corner of my mouth.

"I don't like this," Isadora said, and she leaned forward slightly. While her jacket covered the gun she'd picked up downstairs, I caught glimpses of it every time she so much as twitched.

I was uncomfortably aware of the several attendees who had turned in their seats to watch, openly curious.

The man reached us. I could hardly breathe. Was he about to escort us from the room? Shoot us himself? Call for someone to question us?

"Our founder noticed you are without paddles," he said, reaching into his coat's inner pocket. He handed us the slim boards, cracker thin. Then he dug into his pockets and produced two black masks. "We also require everyone to wear these."

Isadora took both and wordlessly handed me one.

"Gracias," I said. "I mean, thank you."

"Yes, thank you," my sister added.

He nodded, pale eyes flickering between us. "We must have missed you two when the gate opened."

"Must have," I said.

"Everyone is required to check in before walking through the gate."

"Sorry. We were in a hurry to find seats," I said quickly.

He dipped his chin. "It won't happen again, ladies, should you wish to attend the next."

Then he quietly moved away. I glanced to the first row, but the founder had already dismissed us and was facing the front of the room again.

Phillip cleared his throat. "Now that we are all settled and quite comfortable, it's time to go over the essential details. As always, here are our rules: One, you are never to reveal the location of the gate you have walked through. Two, all payment must be rendered in twenty-four hours. No exceptions. Should you fail to do so, the item will go to the second-highest bidder. We will, of course, provide an address where you may send the funds. Three, any person found to be guilty of revealing the identity of anyone attending the auction will be brutally dealt with." Phillip gave a thin-lipped smile. "You have been warned."

I shivered as I tied my mask and then helped my sister tie hers.

"Let's begin with the auction," Phillip continued. "I'll be presenting our customary lot of artifacts acquired in Egypt. But first, we have two unique items that have been recently discovered that I'd like to show you all." He placed the amulet back onto the stand. "The first item open is this extraordinary heart scarab; its size is a little over two inches in length," he said. "And as I've shown, there are rows of hieroglyphs on the bottom, and our scholars believe it to be a protection spell for the recently deceased. Opening bid is one thousand pounds."

Immediately, several paddles swung up into the air.

"I don't recognize that one, do you?" Isadora whispered.

I shook my head. "No. I don't think it belonged to Cleopatra," I whispered back as the auctioneer accepted bids, the number going higher and higher. "I wish I would have thought to ask Farida to take pictures of the room and everyone in it."

She nudged my side and then pointed with her chin behind us. I craned my neck to find Farida quietly taking pictures from the corridor. She met my gaze and smiled a grim sort of smile before disappearing again.

"Sold!" the auctioneer yelled. "For sixteen thousand pounds to the lady with number forty-three."

"What if Mother decided not to sell at the gate?" Isadora asked. "What if she decided it was too risky?"

I pondered her question. Mamá had gone rogue, betraying the people she worked for, but she still needed to move the artifacts. I couldn't know her reasons behind why she did what she had done, but if it were me, it seemed riskier to hold on to objects that the department of antiquities was now looking for than to try to sell them via an established market.

"She'll be here."

Isadora's blue eyes flickered across the room at the other attendees. "Do you see anyone that might be her?"

I did the same slow perusal, and with a sinking heart, I realized it was too difficult to distinguish one lady from the next. There were one or two that had her same hair color, same slight build, but I couldn't confirm with any kind of certainty. She might not even be here herself. It'd be stupidly reckless to appear in the same company as the man you had double-crossed.

But if she wasn't here, how was she planning on selling what she stole?

It occurred to me that she might have sent an emissary. It was a plausible idea and I leaned closer to tell Isadora, but then someone appeared onstage carrying something blue in his gloved hands. The shape looked familiar and my breath caught at the back of my throat. It was only a quick glimpse of the relic, but it was enough to make my blood simmer under my skin. I didn't pay any attention to the man handling the priceless artifact; I only cared about the familiar item. He placed it onto the stand before walking offstage, and I breathed a sigh of relief at finally being able to get a better look.

A moment later, I couldn't breathe at all.

It was a statuette of an asp, made of Egyptian faience. My heart thrashed hard against my ribs, and I was assaulted by a sharp, painful memory. A forgotten tomb underneath a temple. The island of Philae, surrounded on all sides by craggy rocks and beyond; the Nile River, sweeping past in a blur of blue and green. Hot sand that I felt through the leather of my boots, and my fingers stained in charcoal. Whit hovering nearby, cataloguing artifacts, and the sound of Abdullah and Ricardo arguing over something or another.

"Isadora," I whispered. "That's from Cleopatra's cache."

Her brow puckered. "Are you sure? I don't recognize it."

"I am certain." I clutched the paddle in my hand. "Because I drew it."

She sat back in her seat, for once coming close to a slouch. "If Mother isn't here, what good is it, though?"

My mind raced, the answer bubbling to the surface. By the time the auctioneer made his remarks, describing the object and the opening bid, I knew exactly what to do.

"Bidding begins at two thousand pounds," he said.

I raised my paddle. "Five thousand pounds." Isadora loudly coughed, her delicate face turning red. With my free hand, I slapped her back. "She's fine, though the dust in this room is frightful."

The founder turned in his chair and looked at me. I could have sworn I saw a smile on his face, before he resumed facing forward. After a moment, he stood and exited the room.

Phillip rearranged his surprised expression, though he couldn't quite hide the excitement from his voice. "Five thousand to the lively young lady at the back. Do I hear five thousand two hundred pounds?"

Someone in the middle row raised their paddle.

"Five thousand two hundred," Phillip said. "To the gentleman with the green coat. Do I hear—"

"*Ten thousand pounds*," I said.

Isadora muffled her gasp. "Need I remind you that you don't have any money? Your scoundrel of a husband went through it all in less than a day."

I ignored her, waiting to see what the auctioneer would do. In the row ahead of us, several attendees had swirled around to gape at me. A few whispered farther up, no doubt wondering what was so special about the asp statue.

"Ladies and gentlemen," Phillip said. "I suppose I ought to mention where this little statue was found, hidden for two millennia in a burial chamber for one of the most famous rulers of ancient Egypt." Several auction attendees leaned forward in their seat, their interest palpable. "The search for this ruler's tomb has captured the imagination of the entire world, akin to the search for Noah's ark and the Holy Grail. Are you ready to know the answer?" Phillip smiled smugly, a man who knew he held his audience in the palm of his hand.

"This asp was discovered alongside a pharaoh of Egypt, a woman of legend and renown." Someone audibly gasped, while a ripple seemed to spread through crowd, as if they had been dreaming but were now awake and alert. "This same woman, long believed to be a talented Spellcaster, was the descendant of a famous alchemist who made the astonishing discovery on how to turn lead into gold. Rumor has it that she wrote the instructions down on a single sheet of parchment." Phillip shifted, turning to address the other side of the room. "No one has found it—*yet*. But perhaps this asp's final resting place will give us a clue to its whereabouts."

"How?" someone yelled.

Phillip pivoted again, locating the man who had shouted the question. "Because of all the places where the Chrysopoeia could be, why not with the alchemist's descendant? The news will break in all the newspapers soon, but for now, you have the pleasure of hearing it at the gate first: Cleopatra's tomb and an incredible assortment of valuable treasures have been found!"

Phillip smiled, pausing for dramatic effect as the crowd teemed with unbridled enthusiasm. "Now, shall we resume the bidding?"

"Ten thousand five hundred pounds," someone said, waving their paddle.

I glared at the individual, my own paddle already high over my head. "Fifty thousand pounds."

The room hushed. Isadora sank farther into the chair, softly groaning.

"Fifty thousand pounds," the auctioneer repeated faintly. He cleared his throat and shook his head, as if disbelieving his own words. In a stronger voice, he said, "Do I hear fifty-one thousand pounds?"

No one stirred.

"No?" Phillip asked. "Fair enough. Sold! To the young lady, apparently a Cleopatra aficionado."

The same young man walked onto the stage, wearing gloves, and carefully removed the statue. Though he wore a mask obscuring his face, his auburn hair glimmered in the candlelight. He was wearing a different shirt than the one I'd seen him in earlier, and while he never once looked in my direction, I could sense his ire.

My rascal of a husband.

"That's Whit," Isadora said in astonishment. "Isn't it? Wasn't he wearing a blue shirt earlier, though?"

"It is Whit," I confirmed grimly. "And he was wearing blue. He must have ruined the other or found a spare to use as a disguise."

"What on earth is he doing?"

I massaged a growing ache at my temple, a yawning pit deep in my belly. When was I going to learn to take better care with my thieving husband? This auction presented many temptations for him, since money was what he was after. "He might be stealing the asp."

"*What?*"

Whit disappeared into another room, as the throng of people chatted, several continuing to openly stare at me. Which, I suppose, I couldn't blame them for. I had caused quite a stir. I jumped to my feet, intent on following after him, but someone cleared their throat from behind me.

I turned in surprise. It was the same man from before, the one who had given us the masks and paddles.

"Excuse me," he said. "But the founder would like a word with you." His attention flicked toward my sister, who stood, but the man shook his head. "No, not you. Only this one."

WHIT

My wife's plans would be the death of me.

I watched her sitting primly next to Isadora, her mind probably whirring with one reckless idea after another that would get her killed. I frowned, forcing myself to turn away, following after Farida as she snapped photographs of closed doors and different sections of the wall. Sometimes she gently tapped areas, and when she heard a particular sound, Farida smiled to herself before clicking the button on the side of her handheld camera.

"I'm going to explore upstairs," I whispered as I brushed past her.

"I'll be up shortly," she replied, "as soon as I've taken enough down here."

I nodded over my shoulder and climbed up the rest of the way. The third floor was somehow even worse than the other two. A layer of packed dust and grime coated the paneled floors, the rugs having been kicked aside at some point. The smell boasted of the dank and moist, and I winced as the potent stench worked its way up my nose. I moved silently, my boots hardly making a sound as I checked open rooms that were in the same dilapidated state as the rest of the house. One room was locked, and I raised my leg, preparing to kick the door in, but then I shook my head.

Too much noise. Farida and her magic camera could take care of this one.

The sound of the auctioneer calling out broke the quiet as I crept closer to an open space that looked down into the second floor's proceedings. I walked the rectangular perimeter, taking care to keep to the shadows. From a certain angle, I could see Inez in her seat. She should never play poker. That girl wore everything on her face.

I pushed her far from my mind and focused on trying to find the rest of the relics. I was just about to leave the balcony area when a man approached Inez. She held her ground, but even from where I stood, I could see fear etched across her tightened brow. The knife tucked within my boot was in my hand in a matter of seconds, the handle digging in my palm. I approached the railing, readying to hurl it at the man should he even look at her wrong.

Lifting the knife, I exhaled slowly. My feet were already arranged in the exact position I'd need to generate enough force to send it flying into the man's neck. Seconds ticked by.

He had no idea how close to the grave he was.

But then he gave Inez a paddle and a mask, and I relaxed marginally. It was only when he walked away that I tucked the weapon back inside my boot. My attention flickered to the stage where the item for sale rested on a platform. It looked like an expensive piece of jewelry, with a long golden chain, gemstones glimmering in the soft candlelight.

I was more interested in the employee who had brought the item onto the stage.

An idea took shape in my mind as I walked away from the railing. I found more stairs, and I descended quickly. This wing of the house was marginally louder—sounds of quiet conversation and people walking drifted in my direction as I made my way down a long corridor. Like the other wing, the hallway opened up to many more rooms, some doors left open, others closed. When I reached the end, I peered around the corner. Two men stood facing the other direction, talking in hushed tones. I crept closer.

The sound of the bidding began, not too far off. At a particularly loud interval, I raised my hands and shoved their heads together. Hard. They slumped to the floor, and I dragged their unconscious bodies into one of the empty rooms.

"What are you doing?" someone asked from somewhere behind me.

I tensed but walked out of the room, closing the door after me. A short man stood in one of the open doorways farther down, looking at me curiously. "Aren't you supposed to be guarding this room?" he asked in an English accent, jerking his chin behind him.

It was hard to check my amusement, but I managed. "I thought I heard something." The short man took a step in my direction, but I held up my hand. "Only rats. I took care of them."

He regarded me warily before shrugging, then he went back into the room, evidently dismissing me. I followed him inside and stopped short. Wooden crates, the majority of which were nailed shut, covered nearly every foot of floor space. Empty bottles of wine littered the surfaces, along with stacks of old newspapers. Presumably used for additional cushioning for the antiques.

The short man was still eyeing me suspiciously. He fidgeted and swallowed hard, eyes darting nervously toward the door. "I haven't seen you before."

Tension seeped into the room, and I got the distinct impression he was trying to catch me unawares. Any sudden movements on my part would alarm him, and we were too close to the auction. I couldn't risk him yelling for help. My attention flickered back to the newspapers. Nonchalantly I pulled the top stack and pretended to read the front page.

"I was only just hired," I said casually, thumbing through the pages of *The Egyptian Gazette*. I recognized this particular press. Every article was written in English and represented the interests of many European countries who invested in the archaeological pursuits of their countrymen or in the production of Egyptian cotton.

Whatever. I didn't pick it up for reading.

"We have to work, you know," he said, annoyed.

"Then tell me what to do," I said, rolling the paper tightly at a diagonal until it narrowed into a sharp point.

The short man indicated to one crate stacked atop another. "This one's next."

He pried the lid off with a crowbar, and I drew closer, my pulse ticking hard, the rolled-up paper in my fist. I peered into the crate, aware of the anxious man standing on the other side, breathing heavily. Nestled inside the wrapping was a blue statue of an asp. For a moment, I was back underground, inside Cleopatra's final resting place. Inez knelt in front of a row of figurines, her charcoal pencil clutched in one hand while the other gripped a journal. I'd seen this statue in the treasury; I was sure of it—sure, too, that Inez had drawn an illustration of it.

I lifted my eyes, only to meet my companion's shrewd gaze and a dagger in his right hand.

"You've seen it before," he accused. "Where are the other two men?"

"I told you," I said calmly. "I took care of the rats."

The man leapt around the crate, jabbing the knife. I blocked his movement, but the tip dragged along my arm, ripping my shirt. I glared down at the long scrape in annoyance.

"This was my most comfortable shirt," I muttered.

He swung the knife again and I sidestepped, cracking a hard hit to his right eye. He moaned, and now the dagger came at me wildly in downward arcs. I swerved out of reach, barely avoiding the edge of the blade.

"Oh, for fuck's sake," I hissed. "*Enough*."

The short man came at me again, eyes wild. The edge of his weapon scraped against my other arm—I cursed, pivoting, and then I drove the tip of my pointed newspaper up through the underside of his chin. His eyes widened as blood spewed out of his mouth. With my index finger, I gently poked his chest, and he toppled over in a messy heap.

I glanced down at my shirt and sighed. There'd be no cleaning it now. Quickly, I dragged the man into the room where I had knocked the other guards unconscious. I took off one of their masks and shirts and hurriedly put on both before doubling back to the artifacts. I kicked over a rolled-up rug to cover the blood just as someone else entered the room, carrying a clipboard.

"It's time for the next artifact," he said, wrinkling his nose. "My God, the smell in this room." He pointed to the statuette impatiently. "It's that one, and don't forget to wear the gloves."

"Fine," I said. "I'm right behind you."

I found the gloves on top of another crate and dragged them on before taking the asp out of its nest of wrappings. Then I followed him to the auction room, peering over his shoulder at the clipboard in his hands.

On it were pages filled with addresses.

I smiled to myself before taking the stage.

CAPÍTULO CATORCE

The man looked at me expectantly, brows raised above the line of his mask. The upper portion of his face was hidden, but his lips were pressed into a flat, disapproving line. I got the sense that he didn't like this errand, and that it was perhaps an unusual request to make during the auction.

"The founder wants to see me," I repeated.

Isadora lifted her chin. "Whatever for?"

Perhaps the founder wanted to verify I had the funds or he simply wanted to meet me. Either way, I knew of no way to extricate myself from this situation without drawing notice or suspicion. My idea only worked if I followed it through. "It's all right, Isadora."

She narrowed her eyes at me. "I'm going with you."

"If you'd like," the man said. "But he only wants to see her."

"I heard you the first time," Isadora said coolly. "But my sister goes nowhere without me."

"Suit yourself—but you will wait outside the room while they discuss business."

"That's not acceptable."

The man didn't bother to reply but waited for us to exit the last row, and with an impervious air, he bade us to follow after him. I felt as if I were a child who had misbehaved during dinner and now had to face judgment. He walked briskly, and I felt, rather than saw, the weight of everyone's curiosity as they tracked my movements. Isadora maintained the admirable lift of her chin, but her hand hovered close to her skirt pocket where

I knew she kept her sleek little handgun, a small case of bullets, and the extra gun she'd picked up downstairs.

She was a walking armory.

The masked man led us to the opposite wing of the building, past empty rooms that might have been offices, until he reached the last chamber at the end of the corridor. "Here we are."

He held the door open and waited for me to pass.

Isadora glared at the man, and I lightly touched her arm. "I'll be fine, Isadora." I gave her a pointed look, and slightly raised my eyebrows. If there was trouble, she need only scream for help. Our companions were close by.

She nodded in understanding.

"You'll be all right out here on your own?" I asked my sister.

Isadora shot a cool look at our stoic companion. "I think he means to keep me company."

"He does," the man said, and I caught the faintest hint of amusement.

Satisfied that nothing would happen to Isadora, I walked into the room to find the founder facing away from me, intent on looking out the window. He was the only person within. There were no chairs, not one cushion or bookshelf. Under my feet were dirty rugs, flattened so thin I barely felt them. The walls and ceiling were bare, and the only decoration came from the moldy curtains pushed against the right side of the window. But there was one table and on it were three lit candles, casting sinister shadows from the man faced away from me.

The door was shut behind me and I startled.

The founder turned, his mask still on, hat tipped forward covering the long stretch of his brow. He had lightly tanned skin and a thin mouth that stretched into a crooked smile.

"It seems congratulations are in order," he said. "Miss?"

"It's Mrs., actually," I said. "Thank you. Is there something I need to sign?"

He waved his gloved hand dismissively. "In a moment. All the formalities can certainly wait. I wanted to meet the young woman so enraptured by a snake."

The way he spoke felt familiar to me. It wasn't so much his voice but the sense that I had to be careful with every word I uttered. It felt as if I were playing a complicated game of chess, and he knew every move there was to make while I was still trying to understand the rules. "Well, now you've met her. Perhaps we can handle the particulars? I'd rather be on my way." I gestured toward the window where the night had burned away some of its darkness. The morning light would dawn soon. "The hour grows late. Or is it early?"

The founder smiled at me. "How did you hear about the auction? You weren't issued an invitation."

There was no use lying. He would certainly know how many invitations were sent out and to whom. "From a friend. I couldn't resist attending," I added.

"What friend?"

"I'm not going to break any of your rules," I said. "I'm a collector."

"Are you?" he said. "I thought you were a tourist."

I blinked at him in confusion. "Tourist?"

His lips twisted into a smile. "That's what you told me last time."

Horror dawned upon me. I had seen that smug smile, and his slick tone recalled an unpleasant conversation I'd had earlier. The founder raised his hand and pulled off his glove with his teeth. And there, on his littlest pinky, was the golden ring my father had sent me over the summer, right before he disappeared.

"*You*," I whispered.

The founder peeled off his auction mask to reveal the face of Basil Sterling, complete with his outrageous mustache and condescending air.

Anger swam in my blood, a fast-moving river that made my heart race. This man had given the order to kidnap me, but his henchmen had mistakenly taken Elvira instead—thanks to Lourdes's sly involvement.

"My cousin died," I said, my voice shaking. "She *died*."

"I know," he said. "An unfortunate occurrence that could have been entirely avoided. We could bypass another such occurrence if you cooperate."

Fear crept over my skin, turning it ice-cold. My stomach churned at our close proximity, and the instinct to run overwhelmed me. This man was a monster. I glanced behind me, measuring the distance to the door, and prayed Isadora still stood on the other side of it.

Mr. Sterling chuckled. "I only want to have a productive conversation with you. I promise that you will leave this building unharmed."

I noticed he hadn't included Isadora. "My companion, too."

"Certainly," he said. "*If you cooperate.*"

"You're not letting me go," I said, hating the slimy texture to his voice. I felt as if it were coating my clothes, poisoning the air I breathed. "I've seen your face; I could easily turn you in."

His grin widened. "To whom? The authorities? Mostly made up of my countrymen?"

Frustration ate at me, making it hard to talk. He was right, people I could trust were in short supply. But perhaps Monsieur Maspero could be reasoned with?

Mr. Sterling eyed me shrewdly. "I wouldn't count on Monsieur Maspero, either. I believe he's enjoying the spoils of my efforts. But please, go ahead and try it, my dear. I can't wait for you to discover how few options you have left."

"There must be *someone* in this country who isn't corrupt."

"Everyone has a price."

"You're despicable. A criminal with a license."

He shrugged negligently. "You have no proof."

No, but Farida would. And the knowledge of it helped me stand my ground. He didn't know about her magical camera. He didn't know about Whit sneaking around the corridors. But my mind caught at the thought of my husband. He could be betraying me *yet again* and stealing as many artifacts as he could carry. Even now, he could be strolling out the front door, leaving us all behind.

"What do you want to know?" I asked, inching backward. Any hope of locating my mother disappeared. My plan would never work now. This night had been doomed from the start.

"What does any man in my position want? Information."

"I have none—"

"Tell me where to find Lourdes and her known associate," he said. "A Mr. Fincastle, I believe?"

By some miracle, I was able to keep my face neutral; Whit was rubbing off on me. How on earth did Mr. Sterling know about Mr. Fincastle? Well, I suppose they ran in the same shady circles. "I don't know where she is, or him for that matter."

Mr. Sterling tilted his head, as if he hoped to catch a lie in the tone of my voice.

"That's why I'm here," I said, insistent. "I have no idea of her whereabouts or those of Mr. Fincastle."

"Ah," Mr. Sterling said. "Which is why you bid on the item, hoping to know where to direct the funds."

I flattened my lips, disappointment crowding close to my edges. Of course he would have thought of the same thing. "She gave a fake address," I guessed.

"She's no fool, more's the pity," he said. "Well, it seems you are of no use to me after all."

I stiffened and took another step backward.

Mr. Sterling observed my trajectory and shook his head ruefully. "It seems I'm frightening you. Well, I suppose that can't be helped. It's a shame you think so, since we seem to have the same goal in mind. Think of what we could accomplish together."

"You're not actually suggesting that we work together," I said, aghast.

"It would be the pragmatic course."

"I would never help you, *sir*."

"I can't say that I'm not disappointed," Mr. Sterling said. "But as a gesture of goodwill, perhaps I can return something of yours?" He slid off the golden ring and held it out for me.

I stared at it, my hands curled into fists. "It's not mine. It belonged to Cleopatra."

"But somehow it made it into your possession," he said. "Finders keepers, as they say. Come, come. Is this your way of saying you wouldn't like it back?" He started to slide the ring back onto his pinky.

I couldn't let that happen. That was the last thing Papá had given me, and wherever he was, dead or alive, he wouldn't want this vile man to have it.

"No," I said quickly. "I do."

Mr. Sterling paused and then once again held it out to me. "It's yours, then."

No part of me wanted to draw closer to him, but he had remained on the other side of the room. I crossed it and snatched the jewelry from out of his hand. The magic took a hold of me, at once familiar, and the taste of roses bloomed in my mouth. I felt as if I had become reacquainted with an old friend. The feeling crested, and it took several breaths for me to get used to the tingling sensation sweeping up my arm, making the hairs in its path rise on end.

Mr. Sterling motioned toward the door. "You are free to go, just as I promised."

I fled without a backward glance.

Isadora waited for me on the other side, arms crossed, her foot tapping against the crumbly floor. When I stepped out, she breathed a sigh of relief.

"Where's your companion?" I asked.

"I shot him," she said smoothly.

"*What?*"

"I'm only joking," she said. "I *can* be funny at times."

I looked at her. "Isadora, I don't know how to tell you this except to just say it: that wasn't funny."

She smiled demurely. "Maybe not to you."

"Have you seen the others?" I asked.

"I've been here this whole time," she said. "Guarding the door."

"And Farida? Whit?"

"Assuming Whit hasn't absconded with the artifacts and abandoned us, he ought to be waiting for us at the meeting spot. Hopefully with Farida."

Farida looked nervously upward, hazy light bleeding red against the bruised sky. "Where *is* he?"

We were standing in the meeting spot looking on as the attendees left the building, a steady, quiet stream. We had been the first to leave, quickly walking to the shadowy street corner that opened into the narrow alley. The attendees dispersed in every direction. I looked for Whit, but I didn't see him in the crowd.

"I hate to say this," Isadora said, "but your husband is an unreliable thief who—"

"Who what?"

We spun to face the alley. Whit stood with his hands in his pockets, an inscrutable look stamped across his face. "Go on," he said. "I can't wait to hear the rest of it."

"How did you get onstage?" Isadora asked. "Actually, let's begin with *why* you were onstage."

Whit motioned for us to follow him. "We ought to return to the hotel."

Exhaustion sucked me down like mud, and my steps were slow and faltering. I had been up for nearly a full day and was feeling the effects of little sleep. Farida kept yawning, and even Isadora looked a little bedraggled. Her neat hair had escaped the confines of the tight bun at the crown of her head, and her hem was finally dirty.

"Farida, did you manage to take pictures of the storage room?" Whit asked.

She nodded, yawning again hugely. "Sorry, yes. But it was mostly just of the crates. They don't open them until right before they are presented, unfortunately. There was a crowbar, and I managed to pry open only one of them. Inside was a large statue; the top of the head was the only thing visible from its wrapping. I still took a picture, but I'm not sure how helpful it will be. However, I took care to take photographs of each crate. They were sent on from Bulaq."

"I'm sure whatever pictures you managed to take will be fine. You still took photos of the auction room and everyone attending," I said.

"Who were all wearing masks," Isadora said coolly.

"And most of their backs were turned," Whit muttered.

"What about the auctioneer?" I asked. "That Phillip Barnes fellow. He was facing you."

Farida seemed cheered by this, and then her face fell. "Maybe, except he was constantly moving, wasn't he? What if the image is too blurry and he's hard to identify?"

"We'll worry about that when the time comes," I said. "You might have captured him perfectly."

We made the same few turns, and finally Shepheard's came into view. The familiar front steps gave me a warm, pleasant feeling. Ever since I left Argentina, this was the closest place to a home that I had. Cairo was beginning to wake up, and the street soon filled with all the usual morning bustle. Two donkey carts rumbled across our path, while vendors started calling out their various wares for sell. Someone was selling freshly brewed coffee at a small cart near the hotel entrance, and Whit looked at it longingly but must have decided he was too tired to drink it.

He had remained mostly silent for a long stretch of the walk, and my curiosity was making my head spin. "Whit," I said. "Are you going to make us ask you again? What were you doing onstage?"

"I replaced the poor fellow who was charged with moving the artifacts on and off the stage," he said. "In doing so, when I grabbed hold of the asp and returned it to the room where everything else was kept, I was able to learn where the payment ought to go for it." He dipped his hand into his pocket and held up a small scrap of paper. "I wrote down the address."

I frowned. "I have it on good authority that it's fake."

We had reached the stairs, but at my words, Whit stopped abruptly. "I'd like to talk to you alone," he said. "Please."

The others paused, halfway up. Isadora was watching Whit warily, and when her gaze flickered to mine, there was a question in them. I gave her a slight nod. My sister's face darkened, but she followed Farida inside.

"On whose authority?" Whit asked.

"I had a little meeting with the founder of Tradesman's Gate," I said nonchalantly. "It wasn't pleasant, but it was certainly illuminating."

Whit waited for me to explain myself, his shoulders tense. His voice was flat with barely controlled frustration. "Did he hurt you?"

I shook my head. "No—but he did reveal his identity."

Whit arched a brow. "I don't like the sound of that. Now you're a liability."

The man had made my skin crawl, and I shuddered. "It's Basil Sterling," I said. "We guessed as much, remember?" I held up my hand. "He gave me back the golden ring."

Whit leaned forward and brushed his finger across the flat surface featuring Cleopatra's cartouche. "I suppose he doesn't need it anymore, now that she's been found and her resting place pillaged." A deep groove appeared between his brows as he studied me. "Strange that he'd give you something so valuable."

"I don't think so," I said slowly. "He was trying to bribe me."

"So he wants something, then." Whit's eyes flicked uneasily back to the ring. "Did he say what?"

"He wanted to know where my mother was," I said. "And her lover. I told him I didn't know where they were, and he seemed to believe me."

Whit gave me a narrow-eyed look. "Really."

"I told him the only reason we were there this morning was to try to find an address for Mamá."

Whit rubbed his eyes. "Inez."

"He thought the same thing I did," I said defensively. "It occurred to him that if my mother dared to try to sell one of the artifacts she'd stolen from him, she might provide a forwarding address for the payment. That's why he acknowledged it would be fake."

"Probably so," Whit agreed. "But Lourdes would never have given away the asp for free. She *wants* the money."

I blinked at him. "I *know* that. What's your point?"

He held up the scrap of paper. "I'm saying that this address might not lead directly to *her*, but the next one will. Because if I were her, whatever this address is, I guarantee she's watching it. In no world would Lourdes lose track of the money. Somehow, she's following its progress and waiting for it to go to its final destination." He smiled tiredly. "I think we might have found a way to get to her, despite what Mr. Sterling believes."

He handed the paper to me, and I read the scant few lines of his appalling scrawl.

I slowly looked up at him. "This address is in Alexandria."

Whit nodded.

I recalled an earlier conversation with Isadora when she'd revealed how Mamá divided her time in Alexandria, London, and Argentina. She had a home in the former, so while this wasn't surprising information—it was curious. "If your theory is correct, why send the money to Alexandria? Why put herself far away from every other ancient city of note? Cairo, Thebes, Aswan," I said, listing each off with my fingers. "And isn't Tradesman's Gate typically held here?"

"She could be wanting to start an auction in Alexandria."

"But then why try to sell the asp this morning?"

He considered, one leg bent at the knee, his foot propped on a higher step. "Suppose it was personal?" He must have read the confusion on my face because he pressed on. "Your mother betrayed Mr. Sterling—why? Lourdes might be motivated by the money, of course, but what if it ran deeper than that? What if she's trying to run him out of business?"

"So she flaunts her victory under his nose by trying to sell the statuette," I said, following his line of thought. "And she does need a method to sell off what she's stolen. The gate *is* an established auction, with reputable buyers. Meanwhile, she's moving the rest of the artifacts up north?"

"It's possible," Whit said slowly. "And if I were her, I'd want cash to start up a new enterprise that would directly compete with Tradesman's Gate. She'd need to hire new employees, find a secure location to house all the artifacts, and locate a suitable place to host the first auction."

"Well, she's about to learn that the asp statuette earned her fifty thousand pounds. Whoever her emissary was, they're bound to send a telegram to let her know." I wrinkled my nose. "There's still something I don't understand."

Whit waited, expectant.

"On Philae, she asked me about the Chrysopoeia of Cleopatra, and you're also convinced she's searching for it. If Mamá is intent on opening her own auction, does this mean she's given up searching for the sheet?"

"Something tells me that if Basil Sterling is looking for it, then she won't stop looking for it. With the Chrysopoeia in her possession, she'll have unlimited funds."

"But only if she employs an alchemist," I pointed out. "I can't imagine there are many people living who practice that archaic profession."

Whit shrugged and said nonchalantly, "You'd be surprised."

Another thought occurred to me. "Where does Mr. Fincastle fit into all this? He's her lover, her business partner. Could he be with Mamá in Alexandria?"

"Lourdes might be the one focusing on founding a new black market, while Fincastle could be searching for Cleopatra's Chrysopoeia. The reverse could *also* be true."

"If I were them," I said, "I would take care not to be in the same place. One person in a different city, or part of the country, and the other on the opposite end." I studied him carefully, the sun hitting him square in the face, making his eyes squint. "It seems like a logical course of action to split up," I said, trying to keep my voice casual. "Why don't you stop following me around and continue the search for the alchemical sheet?" And because I was a glutton for punishment, I asked the question I was afraid to know the answer to. Even though it shouldn't have mattered anymore, the words ran out of my mouth unfettered. "That's what you really want, isn't it?"

His expression changed subtly, brows drawing inward, the line of his jaw hardening. He was quiet for so long I knew it must be because he was having an argument with himself. This was always the case with Whit. How much of his inner world did he want to reveal? I used to think that he feared being vulnerable because some truths could be used as weapons against him, but now I knew different. Whit wasn't fearful; he was *scheming*.

He was helping me only because it served his own interests.

He folded his arms across his chest. "Yes, it's what I really want." He locked eyes with me, and my heart stuttered. "More than *anything*, I want that alchemical sheet."

It was as if he'd dealt me a physical blow. Hurt bloomed outward, making my chest feel tight. "I'm going to Alexandria," I said with a finality I didn't feel.

But should have.

My voice snapped him from his thoughts. The corners of his mouth tightened as he leaned forward, so close the brush of his words caressed my mouth. "Not without me you're not."

WHIT

Inez had insisted on visiting Ricardo in prison before setting off to Alexandria, and I had agreed to take her. But of course, nothing was ever going to be as simple as her and me having a quick visit, and an hour before we left, we were joined by the rest of her family: the grieving aunt, the disapproving cousin—the latter of which had done nothing but snipe at Inez and glower at me. When Isadora said she wanted to go, I put my foot down.

We were already going to be a bloody parade.

"Ricardo will punt you out of the room himself," I snarled. "Under no circumstances are you going."

Isadora shot a steely-eyed glare at me and left the hotel room, her back rigid, hands curled into fists.

"Was that *really* necessary?" Inez asked, placing a wide-brimmed hat on her head. She was wearing too fine a dress for the prison. The hem would be up to three inches in dirt and dust. It was the kind of thing Arabella would feel self-conscious about. My protective instincts flared, and I debated letting Inez know the state of the roads, but I bit my tongue.

"Your uncle can't stand her, either," I said. "And if I were you, I wouldn't mention that she's with us. One more thing for him to worry about."

Her lips flattened to a mulish line, but she didn't protest. Thank Christ.

"Let's go," I said. "I'll have enough trouble getting all of you inside once we're there, and I know we're in a hurry."

Inez walked to the door and threw it open, one light hand on the knob. She gave me a sweet smile over her shoulder. "Farida wants to come also."

I sighed.

I hated coming back to this building. It was once a military hospital, and I wouldn't be able to walk the halls without thinking of the friends who'd died within these walls. But now it had been converted to a prison. Instead of a place that worked hard to ensure people were able to leave out the front door, it was now a place where people were condemned to be forgotten.

Ricardo and Abdullah hadn't been tried as of yet, but they were being detained to prevent any fleeing out of the country. Monsieur Maspero assured me they'd be given every consideration for their class and status.

But even so, I worried what state we'd find them in.

And it didn't help that Inez had gone pale the farther we traveled north of Cairo. It was a journey of eight miles to Tourah, the village where the wounded had gone to be treated.

Inez stared at the plain and austere prison building, her face wincing. "Abdullah and Tío Ricardo are in there?"

"It's been much improved." It had been dilapidated, the upper story dated, but it was recently renovated and restructured with well-ventilated wards, new beds and bedding, and the appointment of a well-trained doctor. "Let's go before I change my mind."

At first the warden didn't want to permit all of us to visit Ricardo and Abdullah, but eventually he relented under the severe glares he received from all the women in our party. No one, however, came close to Amaranta's fierce scowl.

I understood why she was Inez's least-favorite cousin.

Eventually we were led by two guards to the third floor of the prison, down a long corridor, and to the last cell on the right. One of the guards opened the heavy iron door, the key making a loud scraping noise. We were all silent, waiting to be allowed inside. Next to me, Inez was practically trembling, I'm sure terrified of what state she'd find Abdullah and her uncle in.

"You have a visitor," the guard said in Arabic. "Actually, visitors, I should say."

Then he stepped aside and gestured for us to enter the cell. I let the women precede me and I was about to walk through, when the guard hissed, "Ten minutes only."

I nodded. I had spare change in my pocket in case we needed more time.

Inez went immediately to her uncle and gave him a hug, arms wrapping tight around his waist, narrower now, thanks to his present living conditions. They'd been inside, two, no, three days. Farida went to sit next to her grandfather, Abdullah, who broke into a wide smile as she leaned into his shoulder. They spoke quietly to each other in Arabic, while Amaranta stood off to the side, her attention flickering from one thing to the other: the gray walls, the squeaking mattresses, the bare floors. For once, her expression had softened to one of compassion, and she crossed the room to sit on Ricardo's other side. He seemed surprised by this.

"I suppose we ought to get to know one another," she said coolly. "My mother and I will be your frequent visitors. Tell me, do you have soap?"

Ricardo gaped at her. "Soap?"

Amaranta glanced around again. "You don't have a washbasin. I suppose that was a silly question."

Inez threw the guard a glare. "Perhaps we can request one."

"This is truly a deplorable room," Lorena exclaimed, the train of her voluminous skirt swishing around her like the bristles of a broom. "This window is so small, the beds too narrow!" She spun around and gasped loudly. "Are you drinking water from *petroleum* cans?"

Ricardo shot me a pained look, and I stifled my smile.

She went on and on, finding something to despair over, while Farida gave Abdullah a few letters she had written to him to be read later. She also had brought several treats, which she dug out from within her purse.

"What have you been up to?" Ricardo asked Inez, eyeing her shrewdly. "You look tired. Have you been ill?"

I had to admire the way Inez could lie with a straight face. All of the strain she carried from our disaster of a marriage dissolved, and if I didn't know better, I would have believed the adoring look she sent me. "The opposite, Tío. I've never been happier."

I knew Inez had a tumultuous relationship with her uncle, but watching him now, with his gaze intent on his niece, the clear love he had for her was more than apparent. But when he fixed a glower in my direction, I received no such love.

That still stung. But my wife wasn't the only one who could act the part. "Glad to hear it, amor."

Inez's eyelid twitched, but her smile did not falter.

Lorena glanced between us in comical alarm. Then she loudly exclaimed, "I've brought you a gift, Ricardo."

I leaned against the wall and crossed my ankles, fighting my amusement. It seemed my wife hadn't informed her aunt of our matrimonial state. Well, I wouldn't have, either. I didn't want to have my ears ringing the whole way home from Lorena's screeching. It was clear she did not approve of me. Probably wanted Inez to have that Ernesto, son of a consul or whatever.

It probably would have been better if she'd married him.

"Here, look," Lorena said, reaching into her silk purse. She pulled out a small bundle wrapped in tissue paper patterned in bright colors.

Ricardo had not lost the pained expression on his face. If anything, it had gotten much worse. "No, really, it's fine. I don't need anything."

Lorena brushed his comment aside. "You'll want this, Ricardo. Now, don't be stubborn, and be a dear man and open it."

Abdullah and Farida stopped their quiet conversation and gazed with interest as Ricardo carefully unwrapped the present. When the last of the tissue paper had been set aside, we all stared at the item. Ricardo appeared horrified. "Is this a *teacup*?"

"It is," Lorena confirmed. "Isn't it beautiful? I think the blue pattern is divine. Don't you agree?"

"Er," Ricardo said, eyeing the porcelain cup as if it were a venomous spider. "I won't be invited to a tea in here, Lorena. What the devil do you expect me to do with this?"

"Well, you don't drink from it," Lorena said.

Ricardo eyed the object that was clearly meant for drinking. “I don’t?”

“Is it magic touched, Tía?” Inez asked.

Lorena nodded. “Yes! I have the matching teacup back at the hotel. Whenever you fill one with water, the other will fill up also but glow with a silvery light. That’s when the receiver knows to look inside. You’ll find the sender on the other end, and you can have a conversation as normal.”

“Brilliant,” I said. “Like Alexander Graham Bell’s telephone.”

“Exactly,” Lorena exclaimed. “But with our faces! Can you imagine? What technology could beat this mode of communication? Not a letter, or a telegram.”

“What happens if no one answers on the other end?” Farida asked.

Lorena’s excitement dimmed. “Well, it’s not perfect magic. The water will glow for a few minutes, but if no one answers, the magic stops and the receiver is left with just regular water. Unfortunately, if the sender tries again before the receiver empties the cup, the water *will* overflow.”

“So if I don’t answer your call, you can call again and again and again, flooding our room with water?” Ricardo asked in an aghast tone.

“You’re welcome,” Lorena said, grinning.

PART THREE

THE BRIDE OF THE MEDITERRANEAN

CAPÍTULO QUINCE

I was dreaming, the golden ring a pressing weight on my finger. I didn't quite know how I knew exactly, but somehow my intuition worked even in my subconscious. My limbs felt heavy, tucked under the bedding, and dimly I was aware that I was encased in a gauzy shroud. The mosquito netting. Cool air rustled my hair, and I sank farther into the soft pillow, squeezing my eyes shut, desperate to remain where I was in the dream.

Cleopatra stood in a softly lit room, rows and rows of scrolls in front of her. Her sheer tunic went past her toes, and the fabric kissed the warm-hued stones as she paced, clearly searching for something in particular. She yanked out parchments, unrolling them quickly, hissing with impatience as she threw them onto the floor, one by one. She went to another shelf and pulled out another scroll, unrolling it, and a moment later, she let out a noise of triumph. Her back was turned to me, so I couldn't see what she was reading; I tried to shift around her, but the memory wouldn't let me. I was confined to the corner of the room, as if she only meant to capture what shelf she had taken the scroll from. The smell of ash and smoke filled my nostrils.

Something burned.

She spun toward the chamber's entrance and called out to someone, holding up a single sheet of parchment. Her face was unlined, her hair glossy and dark. This was a younger Cleopatra than I had seen before. She had none of the world weariness from before, none of the jaded expression lining her features.

This Cleopatra had no idea what was to come.

The memory became hazy. My fingers curled around the edge of the pillow, and I held my breath, trying to stay in the memory. I'd seen something on that sheet.

It looked like a snake eating itself.

And then Cleopatra pulled out another scroll, seemingly at random, and slipped the sheet on top of it and then rolled it carefully, effectively hiding what she'd found. She took both with her as she left, and the memory faded completely.

I opened my eyes, confused and disorientated. Next to me, Isadora's sleeping form shifted, and she let out a little breathless mutter, tucking herself closer to me. I blinked away the drowsy feeling of sleep, cautiously sitting up, and peeled back the netting. The carpet was cool under my bare feet as I padded around the stacked crates toward Whit's narrow cot. He slept on his back, long legs stretched out and over the edge of the bed. His hair flopped onto his forehead; the curved line of his jaw was soft.

He looked innocent while he dreamed. Younger and unburdened, the Whit who had once looked at me with hope and a promise I could trust.

I knelt and poked his shoulder.

Whit jerked, his hand reaching under his pillow and retrieving something shiny. A cool, sharp edge pressed against me, right under my chin. Sleepy blue eyes with only a hint of alertness stared broodingly back at me.

"It's me," I breathed. "Just me."

He turned onto his side, hiding the blade back underneath the pillow. "I could have slit your throat."

I rubbed my neck. "You're a walking hazard, Mr. Hayes."

He rubbed his eyes and said tiredly, "Please don't call me that. We're not strangers. We're not even acquaintances."

"I have to," I whispered.

Whit lowered his hands and peered at me. Even in the dim lighting, I could make out the serious line of his mouth, the narrowed eyes. "Why?"

"Because one day, that's all you'll be to me," I whispered with a quick glance toward Isadora. I didn't want to wake her.

A long silence followed, and then he flipped onto his back. "Did you need something?"

"I had another Cleopatra memory," I said, holding up my ring finger. "She's been busy."

Whit turned his head to face me. "And?"

"She was in a room, desperately looking for something," I said. "At first, I thought it was a scroll, but then she held up a single sheet of parchment. On it was a snake eating itself."

"The Chrysopoeia of Cleopatra," he exclaimed.

"Shh," I hissed. "Don't wake up my sister."

Whit rolled his eyes. "I couldn't care less about your sister."

Frustration licked at my edges. He and I were going to have words about his opinion of Isadora. His lack of trust and courtesy was beginning to grate on me. Whit was the one who *betrayed* me, the one who had lied to me. I almost got to my feet, but the memory had stayed with me, and I knew it was important, that it somehow connected to my mother.

"Will you please listen?"

He opened his mouth to speak, but I held up my hand. "At some point during the memory, I caught the scent of something burning. Right before she disappeared, I looked outward, and I saw a view of the sea, parts of the city." I inhaled, the memory sharp and tasting bitter on my tongue. "It was under siege."

Whit sat up and swung his legs around, planting his feet firmly next to me. His knee brushed against my shoulder. "Can I speak now?" There was the faintest note of sarcasm edging his voice.

"You may," I said.

"The city you saw must be Alexandria," he said. "Cleopatra had a palace close to the water, and if she had inherited the alchemical sheet and was working from it, it follows that she'd keep it close." He thought for a moment. "I could see why she'd be desperate to produce the philosopher's stone. Nothing bleeds money quite like war."

"What war was this?" I asked. "She looked too young for it to be the Battle of Actium."

"That took place off the coast of Greece," Whit said.

He was right. I remembered that particular battle, the warships carved onto the walls of her tomb. It was the beginning of the end, that event was a catalyst for the loss of everything she held dear: her kingdom, her children, and eventually her great love, Marcus Antonius. Chills swept up and down my arms.

"It might have been a fight against her brother, who arrived in Alexandria with his army, bent on seizing the throne from Cleopatra," Whit continued.

"So if she had the alchemical sheet, she might have wished to hide it somewhere. If I were her, I wouldn't want it in my brother's hands."

"Right," he said. "There are about a million places she could have hidden something so precious."

"But at least we have the name of the city," I said. "Cleopatra's Chrysopoeia must be in Alexandria."

"Like I said, a million places to hide," Whit muttered.

"We can eliminate one place for sure," I said. "The royal palace. The memory I stumbled into made me think she was leaving it in a rush to get out."

"Agreed." He paused. "And thank Christ, because the palace is underwater."

"What happened in the end with Cleopatra's brother? Did she defeat him?"

Whit nodded. "Thanks to Julius Caesar."

And thus, her love affair began. I found her story fascinating, but I couldn't help thinking of Mamá and how she could be on the same track, following the same clues. "Perhaps that's why my mother is in Alexandria," I said suddenly, remembering our earlier conversation. "Maybe it isn't to start a rival black market after all."

"Or it could be both. Your mother is an enterprising sort of person." Whit smiled ruefully.

I returned it without thinking. We locked eyes for a beat, and then another. The lighting in the room had brightened considerably since I'd walked over to him, and I could see every line and curve of his face. He regarded me fondly, his shoulders relaxed, his elbows resting on his knees. We had slipped into the natural camaraderie and sleuthing that existed between us from the beginning. It had been so easy to fall in love with him.

And so easy to forget what he had done.

I stood, bristling and annoyed with myself. He would be Mr. Hayes to me and nothing else. I turned to go back to bed, to get what little sleep remained for me, but he caught my hand.

"Wait," he said. "Wait."

His fingers were warm against my palm. I hated the way my body sang in response. "What?"

He released me abruptly, jaw clenching. My tone had been curt and iced over.

"I don't mean to be rude," came an annoyed voice from within the confines of the gauzy cocoon in the center of the room, "but would you two please bloody *be quiet*?"

"I'm sorry," I called out to her. "I didn't mean to wake you."

Isadora harrumphed, tossing and turning until finally becoming still and quiet.

"What did you want to say to me?" I asked in an almost inaudible whisper.

"It was nothing," he said after a moment. "Sleep well."

It was a nice sentiment, but I couldn't fall back asleep, no matter how much I wished for it, no matter how much I tried. All I could think about was the despairing note in Whit's voice and the way he had seemed to pull away from me, wall erected in place. This was what I wanted. He didn't deserve my smiles or my friendship, or any of my thoughts.

But it didn't stop me from wanting to know what he had been about to say. Nor did it stop the twinge of sadness that I'd never come to know it, either.

I planned for the trip to Alexandria. Of course, talking about going to Alexandria was much easier than actually doing it. For one thing, when my aunt found out my plans, she had promptly burst into tears and fled the seating area in favor of sobbing alone in her bedroom.

"Would it kill you to think before you speak?" Amaranta demanded. "I'm tired of cleaning up your messes, *prima*."

She said the word *cousin* as if it were a dirty one, a robust curse, and I suddenly remembered that she only called me prima when I was in trouble. Which I had been ever since I had accidentally splashed tea onto the pages of one of her favorite books eleven years ago. Amaranta really knew how to hold a grudge.

"I'm trying to make things right," I said. "I'm trying to put the right person in jail, so that Ricardo and Abdullah can go free."

What had happened to my uncle and Abdullah had also sent my aunt into hysterics. She had calmed down by the time we visited the prison, but I knew she suffered to see him locked away in a tiny room.

"And going to another city after we've only just arrived is the way to do it?" Amaranta asked, one brow arched skeptically. "*After* we crossed an ocean to get here? *After* we learned that Elvira was murdered? This is your best idea?" she scoffed. "I ought to have known you'd run away."

I bristled. "I'm not running away. Mamá is in Alexandria, and if I have any hope of her spending the rest of her miserable life in prison, that's where I need to be, too."

"And what?" Amaranta asked, her voice rising. "You'll ask her nicely to lock herself up? I know you're reckless, and stubborn, and too curious for your own good," she said scathingly, "but I honestly believed you to be smarter than this."

No one infuriated me more than my cousin did.

"I'm building a case against her," I yelled. "Wherever she goes, she leaves behind a trail of damning evidence."

"*Enough*, both of you," Tía Lorena said. She was pale and drawn, half supported by the doorframe opening up to her room. "For years I've watched the pair of you squabble like children. And you are *not* children anymore. One day, and I pray *soon*, you both will have husbands and households to manage and babies to raise."

My stomach did an odd little flip. I had forgotten to tell my aunt of my doomed marriage. No doubt the learning of it would send her back inside her bedroom in a fit of tears. Perhaps it'd be best if she never found out that particular secret.

She raised a trembling hand to her lips. "Do you really believe Lourdes is in Alexandria, Inez?"

I nodded.

"And there's been no word about—" Her voice cracked. She inhaled deeply, visibly fighting to control herself. "About my brother?" she asked.

Shame rose up my throat, hot and tasting like acid. It killed me that I had no new information about my father. Mamá had lied to me the first time, but I refused to accept anything but the truth from her now. I would make her tell me, by any means necessary. If I was forced to, I'd sic my violent husband on her while I still could.

I shook my head. "Nothing. Only Mamá knows the truth at this point."

My aunt's face hardened. "Then go and find her. Amaranta and I will care for Ricardo and his business partner while you're gone."

Amaranta's lips parted in surprise. "But Mamá—"

"If it were *you* in prison, hijita," she said, "wouldn't you want your family to visit every day? To deliver food? Blankets? To keep you company?"

"I'm not against visiting," Amaranta snapped. "I'm furious Inez is leaving us to bear the brunt of the responsibility."

"Amaranta, enough," Tía Lorena said. "Basta. Ya no puedo más."

My cousin fell silent, jaw locked. I couldn't help feeling that my uncle would rather spend his days alone than have my aunt and cousin descending upon him like clucking chickens, but I refrained from saying so. That revelation might turn my aunt into a puddle of tears. Truthfully, I was moved that she wanted to help me at all.

"I would never be in prison to begin with," Amaranta muttered.

"That's beside the point," my aunt said firmly. "I want to know what happened to Cayo. I must have some way to mourn him. Has there been no word about where his . . . his body might be?"

In no world would I allow her to share my hope that my father might still be alive. Better my aunt thought her brother was dead than to agonize over his whereabouts. Like I did. "No word, unfortunately."

Tía Lorena sighed. "Is there anything else you need?"

I considered her question. There was one thing. "Abdullah's granddaughter, Farida, is worried about him, and if you could include her in your plans from time to time, it would mean the world to me."

My aunt gave me a small nod. I would take my victories where I could get them. Then she surprised me by walking into her room abruptly. I looked at Amaranta, who delicately shrugged. My aunt returned, carrying the magic-touched teacup.

"If you're traveling to Alexandria, then you should take this with you," she said, handing it to me. "That way you can communicate with Ricardo whenever you wish." She smiled faintly. "I have a feeling he wouldn't love hearing from me, anyway."

I forced myself to smile. If my uncle found out I was heading to Alexandria, then he wouldn't be happy to hear from me, either.

The train rumbled along, sweeping past farmland and palm trees as we left Cairo. It was just the three of us in the cabin, Isadora at my side, Whit on the opposite bench, legs stretched out and crossed at the ankles.

"You are crushing the hem of my skirt," Isadora said to Whit icily, tugging at the fabric until he finally obliged her by lifting his boots. "Isn't there an empty compartment you can use?"

"I'm comfortable here," he replied, moodily staring out of the dusty window.

Isadora pressed her lips into a thin line. She dug into her bag and pulled out a book. I wished I had thought to bring one.

Whit jumped to his feet, glaring down at his seat. "What the devil!"

"What is it?" I asked.

Isadora peered at him from over the edge of her book.

He sighed, rubbing his eyes. "Remember when you gave me the teacup for safekeeping?"

I nodded, glancing at his knapsack. My own bag was too full, and so I had entrusted it to him, and he'd wrapped it in an old shirt of his. "Did it break?" I asked, my heart sinking. There went a way to communicate with my uncle.

"No," Whit muttered. "Ricardo was trying to communicate with your aunt—"

"Oh no," I said. "And the cup overflowed, getting your things wet."

He glared down at his pants where some of the water had soaked the material. "Yes."

Isadora laughed, and Whit shifted his glare from his pants to her. She smirked and went back to her reading.

"You should pull out your clothes so they can at least be dry by the time we reach Alexandria."

Whit unpacked several shirts and laid them flat on the bench. Then he sat, stretching his legs, placing them exactly where they had been, crushing Isadora's dress.

"Do you mind?"

"Not in the least," Whit said with a cold smile.

Isadora rolled her eyes, then shifted in her seat, facing away from us and toward the window. "I'd like to read in peace, if neither of you minds."

Whit opened his mouth.

"Where should we stay?" I asked quickly, hoping to turn the conversation from their brewing argument. I wished they would work on trying to find common ground while we were forced into one another's company. "You've been to Alexandria before, haven't you?"

Whit's lips flattened. "I wasn't there for the bombing of it, if that's what you're asking."

"I wasn't," I said. "I only wanted the name of a hotel."

"We ought to stay at Hotel d'Europe," Isadora said, not looking up from her reading. "I've heard wonderful things about the accommodations."

"It was destroyed in the bombing," Whit said. "And anyway, it would have been too expensive. We don't have that kind of money at our disposal."

"And whose fault was that again?" Isadora asked, turning the page.

"I don't see you contributing," he countered. "You've been acting like a parasite ever since you arrived in Cairo."

"Parasite," Isadora repeated faintly. She snapped her book shut and stood up, her back stiffening in cold fury, and strode to the compartment door, angrily sliding it open. Without another word, she stalked off in the direction of the dining car.

"Go and apologize, Mr. Hayes," I said.

"Why should I?" he muttered. "It's only too true. She almost got you killed the other night."

I leaned forward. "She is my sister. *Family*. If you insist on staying, following me around everywhere because of some misguided attempt to make it up to me, or to be reconciled—which will never happen—"

"That's not why I'm here," he snapped.

I lifted a brow. "Right. Of course. You're here because of the alchemical sheet."

Whit folded his arms across his chest, the press of his mouth a flat, mutinous line.

"I haven't forgotten," I whispered. "If it were me or the Chrysopoeia, I know the choice you would make. You've made that clear, unless there's something I'm missing. Something you can't or *won't* say."

He stayed silent, and I kicked his side of the bench. "Well?"

He lifted his eyes, met mine levelly. "You don't really want me to answer that."

"No, I guess I don't." I rubbed my eyes tiredly. "Will you please go and say that you're sorry?"

He eyed me wearily. "It's that important to you?"

"Sí. Ahora, por favor."

Whit left me with my thoughts, and my gaze dropped to my canvas bag. I never went anywhere without it, and if I was going to sit here, I might as well do something useful. With a little sigh, I rummaged through the various items tucked inside: pencils, extra candlesticks and matches, and finally, my journal and that of my mother's. I pulled both out and flipped through the pages of the latter, reading bits and pieces until the words swam across my vision.

Mamá's journal was thick, and I still hadn't studied every page in depth; the beginning section interested me the most. She had plenty of sketches, some of them half-finished, some of them finished in color.

She had a penchant for drawing statues. I came across the nine muses from Greek mythology; Cerberus, the three-headed dog who guarded the entrance to the underworld; and then a man I didn't recognize. At first glance, it looked like Hades, especially with the three-headed dog at his feet. But he wore a crown I'd never seen before and carried a staff that I'd never associated with the god of the world below.

Curious, I retrieved a pencil from within my bag and sketched the intriguing god and his dog, sitting on a peculiar structure. The sketch done, I closed my journal and tucked everything back into my canvas bag. Whit still hadn't returned, and I contemplated going to search for them. Just to make sure they were still alive.

The thought didn't amuse me.

Frowning, I stared out the window. We had left the city far behind, replaced by long stretches of golden sand that glimmered under the brutal rays of sunlight. The train cut through the unforgivable terrain, and with every mile crossed, I wondered where we were going to sleep, and how we were going to eat.

And just how long we would last, searching for my mother with limited funds and short tempers, and with two people who couldn't stand the sight of each other.

I sighed, leaning back against the seat as a sea of cotton fields, villages, and gorgeous mountains enclosing the Nile River swept past my window. The train rumbled onward, my worries chasing me every foot of the journey to Alexandria. The bride of the Mediterranean. But I enjoyed none of the scenery.

Instead, I tried not to despair.

WHIT

I started after Isadora, watching her skirt swish as she hustled toward the dining car. She sat at one of the available tables, hands primly folded on the tablecloth. Her posture was perfect, but I knew the secrets that could be hidden behind perfect manners.

I sat down across from her, scowling. "It's time we have a chat."

"I'm busy at the moment," she said coolly. "I'm going to have my tea."

"I want to know what game you're playing."

Isadora raised her brows faintly. "Game?"

"Don't try to tell me that you weren't deliberately leading Inez into the worst part of Cairo, or are you really going to sit there and pretend that you care a whit about her?"

She widened her eyes. "That was an accident! It may come as a shock to you, but my father allowed me to accompany him to his various job sites. Not all of them were at fancy hotels and stately mansions. I recalled the old government building being run-down and made an educated guess on where to go."

"A guess," I said, my anger spiking. "You risked everyone's life on a guess?"

"It wasn't like Inez could ask for directions," she snapped. "It would have drawn too much attention."

I tried another line of questioning. "Where is your father?"

Isadora fell silent. She met my gaze unflinchingly. Not fainthearted, this girl.

"Well?"

"I don't answer to you."

I slapped the table in frustration, and she jumped.

If Inez were here, she'd demand I apologize for that, too.

"Do you really expect me to believe you have had zero contact with him?"

"Why not?" she asked. "It's the truth. My God, what happened to you to mistrust everyone, to believe the worst of people?"

Growing up in a house that held no warmth. Joining the military at fifteen. Being sent off to battle in the desert. Too late to save General Gordon, and then being court-martialed for even attempting it. But I would never have said that out loud. She would turn any word I said against me.

"Why don't you make another guess?"

"I told you—I don't know. Stop asking me."

I studied her, on the edge of her seat, barely holding on to her prim exterior. Twin flags burned on her cheeks, and a vein stood out on her brow. It would be too easy to set her off. People always revealed more than they should while on the defense. "You know what I think?" I began softly. "I think your father learned the truth about Lourdes and decided she wasn't worth the bother. I think he's searching for a way out—"

"No," she said.

"Maybe he'd rather take his chances somewhere else, rather than stay with a cold-blooded—"

"Do not finish that sentence," she cut in, the red blooming across her cheeks turning mottled.

"Maybe he's looking for another woman. Someone less complicated, more loyal. Not a bitch who—"

She stood and reached across the narrow table, her hand held high. I froze, silently goading her to finish what she started. I dared her to strike me.

Isadora panted in outrage, her anger coating her pale skin in a thin layer of sweat. We were locked in this sickening tableau, each of us not moving, barely breathing.

I waited to see what she would do.

She waited to see if I'd let her slap me.

I arched a brow.

Her lips twisted, her arm trembling as if she fought a battle against it. Eventually, she lowered her hand and resumed her seat. Isadora laid her palms flat on the table, her eyes brimming with white-hot anger. "Papa loves my mother. He never lets her out of his sight. I can't imagine he's far away from her."

"Ever?" I asked softly. "I hardly believe—"

"*Ever*," she snapped. "They are devoted to each other."

"Fine," I said flatly. "Then tell me why you followed me to an opium den the other night." I threw that sentence out there from out of nowhere, hoping to surprise her into giving herself away. Everything she did felt calculated to me, despite what Inez might believe.

Isadora blinked.

I leaned forward, narrowing my eyes. "You *were* there."

She shifted away from me, her arms folding across her chest, an air of offended silence swirling around her like artillery smoke. "I don't know what you're talking about, but it doesn't matter, does it? You've already decided who I am, no matter what I'll say."

My frustration grew. She ought to work for imperial Britain as a spy. The chit would be their most treasured asset.

She stared at me, her gaze unwavering. "I don't care if you believe me, I don't care if you think the worst of me. What I *do* care about is Inez. Consider what will happen to me if we are successful in our efforts? Both of my parents in prison, or worse. I will be alone, without family except for Inez. I would never jeopardize our relationship, and while I have made mistakes, they were unintentional." She leaned forward, her blue eyes latched on to mine. "Are you really going to sit there and judge *me* for my actions? After what you've done?"

Doubt crept into my mind. I had great instincts, and there was something off about this girl. But what if I was wrong about her? It was a good thing, then, that I had more time to figure her out. "You can play your little games, but I'm warning you: if you hurt Inez in any way, I'll make your life hell."

"Inez is already in hell," she said, standing. Isadora smoothed the wrinkles on her skirt and stomped off, chin lifted high. For the second time in as many minutes, she walked away from me in a huff. I sat at the table, thinking, considering, piecing together everything I knew about her and every word she'd ever said long after she'd gone. Egypt swept past the window in a monochromatic blur, but I barely noticed.

Because I finally put together a part of the puzzle I hadn't seen. Something she had just revealed—but hadn't meant to. I wanted to run back to the compartment to tell Inez, but doubt niggled at the back of my mind. If I was wrong, Inez would turn away from me further. I had little hope of a reconciliation, but as long as there was a chance, I couldn't afford to jeopardize it.

CAPÍTULO DIECISÉIS

From the station, Whit hired a carriage to take us and our luggage to Hotel Abbat, a handsome building with columns and tall windows overlooking a square. Whit paid the driver, who helped us unload our trunks, and together we all walked into a cozy lobby, and while not as grand as the one in Shepheard's, it had plush seating and a long wooden counter where several workers helped other travelers. Upon further inspection, I found a lush interior garden with blooms that pleasantly scented the air. A sign written in French directed guests to luxurious baths, or to a reading room. There was even a smoking room.

Alarm swept over me. I reached for Whit's arm and hissed, "We can't afford this."

"Since the bombardment, everyone's prices have dropped," Whit whispered back. "This is a comfortable second-class hotel, the only one of which I felt was appropriate, given Alexandria's current state."

"Current state?" I asked.

"I'll explain later," Whit said, leading us to the front desk.

The hotel attendant, a young German named Karl, quickly set us up with a room. It had a fixed price of fifteen francs per day, which included lodging and board but excluded liquor. I expected Whit to protest, but he remained silent on that score. The accommodations were much cheaper than I'd set aside for—an enormous relief. We had used the money I'd received from the first-class passage refund to book this suite for the next week and it thankfully also included all three meals, tea, and coffee.

If Whit despaired about sleeping on a cot, he didn't dare show it.

He and Isadora walked off to explore the rest of the lobby, but I remained with Karl while he shared more information about the hotel and suite. When he finished, I asked, "Would you be able to send a telegram?"

He nodded and procured a slip of paper, an envelope, and a pencil for me. "I'll send it to the telegraph office after you're finished, it will be wired within the hour. The price is five piastres per ten words. Is that acceptable? Yes? Good."

"Thank you," I murmured as I scribbled a quick message to Farida. I gave her the name of the hotel and our address and begged her to please send word if any new photographs were mailed to her. I stuffed the note into an envelope and handed it to Karl, along with payment.

Then I went to find my companions. They were standing off to the side of the lobby unoccupied by other guests. "The room is ready for our use," I announced to Isadora and Whit when I joined them.

They stood coldly staring at each other, Isadora with her arms folded tightly, Whit's looming presence grim and serious, every line of his face steeped in suspicion. Neither had spoken to the other since they'd returned from the dining car on the train ride to Alexandria. I hated the tension that existed between them, and my only consolation was that Whit wouldn't be in my life long enough to truly drive me mad from his cynical view of my sister.

Even so, it grated.

Isadora's blue eyes shot to mine. "Will they bring up our trunks, do you think?"

I nodded. "Already in process."

"By the time we arrive back from our outing, everything should be in order, then," Isadora said in approval.

"*Our* outing?" Whit repeated. "What the hell are you talking about?"

"Mr. Hayes," I said, ignoring the strain appearing along his eyes, "we're going to pay a visit to the address you found. Don't tell me you've forgotten already."

"I haven't," Whit said curtly. "But we can't all go. It'll be faster if I run the errand on my own. Not to mention that I'll draw less notice."

I opened my mouth to protest.

"You know it's true," Whit said. "The quicker I can accomplish our goal, the better. And what would happen if we ran into one of your mother's associates? I can't sneak around with the two of you at my heels. It'd be close to impossible to make your lovely bulk disappear." His blue eyes flicked downward, carefully assessing the way my dress hugged the curved lines of my body.

When Whit lifted his eyes, they burned, twin fires that crackled and hissed sparks.

He hadn't touched me since our wedding night—and I was glad of it. Part of me knew what would happen if he crossed that line: I'd have to fight myself tooth and nail to walk away. A battle I wasn't sure I'd win. And wasn't that sobering?

"You're going to have to figure something out," I said. "Because my following along was one of my conditions, remember? Or are you going to show me, again, that your words are empty?"

Whit locked his jaw.

"I have an idea," Isadora said. "Why don't I stay and unpack our bags, Inez? That way you can accompany Mr. Hayes to the address."

"You're going to willingly stay behind?" Whit asked slowly. "What are you planning?"

"What nefarious scheme could I be planning in unpacking the trunks?" Isadora demanded. "Do you think I'll rip holes in your socks?"

"You are not to open my trunk," Whit said. "It's locked, anyway."

A headache bloomed in my temples. It occurred to me that we were perhaps making the situation more complicated than it ought to be. I held out my hand to Whit. "May I have the address, please?" This halted the argument between them.

"Why?" Whit asked.

"I have a plan," I explained.

"Of course you do," he said.

He'd said the words with a warm glint in his blue eyes. A compliment I ought not to pay attention to, but it dislodged some of the tension I'd carried from the moment we stepped inside the hotel.

Whit handed me the scrap of paper. "Are you going to enlighten us?"

"If the idea has legs to stand on, then yes," I said pleasantly. I glanced behind me to the check-in counter and retraced my steps to speak with the concierge. "Excuse me, Karl."

"Yes, Mrs. Hayes," he said. "How else can I help to make your stay more comfortable?"

I glanced down at the address. "Well, we are here to see the sights, of course. And a friend recommended I pay a visit to this address. Is there a church close by, or perhaps an obelisk?" I slid the paper to Karl.

He read the scant few lines, frowning. "This area is close to the Place des Counsels—one of the casualties from the bombardment. It is still much destroyed, lots of rubble, buildings blown apart, though some parts are under repair." He glanced at me apologetically. "I'm afraid there's not much to see in that area."

I pressed my lips together, considering. My mother wouldn't have provided an address that went nowhere. "Surely there must be something?"

"Only the bank," he said. "A department store and a couple of grocers. That's the extent of it."

It was exactly what I had been looking for, but I didn't let my face show it. Instead, I slumped my shoulders in obvious disappointment and returned to my companions—who were still not speaking to each other.

"The address is a bank," I said triumphantly. "Near the Place des Counsels. This is where my mother is having money wired to."

"Except you never actually wired any of the money," Isadora said. "How will we find her? We can't watch the bank, day in and day out. We don't have the money to stay in Alexandria that long." She threw Whit a pointed look.

He remained stone-faced. I wasn't going to defend him, though the constant arguing between them *still* wasn't helpful. What I wanted was a solution. The faster we found my mother, the more information we could collect, the better to build a case against her. My uncle and Abdullah could go free, my mother would pay for her crimes, and all of the artifacts would have to be returned to the antiquities department.

And in the middle of all that, I'd somehow force her to tell me the truth about my father.

I knew now how to detect her lies, uncover her half-truths, parse through her false speech. I was becoming an expert in digging up my mother's secrets. Even now, I heard her voice in my head, asking me for help.

I knew how to sound like her. I knew how to talk like her.

"I think I might have come up with something," I said slowly.

They turned to look at me expectantly.

I detailed exactly what I wanted to do. Isadora responded with her characteristic hesitation while Whit loudly proclaimed that it was the worst idea he'd ever heard, that I was putting myself at too much risk.

Which was exactly why I knew it was the best option left.

As promised, Isadora stayed behind at the hotel to unpack, while Whit and I hired a carriage to take us to our desired street, the roof open to allow fresh air. The sun bore down on us, and I was thankful for the large hat I wore that blocked most of its harsh rays. I smoothed down the wrinkles of my best skirt and straightened the lapel of my jacket. I'd purposefully chosen something that made me look older. Isadora had even styled my hair in a more mature fashion, neat and coiled at the crown of my head. I had added bright rouge to my lips and darkened my eyelashes.

Whit had lost the power of speech when he had seen me. I didn't know if it was a good or bad thing and ultimately decided that it *should not matter.* I settled back against the seat, idly watching the other carriages on the street attempting to navigate the debris on the road. We were driven through the once-great city square, left ruined and in utter destruction by the bombardment of the British.

"I wonder what it looked like before," I murmured.

Whit pointed to one end, a mass of debris and tangled telegraph wires. "That was once the Hotel d'Europe, one of the nicest places I'd ever had the pleasure of staying in."

"When were you here?"

"I passed through when I first came to Egypt," he said, shifting his hand to point somewhere else. "Here was the French and English consulate; there you can see part of the entrance still standing, and some of the walls. But the interior was completely gutted."

"This must be strange," I commented. "Seeing the city this way when it existed more splendidly in your memory."

"It is," he said, "but stranger still for those profoundly attached to Alexandria. It must have been devastating. Humans can be so careless with beautiful things: lives, animals, art. Nothing is safe from our hands."

"How many people died by the end?"

"Thousands," Whit said grimly. "The British had significantly fewer casualties than the Egyptians."

We were sitting across from each other, his long legs stretched onto the opposite bench. This kind of proximity would never have been allowed if we weren't married. A state that I had only enjoyed for less than twenty-four hours. It amazed me how life could change in an instant. Hearing him talk of the war always made me think of everything he must have witnessed in between boyhood and becoming a man. I wanted to know this side of him, and my curiosity flared with a dozen questions.

But I forced myself to stay silent. The more we talked, the harder it would be to walk away.

And there was no question that I would.

"I don't expect you to forgive me," he said softly.

I startled but kept my attention on the shattered remains of the plaza. I hated that he could guess my thoughts with such precision. I especially hated it because I never knew what he was thinking.

"Or to believe anything I have to say," he continued. "But I do have a plan to make things right between us."

Oh, I didn't doubt it. His guilt would govern every one of his actions, and I was sure he'd bleed himself dry to be rid of it. He didn't care about me other than to ease his own conscience. And he had led me to believe there was more between us than camaraderie. I had been a fool to fall for his scheme, but a small part of me yearned to hear that his feelings had run as deep as mine.

But he never spoke of love. Only friendship.

"What is it that you hope for you and me?" I asked quietly. "When all of this is behind us?"

Whit observed me, considering his response. When he spoke, it was carefully. "I have no expectations. No hopes."

Exactly what I thought.

I gripped the edge of my seat, breathing slowly. It surprised me how his words could still hurt me. That there was a part of me that still wanted to believe he would fight for me, for his heart, for us. That he had loved me, that what we had was real.

My God, I was delusional.

The driver expertly wheeled us onto another street, labeled in French. This one had survived the bombing, two-story buildings lining the path, homes above and businesses below. We passed a hairdresser, two markets, and then the driver whistled, pulling on the reins. He gestured to our left, indicating we had arrived at the bank.

Whit jumped out first and then helped me down.

"Now remember," I said. "You're my personal guard. Do not speak."

He leaned forward, eyes narrowed. "Do *not* tell me what to do. If someone points a gun at you, I will have words to say about that."

"That's not going to happen," I said. "The only thing that could is us getting escorted out of the bank."

"Yes," he muttered. "By the bloody bluejackets."

"The what?"

"Part of the tribunal the British set up after the bombing to restore order," he said. "Now, Olivera, remember to say as little as possible. You don't need to explain yourself, nor launch into superfluous details no one asks for. Just say what you came to say. That's all."

"Yes, I'll remember," I said, my nerves taking flight deep in my belly. I felt as if I had a flock of butterflies invading my person. "Anything else?"

"Maintain eye contact," he went on. "Let him know that you're an important person *without* saying you are important. Keep your back straight, don't fidget, and be confident. And one more thing."

"Yes?"

He smiled. "I thought you didn't want me to talk."

If I could, I would have hit him right there on the front steps of the bank. "You are so exasperating," I said, turning to face the front door. A large rectangular room filled with wooden desks and low chairs greeted us as we walked inside. Several workers stood at the entrance. Some of them walked forward, dressed in tailored suits and pressed shirts, shoes gleaming. They spoke a mixture of Italian and French. I spoke neither, but then one of them began in clumsy English.

"Yes," I said instinctively. "I'd love your help."

He motioned for us to follow him down a narrow corridor that opened to various offices. Whit was a silent and formidable shadow. Many of the attendants looked at us with apparent unease as we walked past. With a quick glance over my shoulder, I found Whit scowling.

"Behave," I whisper-yelled.

"I am Romero," the bank employee said. "Is this your first visit to Alexandria?"

I caught myself before nodding. "No. I've been here plenty. I love seeing all the sights."

His dark brows reached his hairline. "The sights? Most travelers bypass the city altogether in favor of the pyramids or temples found in Upper Egypt. All we have is a field of ruins."

My confusion must have shown because he pressed on.

"The city has shrunk since the time of the Greeks and Romans, and what's left are toppled columns and bumpy stretches of land that no one has excavated. It's a pity—I'm sure there's lots to be discovered beyond the city limits."

"Perhaps it's only a matter of time," I said.

Romero stopped in front of a thick wooden door and, after opening it, gestured for us to walk inside. The walls were covered in a muted wallpaper depicting swirls and filigree, and a leather couch offered comfortable seating. Sitting across from it was a sturdy antique desk with ornate carvings around the legs.

"Would you like tea? Coffee?" Romero asked.

"I'm fine, thank you," I said. "I really am in a hurry."

He rocked back on his heels, nodding. "Then how may I assist you?"

"Well, I have an account here," I began, "and I'd like to update my address from the previous one listed."

He blinked. "You have an account with us?"

I nodded, maintaining eye contact and a sweet smile. "That's right."

Romero's confusion persisted. "What is your name?"

"I am Lourdes," I said, pausing before admitting my last name. What if my mother hadn't used it? What if, instead, she had used her maiden name? Or gone by Mr. Fincastle's name? I thought frantically about what alias she might have chosen for herself. She was living on her own terms and a life that she wanted. What name would she have given herself?

Sweat beaded at my temples as I fixed the smile on my face as if with adhesive.

"Lourdes . . ." Romero waited expectantly.

Whit stood behind the couch since it wouldn't have been appropriate for him to seat himself next to me. I could sense his frustration in not being able to help me.

"Oh, I recently married, and I was about to give you the wrong name," I said with an embarrassed laugh. "It's Fincastle."

Romero's confusion cleared. "That name sounds familiar. Please forgive me; I've only been working at the bank for a few months. Wait a moment while I retrieve your file." He left, shutting the door quickly behind him.

I stared straight ahead, unwilling to let my guard down.

"Do you think he believed me?" I whispered.

"I don't know," Whit murmured. "Though it was a great performance."

"I used to act in plays with my father," I said.

"The practice paid off." He paused. "What made you choose Fincastle?"

I licked my dry lips. "It occurred to me that if my mother used her maiden name, my uncle could have easily located her. Asked around after that name in the nice hotels and expensive restaurants. But since he didn't know who her lover was, I assumed Fincastle was a safe guess."

"Brilliant," he said.

A flush spread across my chest, making my heart skip. "Are we going to be arrested?"

Before Whit could answer, the door opened and Romero walked

through, carrying a slim leather case. He returned to the seat at his desk. "What address would you like to leave with us, Mrs. Fincastle?"

"Well," I said, letting out another embarrassed laugh. "That's part of the problem, actually. I'm so silly! You see, I have various properties, and I'm afraid I don't recall which one I used when I opened this account. If you could remind me, I can confirm if I need to update the file. It's possible you have the correct one. I just want to ensure there are no mistakes—that's all."

"I see," Romero said, a faint frown line appearing between his dark brows. "Why don't you give me the address you'd like, and I'll cross-reference it here?" He tapped the leather case, smiling faintly. "I think it will be easier."

"No," I said, bristling, "I think *my* way would be easier. Please just share the address with me—"

Whit made a small noise at the back of his throat. I hadn't realized that I'd raised my voice.

"Well," Romero said, his smile fading, the frown line becoming more pronounced. "I disagree. The address?" He produced a pen from his jacket pocket.

I fanned myself, thinking hard. "I believe I might have used the one by the coast?"

Romero's eyes flicked downward. The corners of his lips twitched. "That's not the one. Since you seem to be having trouble, why don't you return with your husband? I can't make any updates to your file without him, in any case. But again, if you leave the new address with me, I'll happily correspond with him to make sure nothing is untoward."

Damn it. "Why would anything be untoward?"

"Why, I don't know, Mrs. Fincastle," Romero said mildly. "I'm only letting you know that we have certain systems in place to guard against fraud—of any kind. And as we are a foreign bank, foreign rules apply, and the fact of the matter is that one of them applies to your husband being present for any account changes. Even simple ones like an address. If you'd like, I could bring in my manager to discuss the issue you're having."

"I'm not having any issues," I said through gritted teeth.

Romero stood, clutching the file. "All the same, I'd feel more comfortable having him present as I don't want to cause any unnecessary stress or confusion."

Those were the last words he spoke. Whit cleared the couch and tackled Romero. They landed with a heavy thud onto the plush antique rug decorating the floor, Romero letting out a muffled yell before Whit struck his cheek. The banker's face slackened as he went unconscious. The leather case fell onto the floor as Whit arranged Romero onto the couch, making him look as if he were sleeping.

"Hurry up and look for the address," Whit hissed.

I scooped up the file and opened it.

The pages were blank.

WHIT

Inez flipped the file around so I could see. Every single page was empty of any writing. She walked toward me and peered down at the fallen bank employee.

"The devil damn me," I said.

"Now what?" Inez asked. "The other employees are bound to notice Romero's unconscious state."

"He looks like he's sleeping."

She pointed to Romero's face. "There's blood coming out of the corner of his mouth. It's dripping onto the floor."

I squinted. So there was. Using the hem of his shirt, I cleaned up his face. Now he looked like he was sleeping. We only had a few minutes to think of a new plan.

"Whit," Inez said, her tone curious.

"I'm thinking," I said, hands on my hips.

"No, I know," she said, her voice sounding breathless. "Why is the rug glittering?"

I glanced down in alarm. The woven fiber was shifting under our boots, darkening in color, clearly magic touched. "Move off."

"Well, I'd love to, but I *can't*," Inez said. She lifted her leg and the rug came up, stuck to the sole of her shoe. "It's turned into a kind of adhesive. I'm stuck."

My boots were also glued to the sizable rug. "It has an old spell attached to it," I hissed. "Don't let anything else touch it. Watch the hem of your dress."

Inez bent and gathered the fabric, tying it off into a knot, displaying a good portion of her legs. I glanced away, aggravated. We were stuck, and someone was bound to come looking for Romero if he didn't turn up in a reasonable amount of time.

Inez tried dragging her feet, her arms swinging, but that only made the rug shift forward an inch. She glanced at me, annoyance stamped across her features. "Don't just stand there! We have to get out of this."

"Obviously."

She tried moving again, yanking the rug several inches and succeeding in unbalancing me. I swung my arms out, caught myself from falling. "Olivera, *stop*. We have to work together."

Inez glowered at me.

"Trust me—"

"Trust you?" Inez scoffed. "Consider our past."

"Consider our present," I retorted, gesturing at the infernal rug.

She bit her lip, eyes filling with a nervous and raw confusion that tore up my insides. I would get us out of this predicament, but she didn't know that. Not after what I had done to her. I suddenly felt like howling with frustration. At myself, at this ridiculous situation that we were in. Years of training allowed me to hold on to whatever shred of calm I could muster. I inhaled deeply. "I know it's the absolute last thing you want to do," I said. "But if we're going to get out of this, we have to—"

"What do we do?" she asked in a voice I recognized all too well. It was the one where she fought to keep her tone moderate, but I knew she'd rather be yelling.

The feeling was mutual. "I can't use my knife to cut the rug—it will only stick to the fibers," I said. "Can you, *very carefully*, step out of your shoes and stand on top of them?"

"But then I'll be in my stockings," she protested.

"Do you have a better idea?"

"No." She sighed and then bent forward, fingers working quickly to unlace her boots. She then slowly slipped out of her shoes, gingerly stepping on top of them. Her stockings worked against her, and she kept slipping on the leather.

"Can you jump off?"

Inez eyed the edge of the rug. It was a large woven monstrosity, and she was probably four feet from the corner. "Maybe?"

"Wait," I said, already picturing her falling onto her hands and knees. "Jump into my arms instead."

She tensed, the lines of her face steeped in distrust. She no longer believed I could keep her safe. Or maybe the thought of my holding her was so off-putting she'd rather remain stuck to the rug.

Either way, it stung. More than I wanted to admit.

"I'm going to toss you onto the couch," I said quietly. "From there you can climb up and over, avoiding the rug entirely."

"You are loving this, aren't you?" she asked. "Getting to act like the hero after what you did."

"I'm not a hero," I said. "I've never said I was."

She opened her mouth, no doubt to argue with me, but I cut her off. "Jump. I promise I'll catch you."

Inez gave me no warning, but I was ready for her anyway. She launched herself forward, and I caught her around the waist, boosting her up, flipping her around so I could cradle her.

She tilted her chin upward, her ever-changing eyes meeting mine. We stared at each other for a long beat, her expression guarded, mine probably even more so. Then I bent my knees slightly and tossed her onto the sofa. She bounced once, twice, and she let out a surprised laugh.

"Gracias," she said, breathless.

"Anytime," I muttered, tugging at the laces of my worn boots. I hated to leave them behind—they were my favorite pair. I slipped out of the shoes and leapt, landing with a thud onto the wood floor beside Romero.

"What do you think activated the spell?" Inez asked.

I thought for a moment. "Blood perhaps?" I pointed to a few drops staining the surface. "It's actually clever to use the rug as a deterrent for thieves. I bet the owner found several such ordinary objects and placed them in all of the rooms."

Inez spun around, eyeing the various knickknacks strewn about. There were paintings and quills, picture frames, stacks of paper. Anything could be enchanted.

"What now?" I asked, gesturing toward Romero.

"I could say he fainted," Inez said suddenly. "And call the others in? Perhaps someone can run off for help?"

"Or we could just leave as if we've concluded our business," I said.

"I'm not leaving without the address," she said fiercely, alchemical eyes burning gold. "While I bring in as many people in here as I can, you go sneak into the other offices and find my mother's file." She gripped my lapel. "*Por favor*, Whit."

As if I had any right to deny her anything at this point. "Better put those acting skills to use, Olivera." She lifted her chin and squared her shoulders.

Inez against the world.

"Say that he fainted and hit his head on the way down. It will at least help explain why the spell might have been activated and why we're not wearing shoes."

Inez nodded, moving toward the door. She placed a light hand on the knob. "Ready?"

"Ready."

Then she tugged at her hair until some strands escaped, and her expression changed to one of horror. She swung open the door and screamed at the top of her lungs, "*Help!*"

My wife knew how to be dramatic. I could hear her crying and carrying on all the way down the hall. I had finally found the cabinets where all the files were hidden and was thumbing through them one by one. The bank didn't have many clients, but even I recognized some of the high-society names.

"What are you doing in here?"

I turned to find one of the bank workers standing within the doorframe.

"I'm looking for an address," I said, almost apologetically. This room had exactly one desk, covered in notebooks, stacks of receipts and paper, stationery, and one silver candlestick, which would do nicely. I didn't want to use my knife if I didn't have to.

He stepped inside, anger etched across his brow.

"I'm almost done," I said politely. "If you'll just—" I threw the candlestick at his head. The man crashed to the floor, his mouth gaping. I turned around to rummage through the files and finally found the one I was looking for.

Lourdes Fincastle.

Time to get my theatrical wife before someone offered her a job onstage.

Why was there never a cab when one needed one? I glanced up and down the street, Inez panting next to me. I had to hand it to her—she had cried, had pretended to faint *herself*, and then she had allowed smelling salts to be used on her. A bank employee had, indeed, run off to the medic, while another had dashed off to buy us new shoes. We would be long gone before they returned.

I looked back at the bank uneasily. Someone was bound to come running out when they discovered the second unconscious man in the back office. I gestured for her to follow me down the block.

"Did you get it?" Inez whispered breathlessly. "The address?"

"Of course," I said, and winced when she cheered. No one was louder than my wife. "Now all we need is someone to take us back to the hotel."

"It isn't too far," Inez said. "Why don't we keep walking?"

"You'll ruin your stockings," I warned. "The road is very dusty."

"I don't care," she said. "We have an address. Someone could throw mud at me, and I wouldn't complain."

"Who on earth would throw mud at you?" I asked, slanting a look at her.

"Can I ask you something?"

"Do you mean something *else*?" I asked in amusement. Without thinking, I reached forward and tucked a wayward curl behind her ear.

She flushed but didn't look away from me. "Why is it so hard to stay mad at you?"

Tension pressed down hard on my shoulders. "Because I did it to save my sister?"

"It must be part of your charm," she remarked. "To be able to do a horrible thing and get away with it."

"Have I gotten away with it?" I asked, my breath catching.

Inez picked at the hem of her jacket sleeve. "I've never been one to stay mad for too long. Eventually, my anger fades into profound dislike for the other person. Being furious is exhausting, and you particularly don't make it easy. You're too . . ." She scrunched her nose. "Likable, I suppose. Like a puppy."

"Thank you?"

"Like a mischievous, sneaky, untrained puppy," she amended. "But here's the thing, Whit. I may not be mad at you, but I have not forgiven you. I don't think I can. It *hurt* me too much. Because I really loved you."

I hadn't just lost a friend or a wife. I'd lost Inez's love. Something I didn't know that I'd had. I closed my eyes, wishing I could scrape that truth from my mind, because it was tearing me apart. I opened my eyes slowly, in time to see a small smile on her perfect mouth. Small, but brave and edged in sadness. I'd done that to her.

"I understand," I whispered.

Inez tucked another wayward curl behind her ear, her fingers trembling. "I know you're motivated by your guilt, and I believe some part of you must grieve for the loss of our friendship. It will never be the same, and actually, we won't *ever* have one again. No matter how well we get along, no matter how good of a team we make. All of that doesn't matter. Those are superficial things. Because this is our new reality: you have well and truly lost me." She peered up at me gravely. "You do know that, don't you?"

I was oddly lightheaded. As if I wasn't getting enough air. "I do."

Inez nodded, her face pale. "And the truth is, maybe losing me isn't significant to you. It might be a shallow wound that will heal over quickly, not even leave a scar." She inhaled. "But the hole in my heart won't ever heal."

"Why are you telling me all this?"

She licked her lips, and I fought valiantly not to stare. "Because despite us working together, acting like friends, we're not. And I needed you to know that I have more respect for myself than to ever allow you back in."

"Inez—" I broke off, stomach lurching. A figure walked on the opposite side of the street. She was dressed resplendently in a bright gown, swinging a parasol in a girlish way that made her look years younger. Inez followed the line of my sight, and I slapped my hand over her mouth before she could cry out.

We both watched as Lourdes crossed the street, heading directly for the bank.

She was about to step inside when someone let out a sharp three-tone whistle.

Lourdes froze, one foot poised above the front step. Slowly, she turned, opening her parasol in one fluid movement. She looked both ways before darting back across the street and disappearing around the corner.

Someone had warned her off.

CAPÍTULO DIECISIETE

I'm telling you," Whit seethed. "Isadora was here! She followed us and warned off your mother."

I huffed along his ground-eating strides. We still hadn't managed to secure a carriage back to the hotel, though it hardly mattered since Whit would get us there in minutes, given his quick walking.

"You're being ridiculous," I said in between deep breaths. "She would have had to have found another carriage to follow after us and then pay for it, but with what money? Her father never gave her any."

"According to *her*," Whit scoffed. "Consider the source, Olivera."

I took hold of the crook of his elbow. Enough was enough. I pulled hard and stopped, swinging him around. He was devoid of any perspiration, his breathing even and steady, while I'm sure my face glowed with dripping sweat.

"You would have noticed if she was following us," I said. He opened his mouth, but I beat him to it. "And say she went by foot, don't forget—she doesn't know the city well."

"Again, according to *her*." He leveled me with a pointed look. "Her mother lived here for half the year. Wouldn't she know the area?"

I exhaled, frustrated. "Women don't have the freedom to explore cities like men do."

Whit pulled his arm free gently and continued his brisk walk to the hotel. We were only a block away at this point, if my memory served. "So you think what, exactly? That she's with us to report back to Mamá?"

"She could be reporting to your mother, yes," Whit said. "She could be trying to sabotage our search for her."

"But she's been helpful," I protested. "Recall, also, how she shot the man who was about to attack me."

Whit had no reply for this.

I poked his back. "Listen to me, Mr. Hayes—"

"Stop calling me that," he said tiredly. "I can't stand to hear it from you." I blinked at the broad expanse of his shoulders. His bleak tone caught me off guard. We crossed a street, our hotel coming into view. Guests mingled out front, skirting around horses and donkey-pulled carts.

"I only want to say that I need you to stop bickering with my sister, to trust her as much as you can, because the alternative is stressful for me."

"Do you agree with me about what we just witnessed? Your mother was warned off from entering that bank."

"I do," I said softly. "But don't you think—"

"Don't *you* think it's strange that your mother was warned at a location only your sister knew we were visiting?"

"The hotel clerk also knew," I pointed out.

Whit threw me a disgruntled look over his shoulder. "So your mother is having our hotel watched? We only just decided on that particular one. How would she have known?"

"I admit it's unlikely," I said. "But what if there's a more plausible option? Someone we keep forgetting about?"

Whit was silent, still moving quickly. My skirt dragged behind me as I fought to keep up.

"You're talking about Fincastle," Whit said finally.

"Exactly."

He muttered something under his breath.

"Admit it," I said. "My idea is more probable than your far-fetched one."

"Olivera," Whit said. "We are about to reach the hotel. If she's in the room, with the trunks unpacked, then I might *possibly* agree with you. Maybe it *was* Fincastle warning Lourdes outside the bank. But I'm telling you, Isadora won't be there. I would bet my health that she's racing to intercept us even now."

I had never wanted anyone to be more wrong. "Well, if that's true, I suppose we better hurry."

Together we bolted inside the hotel, startling the few people milling within the lobby. Whit was faster up the stairs, confound my corset, but I managed to catch up to him by the time he was outside our bedroom door. He looked at me grimly. "Ready?" he whispered.

I nodded, breathing hard. I was sure I looked like a street urchin.

He swung the door open.

Inside, Isadora was bending over a nearly empty trunk. She pulled out one of my dresses and began shaking out the wrinkles. Her hair was perfectly styled, her clothing neat and dust-free. My sister looked over at us and raised her brows.

"The damn teacup overflowed again," Isadora remarked. "I had to mop up some of the water, but not before it soaked your bag again, Mr. Hayes."

"Oh *no*," I said. "I hate that I missed his call. *Again*. What if something happened?"

"Well, I couldn't answer, since he wouldn't want to speak with me," Isadora said. "But he sounded more annoyed than in actual duress. He kept calling and calling . . . The only real danger was the carpet became soaked in the process."

Whit glared at her. "And my knapsack. Which I left *on the bed*."

Isadora tilted her head. "You are mistaken. It was on the floor, right by the nightstand." She pointed to said nightstand where the teacup, now empty, stood. "The water dripped right onto it, I'm afraid."

Then she turned to me and asked, "Well? How did it go?"

To Whit's credit, when he recounted our adventure at the bank, he didn't accuse her of warning our mother away from going inside.

"What happens now that we have the address?" Isadora asked.

"We head there directly," I said. "Now, if possible. Because someone alerted Mamá to our presence earlier, she might take refuge at this address, hiding herself away, thinking she's safe."

"Then we are to confront her," Isadora said, her face pale and miserable. "Today."

"Before she disappears again," Whit said.

I reached for her hand, hoping the gesture might give her courage and comfort.

We dressed for the outing; Isadora borrowed a darker-hued dress from me, and I put on my widow disguise. Whit donned a gray shirt, the smudgy color reminding me of one of my charcoal pencils. My stomach rumbled, and I realized it had been hours since I'd last eaten. I looked longingly toward the hotel's dining room entrance as we exited the lobby. But there was no time—I sensed my mother wouldn't stay in one place for long.

Whit hired a carriage, and the three of us climbed inside, Isadora and I squished on one side, him on the other. Pressure gathered along my shoulders, and I tried to steady my breathing. The last time I'd seen my mother, she was in a small boat, sailing away from Philae with all of the artifacts I had personally given her for safekeeping.

Those same artifacts would pass through the gate, never to be seen in Egypt again, if we didn't locate where she had hidden them.

"Are we knocking on the front door?" Isadora asked suddenly, breaking the quiet. "What exactly is the plan?"

"We break in," Whit and I said at the exact same time.

He shot me a smile, which I ignored, and then addressed Isadora. "If we knock, we alert her to our presence, and she has time to make her escape."

"Of course," Isadora said, flushing. "I wasn't thinking."

My sister fidgeted in her seat, clasping and unclasping her hands. It occurred to me that she'd be dreading this moment, when I was looking forward it. She had only recently learned of our mother's involvement, while I had experienced it firsthand. Her composure had completely deserted her.

"When was the last time you saw her?" I asked gently.

"Back home in London, right before Papa and I left for Egypt. She sent us off," Isadora breathed. "I never thought I'd see her *here*. She would pick us up at the docks, like she promised."

"You said they're always in each other's company," Whit said softly.

I looked at him, furrowing my brow. I hadn't heard her say such a thing. I was about to object to his pointed question when Isadora beat me to it.

"Of course they don't spend every waking moment together," she said, exasperated. "I was trying to make a point about the depth of their commitment."

Whit flattened his mouth and looked away. He sat the rest of the way in contemplative silence. No one else spoke; I was locked inside my own thoughts, my nerves governing the slam of my pulse against my throat.

I was *so* close to finding her.

While inside her accommodations, we'd find everything needed to complete our case against her. There would be some trail of her trying to fence the relics, addresses and phone numbers of potential buyers, and damning correspondence from her subordinates.

Soon, I'd have the truth about my father and what she did to him.

I hadn't lost hope that he was alive somewhere in Egypt. Holding on to survival by a thread, locked up somewhere.

If he was alive, I would rescue him.

If he was dead, I would bury him.

Either way, I would know the truth.

The driver pulled up to a plain residence, its only adornment an iron gate that opened up to a narrow path. At the end were steps leading up to an equally plain wooden door. It did not seem like the kind of place my mother would live in. Where was the garden? Potted flowers? She loved all things green, but this place reminded me of the desert. Tawny-colored stone, austere but functional design. There was no elaborate knocker to greet us. Not that we would have used it, but I kept remembering the golden lion we had at home, roaring at anyone who dared to visit. Mamá loved her luxuries. Even on Philae, she insisted on bringing rugs and furniture, mirrors, porcelain washbasins, and the finest bedding made of Egyptian cotton.

"I see a little side terrace," Whit said. "We'll go in through there."

Isadora walked alongside me as we followed Whit to the house. She had lost the pale cast to her skin, as if all the tension and worry she carried had melted off her. Her chin was lifted high, shoulders straight and sharp. When she met my concerned gaze, she nodded, a determined glint shining in her eyes.

This was the Isadora I knew. A girl who'd meet the world with a polite smile and a handgun.

Whit demonstrated another one of his many talents by picking the lock to the side door, swinging it open in mere seconds. Even my sister looked impressed.

"Can you teach me how to do that?" Isadora asked.

He ignored her and instead glanced at me, face grim, and I nodded, urging him to go inside. We followed after him, and I squinted, waiting for my eyes to adjust to the sudden darkness. I wasn't surprised to learn that Whit had brought a handful of supplies, and after rummaging through his leather knapsack, he pulled out short candles and matches.

He handed one to me and Isadora. I hurriedly lit both, desperate to find Mamá. The flame illuminated enough of the room for me to catalogue my surroundings: It was a small sitting area, with simple but comfortable-looking chairs upholstered in bright patterns. Under my feet were layered rugs, clean and well-made. The walls were bare, but the entryway had elaborate wooden casings. On the low coffee table sat a half-filled cup of tea, and judging by the swirls of steam drifting upward, it was still warm. I shot Whit a quick look—he was already moving out of the room, knife in hand.

"Don't hurt her," I whispered.

He ignored me, disappearing into the next room.

Isadora followed after him, nearly tripping over one of the seat cushions stacked on the floor. I was right behind her, checking the other rooms as we went. Whit found stairs leading to the second story, and he climbed them two at a time. I raced after him, and we checked the rooms on that level.

"I don't think there's anyone here," Whit whispered. "Where's Isadora?"

I turned around, frowning, surprised to notice her absence. "I thought she was right behind me." My brow cleared. "She must be downstairs."

He brushed past me, taking the stairs to the bottom floor. I let him search for her while I explored the first room next to the staircase. A made-up bed sat in the center, and in the corner of the room were several potted palms and ferns. This was the mother I knew, the one who could patiently tend to soil, or coax a dying flower back to life. On the opposite end of the room was a wooden dresser, a mirrored tray resting squarely in the middle. I walked to it, a loud rushing noise ringing in my ears. On the tray was a perfume I recognized. I lifted the glass bottle, sniffing delicately. It was from Paris, and it smelled like sweet vanilla. A scent that would forever remind me of my mother.

I hastily put the perfume down, my mind reeling.

She had made a home here.

Hurt bloomed under my skin. Mamá shared this bed with her lover. They had made a life together, complete with another child. A daughter to replace the one she'd abandoned. The enormity of what she had done to Papá and me weighed heavy, and I slumped onto the bed, trembling. My eyes fell on a wooden wardrobe, which was partially opened. Dresses like the ones I'd seen in Cairo overflowed from the tight space.

They were brighter, lower cut, more ruffled and girlish. My mother wasn't that much older than me—only thirty-nine—and she seemed to be grasping at her youth, at the life she had yet to live. And this was how she chose to spend her days. Cheating on Papá for years and years, forbidding me from joining her in Egypt. Selling priceless historical objects of cultural significance to the highest bidder.

I hardly recognized her.

"Olivera!" Whit called from the bottom floor.

I stood on shaking knees, an ache piercing my heart. My family had fallen apart, and I had foolishly tried to create another with a man I'd known for a handful of months. I felt destabilized and so, *so* angry for what my mother had done.

And she didn't have the courtesy to be here so I could yell at her.

I trudged down the stairs, fighting my emotions with every step. Crying wouldn't help. Yelling wouldn't save my uncle and Abdullah from the Cairo prison. The sound of Whit and Isadora arguing pierced the gloom of the empty house. Their voices drew me to their location like a peevish siren. They were in a library, comfortable chairs grouped over plush rugs, small cylinder-shaped tables standing on either end.

Shelves laden with dozens of random objects covered the four walls: books; apothecary jars; bottles of ink; stationery; statuettes and figurines of various Egyptian gods and goddesses and animals; picture frames showcasing sketches and paintings of various monuments and temples; bits of mismatched jewelry; ribbons; pins; scarves; old journals and stacked books, some falling apart at the binding; ladies' hats and various gloves. Curiously, there were chipped cups and rusted silverware and several teakettles. The amount of clutter taking over nearly every available inch astounded me.

"Tell me what you were doing in this room before I walked in," Whit demanded.

"I was searching for clues," Isadora snapped. "Isn't that why we're here? I'm becoming quite exhausted by your constant hounding and suspicion. Inez, won't you please talk some sense into him?"

I rubbed at my sore temples, pressure building behind my eyes. "Have either of you found something useful? Or have you been arguing this whole time?"

Isadora had the good sense to appear sheepish, but Whit remained stone-faced. Finally, he muttered, "Most of the objects are magic touched. I don't know how helpful they'll be, however."

My attention swerved back to the shelves. Mamá had been an avid collector of magic-touched items ever since I could remember. Wherever she traveled, she always found something to bring back home. Her favorite pieces came from Paris. She once told me the spells attached to the objects were mischievous in nature. It amused her greatly to find a music box that only sang lewd sea chanteys. But staring at the hundreds of items littering the shelves, I began to realize I'd severely underestimated her ability to hoard.

"Perhaps there's something here that might point us to where else she could be? Or maybe what she's doing here in Alexandria?" Isadora asked.

Whit met my gaze, raising his brow faintly. We both suspected my mother was looking for the Chrysopoeia of Cleopatra. If she somehow figured out how to transform lead into gold . . . I shuddered to think what she'd do with that kind of wealth.

That kind of power.

"There are more journals piled over here on the chairs," Whit commented. "Why don't we take our time and look through everything? Olivera, if you see anything worth keeping, shrink it."

Reflexively, my hand went to the scarf around my neck.

"We're just going to stay here all night?" Isadora asked. "What happens if Mother comes back?"

"We'll all take tea together," Whit said.

Isadora glared at him. Whit dropped to the floor and began thumbing through the journals and old books. Isadora read through letters, and I perused the shelves slowly. This turned out to be a messy task. The teakettle whistled flames when I touched the handle; various figurines loudly sang lewd songs, reminding me of that old music box; most of the scarves behaved like chameleons, changing color and shape based on what they touched; the bottles of ink were actually medicine, and I shrunk them all down, recalling a story my uncle had told me back on Philae. Mamá constantly worried about getting sick, but then she had found a cache of ink bottles that held the remnants of healing spells. Now she could cure anything: broken bones, heat rashes, fevers, chills, stomach pains.

I felt no qualms in taking the stash.

There was also an earring that seemed to magnify the noise in the room (Whit quietly reading to himself sounded like he was bellowing right in my ear), a bracelet that warmed up my body temperature, and several charcoal pencils that were tied up in a ribbon. I didn't know what they did, but I could always use more of them.

I turned away from the shelf and went to one of the chairs, moving the large stacks of paper to make room. An icy claw of dread pierced me. Somewhere in Alexandria, Mamá was hiding with hundreds and hundreds of artifacts, preparing for them to be sold.

"Where could she be?" I fumed.

"That," came a voice from the doorway, "is a very good question."

Fear pricked my skin. I knew that voice, the greasy quality to it, as if every word was dipped in a vat of oil. Slowly, I lifted my gaze.

Leaning against the frame nonchalantly was Mr. Basil Sterling.

His hand held a pistol pointed at my heart.

CAPÍTULO DIECIOCHO

Mr. Sterling straightened and took a step inside the room, his presence seeming to take over the space, darkening the corners, dropping the temperature to a frightening chill. He wore his usual three-piece suit, dark trousers, matching jacket, and a vest that buttoned over the curve of his belly. I didn't have to look at his shoes to know that they were polished to a shiny gleam. His outrageous mustache quivered in amusement as he took in our astonished expressions.

"I would not reach for your knife, Mr. Hayes," said Mr. Sterling in his nasally voice, adjusting his spectacles. "In fact, why don't you raise up your hands high for me?"

A muscle jumped in Whit's jaw. His eyes flicked to the barrel of the pistol and then up to meet mine. He let me see his fury, twin blue flames. I knew what he was capable of, knew the kind of damage his hands could wreak.

But he would not risk me.

And slowly, deliberately, he raised his arms, palms in a tight fist.

"Young lady," Mr. Sterling said, turning his attention to my sister, "if you'd please mimic our young hero, I'd greatly appreciate it."

Mr. Sterling had followed us here, presumably looking for clues to Mamá's whereabouts. He'd take everything he could carry. Instinctively, I reached for the first shrunken object in my pocket and slipped it into my mouth. It seemed to be one of the tiny ink bottles I'd snatched from the bookshelf. Next, I reached into my other pocket and stuffed tiny pages underneath the collar of my dress.

"*Now*, young lady," Mr. Sterling repeated, thick brows pulled into a tight frown.

Isadora's lips pinched. Mr. Sterling studied her, his brow drawn into a straight, perplexed line. He seemed to find her familiar but couldn't quite place how he would know her.

"Have we met?" he asked finally.

Isadora shook her head, anger bleeding out of her like an open wound.

"You look like a lady, but as you're in the company of a disgraced soldier and the daughter of my enemy, it's highly likely that you'd have no qualms about shooting me in the face."

My sister's voice rang out, cool and confident. I was never more proud of her. "You would be correct."

"*Hands*," Mr. Sterling repeated.

Isadora raised them higher.

"Marvelous," he said. "Now, Inez, I can see that you have many questions, but they'll have to wait. What I'd like to do is collect what you've discovered . . . Ah, here they are," he said, stepping aside to let several men inside. "I'd like everything boxed up." Mr. Sterling's thorough gaze missed nothing, roaming over the shelves, assessing the stacks of books and journals; all the while, his gun remained steady and aimed at the level of my heart. He would shoot me without hesitation. I was, as he said, the daughter of his enemy. An agent of his who had gone rogue. What better way to hurt my mother than to murder me? My throat went dry, and I suddenly wished I had never come to Egypt. Elvira would still be alive. I would have never fallen in love with a thief. Abdullah and Tío Ricardo wouldn't be detained in prison. But if I hadn't come . . . I would have never known that I had a sister.

My attention swerved to Isadora.

No matter the cost, my sister would leave this house alive. I would do anything to keep her safe.

"I suppose I owe you my gratitude," Mr. Sterling said, as his men packed up the room. "I would have found Lourdes's hiding place eventually, but it would have taken me longer without your assistance."

"My assistance," I repeated, speaking carefully around the bottle of ink under my tongue. "I haven't helped you; I never would or will."

Mr. Sterling stared at me, faintly smiling as a parent would to a willful child with foolish ideas. "I believe it was Henry James who said, 'Never say you know the last word about any human heart.' Inez, you are far too young to speak in absolutes."

His admonishment chafed against my skin.

"I did not help you," I said through gritted teeth.

Mr. Sterling smiled wider. "You led me straight here."

I furrowed my brow in confusion, glancing quickly at Whit. His fury radiated off him in strong waves. "You've been following me?" I asked.

The repercussions slammed into me. Did he know where we stayed? Had he been at the bank?

That meant Mamá had eluded not only me and Whit, but Basil Sterling.

"Every step of the journey," he said in his oily voice. "Now, I'd like everyone searched," Mr. Sterling ordered. "No doubt you'll find several things in miniature tucked in pockets and in their bags."

I gaped at him. How would he have known about Mamá's scarf? The answer came a second later. They worked together, and knowing my mother, she must have used the magic at some point when collecting artifacts.

The men advanced, three on Whit, and two on Isadora, and the last on me. He was tall, and his breath stank of tobacco. He forced me to empty my pockets, and he grabbed all of the little ink bottles and charcoal pencils and the single earring. Anger detonated inside me, potent enough to make me want to scream until I had nothing left.

"Why don't you and I have a private chat?" Mr. Sterling said. With his free hand, he crooked his finger at me, and the other still maintained a firm grip on his weapon. "Hurry along, my dear."

"I'm not your dear," I said. "I'm not your anything."

"Well," Mr. Sterling said in a hard voice, "you've certainly been useful."

I glanced at Whit, unsure of what to do. He was already watching me, his face hard, rage burning in his blue eyes, that wave of fury enveloping me tightly. Each of the men surrounding him had a gun pointed at him. My mouth went dry at the sight.

"That's right," Mr. Sterling said from the doorway. "If you don't cooperate, your husband"—Whit let out a snarl—"won't come out of this situation alive."

I clenched my jaw and mouthed goodbye to my sister and then to Whit. No part of me had forgiven him for what he had done, but this wasn't the farewell I thought we'd have. He regarded me silently, frustration etched in every taut line of his body. Then I turned and followed Mr. Sterling to the front of the house. As quietly as I could, I snuck the ink bottle from under my tongue and tucked it under the high collar of my dress. It was as big as a nib, and I barely felt it touching my skin.

That was at least one thing he couldn't take from me.

Mr. Sterling led us to the little sitting room we had initially passed through when we entered the house. Somehow, he seemed to lord over whatever situation he was in. The memory of when he and I shared a cabin during the rattling train ride from Alexandria to Cairo still haunted me. He had condescendingly dismissed my every word, as if I were an ignorant nobody—or worse, an ignorant woman. To him, I was a grievous offense.

"Have you given any thought to our last conversation?"

His question robbed me of speech for several seconds. That he would honestly believe I'd consider his suggestion that we work together to find my mother was outrageous. There were one hundred other things I'd rather do, like, say, swallow one of Mr. Edison's lightbulbs.

"I have not," I said. "I'd rather never think of you at all."

Mr. Sterling studied me in an assessing way. His eyes never drifted lower than my face, but I felt as if his perusal had left me dirty. Like he was looking into my soul to find anything that resembled his own black heart.

"My answer is *no*." I folded my arms, my gaze flicking toward the pistol in his steady hand. "An emphatic no. I suppose now you're going to threaten my companions again if I don't cooperate," I added bitterly. "It's a weak and unimaginative human being who resorts to violence to get what they want."

"And what would you suggest?" he asked softly.

"You only have to look backward to see that most people who governed by fear and malice didn't last long in their position of influence," I said. "They faced revolutions, rebellions, skirmishes, wars, and assassination attempts. But leaders who inspired their subjects were beloved and championed and protected." I narrowed my eyes at him. "Trust me that you will meet a disastrous end. I don't agree with my mother on many things—maybe all things, actually—save for one. I understand why she double-crossed you."

I thought my outburst would send him into a deranged fury, but he regarded me in cold, contemplative silence. "Something tells me," he said finally, "that you will change your mind."

"I'll die first," I seethed.

He eyed me in amusement. "You're quite dramatic, aren't you?"

Sometimes I could be, but right then, I had meant every word.

Mr. Sterling's features twisted, and he hastily yanked a handkerchief from within his pocket and coughed loudly into it. The hand holding his pistol wavered, and I took a step toward the door, but then his coughing subsided, and he steadied the gun.

I froze, my gaze locked on the barrel of his weapon. My knees trembled, and I fought to keep myself upright. I had always thought of myself as brave, but after losing Elvira and seeing firsthand what this weapon could do, my terror gripped me by the throat.

I would never not be afraid of guns.

"Is that your final answer?" he asked.

Would he shoot me if I said yes? Time ticked by in tense seconds. I licked my dry lips and whispered, "I will not change my mind."

Mr. Sterling stared at me for one long, measured beat. Question after question slammed into me. How long would it take me to reach the hallway? Would he aim for my heart?

Was this my last breath?

Mr. Sterling smiled faintly and then pointed to the room's exit and said, "Let's join the others. We have a lot of packing to do."

I blinked at him in confusion, not understanding his words. And then realization dawned, and I let out a slow exhale. He wasn't going to shoot me in this room. My brow furrowed. *Then why bring me in here? Why pull me from the others?*

"If you had agreed, I couldn't have the others knowing," Mr. Sterling said, reading my thoughts. He motioned for me to walk ahead of him, and I did, my shoulders tense, convinced that he was going to shoot me in the back. My movements were stiff, and I constantly looked over my shoulder to find the barrel of his gun pointed between my shoulder blades.

"I'm not going to pull the trigger," he said from behind me, amusement lacing every syllable. "Think of the mess, and besides, you are an essential piece of my elaborate plan. You help me more than you could possibly fathom."

A sharp chill pricked my spine. "What do you mean? How am I helping you?"

"Think it through," he said, almost encouragingly.

Mr. Sterling had far-reaching hands and unlimited resources. He knew where we were staying, maybe even our room number. He could have learned about my aunt and cousin's arrival. Perhaps *he* had a hand in Abdullah's and Ricardo's arrests.

The amount of catastrophe this man was capable of staggered me.

"Is there no one here you haven't corrupted in some way?"

Mr. Sterling remained silent, but I sensed he enjoyed watching me squirm. I was nothing but a cog in the elaborate machine he was building to punish Mamá for what she had done to him.

Every awful thing always led back to my mother.

I wanted to be rid of her, to cut ties with her and forget how much she'd meant to me. Forget how many years I spent trying to be like her, trying to please her. It had all been a lie. She wanted me to be someone perfect, a girl with flawless manners who knew exactly how to behave and what to say.

The girl my mother never was.

It killed me to see Mr. Sterling's men boxing up all of her possessions. Every single item was a potential clue, a way to find her. And he was taking that away from me. Whit and Isadora watched in helpless silence, forced to stand in the corner of the room, their hands up high over their heads. My sister's arms were shaking from the effort.

It was enough to make me want to scream.

Whit met my gaze, his eyes drifting over me slowly, assuring himself I was all right. He raised an eyebrow, and I nodded imperceptibly. I put aside my frustration with him and concentrated on how we could all get out of this situation alive.

I didn't want to lose either of them.

"The ring looks better on you than it ever did on me," Mr. Sterling remarked casually.

I curled my hands into tight fists, my heart slamming against my ribs. This ring reminded me of Papá, and I didn't want Mr. Sterling to touch it. I hated that he was studying it now.

"I promise you'll always think of me when you look at it," Mr. Sterling said shrewdly, once again reading my thoughts easily.

It unnerved me that I was unable to hide my feelings from him.

When they were done, the men carried everything out of the house in multiple trips. Then it was just the three of us in the bare room—even the furniture and rugs had been taken. Mr. Sterling and his companions aimed their pistols at us.

Whit took a half step in front of me, covering as much of me as he could. But it didn't matter—the bullets would find the three of us no matter where we stood. There was nowhere to hide. Mr. Sterling had said he wouldn't harm me, but I didn't trust a word of what he said. If he had been telling the truth, I wouldn't let him shoot Whit or Isadora—I'd scream and carry on as if it were the end of the world.

To me, it might as well have been.

Mr. Sterling pulled out a slim silver case from within his jacket pocket. He opened it to reveal one calling card, printed on thick speckled paper. "Please take one."

He held out the case to me.

I eyed it warily. "The last time I took something from you, things didn't end well for me."

Mr. Sterling smiled, his lips twitching beneath his mustache. "When you change your mind, you only need to rub your thumb across my name. I have a matching calling card, made from the same magic-touched paper, and my name will glow from your call. I will come to the hotel as soon as possible."

"I won't use it," I said.

He took the card and slipped it into the pocket of my skirt. "Possibly, but I will make you a promise, Señorita Olivera. If I find your mother, I will use the card to let you know. I don't think you'll be able to resist coming to me then."

With a dip of his chin, he and his companions walked out, as if leaving an elegant soiree. I turned to Whit and Isadora, reeling from the day's events, but Whit abruptly went to the window. He unlocked it, yanked it open, and swung one leg over, then the other.

"Where are you going?" I asked.

"Meet me back at the hotel," he said hurriedly. Then he walked out of sight without a look in my direction.

"How rude," Isadora said disgustedly. "Would it kill him to have said please?"

I walked to the window and leaned out as far as I could. He was long gone, and I frowned into the darkness. He wouldn't have left us here if he didn't have good reason. Shrugging, I faced my sister.

Her expression was grim. "That was the man Mother betrayed, wasn't it? Mr. Sterling?"

I nodded. "Yes, it was."

"Pity I couldn't shoot him," she said with real regret.

I stared at her, her bloodthirsty comment at odds with her delicate features, softly rounded cheeks, wide blue eyes. "How many people have you killed, Isadora?"

"A few, along with that crocodile," she said.

The memory of those obsidian eyes stalking me made me shiver, goose bumps flaring up and down my arms. Suddenly, I wanted to run from this dark, bare room. I wanted warmth and sunlight and to never look down the barrel of a pistol again. We had done a thorough search before Mr. Sterling's arrival and with him taking everything of note, it was unlikely we'd find anything else.

"Shall we head back?" I patted the collar of my dress. "I have some things we need to go over."

Isadora smiled, raising the hem of her skirt. She bent and retrieved folded-up pieces of paper tucked inside her shoe. "Excellent. So do I."

We linked arms and together went out into the night. Isadora vented her frustration at losing so much material to parse through, and she comforted herself by coming up with a variety of insults aimed at Mr. Sterling. He was a vile toad in one breath, and an infected wart in another. But the whole way back, I barely listened, my mind dwelling on one disturbing question.

How did Mr. Sterling follow me all the way from Cairo without any of us noticing?

WHIT

I peered around the corner of the house, squinting in the dim light provided by the two gas lanterns illumining the street. The bastard traveled in style. He had come in a black-paneled, enclosed carriage outfitted with brass door handles, two lamps, and folded seating available in the back for extra passengers. His transportation could hold up to ten people easily. The horses fidgeted, restless. Even they looked expensive. The driver matched the transport—elegant dark clothing, polished shoes, long leather whip. Sterling climbed inside, saying something to his companions, but I was too far to hear whatever it was. They loaded all of the boxes they'd taken from Lourdes's house, oblivious that they were being watched.

How do you like being followed, asshole?

It grated that I'd somehow missed his goons dogging our steps since Cairo. Except—there hadn't been anyone suspicious on the train, nor at the train station when we'd first arrived in Alexandria.

I knew because I'd made sure to look.

So then how had he done it?

The answer would have to wait. I crept closer, running quietly, my knees bent, keeping as low to the ground as possible. My steps on the dirt path hardly made a sound as I drew near to the back of the carriage. The driver clicked his teeth, and as Sterling's men climbed aboard the front to join the driver, the brougham lurched forward, and I lightly stepped onto the back bar, folded down the seat, and made myself comfortable.

We ambled through the city, navigating the streets with ease, crossing paths with travelers on foot, on donkeys, on horses. At last, we came to a nondescript section in Turkish Town, overlooking the eastern harbor. I took advantage of the road's bumpy surface to hop off the seat. They continued on without me, but I followed at a distance, until they eventually stopped at a building that had a shop at the bottom floor and an apartment on the upper one. They all exited the transport quietly, Sterling's guards looking up and down the street, before carting Lourdes's belongings inside. I made sure none of them saw me as I drew closer, hiding in the alley directly opposite from Sterling's headquarters. They were talking, and my ears strained to hear their conversation.

"Mr. Graves, I expected better from young Collins . . . Has he not . . ." Sterling said, the sea air snatching some of the words before I could hear them.

The man named Graves peered down the street, squinting. "Here he comes now."

I crouched low to the ground, completely hidden in the shadows. A man drew near, shoulders hunched, cap sitting low on his head. He seemed to be dragging his feet, as if he already knew the outcome of the conversation he was about to have with his employer.

He didn't see Graves pull out his revolver until the last second.

Shit.

"You led us to the wrong location," Graves said in a mild tone. "If it weren't for . . . we wouldn't have found . . ."

The man held up his hands. They shook so violently, as if he stood on quicksand and he knew it was only a matter of minutes before the sand overtook him. He couldn't have been more than sixteen, eighteen at the most. "Honest mistake."

Graves looked to Sterling, who nodded almost imperceptibly.

Sterling disappeared inside as the shot rent the air, cutting through the quiet night like the slash of a knife. Graves barked, "Throw him in the sea!" as the sound of surprised exclamations came from various directions. Windows were opened from neighboring buildings, and some people looked below at the scene. Many turned away, snapping the shutters closed. Given their reactions, Sterling having men murdered must have been a common occurrence.

The neighbors knew to stay out of his way.

My palm stung, and surprised, I glanced down to find that I had taken hold of a rock. Slowly, I set it onto the ground and wiped my sore hand on my trousers. I watched Graves orchestrate everyone's departure. Some left on foot, others on horses. Only he and the carriage, the team of horses, and the driver remained.

Graves eyed the street, his gaze flickering from building to building. His attention fell on the alley where I crouched in the darkness.

I stayed absolutely still, my breaths steady and deep and silent. He couldn't see me, but somehow it felt as if he were staring right at me. Then he turned, climbed inside the carriage, and gave the order to depart.

Still, I did not move, even as they turned off the street.

Finally, I slowly stood, my mind back on Sterling.

He was inside that building, probably not alone. I'd have to take care not to make a sound seeking entry. The exterior was exactly like the others, the upper level overhanging the narrow street, windows adorned with ornate casings and shutters. The stone blocks composing the walls would be easy to climb, with many footholds to gain purchase. Sterling had lit the lamp in one of the rooms, most likely his bedroom as he readied for sleep.

Briny sea air filled my lungs as I waited.

A half hour later, the windows went dark.

I found his office easily on the second floor, situated at the back of the house. Sterling's snores drifting from the level below were loud enough to disguise any noise I made. I found a tray piled high with candlesticks and matches, and I lit one, my eyes adjusting to the light after a moment.

The room was a mess.

Stacks of books, bottles of liquor, maps. On his shelves were jars of various medicines and tinctures, shoe polish, what appeared to be different mustaches—long, short, in varying hair colors—several pairs of spectacles, bottles of tooth powder, boxes of matches, hats, empty vases, and jackets. Clearly, like Lourdes, he collected random objects that were magic touched. I peered around the room, gathering more information. Sterling wore cologne and liked his tea. Empty cups sat on nearly every available surface. He didn't employ a maid. Curious.

He seemed to spend a lot of time in this room, reading, finishing getting ready for the day.

His men had dropped off the boxes filled with Lourdes's things, and they were stacked high. I rolled up the sleeves of my shirt, exhaustion hitting me like a cannonball. I shoved it aside and got to work, hoping to find anything that was damning, anything I could leverage, anything that I could use to help Inez.

An hour passed, then two, the candle burning low, as I looked through every drawer, most of the boxes, and every sheet. I found nothing proving his criminal activities. He was a corrupt antiquities agent who had founded the most lucrative underground black market in Egypt. There had to be *something* here. A drawing of the gate. Past invitations with the date and time stamped on the bottom. Receipts of payments he'd received with every one of his sales.

Everything seemed to be in here, except for what I wanted to find the most.

There were no stolen artifacts. No talismans, not one amulet. Not even the fake kinds one can buy at markets geared toward the tourists.

My frustration mounting, I packed up one of the boxes to go through with Inez, opened the window, and then dropped it outside. I threw a leg over the railing and climbed down, my breathing slow and even. I reached the ground with no issue and bent to retrieve the box. While carrying some of Lourdes's things to the hotel, something niggled at the back of my mind. I could picture that room exactly as I found it, every item laid out before me.

Nothing seemed out of the ordinary.

But my gut told me I had seen something and missed its significance entirely.

CAPÍTULO DIECINUEVE

We got straight to work upon reaching our hotel room. I resized all the items we'd taken from my mother's home back into their regular proportions, and together with my sister, we laid everything out on the bed.

We made quite the team.

I rolled up my sleeves and gave everything a cursory glance. I refused to believe that there wasn't something in this room that could help us find my mother. It was only a matter of studying each sheet carefully.

Or so I kept telling myself.

It occurred to me that we could potentially return to Mamá's house and wait for her—but I recalled the way she had been warned away from the bank. Someone was watching our movements and my guess was it was her lover, or at the very least, he'd employed a thug to observe us. Best not to go back—unless we had no other options.

I sank onto a stretch of space on the bed that wasn't covered by one of my mother's things as Isadora scooted a stool closer to me. A knock sounded on the door and my eyes flew to hers in surprise.

Isadora jumped up, reaching for the gun she'd taken from the night of the auction. She'd hidden it under a pillow on her side of the bed.

"Who is it?" she asked.

"It's me."

My sister unlocked the door and swung it open, revealing a very dusty and disheveled Whit. He carried an enormous tray with him on one hand, laden with covered dishes, and a box filled with stacks of paper with the other.

"Is that . . . ?"

"Yes."

Somehow, he'd found more of my mother's things. "How did you—"

"I'll explain in a moment," he grunted.

"I suppose you wouldn't like me to shoot him?" Isadora asked in a wistful tone, stepping aside to let him through.

I stood, my nose picking up the scent of bread and lemon, fresh herbs. My mouth watered. "Not today."

Whit scowled at Isadora as he walked past her. "No falafels for you."

Isadora perked up. "Where did you find falafels at this time of night?"

"The kitchen in the hotel is well stocked," he said. "I found hummus, tomatoes and cucumbers, bread, and a pitcher of lemonade. I also stopped by the front desk and checked for any messages and discovered a telegram for you, Olivera."

"A telegram!" I exclaimed and held out my hand for it.

But he ignored me as he looked around for somewhere to set the tray, saw that every available surface was occupied, and then, shrugging, he dropped to his knees, gently placing the food and my mother's things onto the carpeted floor. I settled next to him with an inelegant thud, while Isadora daintily picked up her skirt and gracefully sat, her knees bent, ankles crossed. She tugged the box toward her, curiously peering inside.

Finally, Whit dug into his pockets and handed me the sealed envelope. Eagerly, I opened it and read the first line. When I saw that it was addressed to the three of us, I switched to reading it out loud.

INEZ & CO—RECEIVED YOUR LETTER STOP RICARDO SAYS TO PLEASE ANSWER HIM WHEN HE CALLS OR HE WILL PERSONALLY FLOOD YOUR ROOM STOP

Whit covered his eyes with an exasperated groan, and I winced, my gaze automatically flickering to the cup on the nightstand. Mercifully, it was empty.

"Keep reading," Isadora urged as she began filling up her plate.

My attention returned to the telegram, and I cleared my throat and began again.

RICARDO AND GRANDFATHER ARE BEING
TREATED ABOMINABLY IN PRISON STOP

My voice cracked and I valiantly pushed on, reading the line again, as if the letters would magically rearrange themselves into something that didn't make me imagine the worst. My uncle and Abdullah covered in scrapes and bruises. Frequently beaten and left to starve. It was enough to send me into a despairing spiral. A curious numbness settled over me, stifling and heavy. I squeezed my eyes shut.

A soft hand touched my arm.

Slowly, I opened my eyes and stared blankly at Whit.

He withdrew, his jaw locked. He kept his expression impassive, but I sensed his turmoil, his raw frustration about what was happening to them and not being able to do a thing to stop it.

"What else does it say?" Isadora asked quietly. "Or would you prefer me to read it for you?"

I licked my lips, shaking my head. "I can do it."

A soft laugh escaped me as I quickly scanned the rest of the text. Then I read the rest of the message out loud.

AMARANTA HAS YELLED AT MONSIEUR MASPERO COMMA
I THINK HE IS AFRAID OF HER BECAUSE HE HAS
MOVED THEM INTO A LARGER ROOM STOP
KAREEM IS IN CAIRO AND HAS FOUND A WAY INTO
THE PRISON STOP HE HAS SNUCK RICARDO AND
GRANDFATHER BASKETS OF FOOD AND CANTEENS OF
WATER DO NOT ASK ME HOW STOP KODAK IS TAKING
TOO LONG COMMA WILL FIGURE OUT HOW TO DEVELOP PHOTO-
GRAPHS AT SHEPHEARDS STOP THE STAFF ARE HELPING ME
LOCATE WHAT I NEED STOP BE SAFE COMMA FARIDA

I lowered the telegram, and stared blankly ahead, feeling profoundly grateful for Kareem and Farida. A part of me wished I was there with them, helping in some way. In Alexandria, I could do nothing. Well, actually, that wasn't quite true.

We had Mamá's things, her private papers, her ideas written down, clues to where she might be or where she might have hidden all the artifacts. We had her journal.

"Let's start our search," I said. "Again. There might have been something we missed."

"Food first," Whit said sternly. He uncovered the trays and I groaned, my stomach rumbling loudly. I hadn't realized how hungry I was. Whit had brought a feast of warm pita bread, minced meat spiced with cumin and garlic, fresh cucumber and tomatoes, creamy fava beans, and a bowl of hummus with a generous drizzle of olive oil.

"Gracias," I murmured.

"You're welcome," he said with a small smile.

I forced myself to keep my face blank.

His smile faded, and I busily grabbed one of the falafels, dipping it into the hummus. It tasted creamy and delicious, and while the falafel was cold, it still had a great herby flavor. I felt Whit watching me, but I refused to glance at him. The tone of his voice had sent a warm shiver through me, and I couldn't afford to be foolish again. I had fallen in love with him without the slightest resistance, a gullible little idiot, attracted by the sense of danger he oozed, charmed by his roguish personality, and taken in by his heroics.

For the millionth time, I held on to one reality: he did not love me. It was a curse written on my heart, and every time I thought of it, I felt as if I bled from an open wound. It had all been an act. He was only here out of some misguided sense of responsibility and guilt. That, and he wanted to find the alchemical sheet before my mother did. I would repeat those truths until I said them in my sleep. Until they were stitched across my skin.

"There are no glasses," Isadora remarked.

Whit handed her the pitcher. "I beg your pardon. The fine china wouldn't fit on the tray."

Isadora sniffed but took the drink from him. We all began to eat in earnest while we looked through stacks of papers and journals.

"Are you going to tell us where you went?" I asked Whit.

"I followed Sterling back to his headquarters in Turkish Town," Whit said. "He has a man named Graves working for him, one of the men who searched me in your mother's home. Not a nice fellow." He tore a chunk of the bread and piled it high with hummus and slices of cucumber and tomato, and the whole thing disappeared into his mouth. After he was done chewing, his face took on a grim expression. "I watched him murder a young man in cold blood on Sterling's orders."

I set down the pitcher of lemonade, my stomach roiling. Just like that, I lost my appetite. We had come so close to death earlier. All it would have taken was one nod from Mr. Sterling.

"Why did Mr. Sterling let us live?" Isadora asked.

"I suspect because he still needs Inez in some way," Whit said. "What did he say to you when he took you to a different room?"

"He wants me to help him find Mamá," I said absently, reading through the papers Whit had stolen back from Mr. Sterling. "He keeps asking me to join his side."

"Did he have a gun on you?" Whit asked, his voice quietly lethal.

I paused in my reading. "He did. But it didn't change my answer."

"Of course not," Isadora said.

I lifted my gaze, and it automatically went to Whit. He was looking at me, focused, intense, with an emotion swirling in the cool depths of his eyes. It might have been adoration. It might have been frustration. When it came to Whit, I never knew. He dropped his chin, averting his face from mine, attention back on the tray of food.

I stared at him for a moment longer before forcing myself back to the pages. There was work to be done.

"I confess it makes me nervous that Mr. Sterling just let us go," Isadora said. "Do you think you could be wearing anything that might bring him here?"

Whit muttered his reply, but I barely caught it because I'd stumbled across something interesting. For some reason, Mamá had collected a variety of Alexandria maps featuring old street names, the eastern harbor, and especially a place called Pharos Island. They were all done by a Mahmoud el-Falaki. I squinted at one of the maps, trying to make out a peculiar shape drawn on the western side.

"He probably knows where we are staying," Whit was saying next. "My sense is that he's waiting for us to lead him right to Lourdes."

My eye caught on something else when I flipped the sheet. It was another old map of Alexandria, and someone had marked, in pencil, the location of where the Great Library of Alexandria had once stood before it was ravaged by fire. But there were other curious markings in what looked to be Greek. Someone had also drawn a light sketch of a three-headed dog atop a side street, away from the city center. I frowned down at Cerberus, the guardian of the underworld, a memory niggling at the back of my mind. And then I remembered exactly where I'd last seen the creature: Mamá's journal.

I went to my canvas bag and pulled out the sketch I'd copied from her journal while I was on the train. It seemed incredible there wouldn't be a connection between the map of the city and my mother's journal.

"Does anyone speak Greek?" I asked.

Both of them shook their heads as they continued their own searches. I flipped through the rest of the pages but found nothing else of note. I returned to the map depicting the three-headed dog. I didn't know the street, but it was beyond the Arab wall, in an older part of Alexandria, situated in the field of ruins.

"I think I've found something," Whit said suddenly, breaking the quiet. He held up a journal. "Your mother has drawn pictures of the lighthouse of Alexandria several times, with a particular focus on the base. Perhaps she believed there was something hidden there of note?"

My heart began to beat faster. "Is it on Pharos Island?"

Whit glanced down at the journal. "Yes, it is," he confirmed after a moment.

"Is there anything written down?" Isadora asked. "Any clue?"

Whit scowled. "Yes, but it's in Greek."

My sister and I groaned.

"How many drawings of the lighthouse are there in that journal?"

Whit flipped through the pages. "Seven."

That was substantial. "Perhaps Mamá and Mr. Fincastle have found something of note and are secretly excavating?" I asked. Another possibility occurred to me. "Do you think they might have found—"

Whit gave me a pointed look, and I fell silent. He had known what I was going to ask, and he clearly didn't want me to mention the alchemical sheet in front of my sister. There was no reason to keep that information from her.

I opened my mouth but Whit spoke first.

"It makes no sense Lourdes and Fincastle would be excavating there," Whit said. "The lighthouse was destroyed by several earthquakes. It's mostly a pile of rubble, isn't it?"

His words distracted me from my train of thought. "I believe tourists still visit. During my crossing of the Atlantic, several passengers told me of their plans to include the lighthouse in their itineraries."

"Wasn't it Herodotus who said the whole structure had fallen into the sea?" Isadora asked.

"Strabo, I think," Whit said.

"And not all of it disappeared," I said slowly. "It *does* seem a peculiar place to excavate unless . . . some secret room has survived?" I thought about Tío Ricardo and Abdullah, how they were wasting away in a prison, surviving only by Kareem's wily efforts in sneaking them food. I curled my hands into fists. I couldn't wait for Mr. Sterling to come to us, nor could I hide in this room forever out of fear that he'd follow us. I had to do something to help get them out of prison. "I think we ought to go and explore the base of the lighthouse."

Whit considered the idea. "The structure has been weakened by many natural disasters. The whole thing could come down over our heads."

"Perhaps that's part of the appeal," I said. "No tourists will venture inside, which means no interruptions to their digging, no pesky government agents looking over their shoulder. Mamá and Fincastle could be working undisturbed even now . . . getting closer to discovering—"

"Fine," Whit cut in. "Let's go, then. We'll go later tonight, after we all get a few hours of sleep."

"I can't just do nothing while my uncle and Abdullah rot in that cell," I continued loudly.

Whit leaned forward, peering at me intently. "I said fine, Olivera. We'll go to the lighthouse, even if it falls on top of our heads."

"Oh," I said, stymied.

"A rousing speech," Isadora said dryly.

"You're welcome to stay behind," Whit said. "Or better yet, return to Cairo."

Isadora shook her head. "I'm not leaving my sister."

I gave her a watery smile. "Thank you."

Whit rolled his eyes and said, "*Christ*."

The glare that he gave her could have leveled a small town, buildings, trees, nothing would have survived. But it wasn't all anger . . . not quite. If I didn't know better, I would have named his emotion something else entirely.

It looked a lot like jealousy.

But that was impossible. The idea that he was jealous about my relationship with my sister was ludicrous.

Wasn't it?

WHIT

Once again, my wife woke me up in the middle of night. I rubbed the sleep from my eyes and waited for them to adjust to the darkness. "What is it?" I whispered.

"I've had another vision," she whispered back.

"Inez," I said. "Could you be having dreams?"

She was kneeling next to my cot, and at last her features came into shape, enough for me to see that she was scowling. "I couldn't sleep, and I have this habit sometimes of twisting the ring around my finger, and so I was thinking about Cleopatra, and then the next second I was in one of her memories. Do you want to hear about it or not?"

I gestured for her to continue.

"She was at her worktable," Inez began. "And dressed curiously. Usually, I see her in these beautiful outfits, made of expensive fabric. On her feet are bejeweled sandals, and her hair is always adorned by ribbon and pearls. But this time she was in a plain, simple robe—dark in color and with a hood. Her shoes were made of serviceable leather. Sturdy, as if she was expecting to travel a long distance."

"What was she doing at the table?"

"She had the alchemical sheet in front of her," Inez said in her soft voice.

I was suddenly extremely awake. "Was she turning lead into gold?"

Inez shook her head. "But she had all manner of ingredients before her, and she was cutting up roots and mixing various liquids that had a shimmer to them. And she was saying something as she worked."

"She was creating a spell," I said.

"I believe so. I think to protect the alchemical sheet."

"It's possible," I said. "It's what I would do if I had her particular skill set. Her brother might have known about it—after all, he was also related to the famous alchemist. Perhaps Cleopatra felt it necessary to take action against him acquiring it. Was that all?"

Again, she shook her head. "No. When she was done, she spilled water all over it."

"*What?*"

"Shhh!" Inez hissed. "You'll wake Isadora."

My pulse roared in my ears. If that sheet was ruined, I might as well be also. "Explain."

"The ink didn't run; the paper didn't even get wet," she said. "Cleopatra had made the Chrysopoeia *waterproof*."

Dozens of feluccas, schooners, and brigantines bobbed in the harbor, their masts and sails rising high and reflecting the silver glow of the moon. We were the only idiots enjoying the view in the middle of the night, exhausted and nervous. Well, I was exhausted and nervous. Inez had that gleam in her eye that struck terror in my soul. It somehow communicated that she'd pursue her goal, no matter the cost to her life. Come what may, she would see it through to the end.

"Have you paid the driver?" Isadora asked in her cool voice.

I barely heard her. Inez tapped her foot, gazing impatiently across the water, as if she wanted to conjure her mother into existence, standing at the base of the lighthouse. The sea air teased her long hair, whipping it across her face. She didn't seem to notice, every part of her focused on getting to that island. We had gone through Turkish Town, and though we could have continued by land, I thought it best to go the rest of the way by boat; it was harder to follow after us. Isadora had been helpful with navigating the tight turns through the city and had provided several shortcuts on the way to the coast.

I turned to look at her, and she raised her brows expectantly.

"The driver?" Isadora prompted.

"How did you know the quickest way through Turkish Town?" I kept my tone nonchalant, but my mind repeated Inez's earlier words when we argued in front of the bank. If Isadora knew the city as well as it certainly looked like, then she could have easily beaten us back to the hotel after warning Lourdes.

She stared at me, hand on her hip, all the appearance of outrage. "People *talk* to me."

"And?"

"And I've made a few acquaintances at the hotel," she said. "I'm good at collecting information."

"If that's all it is, then why are you angry?"

She took a step toward me, jabbed her index finger in my chest. "Because every time you speak with me, every time you ask me a question, it always sounds like an accusation." She inhaled deeply, nostrils flaring. "And it's *annoying*."

"I won't apologize for it."

"Of course not," she said, rolling her eyes. "But do you want to know what I think?"

I waited, hoping my silence would goad her. People talked more when they were upset, or under suspicion.

"I think you see qualities in me that you yourself possess." Her voice dropped to a pointed whisper. "And you *hate* it. I'd bet everything that I own, all my money, that you can't stand parts of yourself. The eternal distrust, the cynicism, a mind always calculating how to utilize people for your own benefit."

"I don't—"

"You do," she said firmly. "It's what makes you good at your job. We're survivors. By definition, we've done things to avoid hurt, to stay alive, one step ahead of everyone else. We get our way by any means possible."

Every word grated. Because she was right.

"And when we care about someone, we become protective," Isadora said in the same hushed whisper. "We will move heaven and earth to help them, to save them from themselves. Because there are only a few people in this world whom we love, and we'd damn anyone to hell who would dare to hurt them."

She flicked her gaze to Inez, but I didn't follow it. I kept my eyes on her.

"I can see who you are as easily as I see myself," she said. "Now. Back to the matter at hand. Have you taken care of the driver?"

I looked away from her, wishing I didn't agree with her. It was easier to think of her as an enemy. Easier than recognizing all the ways we were similar, and how that didn't stop Inez from trusting her. Because then I'd have to sit with how Inez could no longer stand the sight of me.

A headache bloomed from the sudden emotion that settled over me. Anger, frustration. Grief, too, if I would let myself really feel it. I had no one to blame but myself.

I rubbed my temples, never wanting a cup of coffee more. Our carriage driver waited, yawning hugely, the horses grunting softly. Even they protested the early hour. I gave the lad a handful of francs. "Would you mind waiting for us?"

He looked around, frowning. "Here?"

"Yes," I said, pointing behind me to the island of Pharos. "We want to see the lighthouse."

The driver nodded, though he still seemed perplexed. "At this hour?"

"I don't make the plans," I muttered, giving him more coins.

"You ought to send him away," Isadora said. "It's rude to keep him waiting."

I ignored her and addressed the lad. "We'll be right back. Don't leave us."

We had maybe an hour, two at the most, before the sun showed her face. If we weren't long gone before then, I would scream bloody murder at Isadora, damn the consequences. I stared across the Mediterranean, the sea disquieted and uneasy, as if knowing she was about to be disturbed. Along the water's edge were a slew of rickety boats, tied off at a narrow dock that went out ten or fifteen feet. Beyond, the outline of Pharos Island rose high above the surface, the waves slapping against every sharp edge. The base of Alexandria's lighthouse still stood on the eastern side, even after millennia, an impressive sight despite the loss of the upper structure that had once guided ships by a flame in the night.

"How tall was it?" Inez asked as we walked away from the driver, her attention ensnared by the ancient wonder.

"Mamá's notes said it would have stood at least forty stories high." Isadora shook her head, marveling. "Imagine the building of it! The sweat and toil of every worker."

"Only for an earthquake to send most of it into the sea below," I said dourly. "Nothing beautiful lasts."

"Your cynicism is showing again," Inez murmured.

"I wasn't trying to hide it," I muttered back. Then in a louder voice, I said, "All right, we've seen the lighthouse. Let's go back to the hotel and have tea, coffee, and a decent meal."

A part of me couldn't believe what I was saying. If Lourdes truly believed Cleopatra's Chrysopoeia was hidden in the base of the lighthouse, I ought to explore every inch. But my gut clenched tight, anticipation making my blood thrum in my veins, clamoring for attention. My body was on high alert—enemy-beyond-the-hill high alert.

Something was wrong.

Or *about* to be wrong.

If I learned anything from my time in the militia, it was to trust my gut. And right then, it was telling me to take Inez far from this place.

To ready my rifle and keep a finger on the trigger. I itched for the knife I always carried in my boot, but that deplorable bastard Sterling had stolen it from me.

"We just got here," Inez said. "I'm not turning back now. Mamá might be inside, or if she's not here, she might have left a clue behind. I think we ought to go and explore. Unless you have a better idea on how to find her?"

I folded my arms, tension making my jaw lock. "It's safer to go by water the rest of the way. But it would mean stealing a rowboat."

"It's not that far," Isadora said, scrunching her pointed nose. "A pity we didn't bring a change of clothes. We might get wet."

I didn't bother replying to that nonsense.

Inez pointed to the row of fishing boats. "Let's borrow one of those. No stealing required. We'll return it once we're finished, and I can leave some coins inside, too."

Isadora was already walking to the dock in quick, determined strides, her manner confident and sure, an illusion for the chaos rioting underneath. She reminded me of a Greek tragedy, every character marching toward their doom, wreaking havoc and sowing discord as they went, a deranged pixie sprinkling their destructive energy around onto unsuspecting innocents.

"I still don't trust her," I said with narrowed eyes at said deranged pixie.

"You have made that more than clear," Inez said tiredly. Deep shadows under her eyes belied her exhaustion. When had she had a full night of sleep? When had I? I couldn't remember. "But she's done nothing but help me," she said. "You're welcome to stay behind."

"The hell I will," I said. "And don't think I didn't notice how you used my words against me."

"I was counting on it," she said sweetly.

I trailed after her, trying to ignore her hips swaying as she walked, the way her curls danced in the briny air. Isadora had untied the rope of one of the boats by the time we joined her on the dock. I took over the task, relieved to see oars poking out from under the bench. I helped Inez into the boat, considered pushing Isadora into the sea but instead ignored her as she gracefully stepped aboard. She remained upright, knees bent in sync with the water's sway.

"Will you do the honors, or are you going to have *me* row us over to the island?" Isadora asked, the ice in her voice pronounced.

"I can help," Inez protested.

I took the oars and dipped them into the water. This was such a bad idea. I never should have gone along with it. It would have been better if I had come on my own. "Let's just bloody get this over with."

Inez rummaged through her bag of supplies and handed Isadora a candle and then found an extra for herself. She lit both and they held the lights high, using their free hands to cup the flames and keep them from flickering out from the breeze. Inez couldn't quite manage it, and the fire went out when the wind blew across the boat.

She sighed. "I miss the sandal."

I laughed.

Inez glanced at me, startled, her hazel eyes warm and amused. She hadn't looked at me like that in what felt like years. She quickly averted her gaze, and I yanked my attention off her and toward the lighthouse where it belonged.

We approached the island, and I noted the small bay, taking care to maneuver the boat in that direction. When we were close enough, I jumped out, the water cool against my skin, and guided the boat up the bank. Inez scrambled over the rail, refusing my help, slipping and windmilling her arms to keep from falling face-first into the water. Isadora nimbly leapt over, landing neatly with a minimal splash, and helped Inez up the shore. I put the oars away, and we trekked the steep incline up to the base of the lighthouse.

The craggy rocks pierced my shoes, and for the last stretch, I had to help both of them navigate the path. The ancient building came into view as the dark sky lightened into a navy blue. It was my favorite time of day, the moment right before dawn broke.

"It's enormous," Inez whispered.

"The tallest structure in the ancient world," I said. "At the very top, there used to be a massive mirror that reflected light and could be seen thirty-five miles away."

"You can still see the inscription on this side," Isadora said, pointing to the etching on the light stone. "An offering to the twin guardians of the sea."

"Who were they?" Inez asked.

"Castor and Pollux," Isadora and I said in unison.

We looked at each other in horrified surprise. Inez merely smiled and strode toward the front entrance, her chin lifted, her curly hair trailing down to the middle of her back. "There's the doorway," she said. "Wide enough for two horsemen to ride through side by side."

We walked inside and were met by a crumbling staircase and a large square-shaped area that must have housed chariots and horses at one point. Overhead, parts of the ceiling had fallen. Boulders littered the space, some taller than me. While the lighthouse seemed empty, there were many shadowy corners in which to hide.

Inez glanced around warily, her gaze landing on Isadora. "Did you remember to bring your gun?"

Isadora patted her jacket pocket. "Oh, I must have forgotten my spare when we went to the hotel for supplies."

I studied our surroundings, my gut clenching. I had brought my rifle, which I'd packed inside my trunk, unassembled. It was my least favorite gun—bulky, loud, and a nuisance to load. But something was better than nothing.

It wouldn't do to meet our enemies unarmed.

"Look over here," Inez called out.

I walked to where she stood, peering at a mostly intact wall. An enormous relief was carved into the stone, depicting a Greek god in billowing robes. He wore a crown, and in his left hand, he carried a scepter. At his feet rested a three-headed dog, its teeth bared fiercely.

"Cerberus again," Inez murmured.

"The hound of Hades," I said. "A curious creature to carve onto the wall of the lighthouse. It guarded the entrance to the underworld and had nothing to do with the sea."

Inez was barely listening to me. She had crept closer, her finger lightly tracing the carving, inspecting the lettering at the base of the relief. "There is some writing in Latin. Can you read it?"

"Very little," I said, but I came closer, peering over her shoulder. I tried to ignore the sweet scent of her hair, the brush of her long skirt against the toes of my boots. This was the closest I'd stood next to her since we married. Which had *nothing* to do with anything. I cleared my throat and focused on translating. "I believe the name of this god is Serapis."

She glanced at me from over the curve of her shoulder. "I don't know who he is."

"Abdullah would," I muttered. "I think he's a Greco-Egyptian god." My eye caught another faint line of text. "Wait a moment—there's something else written below his name." Gently, I moved her aside so I could better read the scant lines of text etched into the wall. "He's the patron of Alexandria, and there's a temple dedicated to him in the city."

"Where?" Inez asked sharply. "Because I think I've seen . . ."

A dreamy expression stole over her face, as if she'd stepped into another world. I waved my hand across her eyes. She stared vacantly back at me, not quite alert but still lost somehow. "Inez? *Inez*."

I reached out to shake her shoulders but stilled when I recalled her curious connection to Cleopatra via the golden ring on her finger. She might be viewing one of her memories.

"What's the matter with her?" Isadora asked sharply from somewhere behind me. I barely heard her. My whole focus was on my wife.

"Inez?" I asked again, louder this time.

She blinked, coming back to herself in a matter of seconds. She squeezed her eyes shut and then slowly opened them, meeting my gaze levelly. "Can you see a tower from here?"

"What?" I asked.

"Across the harbor," she said. "Is there a tower? It looks Roman by design."

I turned, squinting through the rubble. There was a section that allowed someone to see across the water and back to the coastline we'd rowed from earlier. "Yes, I think. Why?"

"I was in a memory," she breathed. "Cleopatra was traveling by boat and wearing the same exact robe from last time. I think these two memories are connected. In the first one, she had the roll of parchment on her, and just now I saw her in a little rowboat, only one guard with her. He was working the oars, but they weren't on the Nile River, or even out at sea. They were *underground*."

"What do you mean? Underground how?"

Inez gripped my arm, excitement lit across her face. She was trembling from it. "I mean it looked like there was a network of canals beneath the city of Alexandria, and Cleopatra knew about them *and* where they led to." Inez tightened her grasp. "I saw her reaching a tunnel that had a curved staircase, and after getting out of the boat, she used it to climb up a tower. It overlooked the harbor. And I saw it—"

"Saw what?"

"The lighthouse, her palace. Everything." Inez frowned. "But she wasn't carrying the roll of parchment anymore. I don't understand—she wouldn't have left it in the boat. It's too valuable."

I tried to picture what Inez would have seen. All of these visions were connected. The first had been a frantic search for the alchemical sheet, the second had been Cleopatra, a Spellcaster, creating magic to perhaps protect the Chrysopoeia. At this point, Cleopatra's goal was to hide such a treasure from her scheming brother. She needed help, and history told us that eventually, she went to Julius Caesar—who had stationed himself at the royal palace.

"She was going back to her home," I said.

"Yes, that must be it exactly," Inez replied, grinning. "With her brother hoping to invade the city, Cleopatra would have had to move about secretly. What better way than the underground passageways?"

Instinctively, I understood that she wouldn't have given a Roman general something so valuable to her. No, she would have found a way to keep it hidden.

"Right," I said quietly. "But before getting to the tower, Cleopatra must have made a stop along the way and found a secure place to—"

From the corner of my eye, I caught sight of Isadora approaching.

She held something small in her hand.

A gun, glinting in the moonlight.

She lifted her arm, aiming directly at Inez. Her finger curled around the trigger. My heart stopped.

CRACK.

CAPÍTULO VEINTE

Whit gripped my hand and yanked me behind one of the massive boulders piled one on top of the other. The sound of the shot thundered in my ears. Everything had happened so fast I still didn't know who had fired at us. I tried to picture where we had been standing, where Isadora might have gone. Had she been near us?

"*Keep moving*," Whit said, pulling me at a run. We dodged around the rocks, pebbles and sand kicking up under my heels.

"What about my sister?" I yelled.

Whit shot me a thoroughly exasperated look before tucking me behind a partially buried doorway. He peered around the edge calmly, his rifle in his hands.

I poked his back, and he grunted. "We can't leave her. Let's go—"

"*She's* the one shooting at us," Whit said through gritted teeth. "Now, quiet. I don't think your sister knows where we're hiding."

"Isadora wouldn't—"

Whit glared at me, and I fell silent. He motioned for me to look out into the opening, and as I peered around him, I could make out Isadora picking her way through the debris, the gun in her hand still smoking. My stomach lurched. Whit lowered his gun, bent forward, and then straightened, showing me a rock in his fist.

I gasped. "You are *not* going to throw it at her."

He rolled his eyes and then threw it in the opposite direction of where we hid. Isadora spun around and shot where she had heard the rock hitting the ground.

"Sissssster," she called out in an eerie singsong voice. "Why don't you come out here and we can have a talk, you and I? Only, let me take care of your brute, first. What you see in him I'll never understand."

I stared, riveted, as her expression turned cold and grim. All of her earlier warmth seemed to bleed out of her. I couldn't make sense of her behavior. She loaded her weapon with quick, efficient movements. It wasn't just her expression that had changed. No, she seemed like an entirely different person. Her movements were less polished, less perfect, all traces of the lady she had been gone. Now she walked loosely, her steps long and confident. There was nothing prim and dainty about her. She shoved at her long skirt impatiently, kicking the bulk as she prowled the space.

This person was a stranger to me.

Whit aimed his gun at her, and I instinctively reached out, forcing him to lower the barrel.

"No," I cried out.

Isadora spun again, her gaze unerringly finding mine. I ducked as she fired, and Whit led me out from under the crumbling doorway. My foot caught on an overturned slab of stone, and I tumbled forward, landing hard on my hands and knees. My palms stung, pebbles embedding into the tender flesh.

Isadora laughed, mean and sharp edged. Chills bloomed up and down my arms. I'd never heard her sound like that. She stood not ten paces from me, her gun aimed at my head. Nausea wrapped around me and squeezed. Elvira's sweet face flew across my mind, her wide eyes, the slackened line of her jaw when she'd died.

"Toss the rifle," Isadora said to Whit.

He did without hesitation. Then he held out his hand and helped me to my feet. My knees shook as he brushed the pebbles from my hands.

"It will be all right," he murmured.

"Step away from her," Isadora demanded.

He did but only moved an arm's length from me. If I wanted to, I could reach for him and hold on tight. But I kept my arms by my side, fear coating my tongue like acid.

"Why?" I asked, pushing the word out through my cracked lips. "Why turn against us?"

"She was never on our side, Inez," Whit said in a cool, aloof voice.

Isadora studied me, the soft curves of her face at odds with the hatred steeped in her blue eyes. "I warned you once that you were too trusting, Inez. Too naive to see what had been in front of you all along."

"Stop talking in riddles," I said, my anger flaring. "And don't be condescending to me." My thoughts blurred as I struggled to undo the tangled knots in my mind. Isadora had set out to fool me. To make me believe we were family.

She took what I longed for the most and twisted it into something ugly.

"You've been helping Mamá all along. You have been trying to sabotage us from the beginning," I said, realization dawning. "You led us straight to those men when we were in Cairo, didn't you? You were going to let them kill me."

Isadora remained stone-faced as the accusations piled up against her. I wanted her to defend herself, to tell me it wasn't true. But she was coldly silent.

"You were the one who whistled in front of the bank," Whit said bitterly.

Shame worked its way up my throat.

Whit had been trying to warn me all along. But I'd been swallowed up by the death of Elvira, and I had latched on to the one person I shouldn't have. A venomous snake.

Foolish, *foolish* mistake.

"We couldn't allow you to get too close," Isadora said finally. "Not when we've worked so hard and have come so far to get Mamá away from him."

"Away from who?" I demanded. "Basil Sterling?"

"It was her plan all along to double-cross him, to start her own black market," Whit said. "You've been a part of this from the beginning."

"Yes," Isadora said. "She wanted a new life."

"Why?" I demanded.

"Her old one was killing her, and she needed to be free. From the whole lot of you."

It was as if she'd already pulled the trigger. I took a step back, hunching my shoulders, reeling from Isadora's words. My mother had been so unhappy she had sought to destroy our life, mine and Papá's. Actually, she had gone beyond destruction. She'd turned to murder. "Mamá hired those men in the alley to kill me," I whispered, the horror of it making my eyes burn with hot tears.

If she had done that to me, than she would have had no compunction to do that to my father. It wasn't until that moment that I really believed my mother had had him killed.

He was gone. Well and truly gone.

"Papa and I are her *real* family. The one you've never been a part of," she said. "Whit, if you take another step closer to her, I will pull the trigger. Do you understand me, you deplorable miscreant?"

Whit froze, scowling.

"Listen to me," I said. "Mamá only cares about the money. Otherwise, why would she send you—"

"I sent myself!" Isadora snapped. "Mother has a weakness when it comes to you. It's the only time I've seen her make stupid decisions."

Hope bloomed in my chest. If my mother hadn't enlisted Isadora's help, then she might not know my sister was trying to kill me. "We are family. Surely—"

"You are *not* my family," she cried, pressing closer. "Mother left you behind. She picked *me*. Do you understand? *Me!* I'm the one she trusts the most; I'm the one she confides in. You she liked to keep in the dark, in a different continent. You're deluded if you think she cares for you as much as she does for me." She cocked the gun, her hand steady.

"Inez," Whit whispered, inching closer to me. "The rifle."

I didn't let my eyes flick downward, but I had seen where he had tossed the loaded weapon. It had landed to my left, just ahead of a grouping of rocks.

"Stop moving," Isadora cried.

I flinched at her enraged tone. "Sister, please—"

"*I'm not your sister*," Isadora said through clenched teeth. "No matter how many times Mother spoke of you, no matter how much Mother tried to get me to see you that way. I have done everything to be the daughter she always wanted. Did exactly what she wanted, learned how to exist in the world she created with my father. She promised me her old life was over and that *I* was her whole world now."

"But then she tried to save Inez over and over again," Whit said. "Did she often compare you to her? A daughter you could never compete with?"

"You're trying to make me angry," Isadora said in a silky voice. "Do you want me to lose control? Make a mistake? I think before I act, you imbecile. What else did Cleopatra show you?"

"Think this through carefully," I asked. "Do you really believe Mamá would support your actions?"

"Tell me what you know, Inez," Isadora repeated.

"Do you think she'd love you more if she knew that you were threatening me?" I countered.

"Maybe not," she agreed. "But she can't love a ghost, can she?"

Whit leapt, shoving me aside as she pulled the trigger.

I landed hard on the ground with a surprised cry. Whit groaned, his eyes squeezed shut. He clutched at his side, blood seeping through his fingers.

"No," I whispered. "*No.*"

"The gun," Whit said through clenched teeth.

My knees throbbed as I reached for the rifle, but Isadora kicked it out of the way. "Last chance, Inez. Tell me what you saw."

Desperate, I grabbed a handful of rocks and pebbles and sand and flung it at her. She flinched, blinking rapidly, and I scrambled to my feet as the sound of another shot rent the air. Isadora had missed.

Whit tried to kick her, but she jumped over him, laughing.

"Run," Whit cried hoarsely. "*Run!*"

My heart tore in two as I stumbled away from him. Isadora came after me, shooting wildly, herding me farther from the entrance to the lighthouse. I ducked as another shot thundered behind me. The crumbling steps were ahead, and I rushed forward, wanting to put as much distance between us as possible. I followed the curve of the wall, finding notches wherever I could to gain purchase as I climbed higher and higher. My heart slammed against my ribs, one bruising beat at a time.

"There's nowhere for you to go," Isadora called from behind me.

I glanced over my shoulder, watching in terror as she reloaded her weapon, calmly following in my footsteps.

I stumbled up another few steps, and I let out a sharp cry. So many of them had broken off. Chunks of stone blocked most of the path upward, and I had to pick through the debris while navigating the disappearing staircase. Soon, I'd run out of steps. Sweat dripped down my face. My skirt made it nearly impossible to see what was under my feet, and impatiently, I bent at the waist to grab the fabric.

Another shot rang out.

"So close," Isadora cooed. "You have nowhere left to go."

I reached for a rock the size of my palm and threw it at her. She nimbly ducked, her brows pinched tight. She raised her arm but I threw another rock. It smacked her hand as she pulled the trigger, and the gun fell from her grasp, plummeting to the ground below.

I dropped onto the step, pain shooting from my knees at the contact as the shot hurtled over my head. I leaned over the edge of the step, my eyes stinging. We were thirty or so feet from the floor. Whit was crawling forward, clutching his side but looking up at me, frantic.

"*Inez!* Watch out!"

Footsteps thundered from somewhere behind me, and I reached for another rock but found none small enough for me to throw. Rough hands grabbed my hair hard, and I screeched. Isadora clawed at my face, nails digging deep.

I tasted blood and dust in my mouth.

She held on to me, hands moving to around my neck. The air became tight in my lungs; I couldn't get a breath. Panic made my pulse leap, fighting for oxygen. I didn't want to die. Didn't want to go like this. Tears streaked down my stinging cheeks as I tried to inhale and inhale.

There was no give. No air.

Black spots crowded my vision. I elbowed Isadora hard—

A loud cracking noise startled us both. The stone under us quaked. Blindly I reached for something I could hold on to, felt Isadora loosen her hold on my neck as the steps crumbled. I inhaled sharply, and then coughed from the effort. My fingers found purchase as my body dropped, legs swinging forward and back as I gripped the ledge. Isadora's frightened scream rang, at first so close, right in my ear, but then softer as she fell.

The sound of her body hitting the ground went through me. A loud smack, bones breaking, her scream abruptly cut off, as if someone had slapped a hand over her mouth.

"Shit, shit, shit," I hissed, tears streaking down my face. My fingers were slick with sweat, digging into the stone, but I felt them slipping. "I can't hold on!"

"*Inez!*" Whit yelled from below. "The steps are going to give. Let go!"

Terror gripped me. "I can't. I'm too high!"

I glanced over my shoulder and down below and let out a whimper at the sight of Isadora's broken body. Whit stood directly beneath me, one hand clutching his side, the other raised high, stained bright red. "I'll catch you. Inez, I'll catch you!"

A chunk of the rock gave way, pitching down, and I yelled out a warning.

"*Christ.*"

"Whit! Are you all right? Whit!"

He coughed. "I'm all right. Inez, let go. The rest of the staircase has broken off—I can't climb up to you. Please let go!"

"It's too high—" I choked out, gasping. Another chunk of the stairs broke off with a thunderous crack. I heard Whit scrambling out of the way and then shuffling back to stand directly beneath me.

"Inez," Whit said, his voice calm, working against the panic rioting in my chest. "I'll catch you. Now, *let go*!"

I squeezed my eyes shut, afraid to trust his words. Afraid that he wouldn't be there at the end of my fall. That I'd end up like Isadora, sprawled across the stone, staring blankly upward, limbs twisted unnaturally.

"Inez, you are the love of my life," Whit roared. "I will not lose you now."

My gaze returned to Whit's. He stared at me steadily, face tilted upward, arm still outstretched. He nodded, reassuring me. "I'm right here. Please let go."

I let out a shuddering breath and shut my eyes. I opened my hands and let myself fall. It was only a moment, but it felt like forever. My skirt rippled against my legs. Air whipped around my hair—then the hard collision against Whit, his arms wrapping tight around me as I knocked him into the ground. He rolled us again and again as rocks fell, a lethal downpour of heavy stones. Dust rose around us in a plume.

"Inez," he whispered hoarsely as he pulled me on top of him, away from the jagged rocks surrounding us. His lips moved against my throat when he spoke again. "Are you all right? Are you hurt?"

I inhaled deeply, joyous disbelief making it hard to form a word, a thought.

He gently shook me. "Answer me, sweetheart."

"Are we alive?" I managed after a moment.

"Of course. So dramatic." Whit pushed the hair from out of my face, cradling my cheeks in both hands. "Are you hurt?"

I nodded, my vision blurring. Dust coated his face, and he nodded back. His eyes slid shut and panic stole over me. "Whit. Whit!"

He lay still and unmoving. A deep-red puddle pooled underneath his body.

"Whit!" I screamed. "If you die, I will never forgive you."

He opened his eyes, dazed and blinking rapidly. "I'm fine. I was just resting."

Relief made my head spin. If he could talk, then surely it meant he wasn't injured too badly. He flinched as I scrambled off him. Whit groaned, clutching the right side of his abdomen. Blood stained his blue shirt; his hands were already covered in it.

"You are not fine. We have to get out of here." Instinctively, I covered both of his hands and pressed down.

He hissed sharply. "Get off, get off, get off."

"Don't we have to stop the bleeding?" I cried loudly.

"I have not lost my hearing," he gasped between breaths. "The ceiling is about to come down on top of us."

He tried to sit up, his face bleached of all color. I helped him struggle to his feet, his soft groans piercing my heart.

"I have never been shot before," he said in a marveling tone. "I really don't like it."

He tripped, and I dragged one of his arms over my shoulder. "Just a few more feet," I coaxed. "As quick as you can."

He glanced up at the sudden noise rending the air. "Where is Isadora?"

I looked over my shoulder. Only her hand was visible underneath all of the rubble. It lay motionless. I shook my head at him, and his lips flattened. The ceiling moaned and cracked as more rocks fell, crashing around us.

"Go. Without me, go," Whit said, his lips white. "*Go.*"

What utter nonsense. I held on tighter, and he seemed to understand that in order to save me, he had to save himself. He looked murderous. But then his expression turned to one of resignation and he allowed me to keep helping him. We managed to fling ourselves out of the entrance, Whit clutching his side while I tugged on his free hand, down the rocky path and toward the moored boat. Behind us, the sound of the rocks crashed and shattered, and the ground shook under our feet. I helped Whit the rest of the way, step by step, his movements unsteady and stumbling.

"Wait, wait," he said. "I need a minute."

He fought to keep his breathing steady, but sweat dripped down the sides of his face. His hair lay flat across his brow, and his shoulders were hunched, as if he were trying to protect himself from another blow.

"We have to keep going," I said, reaching for him. "You need medical attention."

Whit nodded and allowed me to shepherd him to the boat. I pushed with both hands, and he watched me helplessly as I struggled to get as much of the boat back into the water as I could. I helped him swing his legs over, to which he let out a truly foul string of curses and then dropped inside.

"Face the stern," he said weakly. "The back of the boat."

I did as he instructed and then looked at him again for more guidance. I took up the oars, placing them back into the hooks and awkwardly attempted to navigate us back to Alexandria's coastline. Whit watched me silently, his breathing shallow. "I wish I could help you."

"Don't talk," I said. "Conserve your strength. I'll get us there."

He smiled faintly. "I know."

Then he tipped his head backward, propping it against the opposite bench, and closed his eyes. I was half-terrified that he'd never open them to glare at me again, half-glad that he was actually doing what I asked him to do. My mind replayed Isadora lifting her arm, hand steady and wrapped around the pistol's handle. Her expression of utter hatred when she pulled the trigger.

Whit had pushed me out of the way. Saved my life.

And he could die because of it.

I clutched the ends of the oars tighter. I wasn't going to let that happen.

Before long, our boat was almost at the end of the dock—I could just see it as the sun dawned, turning the sky a resplendent gold. He would be all right. Our driver was waiting for us in his carriage. We only had to make it back to the hotel where I could order the staff to find a local physician.

Whit would not die.

He cracked an eye open. "You're doing great, sweetheart."

"Stop talking," I snapped. The bottom right of his shirt was covered in his blood. It'd never be clean again. "Do you think I should wrap the wound? I could use a petticoat."

Whit seemed highly amused by this prospect. "Aren't damsels always providing petticoats when the hero is in dire straits?"

"Aren't you always telling me that you're not a hero?" I retorted.

He nodded. "You're right. I'm not."

I looked away. I fought hard to remember the moment I learned he had stolen my fortune. It had felt akin to standing on the Philae sandbank, watching as my mother rowed away from me, leaving me behind, taking hundreds of artifacts with her. I had felt enraged and tricked and manipulated.

My mother had left me to my fate.

But Whit had saved mine.

Twice.

He had told me he loved me—but he'd said that to make me jump, surely. Another attempt to manipulate me. I didn't understand him. Why risk his life for me—a woman who would divorce him? Who, for all he knew, hated him? All this time, I had known that he felt some measure of guilt for what he had done, but not enough to apologize. He had told me himself that he would do the same thing all over again.

However.

Now that he was bleeding, slowly dying in front of me, it was hard to be angry at him. Because somehow, I knew that if he could choose whether or not to save my life, he would jump in front of that bullet for me again.

And again and again and again.

He was being so inconveniently honorable.

I channeled all my fear and anger and frustration into rowing the damn boat.

I paced outside the hotel room, up and down the long corridor. The physician had been inside with Whit for several hours. Only the sound of quiet murmuring broke the silence, and the occasional guest who looked at me curiously, dressed as I was in my widow's garb that was now dust and torn in places. Three times now, the staff had come by to offer me tea and a lunch of hummus and fresh-cut vegetables, but my stomach roiled at the sight of the food (though I did accept the tea).

Another hour passed with no word.

With every step I took, my imagination wrought turmoil in my mind. The blood on Whit's shirt. Isadora racing up the stairs after me—and falling. The sight of Isadora's slim pale hand, the only thing visible from the pile of rocks on top of her slight frame.

She was dead, and I knew that her father would not let me live after this.

CAPÍTULO VEINTIUNO

The door opened, and the physician walked out. He appeared calm and collected. His eyes were kind, and his clipped graying hair reminded me of marbled granite pillars. Two of his assistants followed, carrying bloody sheets.

I tried not to stare at the mess.

"Good evening, or is it afternoon?" the doctor asked, rubbing his tired eyes. "I am Dr. Neruzzos Bey."

"How is he?" I asked, my throat tight. I could hardly speak.

The physician jerked his chin in the direction of the hotel room. "Are you related to this man?"

I shook my head, recalled a crucial piece of information, and corrected myself. "Yes, well, I'm his wife."

"He's as stable as I could make him," he said. "The time spent on the boat and the jostling of the carriage did him no favors. But I managed to remove the shattered bullet. I believe I got all of it, but it's hard to be sure. He has a fever, so I recommend cold compresses throughout the day and night. Try to give him water and make him as comfortable as you can. I'll return tomorrow to check his progress." He hesitated. "I'd prepare yourself. An abdominal gunshot wound is serious. Thankfully, there was no harm to his kidneys or appendix. I can't say the same for a section of his intestines."

Terror seized me. The whole time I had paced outside the hotel room, I reminded myself that Whit was strong, that he had survived battles and other wounds. I told myself that he would live. My hands shook violently.

"Shokran," I murmured, my throat dry.

Dr. Neruzzos Bey nodded and brushed past. I stared at the closed door, my nerves shattered, worry pricking at my edges. I inhaled through my nose, trying to brace myself for the worst. After a moment, my heartbeat slowed to normal, and I straightened my shoulders as I opened the door and walked through.

Whit lay on the bed, his face turned toward me. A faint smile touched his lips. I walked three steps and dropped to my knees next to the bed. His eyes appeared sunken, and deep caverns had hollowed out his cheeks.

"How are you?" His voice was barely above a whisper, and I had to lean closer to hear him clearly. He looked at me wryly, as if he knew to suspect that his days were numbered.

"The doctor is incredibly competent and has given me a list of things to do to make you comfortable," I said.

"That's fine," he said breathlessly. "But that doesn't tell me how *you* are."

"You're the one who's dy—ill. I should be asking you how you're feeling," I said through numb lips.

He seized on my misstep. "Dying? That sounds quite serious."

I waved this off dismissively, and for a moment I was impressed by my ability to seem nonchalant, when my mind screamed with terror. His face had lost all color; his skin was clammy, beads of sweat lining his brow.

"Tell me the truth," he said gently.

"I wouldn't lie to you about this," I whispered. "There was considerable blood loss, and infection has set in. You have a fever, and it might get worse before it gets better. Surviving tonight is critical. The physician is coming back tomorrow."

My fingers itched to smooth the matted hair off his forehead. I fought the impulse with everything in me. A part of me wanted to hold on to my anger because I was terrified of feeling anything else for him. My rage didn't scare me as much as my love for him did. But looking at him now, I realized that I was on the brink of losing him. Nothing else mattered except making sure he lived.

"He tried to draw some of my blood," he said. "I wouldn't let him."

It was a tried tactic to dispel any sickened blood from the body, and it made me nauseous to think about. I started to protest, but Whit had closed his eyes, grimacing. The pain he must have been in.

"Will you have something to drink?"

He opened his eyes, which were bloodshot and exhausted and red rimmed. I made the decision for him and gave him a small cup of tepid water. He managed a few sips before dropping his head back onto the pillow with a groan. A moment later, he drifted to sleep. I pulled a chair closer to the bed and reached for his hand. It burned to the touch. For the next hour, I alternated between holding on to him and attempting to stave off the worst of his fever with cold compresses. He shifted, uncomfortable, sweating. The bedding became wrapped around his waist and legs, and I gave up straightening the sheet.

Horror gripped me as I listened to his strained breathing, shallow breaths that cost him. Every single one of them sounded like a pained gasp. I forced him to take a few sips of water through his cracked and dry lips at regular intervals. My palms turned wrinkly from the constant wringing of the damp cloth. Every time I applied it across his forehead, his chest, tension seeped out of him, and the tight lines fanning from the corners of his eyes smoothed away.

Time passed, but I was only aware of it because the staff would routinely knock on the door with fresh cloths, tea, and simple meals for me. My bones ached from sitting up for so long without food or sleep. I would have suffered much worse to never let go of his hand. His delirium persisted through the rest of the day and long into the night. Several times, he called my name. Lack of sleep made my head spin, but I answered every single time, my voice hoarse from my reassurances.

And then, shortly before the dawn of a new day, Whit's eyes drifted open. He stared at me, squinting.

"I haven't left you," I whispered.

He nodded, relief softening the tight press of his mouth.

"You're being ridiculous," I said. "Get rid of this fever immediately and become well."

Whit's dry lips stretched into a smile, as I knew they would. "Where are your manners, Inez? Say please."

"*Please.*"

He turned his head toward mine. "You have bruises around your throat, and there are scratches on your cheeks."

"Isadora fought like a cat," I said.

"This is why I hate them." Whit didn't lose his faint but determined smile, and my heart flipped at the sight of it. "Dogs are wonderful, and humans don't deserve them."

"Stop talking and rest," I said sternly.

"Too much to say," Whit whispered. "I could murder the bastard."

"Mr. Sterling?" I guessed.

"He just had to take all of the ink bottles, didn't he?"

I blinked at him. Ink bottles? What ink—*Oh!* My cheeks burned. I couldn't believe I'd forgotten. I looked around for the lone bottle I'd managed to shrink before Sterling had arrived. It was on the windowsill.

He followed my line of sight. "You've had the ink this whole time?" Whit asked, eyes wild. "All while that doctor pulled a *bullet* out of my stomach? Tried to *drain* me of my blood? Olivera, do you know that I have a *fever*? You must really hate me."

The words ripped out of me. "No, I don't."

They rang between us, and through the haze of his fever, he looked at me in surprise.

"I forgot all about it," I said sheepishly, trying to move past the sudden awkward tension.

"All I need is a drop," he said, panting. "Your mother would use the tiniest amount on any scrapes and cuts or insect bites."

"Those are all minor wounds." I stood and went to retrieve the bottle. I lifted it, examining the liquid closely. It looked like regular ink, deep black. "Will this work on you?"

He licked his lips. "Worth a try. May I have more water?"

I immediately fetched the glass and carefully lifted his head. He took two tiny sips and then shook his head. "No more."

I eased his head back onto the pillow, my fingers brushing against the damp cotton. "Do I put it on the wound? Or do you swallow it?"

Whit twisted his lips in disgust. "It would taste foul. Pour it in the hole in my stomach."

"What if it makes it worse?"

"Have a little faith in the magic, Olivera," he said, gasping. "You can't possibly make it worse."

"That's not true," I said, but I carefully uncorked the bottle. Whit lifted the corner of his shirt, displaying a stretch of tanned, taut skin. The right side of his body had a bandage covering the wound. He lifted it, wincing, the muscles in his stomach flexing.

"Stay still," I said. "This might sting a little."

"Remember just a drop—"

I poured all the liquid directly into the inflamed, punctured skin. The severity of his wound terrified me, and I didn't think so small of an amount would do the job properly.

"*—Goddamn it!*" Whit hissed through his teeth.

I placed the bottle on the nightstand. "Do you want to be distracted?"

"I'm not a child," he said panting. But then his lips twisted wryly. "Yes, please."

One question burned in my mind. While I had stared at him through the night, one word flickered persistently. "Why?"

Realization moved across his wan features. He understood what I wanted to know. "Of all the questions you could ask me, that's the one you picked?" Whit asked, his voice threadbare. "Do I really have to answer that?"

I thought about it. "Yes."

Whit stared at me. He licked his dry, cracked lips again and asked, "I said it to you earlier. Will you believe me if I say it again?"

"Tell me," I said, afraid to hope, afraid to open the door to let him back in. He had left me with nothing. Taken away every wish for a family with him. I was scared to believe him, but I desperately wanted to.

"Inez," he whispered. "You want to know why I saved your life? I can think of no better act to show how much I love you. This world would not be the same without you in it, and I don't *ever* want to find out what that feels like. If I have to follow you across a desert, I will. If I have to jump into the Nile, again and again, I will. If I have to leap in front of a thousand bullets, I will." He closed his eyes, breath shuddering. "I will always love you."

"You love me," I repeated.

Some of the color returned to his pale cheeks. A deep flush of health and vitality. Slowly, he opened his eyes, and they pierced through flesh and bone, finding the heart of me. They were still bloodshot, red rimmed, and weary. But they did not waver from my own.

"Yes," he said. "I'm yours."

I swallowed hard, fear taking a firm hold of me. I wanted to trust him, but would I be able to?

"I have been for a long time," Whit added softly. Very slowly, he reached across the bedding, fingers stretching to find mine. He flipped his wrist, palm open. I stared at the rough callouses. At his blunt hands capable of death, of rescue. Hands that held mine, that pulled me across a dance floor, held me above water, comforted me in the darkness of a tomb.

Right then, I gave in to what I had wanted to do since I'd seen him lying in that bed, the fever raging war against him. I leaned forward and kissed his cheek, smoothing the hair off his forehead. When I straightened, his eyes had once again drifted closed, the smallest smile on his face.

CAPÍTULO VEINTIDÓS

Morning light seeped into the room and I blinked, hazy from sleep. I yawned, stretching my legs, and discovered Whit was alert. He lay curled on his side, his arm having served as a makeshift pillow for my head. He played with my hair, tucking strands behind my ear.

"How are you feeling?" I asked.

"Have a look." Whit lifted the corner of his shirt. The wound had closed up, and the angry-looking veins spreading outward had faded. He'd have a scar for the rest of his life, but he had stayed and lived. I let out an incredulous laugh and then promptly burst into tears.

"You must be so hungry," I said, mopping up my eyes.

"I want a banquet table to suddenly appear in this room," he said. "I want a mile-long buffet table. I want—"

"Understood," I said, laughing again as I immediately got to my feet and walked out of the hotel room, fighting to keep my erratic emotions under control. One of the hotel attendants was coming down the hall with a tea tray, and I gave him a tremulous smile.

"He's feeling much better," I explained at the sudden alarm on his face. He must have assumed my puffy eyes had meant something different. Had I not used the ink bottle, that might have been the case. "May we have hot water sent up, along with fresh sheets? And he'd like breakfast. Boiled eggs, pita bread, that delicious stewed fava-bean dish. Maybe some rice? Oh, and he loves pan-fried eggplants with lots of honey. Actually, please also bring a bowl of honey. And a pot of coffee!"

He nodded and doubled back down the hallway.

"Food is on its way," I said, closing the hotel room door behind me.

"Let me ask you something," Whit said. "Who in Egypt would know about the underground water passageways beneath Alexandria?"

I blinked at the abrupt subject change. I was still in a Whit-had-almost-died headspace. "I left the room for one minute."

"I don't have a pocket watch, so I'll take your word for it."

"Whit."

"Inez."

"You're supposed to be resting."

"We don't have time for me to have a proper convalescence," Whit retorted. "Abdullah and Ricardo are wasting away in prison, while Mr. Sterling is tracking our every move. Lourdes is one step ahead of us, probably *this* close"—he brought his index finger and thumb nearly together, almost touching—"to finding the alchemical sheet, and if your father is alive, he's probably being kept in some damp hovel somewhere."

"Wait," I said, shaking my head. At the lighthouse, I'd had the strongest feeling that he was gone. "You think there's a chance Papá might be alive?"

"I don't know," Whit said softly. "But if he's alive, then the only reason he hasn't reached out to you is because he physically can't. He might be locked up somewhere . . ."

"I've thought that, too," I breathed, hardly daring to hope.

"I know you have," Whit said. "But I also want you to at least think it's possible that he's gone, Inez."

"You've made your point," I said absently, my mind stuck on what he'd said earlier. He loved me, but he clearly still wanted the Chrysopoeia, though I didn't understand why. "Talk to me about the alchemical sheet, Whit."

He blinked. "*Now?*"

"Now. Please."

Whit shifted, getting slowly to a sitting position. His gaze dropped to his hands, clasped tightly in his lap. "I was never given a choice about who I'd marry. She was always going to be wealthy, an heiress, someone to pull my family out of the hole my parents had dug for themselves."

I went to sit by him. "Go on."

"After I was discharged, I spent a lot of time out at night." He flushed. "I'm not proud of that season of my life, but I did happen to learn of an extraordinary rumor. A single sheet with instructions on how to turn lead into gold, written down centuries earlier by none other than Cleopatra the alchemist." He unclasped his hands, his fingers twisting the bedding, and I reached forward to take his hand in mine. "I became obsessed with discovering where it was."

"Why?"

Whit slowly lifted his face, his eyes meeting mine. "Inez, at first I wanted to find the sheet to get out of a marriage I *didn't* want. Now, more than anything, I want to find the Chrysopoeia to save a marriage I *desperately* want."

"The money doesn't matter to me anymore," I said. "It wasn't about that—"

Whit arched a brow.

"Not entirely about that," I amended. "It hurt that you'd lied, that you'd betrayed me. I wanted a family with you, a life together, and you destroyed us before we really got to begin."

"I'm sorry." Whit lifted my palm and kissed it. "I will never derail us again. It's you and me, darling. Forever."

"I believe you," I whispered, suddenly feeling shy.

Whit leaned forward and pressed his lips to my cheek, the softest brush of his mouth against my skin. Then he leaned back and asked, "Any more questions?"

I shook my head. "You were onto something earlier."

"What was it?" Whit tugged at his hair and then snapped his fingers. "Oh, right. The lighthouse. When we were there, you were just coming out of one of Cleopatra's memories," Whit said. "And you were telling me what you'd seen. At some point, Isadora snapped. She heard something that made her break character and fire her gun at you. I think we were on the brink of making a discovery."

I rubbed my temples, fighting to remember exactly what I'd seen. "Let me think," I murmured. "Cleopatra was in a rowboat accompanied by one guard, and he was rowing while she sat behind him, dressed in a dark robe with a hood. Her hands were on the railing—no, wait. That's not true. She was carrying something. It was . . . it was the roll of parchment!"

"The Chrysopoeia," Whit said. "She had it on her, which makes sense. Her brother is trying to reclaim the throne, and he has his sights set on Alexandria. And who knows? He might have been looking for the sheet, too. He was also a descendant of the famous alchemist."

Another part of the memory surfaced in my mind. "Whit, by the time Cleopatra arrives at the Roman tower, she's no longer carrying the parchment roll. Cleopatra had made a turn before arriving at the palace where she could beg Julius Caesar's help against her brother. That's the moment I remember before Isadora started firing at us."

"Exactly what I remember," Whit said. "Which brings me back to my original question. Who do we know that could help us with the underground passageways in Alexandria?" His expression turned to excitement at the same moment a name popped into my mind.

We said it together: "Abdullah."

A knock sounded as my stomach grumbled. "Hurrah, our food is here. Whit, why don't you fill up the teacup—"

He was already up and moving toward the water basin, albeit very slowly. I went to the door, permitting entry to two waiters who brought in a tray laden with covered dishes, a small round table, and an extra wooden chair. The table was placed in front of the bed, the chair on the opposite side, tucked underneath. Together we arranged the dishes, uncovering the array, the savory aroma wafting through the room making my mouth water. Whit tipped the waiters, and they left us to enjoy our meal.

"How long before they answer?" I asked, eyeing the magical cup.

Whit fixed a plate and handed it to me and then piled the second with a truly spectacular amount of food. "I would think soon. There, see?" Whit pointed to the cup with his fork. "It's already working."

Sure enough, the water within the cup was shimmering silver, and when I brought it closer to me, Tío Ricardo's face appeared, distorted from the constant rippling of the surface.

"Finally," my uncle snarled. "It's been days, Inez. And don't think I don't know where you went. Lorena told me everything. Why the hell are you in Alexandria?"

"You've flooded the carpet twice," I remarked dryly. "We had to walk around the room in our shoes or risk sodden stockings."

"No less than you deserve for making me worry," he snapped. "I'm stuck in this room, and you're a hundred miles away, getting into all kinds of trouble, I'm *sure*. And there's been no word. Do you have any idea how that makes me feel?"

I squirmed, absolutely ashamed of myself.

"We've been busy," Whit said between chewing. Somehow, he'd managed to clear half of his plate of food.

"Is that *Whitford*?" Tío Ricardo asked. "Tell that scoundrel he ought to know better— What *is* it, Abdullah?" My uncle turned his face away, and I heard someone speaking in a muffled voice. Tío Ricardo returned to the cup, rolling his eyes. "Abdullah thinks I'm being too hard on you both. And he sends his greetings and congratulations and I don't know what else. Health for all eternity or some such."

I laughed. "Can we speak to him, por favor?"

"Am I not worth a few more minutes?" Tío Ricardo demanded.

Whit paused in his eating and came to sit next to me on the bed. He pressed his temple close to mine and peered into the cup. "It's important, Ricardo."

"Humph," he said, but disappeared. Abdullah appeared in the cup a moment later, looking tired, his face thinner, beard overtaking the bottom half of his face.

"How are you feeling?" I asked, anxious.

"Much better now that I'm seeing you two," Abdullah said. "I am so happy for you both. You make a great pair. Now, if only there was someone I could introduce Farida to. I'd love to see her settled down with the right person—"

"Abdullah," Whit broke in firmly. "We have something we need to speak to you about."

"Oh?"

Quickly, we relayed each of the memories I'd seen, skipping over the events at the lighthouse. My uncle didn't need to hear about Isadora or Whit getting shot. He'd have questions, and neither Whit nor I had time to reassure him.

And anyway, it would be a lie.

I didn't know if either of us would make it out of our present peril alive—a truth that turned my stomach into tight knots. I shoved the worry aside, concentrating on what Abdullah was saying.

"Underground canals?" Abdullah asked. "You must be talking about the ancient cisterns of Alexandria."

"Cisterns?" Whit asked.

"From the days of Alexander the Great when he founded the city, naming it after himself, of course. He was heavily involved in the planning of the city, which included making sure the inhabitants would have access to water. There are hundreds of cisterns that provided the water supply for Alexandrians, and they were connected by a series of canals fed by the Nile. But the canals weren't just used for water—I believe it was Julius Caesar who sent his soldiers below to keep their movements secret when he was quelling the rebellion of Cleopatra's brother Ptolemy the thirteenth."

Whit and I glanced at each other, and I could sense we had been struck by the same thought. It was Cleopatra who had told Caesar about the underground waterways.

"So the underground canals run throughout the city," Whit remarked.

"Yes," Abdullah said. "By the way, everything I know about this underground network of canals I know because of the tremendous work of Mahmoud el-Falaki, a man of many talents: the court astronomer, an excavator, a physicist, and a mapmaker. He was tasked with creating a map of ancient Alexandria, and he was able to correctly place ancient buildings where they were situated in antiquity. Of course, no one in the English-speaking world believes him or has given him the credit he deserves," Abdullah said sadly, shaking his head. His face blurred from the movement, the water rippling sharply.

While all of the information was fascinating, it didn't help us pinpoint where Cleopatra could have hidden the alchemical sheet on her way to the royal palace to request an audience with Julius Caesar. "I don't suppose there's anything else hidden down there," I said.

"Well, now that you mention it," Abdullah said slowly, "there's a story repeated among some archaeologists. But it's just a rumor and not founded on any evidence—only a few scraps of ancient written history."

I leaned forward, excitement pulsing in my throat. "What rumor?"

"The Great Library of Alexandria was one of the most famous libraries of antiquity. It was dedicated to the nine muses of the arts and was a center of learning. It housed thousands of scrolls from not just Egyptian history, but the histories of dozens of countries. Unfortunately, Julius Caesar set fire to Egyptian ships in the harbor, hoping to block Ptolemy's fleet, but the fire spread to a warehouse affiliated with the Library where thousands of scrolls were stored," Abdullah said. "Some historians estimate around forty thousand scrolls were lost."

"That's terrible," I exclaimed, thinking of Cleopatra and how she must have felt to see parts of her city catching fire.

"Well, because of that event, more priceless documents went to the daughter library at the Serapeum, an ancient temple dedicated to Serapis," Abdullah said. "Many of the scrolls from the Great Library were moved there for safekeeping, but here's the interesting thing—there's rumor of a secret library where some of the most treasured papyruses were hidden."

"A secret library?" Whit repeated.

Abdullah smiled. "The lore says it's somehow connected to the Serapeum."

"Serapis and his loyal companion, Cerberus," I said, my gaze dropping to the box of my mother's things. I knew I'd find a map of the ancient city of Alexandria tucked inside, where on a little side street, someone had drawn the figure of the three-headed dog.

"Yes, the two are often connected," Abdullah said. "In fact, I believe there is a carving of Cerberus somewhere at the lighthouse. Interestingly, visitors to Alexandria first had to pay a toll to enter the harbor. Any scrolls or papyruses they brought with them had to be sent to the library in order to be copied. This was how the Great Library became what it was."

"And some of those scrolls moved to the secret library," Whit said. "Could it be underground?"

Abdullah tilted his head, shrugging. "Who knows where the library hides?"

Whit immediately wanted to visit the Serapeum, but the physician arrived, determined to see his patient. I think he believed to find Whit at death's door and was quite astonished to see me yelling at him to stop putting on his boots.

The physician ordered me from the room, since I was apparently aggravating his patient.

I stood in the hallway, hearing the heated back-and-forth between the two, even with the door shut. I knew I ought to go back inside, but something held me back. Instead, I went to the lobby, my steps slow and meandering. Whit would live, and now I didn't have the faintest idea of what to do next. Sometime during the night, when he held on to my hand in a death grip, I had forgiven him for what he had done. It seemed he would always do the extreme to help the people in his life. Steal a fortune to save his sister. Jump in front of a bullet to save me. Fight crocodiles.

The lobby was silent; it was too early for guests to venture out to see the sights. I slumped into one of the available low chairs and stared blankly around me, overwhelmed. One of the attendants took pity on me and brought over a pot of tea, which I sipped as my thoughts whirred.

Isadora was gone, and at some point Mamá and her lover would find out what I had done. They would come after me, seeking revenge, no doubt. I didn't know what my mother would do, and again I thought of Mr. Fincastle and his wide assortment of weapons.

The truth of my situation stared me in the face. Elvira was murdered. Isadora was on that staircase because of me. During the long hours of the night, despair had kept me wide awake at the thought of Whit dying from the hole in his stomach.

Death followed after me no matter what I did.

Terror gripped me so fully my body quaked from it. Because in my heart, I *knew* if I persisted down this path, someone else would die.

I would not risk Whit's life ever again. He was recovering and on the mend, and he was the only one I had left who would stubbornly stay by my side. Even if it killed him.

Everything inside me rebelled at the idea of going after my mother. Except, my uncle and Abdullah would rot in prison for the rest of their lives if I didn't pursue her.

But why did it have to be *me*?

There was someone else who could do that for me. Slowly, I pulled out Mr. Sterling's card and looked at it, contemplating my options. Whit would not want me to contact him. But if I gave Mr. Sterling the means to find my mother, then I created a real chance for Whit and me to get out of this horrible, messy situation alive. I would do anything to not go another day wondering if Whit would live to see tomorrow.

But the idea of turning to Mr. Sterling for help disgusted me.

My whole life, I worked to earn my parents' love and approval. I contorted myself into who they wanted me to be, sure that if they saw the real me, they'd try to change me. It was exhausting constantly pretending, constantly biting back my words, silencing my opinions. When I came to Egypt, I had made my own decisions, and sometimes they had been disastrous, but they were *my* mistakes.

But I fell into the same pattern I always did. I blamed myself for what my mother had done with those artifacts. No grace, no quarter, no understanding. I was done trying to be perfect, done trying to be someone I wasn't. I had instincts that I needed to learn how to trust. And if I took a wrong turn, I was smart enough to look for a better way to go.

Which brought me back to this annoying crossroad. I still didn't know how to save everyone I loved in my life.

"Excuse me," one of the hotel workers said. "Your husband is asking for you."

I looked to the hotel entrance, gripping the card. Then I deliberately tore it in half.

With a shaky breath, I stood and gave the employee the torn halves. "Will you throw this away for me?"

"Of course," he said.

Then I turned my feet in the direction of where Whit waited, and I began to walk.

Whit was sitting up on the bed in clean sheets, drinking coffee, hair damp from his quick bath. When I closed the door behind me, his hands tightened on the handle of the cup almost imperceptibly. He seemed nervous. My watery eyes blurred as Whit patted the space next to him. I went to him, sinking onto the bed, and then leaned against his shoulder. Whit used his sleeve to wipe my face, murmuring soft words, somehow tugging me closer so that I sat across his lap. He smoothed the hair from off my face and leaned down to brush his lips against mine.

Need flared between us.

"Come here," he said, voice hoarse with want.

I glanced at our position, my legs draped over his thighs. "How can I be any closer?"

Whit leveled me with a demanding, impatient look.

That look shot fiery sparks to every corner of my body. It felt like it had been so long since our first time together. That night, he'd taken off his jacket and his boots, laid his gun on the nightstand, and removed his hidden knife. He'd made a handsome armory. This time, he wore only his trousers and a shirt already mostly unbuttoned. There were no weapons between us.

I missed every moment with him more than I had wanted to admit when I'd been so angry at him.

I raised my hand and wrapped it around his neck as he deftly lifted me so that I could straddle him. His mouth moved against mine, kissing me deeply, hungrily, as if he wanted to show me that he really was all right, that he had truly escaped death. I sank my fingers into his hair while his hands drifted down my back until he cupped my bottom and moved me closer. He pressed hot, open-mouthed kisses up and down my neck, and I shivered.

"I love you," he whispered against my skin.

I leaned backward, far enough so that I could stare into his eyes but close enough to still be in the circle of his arms. His hand slid to my thigh, and he tugged my skirt over my knee. Slowly, I unbuttoned the tiny row of buttons on my shirt. Whit fixated on every inch I revealed. He leaned forward and pressed soft kisses on my skin while his fingers drifted higher and higher. A gasp worked itself out of my mouth as my forehead dropped onto his shoulder. I reached for his trousers, and he helped me shift clothing aside before positioning me right where he wanted.

He lifted his head, a silent question in the depths of his blue gaze, and I nodded, breathless. Our wedding night felt like forever ago; I had been nervous, on a mission to outwit my uncle. But tonight was about me and Whit, and the rest of our lives, or however long we had left. I was safe, I was loved. He cupped my cheek and brought my face close to his, kissing me with a tenderness that felt raw and vulnerable. I sank onto him, and his lips moved to brush the shell of my ear as he whispered, "Good girl." Then we were moving together, that last bit of distance between us gone forever.

Whit was my husband, my best friend.

He murmured soothing words against my hair, his hands drifting once again behind me, rocking me slowly. "*Inez*," he said, and my name was a whispered prayer in his mouth. He kissed me deeply, feverishly.

I forgave him, again and again.

He splayed his hands tight against my lower back, and every thought skittered out of reach. I only knew the tender way he stared up at me, the way he kept me close, and the inescapable feeling of losing control as my body took over. I let it, giving in to him freely.

Nothing else mattered except this moment.

I wanted a million more, and I would do *anything* to have them.

We gave ourselves one day together.

One day for Whit to recover fully, for his wound to heal as much as possible, for me to grapple with Isadora's death, and what it meant. We spent most of the day in bed, sleeping and sometimes not sleeping, and somewhere in between, making plans for what came next.

The next morning, the sharp sunlight illuminating our room woke me. I blinked, my cheek pressed against Whit's bare chest, which was rising and falling steadily. He was still resting. Carefully, I shifted away from him so I could look at his wound. It was puckered, the skin less irritated, less of an angry shade of red. The magic had worked, aided by a full day of rest. His soft snoring diverted my attention from his chest and up to his face. Auburn eyelashes fluttered above high cheekbones. His mouth was soft, his wavy hair tumbling across his forehead.

He'd wake up hungry, wanting a full ration of breakfast and black coffee. I could easily arrange that, and with my own stomach growling, the sooner the better. I moved off the bed gingerly, not wanting to wake him. I pulled on the first shirt I could get a hold of and my long linen skirt, which was an olive-green shade that I particularly loved. Stocking and boots came on next, but I left my hair unbound and wild.

Quietly, I collected my purse for the tip and then I opened the door a crack and slipped out of our room. The corridor was empty and still as I made my way downstairs, but the lobby had a few guests dressed for the day. Some stood next to their trunks; others held printed guides for sightseeing.

When all of this was over, I would make Whit take me to every single country I'd been dreaming about visiting since I was a little girl. There were so many cities and ruins I wanted to explore, different foods I wanted to try.

We only had to survive what came next.

I hailed down a hotel worker, another German, who took my order on a slip of paper. "Scrambled eggs, two—no, *three*—portions. Pita bread, honey, butter," I said. "Coffee, black, please, and I'd love any fruit you have that's in season."

"Very good, miss."

"Mrs.," I corrected, smiling.

"Is that all?"

"Room two hundred and six," I said. "Thank you."

He nodded and strode off to the kitchens. I turned toward the grand staircase, but a soft voice in my ear stopped me cold. Something dug into my lower back.

"Hello, Inez," a man whispered. "What you feel is my pistol. Cry for help, and I'll shoot you. Make eye contact with anyone, and I'll shoot you."

I tried to turn, but he pressed his weapon into me farther, and I gasped.

"Not another sound," he said. "We're going to walk out of the hotel without any fuss. Understand?" He jabbed the barrel of his gun into me again. "Or I'll walk up to room two hundred and six and shoot your husband." He leaned closer, his breath skating across my skin, making it crawl. "That was your room number, wasn't it?"

I swallowed hard, unable to rid my mind of the image of Whit bleeding, his hands stained red, gasping for breath, his face turning pale and cold.

"Are you going to cooperate, Inez?"

I nodded.

"Then let's go," the stranger said. He came to stand next to me, placing his free hand around me, the gun hidden underneath his jacket but still pressed tight against my side. I recognized him—he was one of the men who had been with Mr. Sterling. It was then I understood the trouble I was in.

"One foot in front of the other."

Trembling, knees shaking, and palms damp with sweat, I did as he ordered, my only thought on saving the one person who mattered most to me in the world.

Whit. Whit. Whit.

PART FOUR

A RIVER FLOWS UNDERNEATH

WHIT

My wife was gone when I woke. I sat up, bleary-eyed, blinking at the space where she ought to have been sleeping. I glanced around the empty room, at the drawn curtains, and felt that something wasn't right. My gut clenched as I swung my legs off the bed.

That first step hurt.

But I pushed through the unsteadiness, finding my boots under a chair, my shirt slung over the dresser. I tugged it on and then strode to the window to let the sunlight inside. I squinted, waiting for my eyes to adjust to the sudden brightness. Slowly, the room came into focus. Everything looked normal, the trunks stacked.

Her purse was gone.

Where the *hell* was she?

Last night replayed in my mind. I had told her that I loved her. She never said the words back to me. Fear worked itself in my stomach. Maybe she realized she could never forgive me for what I had done.

And so she left me.

Panic tore into me. I tugged on my shoes, shrugged into my jacket, wincing slightly. The gunshot wound had healed as if several months had passed, but it still felt a little tender. I would go after her and get down on my knees if she wanted.

I raced out the door, chanting her name.

Inez. Inez. Inez.

CAPÍTULO VEINTITRÉS

Carriages rumbled up and down the street, and donkeys laden with their burdens crowded the lane, while vendors selling juice and spices and bread called out their prices. The bustling noise surrounded me, and the urge to yell for help overwhelmed me.

"We wait here," the man said.

I licked my dry lips. "What does Mr. Sterling want?"

"Quiet," he said, removing his hand from around my shoulders. The gun stayed where it was, half-hidden. He reached into his jacket pocket and pulled out the same card Mr. Sterling had given me and traced the lettering printed on the surface with his thumb. "He won't be long now."

He was older, and his manner was grim and jaded. Everything about him was dour: his clothing, the turned-down corners of his mouth, the vacant emptiness in his watery blue eyes.

I glanced around nervously, my hackles rising. Despite the morning sunlight, a chill skipped down my spine. A sleek brougham painted black approached. One could trust Mr. Sterling to choose the most formidable transportation available. The driver pulled to a stop in front of us, and through the window, I caught sight of the person I least wanted to see in all the world.

The door opened, and Mr. Sterling leaned forward, tipping his hat to me in mock salute. "Hello, Miss Olivera," he said in his nasally voice. "Won't you come in?"

I eyed him warily, conscious of the gun pressed into my side. Would he truly have his associate shoot me in the middle of the street?

"I really would," Mr. Sterling said, as if I'd asked the question out loud. "I've reached a point of no return, I fear. Now, I'll ask you one more time. Won't you come in?"

"No, thank you; I'd rather stay where I am," I said. "You're here for a reason, I'm sure. Why don't we have our discussion right now?"

"Mr. Graves, if you would?"

The man took a hold of my arm while jabbing me again with his pistol. "In you go, Inez."

"No," I said, squirming. Mr. Sterling was here for a reason—and he was bluffing. He had to be. He wouldn't shoot me before he got what he wanted. And clearly there was something I had that he needed. I wouldn't go easy.

I opened my mouth, inhaling, a scream gathering deep in my chest.

"Remember your husband," Mr. Graves said. "If you don't cooperate, he dies."

My voice abandoned me, and my terror returned. Mr. Graves pointed to the open carriage with his chin, and I took a wobbly step forward, and then another.

I hesitated. Whit would not want me to go anywhere with Mr. Sterling of all people, not for his sake. I heard Whit's roaring protest in my mind. I blinked when I heard that distinct shout again.

Actually, that *was* Whit roaring.

I half turned in the direction of the hotel to find him racing toward me, shouting my name. Mr. Graves let out a sharp curse. The stab of the gun at my side decreased in pressure. Mr. Graves shifted on his feet, turning.

No, no, no.

Instinctively, I spun around and climbed inside the carriage, dropping onto the bench opposite Mr. Sterling. Whit abruptly stopped in his tracks, sand spurting. His jaw dropped, and anguish stole over his face. My heart shattered. I knew what this would look like to him. Mr. Graves came in after me, the pistol in his hand aimed at Whit.

"I'll cooperate," I said. "Please, shut the door. Please."

Mr. Sterling nodded, and Mr. Graves did as he was ordered. Mr. Sterling struck the roof of the carriage twice and the driver clicked his teeth. We lurched forward, gaining speed. I looked out the window, catching sight of Whit as we rolled past him.

"Inez," he yelled, frantically trying to get to me. He skirted around the hotel guests gazing at the scene in unabashed astonishment. "*Don't*—"

"Lo siento," I said. "Go back! Please!"

This, apparently, wasn't a sufficient enough apology, because Whit ran after us, cursing at Mr. Sterling with every step.

"He's a determined young man," Mr. Sterling commented. "Your brute."

"He's not a brute," I said sharply. "You're the one with a *brute*." I inclined my head in the direction of his employee.

"Mr. Graves comes everywhere with me," Mr. Sterling said. "He even carries my guns."

He smiled dourly in my direction, like a crack of lightning that heralded an approaching storm. Whit had seen Mr. Graves murder that young man in cold blood. I scooted as far from him as I could, clutching the handle of the door so hard my knuckles turned white.

The carriage picked up speed, and my stomach twisted in knots. I had only thought of keeping Whit from dying, but now unease flared as I fully realized my situation. "Where are we going?"

"To my office."

"Why?" I asked. "Whit won't stop looking for me. He'll involve the authorities."

"No one can touch me in Egypt, Inez. I thought you knew that. And as for your persistent husband, my men will pick him up at the next block."

I leaned forward, anger blooming in my blood. "If you hurt him, I won't cooperate. I'll make your life miserable—I swear."

Mr. Sterling looked at me passively. "What makes you think you can tell me what to do?"

"Because," I said, "there's obviously something you need from me. Why bother with kidnapping if that weren't the case?"

His lips parted in surprise, then they stretched into a wide grin, his ridiculous mustache twitching. "I got tired of waiting for you to call."

"I ripped your card in half," I said, seething.

Mr. Sterling's eyes flickered to the silent Mr. Graves. A wordless conversation passed between them and then Mr. Graves nodded. A sharp prickle of alarm stabbed the back of my neck. I moved to the door, managing to get it open, but rough hands grabbed me from behind, dragging me backward. I struggled, legs kicking, and I screamed as loud as I could.

Mr. Graves slapped a damp cloth against my mouth and nose.

Three breaths later, my vision dimmed.

And in the next, it went fully black.

I woke slowly, a headache pounded near my temples. Groaning, I sat up, rubbing my brow, swallowing hard. My vision spun as I stumbled to my feet. I was in an elegant room with dark paneled walls and expensive rugs layered on top of one another. A handsome wooden desk faced a leather sofa. I looked at the creased velvet pillow I had been lying on and shuddered, knowing someone had laid me down and covered me with a blanket.

The door opened, and Mr. Sterling strode in, carrying a tray with a steaming teapot and two empty cups. He set it down on the desk and said, "I'm glad you're awake. I trust you had a nice rest?"

"A nice rest," I repeated, shaking my head, feeling sluggish. "You had me *drugged*."

"I couldn't let you discover the location of my office," he said, sounding almost apologetic. "And you look exhausted, if you'll permit me to say so. I think the sleep did you good, even if it was forced."

"I want to go back to the hotel," I said firmly. "Take me there at once."

Mr. Sterling carried the chair tucked under the desk closer to the sofa and then sat down. "I've made other plans, I'm afraid. Let's have tea, and we'll have our discussion. You did tell Mr. Graves you'd cooperate, if you recall."

I opened and closed my mouth, confused by his almost solicitous manner. "Will you take me back to the hotel once we're through?"

Mr. Sterling smiled and gestured to the couch. "Have a seat, Miss Olivera."

"Obviously, you've doctored the tea," I said stiffly as I positioned myself on a cushion. "I will not be drinking or eating anything you offer."

"It has not been tampered with," he said. "Watch carefully."

He poured the tea, filling both cups to the brim. Then he lifted his own and took a long sip.

"I still won't drink the damn tea," I said.

"Well, now you're just being stubborn," he said. "But suit yourself."

He took another sip of his tea, set down his cup, and then proceeded to drink from mine. After proving his point, he settled back against the chair and raised his eyebrows. "You've been up to your usual tricks, searching for clues, getting into scrapes. I have a hard time believing you haven't made any headway in finding out where Lourdes might be."

"I don't—"

He held up a hand. "Before you lie to me, consider who you're speaking with. I have a great many resources at my disposal, I'm well-connected, and I have the funds to employ however much manpower I need in order to get what I want. I only need to say the word, and your husband is dead. I'm in control, not you." He dropped his hand and regarded me shrewdly. "Now, do you want to reevaluate your response and adjust accordingly?"

His unwavering stare unnerved me, while the panic I felt over Whit's safety made me break out in a cold sweat. This man was a liar, a murderer. All my instincts were screaming at me to get out of this room and run for my life. But I couldn't—not without ensuring Whit would be safe from Mr. Sterling's plans.

"You're very confident in my sleuthing," I said. "Suppose I don't know where my mother is."

"Oh, but I think that you have some idea."

"And if I were to share this idea, how do I know that you'll leave Whit and me alone?"

"Because you don't have any other options," Mr. Sterling said. "You've reached the end of the road, *Inez*."

I lifted my chin. "If you hurt Whit, I will never tell you what I know. If you kill me, then you're back where you started. I think you need me more than you're letting on, *Mr. Sterling*."

His dark eyes gleamed with emotion—one I couldn't interpret. He almost appeared to be entertained, as if enjoying a friendly competition.

"All right, Señorita Olivera. What are your terms?"

"First, I'd like to remove myself, and my husband, entirely from this situation," I said. "After today, I never want to see you again."

"What else?"

"Second, I'd like all the artifacts my mother and Mr. Fincastle stole returned to the antiquities department. Hopefully, they will make these storied objects accessible for all, though I have a suspicion that won't be the case. However, better the artifacts and Cleopatra herself are in the hands of the government than sold, piece by piece, to the highest bidder."

Mr. Sterling opened his mouth to reply, but just then, he was overtaken by a fit of coughing. He pulled a handkerchief from his jacket pocket and wiped his lips. Before it disappeared, I caught sight of blood on the fabric.

"You're ill," I said.

"I'm ill," he confirmed. His expression remained devoid of any emotion. "Is that all you want?"

"In exchange for the location of your enemy? Absolutely not," I scoffed. "Third, my uncle has been charged with the theft of Cleopatra's sarcophagus and all of the artifacts residing in her tomb on Philae. We both know my mother and her lover, Mr. Fincastle, were responsible. Once you find my mother, I want you to send her to Cairo where she will face judgment for her crimes so that my uncle and his business partner will go free and have their reputations restored."

"But I don't want Lourdes in prison," Mr. Sterling said mildly. "I want her dead, *and* her annoying associate."

"Then we don't have a bargain," I said firmly. "The authorities will need her alive for questioning, and I won't share what I know if you can't guarantee my mother will make it to Cairo alive." I stood up, smoothing my skirt, and gave him a wintry gaze I hoped would freeze any protest he might make. "Now, take me back to the hotel."

Mr. Sterling regarded me thoughtfully, and then he said, "Sit back down, please."

The mildness of his tone alarmed me. It would have been better if he'd shouted; then I could have truly understood who I was dealing with. Still, I kept my chin raised, my shoulders straight, and shook my head. "I demand to be taken to my hotel."

"You'll want to hear what I have to say. I think you might be pleased with the counteroffer," he said. "Now, will you sit?"

"No. I insist you take me back and—" I broke off, my curiosity flaring. "What is it?"

He nodded as I sank down onto the sofa. I eyed the empty teacup wistfully, wishing I hadn't been quite so stubborn. I was thirsty, but I would be damned if I asked for something to drink now.

Mr. Sterling leaned forward and poured himself whiskey from a decanter on the coffee table, next to the pot of tea. "I will allow your mother to rot in prison, and I will force her to reveal where she has hidden Cleopatra and her cache. But Inez? I will keep it all."

My lips thinned. "That is not—"

"Think it through. You and your husband will be kept safe; your uncle and his business partner will be freed and vindicated."

I tried to protest, but he held up his hand.

"Furthermore, I will personally see to it that your aunt and her daughter, along with your cousin's body, are safely returned to Argentina. Do not forget that you have made enemies here, Inez."

My breath whooshed out of me, and the memory of Elvira dying flooded my mind. I had fought so hard not to remember her lying on the sand, her face destroyed by a single bullet.

"You tried to kidnap me," I seethed, "but took the wrong girl instead."

"Because *Lourdes* had marked her. She sacrificed your cousin, selfishly trying to save your life." His voice dropped to a coaxing whisper. "Accept my terms, and everyone you care about will be saved."

The weight of our conversation pressed against my chest. Everything hinged on what I said next. The terror of messing up overwhelmed me. More than anything, I wanted to be able to look over my shoulder and find Whit, my uncle, or Abdullah standing behind me, telling me what they'd do.

If they'd risk everything on Mr. Sterling's word alone.

"Come now, Inez," he said in that same coaxing whisper. "What's it to be?"

WHIT

That woman was going to be the death of me.

I stared after my wife, hardly believing my eyes. She had willingly climbed into that bastard's carriage. I ran after it, yelling her name until my lungs burned. Why would she align herself with Mr. Sterling? She *wouldn't*. Doubt crept in, and I fought hard to beat it back. It took me a full minute to think it through logically, to make sense of her actions.

I *knew* Inez. She was resourceful, reckless, curious. My wife had conviction and cared deeply for the people in her life. Her family. And that was me.

I was her family.

The night we shared swam in my mind. How she had clung to me, afraid that I'd disappear. That the magic wouldn't work, that I'd end up worse than before. She had gripped my hand through the worst of it, as if by her touch alone she'd save me from death.

Inez was scared. So she'd come up with a plan, a desperate one. One that clearly didn't involve me, but tough shit. All I could do was show up if she needed me.

I only had to prepare for all eventualities.

Three knives, two pistols, and one rifle, the latter of which I tucked into my scabbard strapped to my back. There was the tiniest amount left of the magic-touched ink and I dribbled it onto my wound, howling silently at the wretched sting. I rolled up the sleeves of my shirt and then took one last look, searching for anything else I might need, before locking the room behind me. The lobby was nearly empty as I strode past the front desk, but as I reached the entrance, I stopped, arrested by a sudden thought.

I stood frozen, silently considering.

The consequences would be severe if I was wrong. As in, Ricardo and Abdullah could remain in prison for a *very* long time. But I thought of Inez and what she'd do. My wife was a risk-taker, but more than anything, she had faith in herself.

My gut was telling me to proceed.

I turned and flagged down one of the hotel attendants.

"I'd like to send a telegram," I said.

"Certainly, sir," he replied. "By when?"

"Now."

He nodded and went to retrieve a card and pencil. He gave me both and said, "I'll have someone go to the office as soon as you finish."

I looked down at the blank sheet, took a breath, and began writing. The hotel clerk handed me an envelope, and I tucked the note inside and gave it back to him.

"Thank you," I said.

Mr. Sterling's men were waiting for me the moment I stepped outside of the hotel. Three of them—one with pale blue eyes, another who wore a checkered shirt, and the last with shoes that had been polished to a glossy sheen.

I held up both hands as I walked down the steps, taking each one slow. "Hello, gentlemen," I said pleasantly.

They tensed, raising their arms, hands curled into fists.

It would be quite a show out here in the middle of the dusty street. Using my rifle was out of the question. Already, several onlookers gathered, while women hustled their children out of sight. Polished Shoes came at me first, throwing a punch that I easily sidestepped. I used his momentum against him, yanking him forward, and he stumbled, body bent at the waist, and I slammed my elbow into the middle of his back. He went down hard on his knees, and a swift kick to his ribs sent him toppling over, moaning.

"Who's next?"

The last two rushed forward, fists swinging. I threw my leg around the shorter one's neck, forcing us both to the ground. Checkered Shirt gasped, fighting for air, his neck in the crook of my bent leg. Pale Blue Eyes aimed a kick to my side, and pain shot through to my limbs. Grunting, I clenched my thigh muscle, and Checkered Shirt ceased struggling.

Pale Blue Eyes dragged me up by the lapel of my shirt, and I stumbled to my feet as he threw a punch below my rib cage. I gasped, eyes watering from the sharp ache. I inhaled, focused on my anger, and lurched forward, snarling as I grabbed the back of his neck and brought his face sharply down onto my raised knee. His nose broke, and he crashed to the ground, blood pouring from both nostrils. I used my elbow like I'd done to the other guy, but this time aiming for his upper back, and he dropped with a loud thud.

I straightened, breathing hard, and wiped the sweat off my face with the back of my hand.

One man down, groaning, clutching his ribs, and the last two unconscious. Not bad, considering I almost died recently. I glanced up the street, but the carriage was long gone. That didn't matter.

I knew exactly where that bastard took her.

CAPÍTULO VEINTICUATRO

Don't make me ask you again, Inez. I have no more patience for the little games you play," Mr. Sterling said.

He was more persuasive than a siren luring sailors to their doom. I looked away, biting my lip. No part of me wanted to agree to his counteroffer. However, once my uncle and Abdullah were free, I could go to them and tell them everything I knew about Basil Sterling. How he operated, the name of his known associates, the location of the gate—at least the one I had attended. They'd take the information, and then the search for him could begin, and maybe he'd end up in a cell next to my mother. There was still time to involve the authorities and save Cleopatra's cache from his greedy hands.

"I accept," I said.

"Now, tell me where I can find her."

"She's excavating in a library."

He straightened, his exasperation making his mustache twitch. "Do you take me for a fool? The library was destroyed. Several times."

I nodded slowly. "The one above ground, yes. But there's another."

"Another library?" he asked flatly. "Where?"

"What survived of the collection was moved to the Serapeum," I said. "The daughter library of Alexandria."

He brushed this aside with an airy hand. "Everyone knows that."

"I'm sure you're right," I said. "But did you know my mother is excavating underneath where it had once stood?" I had to force the rest of what I knew past my lips. "There is a system of subterranean canals that lead to an underground secret library."

"You're lying," he said. "I know all about the hundreds of cisterns beneath the city streets, but the Serapeum does not have a secret entrance that leads below ground. That area has been pillaged for centuries. I think I would have discovered an underground library before Lourdes."

"Perhaps she is more clever than you," I said coolly. "I never said the entrance was at the Serapeum. The entrance is several streets over from the ruins, marked somehow by Cerberus. It will lead down to the canals, and the library might be close by from there."

"Might be," he repeated, his tone steeped in skepticism.

"It's the strongest lead I have."

"You're telling me that there is an underground library, and the way to get there is by navigating the sewers of Alexandria?"

I nodded. "Like I said, it's the best clue I have."

"How do I know you speak the truth?" he demanded. "You are too wily by half."

"How do I know you'll keep your word?" I countered. "You're too despicable by half."

He stared at me for a long moment. The seconds ticked by, and I kept my eyes trained on his face, searching for any clues as to what he was thinking.

"Well, then," he said finally. "I suppose we have to trust each other. Excuse me a moment," Mr. Sterling said, getting up and striding to the door. He disappeared, and I bent forward, exhaling deeply.

I felt as if I had made a deal with the devil. I jumped to my feet and began to pace, worrying my lip so hard I almost drew blood. Eventually, more tea was brought, along with a plate of food. My stomach raged at me to eat the pita bread and hummus, the fresh tomato-and-cucumber salad drizzled in olive oil and finished with chopped herbs. But I resisted the temptation.

It might be poisoned.

Instead, I kept walking, throwing a disgruntled look at the locked door and window.

When Mr. Sterling finally returned after what felt like hours, I had to restrain myself from throwing the plate of food at his face.

"You've been gone for hours," I hissed. "It's time for me to go."

"I had Mr. Graves verify your information," he said smoothly.

My breath caught in my throat as I waited to hear the verdict.

"It is as you described," Mr. Sterling said finally. "Very clever of you to put it all together. We found Cerberus at the entrance. It does seem to connect to a larger system of canals."

"Did you find the underground library of Alexandria?"

Mr. Sterling looked at me for a moment, then his eyes dropped to the food. He frowned. "You haven't touched your meal."

"Did you?" I pressed.

"I think it's high time we go and have a conversation with your mother."

"*What?*" I gaped at him. "You found her?" I thought about what that could look like—my mother furious that I had not left Egypt after she had sent me the first-class tickets, and then her volatile gun-loving lover, Mr. Fincastle, more than likely blaming me for Isadora's death.

And Whit and I caught in the middle.

"I told you," I said through gritted teeth. "I don't want to be a part of—"

"But you already are," he said gently. "You've been a part of my plan from the very beginning. You see, Inez, I'm the reason why you're in Egypt at all. I did the one thing I knew would hurt your mother."

"What are you talking about?"

"We're connected in more ways than one," he said, using his chin to point to the golden ring on my finger. "Or did you really think I gave it back to you for no reason?"

I glanced down at it in shock, my mind protesting.

"Some of the magic had also clung to *me* when I first put it on, and I was able to track you down by paying attention to the way the spell sang in my blood, calling to be reunited with that ring. Astonishing, isn't it? A phenomenon that doesn't happen with every object that passes hands, but when it does, a curious link is formed. I believe that same link helped you to discover Cleopatra's tomb. Isn't that right?"

"That's how you followed us to my mother's apartment. It's how you knew where we were staying." I couldn't get the ring off fast enough. I flung it at the chair, disgusted that he had tracked me down as if I were a hare.

"I wondered if you would indulge in a childish fit," he said coldly. "Put the ring back on."

I squared my shoulders. "No."

"Do it, or I'll send Mr. Graves after your young brute."

Revulsion rose up my throat. He was unconscionable. A man without morals or any sense of right or wrong. Clenching my teeth I went to go pick up the ring, but I refused to put it back on. I wanted to fling it far from my person.

As if sensing my thoughts, Mr. Sterling chuckled softly. "Oh, I'm afraid the damage has already been done."

It was as if the worst parts of myself were laid bare at his feet. Guilt gripped me tightly as I shoved the golden ring back onto my finger. He was talking about Cleopatra's tomb.

"Don't feel too bad, señorita," he said. "I wanted you to find her all along."'

The room began to spin. I hadn't noticed before, perhaps thanks to the chloroform, but Mr. Sterling had switched his speech pattern. He no longer spoke in a loud, bombastic way. His voice had turned mild, almost sedate. "I don't understand," I said in a breathless whisper. "What does all this mean?"

"I'm afraid you've been caught in the middle of a war I've been fighting against your mother. But I think it's time for the truth. Don't you?"

He sounded like someone I'd spoken with before. Elegant and refined. I could picture the swirl of tobacco smoke, see a leather chair and the decanters of whiskey lined up on a shelf. "Why are you talking differently?"

"Let me ask you a question, Inez."

I stiffened at the informal tone, at odds with the way he had been speaking to me.

"Do I seem at all familiar to you?"

His question confused me. We had met months ago, on that awful train ride from Alexandria to Cairo. I frowned at him. "In what sense?"

Mr. Sterling smiled faintly. "In the sense that matters." He reached up and tossed his hat to the floor. I stared at it, completely taken aback.

I hadn't expected him to—

He lifted his hands to his balding head and began peeling the skin. I watched, half-transfixed, half-disgusted, as he kept pulling at his scalp to reveal dark hair, shot through with silver, covered by a bald cap. He regarded me intently, light eyes fixed on mine. His hair fell in disorderly curls across his brow, and a feeling of trepidation stole over me.

Mr. Sterling fingered the end of his mustache and slowly tugged it off. He dropped the mustache onto the floor, but I barely noticed. A shimmer of magical energy pulsed between us, faint, like the softest brush of cloth against skin. His light eyes, a cool green, darkened into a rich brown.

I watched in horrified silence as Mr. Sterling became someone else entirely.

WHIT

I wiped the sweat off my brow as I peered around the corner of the same back alley I'd stood in in Turkish Town, mentally cataloguing my injuries. The gunshot wound was taken care of, thanks to the ink bottle. The brawl outside the hotel had left me with a sore jaw and bleeding knuckles. There might be some damage to my ribs—I felt a tug deep in my side.

So essentially, I was fine.

Sterling's building looked innocuous, but I knew my wife was inside. I ducked out of the alley and crept closer. The front door opened, and I quickly ran to the other side of a donkey cart, parked close to the entrance. Mr. Graves stepped out of the house.

"Send messages out now," he said. "I can have ten men meet us at the entry point. If the girl isn't lying, that is."

"I don't think so," Sterling said, appearing behind Mr. Graves. "Where is the carriage?"

"Just around the corner," Mr. Graves replied.

My eyes flicked to the front door, left open. I hadn't seen Inez come out.

"Do you want me to take her with us?"

Sterling shook his head. "No. She'll stay behind in the house with me. We'll bring her later once I understand what we're dealing with. I'll wait for your return before I speak with her again. Don't be gone too long; I'm impatient to finish this." He turned away and disappeared into the house.

The carriage pulled up behind the cart. I shifted, moving around so as not to be seen while Graves climbed into his transport.

I could run inside that house and shoot anyone who crossed my path to save Inez. But it was risky, and she could be caught in the cross fire.

Or I could follow Mr. Graves and see where he would be taking her.

The driver clicked his teeth, and the horses lurched forward. Once again, I moved out of the way, considering my options.

Just as the carriage made a turn down the street, I took off after it in a dead run.

CAPÍTULO VEINTICINCO

Thunder roared in my head. I blinked once, twice, as the room spun again. Mr. Sterling became a man I had loved all my life. A man I had looked up to, a man I'd played with as a young girl, dressing up to perform Shakespeare for the household running the estate in Buenos Aires.

He removed his jacket and the padded belly around his middle, balling them up and tossing them over his shoulder, revealing his rangy build. Tears burned in my eyes, scalding my cheeks as they dribbled down to my chin while I stared into his face.

My father looked back at me, smiling slightly. In his soft voice that I would recognize anywhere, he said, "Hola, hijita."

I bent forward, cradling my stomach. My breath caught in my throat, and I struggled to remain on my feet. I remembered the moment when I'd first read Ricardo's letter back in Argentina, how my throat had felt tight, as if I'd been screaming for hours. It was the same now, and I couldn't get a word out, couldn't take a deep enough breath.

Papá was alive. Alive exactly like I'd hoped. Except he was Basil Sterling, someone I *hated*. The man who had founded Tradesman's Gate.

A criminal, a liar, a con artist. A thief and a *killer*: I recalled Whit's words from the other night when Mr. Sterling—Dios, when *Papá*—had given the order to kill that young man in the street.

Papá coaxed me to the chair, and I dropped into it, the weight of my realization sitting on my shoulders like granite. He laid his handkerchief onto my lap, and I wiped my face and blew my nose. Then he bent and slid his arm around my shoulders. He smelled different, astringent and slightly chemical; instead of a library, I pictured a laboratory. Papá rubbed my back, but I pushed him away.

"Don't touch me," I said.

If he touched me again, I knew somehow my throat would let me scream.

His arm fell to his side, and he eyed me warily.

I didn't want his comfort, or his acidic scent, or his damn handkerchief. I wanted my father, and not this stranger who profited off history that wasn't his own. Not this stranger who was a *murderer.*

But whoever I thought my father was, whatever I had believed, was lost to me forever. All it took was a few seconds, the time it had taken him to remove his appalling disguise. It was incredible how life could pivot so sharply. How someone you thought you knew could turn into a stranger in the space of a breath.

"How long have you been Basil Sterling?" I choked out, my throat still too tight. "How long have you been a *criminal*, Papá?"

He must have read the disappointment in my face because with every word, he became more and more withdrawn. My parents never argued in front of me, but I certainly had raged against them. In anger, Mamá became coldly stern and unmoving. If pushed, she was a screamer. Papá never shouted, never raised his voice above a moderate tone. He would use logic to wear down my arguments. He would reason and coax and turn factual or quote literary giants to support his arguments. I learned early on that it was hard to fight with someone smarter than you.

"How long have you been *him*?" I said at his stubborn silence. "*How long?*"

"I have played the role of Basil Sterling for many, many years," he said. "At first, it was because I grew increasingly frustrated by the antiquities department's inability to staunch the flow of artifacts leaving Egypt. As a government agent, I witnessed firsthand the corruption, and I vowed to stop it—from within."

"How noble of you," I said scathingly.

He ignored my tone. "As I acquired many relics of historical value, I developed quite a name for myself. I knew real power." His eyes gleamed. "Suddenly, dignitaries and collectors wanted what *I* had. At first, I sold anything chipped or defective in some way. Then duplicates, redundancies. Multiple statues of the same god—that sort of thing."

My father always had an eye for business. "And so the money came in."

"The money came in," he affirmed. "I was down a road I never thought I'd travel, and one day I realized that I couldn't turn back." He sat down on the sofa, hooked his foot around the leg of my chair, and dragged it forward. We faced each other as we normally would when we'd discuss our favorite plays or the latest performance at the opera house. I used to ache for his attention, for his love, but looking at him now, I only felt a deep repulsion. "By then, it was too late. I'd done too much, and there was no going back," he said softly. "I had no choice but to keep up the persona."

"There's always a choice—"

"Don't misunderstand me," he said sharply. "I didn't want to turn back."

"So you founded the moving gate," I said bitterly. "And turned away from everything you taught me—respect for our histories, never to cheat or steal or commit murder. Was Mamá a part of it from the beginning?"

He leaned back against the sofa, folded his arms across his chest. The line of his shoulders was tense, his jaw rigid. "Not at first, but she caught on eventually. When she did, I had to loop her into my plans. She had a knack for bringing people together. Forging connections. She persuaded me to grant favors, give discounts." His lips twisted. "Soon, I had the most influential people in my pocket. That was all your mother."

"Then what happened?"

"She proved untrustworthy."

Once again, I thought of the man my father had sentenced to death for making a mistake. Someone who was probably in over his head, not knowing he dealt with the devil.

I was suddenly sitting too close to him. This room felt too small with him in it. But my mind spun with questions, and I wanted to know more. "You mean the affair."

"It was more than that," he said. "But essentially, yes. She failed to report back regularly, failed to show up when I needed her. She became too busy for me, and her visits to the excavation sites were infrequent. When she did turn up, her behavior was unacceptable."

"What do you mean?"

Papá looked at me steadily. "That part will have to remain between me and Lourdes. Suffice it to say, I found her cold demeanor off-putting. During her last visit, I followed her back to Cairo and discovered the affair." His fingers dug into his arms, knuckles turning white. "I learned of her little family, complete with another daughter. It wasn't until I met her here in Alexandria with you that I put together who she was. A charming little reprobate. Isadora was her name, wasn't it?"

Mutely, I nodded, noting his use of past tense. Briefly, I wondered how he had known what happened to her at the lighthouse. But an event like that would not have gone unnoticed for long.

"Well," Papá said with an icy smile, "I can't say I'm sorry she's dead. How did she die? Does it have something to do with the bruises on your neck?"

I remembered the way Isadora had wrapped her hands around my throat and squeezed, the panic I'd felt the moment I realized I wasn't getting enough air. "She fell," I said, my voice hoarse.

"She fell," he repeated. "And the bruises?"

"It doesn't matter anymore," I said.

"It does to me."

I brushed this aside. If his words were supposed to reassure me of his fatherly devotion and protection, it was too late for that. I didn't want either of those things from him.

"Finish telling me about Mamá," I said. "What happened after she betrayed you?"

Papá studied me, and I could tell his mind was working furiously. "I know you've questioned our decision to never bring you with us to Egypt. Throughout the years, you would beg, cry, rage at us to let you come along."

"I remember."

"It was your mother's idea to never let you come with us, and I went along with it, because, well, I understood her reasoning. I gather you would have made up some reason for why she wanted you to remain in

Argentina?" He unfolded his arms and leaned forward, elbows resting on his knees. I was struck by our similarities, the way our hair curled wildly, our inquisitive and curious natures. An ache bloomed in my heart, tearing it wide open.

A yawning wound I knew would never heal properly.

"Inez?"

I shook my head, tried to clear my thoughts. "Mamá felt it was too dangerous," I guessed.

Papá nodded. "Yes. We've acquired many enemies during our joint venture. But that wasn't the main reason. Or to put it differently, we each had our secret reason for why we didn't want you to come to Egypt. Your mother didn't want you to see who she really was—an adulteress, a thief. She wanted you to have the idea she had shaped of herself, perfect in every way. A real lady." His tone had turned caustic. "Respectable, admired."

"And your reason?"

Papá smiled. "That will come later. But suffice it to say, it all hinges on what you do next."

"I don't understand."

"I don't need you to right now," he said. "What I do want you to understand is that your mother tried to destroy me. And so I retaliated, hurting her where she's most vulnerable by doing the worst thing I could think of."

"What was that?"

"I made sure you would come to Egypt."

There was a knock on the door.

Without looking away from my face, Papá said, "Enter."

Mr. Graves peered around the door. "It's time. Everything is set up."

"Is she there?" Papá said, his dark eyes still trained on mine.

"They both are."

Papá stood up and extended his hand toward me. "It's time to go, Inez."

"I don't want any part of this . . . this war between you and Mamá. I gave you what you wanted. Now you must honor our terms and send her to Cairo so—"

"There is no honor among thieves," he said. "You are coming with me, hijita."

Mr. Graves came forward, a pistol in his hand.

"You would shoot your own daughter?" I whispered. I couldn't believe that he would actually do something so horrific.

Papá looked me over, studying the lines and curves of my face. "I raised you as my own. But ever since I found out about the affair, my plans for you have shifted. Your mother is a whore, and I don't believe Mr. Fincastle was her first paramour."

"No," I whispered. "You don't think . . ."

"I'd be a fool not to ask the question," Papá said gravely. "Whose daughter are you? Mine or someone else's? You very well could be my own child. My own blood." Then his face hardened; deep lines flared outward from the corners of his eyes. "But you might also not be." He flicked his head toward the door, and then motioned for me to get up. I obeyed in a kind of daze. "Either way, why don't we go ask your mother?"

I felt as if I'd been dealt a mortal blow, but somehow, I was still expected to walk and talk and take orders. I was still expected to breathe after he casually stated that I might not be his flesh and blood. Yes, I mostly favored my mother in my looks, but I never questioned whether I was his child. We both loved reading Shakespeare, getting lost in stories, or learning about the past.

It couldn't be true that I wasn't his daughter.

But even if it was, would he murder a child he'd raised?

Mr. Graves jabbed the tip of the gun deep into my back, and I jumped.

"I'm afraid I have more patience than he does," Papá said. "I would do as he says."

Then he collected his disguise from off the floor and once again became Mr. Sterling. As he fixed his awful mustache, realization slowly dawned on me.

My father had died the day I received my uncle's letter. There would never be a moment when I'd look at Papá and not think of Mr. Sterling, his alter ego. A man he'd created who used violence to get what he wanted, lies to become more powerful, and coercion to acquire information.

The man I had loved all my life was gone forever, and what killed me most was that I had never known who Papá was at all, or what he was capable of.

If I had, maybe I could have protected myself from ever loving a monster.

We took another carriage, and once again I found myself seated next to Mr. Graves. They blindfolded me. They must have believed that with the gun pointed in my direction, I would not make a fuss. But I was reeling from our conversation, and I couldn't sit still. I wanted out of the brougham; I wanted out of my father's heinous plans.

"Do *not* fidget, Inez," Papá said.

I swallowed hard. "Why didn't you reveal who you were earlier?"

"You had only just arrived, and I needed to see how you would fare," he said. "I watched you from afar and observed who you were without your mother or me there to guide or admonish your behavior. I sent you the golden ring, wondering if the magic would leach into you, like it did me."

"Is that the proof you were looking for?" I asked bitterly. "To confirm our blood was the same?"

"It certainly helped, but magic is fickle, and I couldn't rely on it entirely," he said. "I kept tabs on you while you walked through the bazaar and felt joy when the magic lured you to the same trinket vendor I had visited." His voice dropped to a disappointed hush. "But then you disappeared. No one knew where you had gone. My men searched your hotel room and found that you'd left your trunks behind. Clothes, books, most of your art supplies."

That was when I had stowed away on the *Elephantine*. "Why didn't the magic lead you to me?"

"You'd traveled too far," he said. "And I realized you must have gone with Ricardo to a secret excavation site—which could have been anywhere in Upper Egypt. Thanks to his brute aide-de-camp who spread rumors of several dig locations down the Nile."

Whitford. I couldn't help my small smile.

"A dishonorably discharged soldier for a husband. I'm so proud, Inez."

I flinched at the harsh reprimand.

"That is your mother in you," he continued. "When I'd found out that she had stolen Cleopatra from me, that you had helped her—well, I admit I lost my temper."

"Cleopatra never belonged to you," I said. "She doesn't belong to anyone."

"Well, thanks to you, she's in your mother's ignorant hands. I realized then that you were doing more damage to me than I had anticipated. I had hoped you'd act with more sense. But you disappointed me, Inez."

"Is that when you ordered my kidnapping?"

Papá tugged the blindfold off me. I blinked several times, waiting for my eyes to adjust. It didn't take long; a quick glance out the window revealed a darkening sky. We were in the outer city limits of Alexandria, the field of ruins spreading out in every direction. Fallen columns and small hills peppered the expansive area. I turned my attention back to my father.

"It was," he said. "I saw you at the New Year's Eve party and gave the order for a dark-haired young woman in a gold dress to be brought to me. But your mother intercepted my men and marked the wrong girl. I had no use for Elvira."

Fury tightened my hands into fists. "You had her killed."

"No," he said. "Your uncle did when he refused to tell me where Lourdes had gone."

"He didn't know," I exclaimed, leaning forward.

Mr. Graves swung his arm forward and pushed me back against the seat with a violent shove. I gasped, trying to wiggle away, but he wouldn't budge.

"I was sorry to hear of her death," he conceded. "Entirely avoidable."

I let out a sob, shutting my eyes. It didn't matter—tears swept down my cheeks, and I hated my display of emotion, of vulnerability. He didn't deserve it.

Mr. Graves let me go, and I slumped forward, shuddering.

"When I made my offer for you to join me in my search for Lourdes, it was a sincere one," Papá said. "I had hoped you'd have seen through her charms to discover the snake underneath. But you've stubbornly resisted the olive branch I offered, time and time again."

"It would have been better if I believed you to be dead," I whispered. "Why didn't you stay that way?"

Papá caressed my cheek, but I jerked out of his reach. "Do you want to know my reason for having you stay away in Argentina?"

It wasn't a question. I really ought not to give him the satisfaction, but I couldn't help asking, "What was it?"

"It's simple, Inez," he whispered close to my ear. "I've built an empire, and I didn't know if I could give you the keys to my kingdom."

"That's why you kept asking me to join you," I said. "You were hoping to see . . . what, exactly? If I was corruptible?"

"I need an heir. Someone I could trust to help with my legacy."

I shook my head, inching away from him. "I want nothing to do with you."

"You might change your mind," he said mildly. "After our conversation with your mother." He turned in his seat, peering out the window. "Ah. I believe we're here. Time to go underground, Inez."

He opened the door and took the crook of my elbow in a firm grip and led me out and down onto the street. Dread built up inside me, brick by brick, as my father tugged me toward a nondescript well, big enough for one person to fit through. I took a closer look, and to my amazement, someone had carved the word Cerberus along the lip of the well.

Behind me, I sensed Mr. Graves's looming presence. A glance over my shoulder confirmed him hovering close, carrying two lanterns. He handed one of them to my father.

Papá eyed my clothing. "I'm afraid you won't be comfortable traversing the canals in your current dress."

"As if you care about my comfort," I snapped.

Mr. Graves gestured toward the gun in his holster. "She ought to go in first."

Papá looked through the hole. "There seem to be steps carved into the stone. I'll climb down first. Keep an eye on her. If you need to shoot, make sure she can still walk afterward."

My jaw dropped as he disappeared below.

After a moment, Mr. Graves motioned for me to follow, the gun pointed at my face. I was confident that I would not still be able to walk if he were to pull that trigger. He lowered the lantern and, with his free hand, shoved me toward the entrance, my skirt tangling around my legs. With a sigh, I bent to grab the hem.

"Slowly," he barked.

I gathered the fabric, and took my time straightening. Then I climbed up and over, my foot easily reaching the first step down into the hollowed-out world below. At the bottom, Papá helped me the rest of the way, and we silently waited in the dark as Mr. Graves brought down the lighting. We seemed to be standing on a raised platform, rectangular in shape.

By the time he made it to the floor, portions of the chamber were illuminated. The sound of rushing water drifted upward, and I gasped at the sight. It was as if I stood in a subterranean Gothic cathedral. We were on the upper level of three stories. Dozens of ancient columns, spaced equidistant from one another to form a grid, were linked by carved arches that framed vaulted ceilings at the top floor. It looked like a massive checkerboard, one on top of the other, with a column situated at every corner. The pillars were capped by ornately carved marble capitals in various architecture styles (Tuscan and Corinthian) featuring delicate leaves. There was no floor, but the top of the arches from the second and first levels provided a narrow path, the width of two feet, to allow passage. My fingers itched to draw the space; I'd never seen anything quite like it.

"Where to?" Papá asked.

Mr. Graves indicated to the left with one of his lanterns. "This way. The rest of the men are waiting for our arrival. Once we pass this section, there is a makeshift wooden platform that extends out to where we need to go."

"And on what level will we find them?" Papá said, walking carefully forward.

"The bottom, right above the river water," Mr. Graves said. "We'll have to climb down at some point with a rope."

I peered over the edge of the platform, the lanterns providing enough light to see the columns directly below us. Farther than that, it remained stubbornly pitch-black.

Pity I only just discovered a fear of heights.

Shuddering, I inched away on shaking knees. Papá stepped onto the walkway and nimbly crossed the first square. On either side was open air, divided by the next square shaped by the top of the arches from the network below. Once he reached the column on the other side, he had to step around the base and aim for the path on the opposite end. It was a careful dance. One wrong step, and gravity would reach her lethal hand to pull you down three stories. Mr. Graves indicated I ought to follow, but I quickly realized my skirt would make it difficult to navigate the narrow path.

To hell with propriety. I did not want to fall into the sewer.

I worked the buttons of my long skirt, but Mr. Graves let out a sharp warning. "Do not. Your father would not like you improperly dressed."

"I might fall."

"Lift your skirt higher and walk carefully. Now *go*."

I let out a shaky breath and once again gathered the fabric. Fear worked itself under my skin, making my heart race. The rushing of the water roared in my ears. I swallowed hard and took the first step onto the path, keeping an eye on my father as he traversed the gloom.

We made our way silently. I gripped my skirt tightly, my palms beginning to sweat. The air tasted stale and wet, the sound of the hidden Nile a constant presence. Every now and then, we passed a large spout that shot water where it met with the sewer below. An eerie waterfall in the near dark.

"Remarkable," Papá called backward. "This used to be Alexandria's water supply, dating to the city's founding. Of course, the water isn't drinkable now, thanks to years of neglect. Can you picture Julius Caesar walking this same footpath?"

I peered up at the crumbled capitals above us. To my left, there were missing pillars, disrupting the grid. "Are these structures safe?"

"Doubtful," Papá said. "I'd take care if I were you."

I glared at his back before dropping my gaze to the path. I could not afford a misstep. Terror gripped me as I inched forward.

"Quicker now," Mr. Graves intoned. "It's not much farther."

Another ten minutes, and Papá reached a section that had a long rope looping around it. He lowered the lantern for a closer look. A system of pulleys provided extra support and leverage. Papá had seemed dauntless, leading us deeper and deeper under the city of Alexandria. But now he stopped and turned to frown at Mr. Graves, who waited behind me.

"Surely there is a better option," Papá hissed quietly.

"There is not," Mr. Graves whispered in his gruff voice. "If you pull, there is an extra loop that serves as a kind of seat. It was the best we could come up with, given the time available."

Papá's lips thinned, but he bent and yanked on the rope, tugging until the extra loop came into view. The sound reverberated like thunder. My father slowed his movements and proceeded more quietly. He situated himself onto the makeshift seat, awkwardly pushing at his fake belly to give himself more room. Papá was not a young man, but his years in Egypt had kept him active and adept at handling the warmer climate.

Papá jumped off the ledge, and I let out a gasp. But the rope held as he swung in the air, anchored by the pulley. He tugged on the rope, one hand over the other, and slowly lowered himself. It took a long while, and my legs ached, tense from keeping balance on the narrow path.

"You're next," Mr. Graves said.

"May I have the lantern?" I asked.

"You may not," he said. "Here comes the seat. Go on, now."

I fought the whimper climbing up my throat, but I stepped forward, slowly, and crossed to the rope. I put my head and shoulders through the loop and tugged it down until it cupped my bottom. I shortened the loop, feeling it tighten. This was, by far, the scariest thing I would ever do. I was sure of it.

"Jump, Miss Olivera," Mr. Graves said in a tone that brooked no argument.

My body quaked as I inched to the edge. I stood far enough from Mr.

Graves, who held the only source of light, so that when I looked down, I saw nothing but pitch-black. I was going to step into utter darkness, suspended in the air by one measly rope.

"Do it," he said, cocking the gun. "*Silently.*"

Whit's face swept across my vision, and I pretended he waited for me at the bottom. I heard his warm voice when he had taken me into the cave to show me a secret painting on the wall, hidden for centuries. A Christmas present for me. He had kept me safe, with a firm grasp on the rope. I pictured him holding it now.

My imagination would not fail me.

I leapt off the path.

CAPÍTULO VEINTISÉIS

I bit my lip to keep myself from crying out. The rope tautened, snapping against the archway. I held on to the loop with both hands as if it were a swing. I leaned forward, balancing, and reached for the other rope, barely visible from the lantern's light. Then I pulled, imitating my father's hand-over-hand motions, and slowly lowered myself down, down, down. The light dimmed with every foot I descended.

By the time I made it to the second level, I could not see at all. I scraped past the footpath directly below the one I just jumped from and kept going. My hands were slick with sweat and the rope burned my palms, but I dared not let go.

More than anything, I wanted Whit to be at the bottom to catch me in case I fell.

I pushed myself to keep going. To breathe through my fear. I wanted this part over, and I never wanted to do it again, as long as I lived.

Hand over hand.

Foot by foot.

"You're almost done," Papá called up softly. "Follow the sound of my voice. A few feet to go."

At last, my boots touched the floor. Tears pricked the corners of my eyes, and I inhaled deeply, shuddering from relief and exhaustion. By the time I stepped out of the loop, flinging it away from me as if it were a coiled snake, my entire body refused to stay upright. Papá came forward, wrapped his arm around my waist, and held me up.

"Don't fall into the water," he said urgently. "Lean against the wall if you have to. I need to send the rope back up for Mr. Graves."

He released me, handing me the lantern, and I slumped against the stone. Three feet in front of me, the walkway ended abruptly, and I could see the rush of water sweep past. We waited for Mr. Graves to join us, and our procession continued with Papá once again leading the way and the odious Mr. Graves at the tail. There was no time to admire the intricately designed surroundings as they set a brisk march that nearly left me out of breath.

"Up ahead, make a right," Mr. Graves shouted over the roar of the water.

Papá made the turn and I followed, nervous energy making me jumpy. I was unprepared for what waited for me: ten men, dressed in various dark colors from black to dour gray; they wore caps perched low over their brows, and most of their shirtsleeves were rolled up to their elbows.

"Where's the library entrance?" Papá asked.

"Up ahead," Mr. Graves repeated, coming to stand in front of the group. "All these men are armed with rifles or revolvers, knives and daggers. How would you like to proceed?"

"Possible to surround the site?"

Mr. Graves nodded. "There's no exterior wall to the library, only one archway that was designated the official entrance, though you can enter from the other canal paths converging at this point. Once you're farther inside, there are walls lined with rows and rows and rows of shelves. This stretch of area is covered by a wooden floor, but sections have decayed and broken off, revealing the water underneath. Seems a curious place for a library."

"A desperate move," Papá mused. Though he whispered, I could still detect the potent excitement threading his voice. "But how else to protect the marvels librarians and scholars amassed throughout millennia? Through countless fires, wars, protests? What an extraordinary undertaking to transfer the world's wealth below ground. I suppose it must have been the Greeks who decided the extreme measure was necess—"

"Sir," Mr. Graves murmured. "I hate to interrupt, but perhaps we ought to press on while we have the advantage?"

The men were huddled, shifting on their feet, restless.

Mr. Graves indicated one of the paths. "Two men with Mr. Sterling, if you please. I'll remain with Miss Olivera at the middle, and the rest follow behind. I want not a sound from any of you. Understood?"

The men nodded and quietly situated themselves as directed. Papá set off, flanked by his two guards, and then Mr. Graves flicked his gun, indicated I ought to follow. I did so, conscious that he remained close, the gleam of his weapon reflecting in the glow from the lantern. To my left, the water roared, creating a humid atmosphere that felt as if I were in a steam room. My shirtsleeves clung to my damp skin.

More than once, Whit's face popped into my mind.

I had left our room to order breakfast, never imagining that in a span of minutes, I'd be forced out of the hotel. He would be furious, desperately searching for me, and I would have given anything to hear him shout at me instead of the steady thud of our footsteps as we followed my father, a general waging war against my mother.

We had to pick our way through debris, columns tumbled to their sides, the ends falling into the water. Giant chunks of stone blocked our path, and we had to climb up and over in order to press on. Sweat slid under the collar of my shirt, and I wiped my face with my sleeve. It was undignified, but I didn't care. It was hard to see when—

My foot caught on an overturned rock, and I stumbled into one of the men who trailed after my father. He windmilled his arms, catching his balance, and then turned to glare at me.

"Bitch," he muttered.

A second later, his eyes widened as he pitched to the side, arms outstretched toward me, fingers grasping air before he tumbled into the water. He screamed as the river carried him away, and he waved his hands desperately, fighting to stay afloat.

"Stop," Mr. Graves barked. He took ahold of my arm, nails digging in, and swung me around to face him. "What the hell happened?"

I gaped at him, stunned by the incident. It had happened so fast. "He fell."

He jerked me forward, his harsh breath blowing into my face. "You pushed him."

"No," I said, trying to wiggle out of his grasp, but his grip never slackened. I'd have bruises marking my skin from his tight hold. "I didn't. I *swear—*"

"He tripped," came a low voice from behind me. "Saw it clearly."

I froze, my lips parting in surprise. Every word of protest died on my tongue. A tremor shook my body, and I fought to keep my wits.

That voice.

I'd heard it whispered against my skin, murmured soothingly in the dark, yelled in exasperation. I'd know it anywhere, even below ground.

"Fool," Mr. Graves said disgustedly. He narrowed his eyes at the man behind me, but then his attention veered to the others surrounding us. "Keep going, and for God's sake, watch where you step."

He tugged me forward, and I tried to look over my shoulder. But I didn't need to—I knew who had come for me.

Whitford Simon Hayes.

A wave of emotions struck me. Relief, because I wasn't alone anymore, followed quickly by terror.

I wanted to yell at him.

I wanted to kiss him.

Since I could do neither, I stayed silent and focused, my thoughts whirring on how to get us out of here. I knew Papá would use me as leverage until he learned where Mamá had hidden away Cleopatra and the artifacts. I also knew that Mr. Fincastle had most likely brought an entire armory to serve as their defense should they be discovered.

I trembled at the thought of a gunfight erupting in such an unstable environment, surrounded by the water below and that which was coming down from the frequent spouts. Dread formed a knot deep in my belly.

Death would find me down here—I was sure of it.

We marched until we came to a tall statue of a man in billowing robes, his hand resting lightly on a three-headed dog. He had been placed in front of an ornate arch, depicting rolls of parchment. Greek letters were engraved following the curve.

"Serapis," Papá whispered. "Astonishing."

My father's face was a frozen mask of triumphant joy. Only his eyes moved, flickering from one thing to another, desperately reading every inch of the entrance. But then he straightened his shoulders and looked to Mr. Graves.

"We take them by surprise," he said. "How many are within?"

"Obviously the two of them," Mr. Graves said. "And three workers and one guard. My impression is they hoped to keep their discovery a secret."

"Excellent," Papá said. "Secure the area, and Inez and I will follow."

Mr. Graves nodded and motioned for the men to walk through. He pointed to the man behind me and said, "You I want with me." Terror scored my heart. I felt, rather than saw, Whit's hesitation. I knew he didn't want to leave, but with my father's armed men surrounding us, he would not risk me.

Finally, he brushed past me, his cap sitting low across his brow. His finger found mine for one fleeting second, hooking around my pinky for one breath. I felt his desperation, his fury in that single point of contact. He released me, and together with Mr. Graves, they walked through the arch.

"It will only be a moment," Papá said.

I tore my gaze from Whit's retreating back. It was then that I realized my father had a pistol pointed at me. My entire focus narrowed to the gun in his hand. That same hand had held me as a child. I lifted my eyes and met his, expecting to see some flicker of emotion. Regret, maybe. Grief. But there was neither. He looked back at me with a mixture of resignation and determination; there was nothing soft about his expression. Perhaps he knew we would always come to this moment.

A father threatening the life of his daughter.

We stared at each other for an interval of time. I didn't dare make any sudden movement; I instinctively knew he would not hesitate to pull the trigger if I became difficult.

"Why?" I asked finally. It felt as if I'd lived several lifetimes.

"You are my leverage," he explained. "If your mother cares more for you than her treasure, I believe you will survive this night."

A shot rang out. Then another. And another. The sound crashed around us, louder than the Nile. My pulse thrummed in my veins, and I snapped around.

My father grasped my arm, tugging me close to his side. "Let's see if we can stop the shooting, shall we, querida?"

Papá lodged the barrel of the gun under my chin, and we walked beneath the arch, passing more columns placed in the same checkerboard pattern. These held guttering torches, illuminating our way. Whole sections of floor were rotting under my feet. Soon, we came to a place where the spaces between the pillars were filled with shelves that held hundreds of rolls of parchment stacked on top of one another. Incredibly, my father ignored every single one, half dragging me along, the barrel pressed hard against the underside of my jaw. Because we still followed the checkerboard pattern, we passed square-shaped rooms through narrow doorways that allowed passage from one to another. The deeper we went, the walls became more sporadically placed, forming larger square rooms, and then eventually, rectangular-shaped ones. I imagined it looked like a veritable maze from up above.

"Each room is labeled by topic," Papá breathed. "We've passed poetry, law, history, tragedy, and medicine. This is *astonishing*."

"Not for me it isn't," I hissed.

"Quiet," Papá said. "I think I hear . . . Yes, that's Mr. Graves."

"Take a left and you'll find us," Mr. Graves called out.

Papá pulled me into the room, the pistol's barrel cold against my skin. Another bruise would bloom tomorrow from Papá's constant jabbing.

Provided I lived to see tomorrow.

The scene before me was a horrifying tableau. The room had opened up considerably, and farther down, the canal came into view. Three spouts poured water, the noise thundering. It seemed to me we were on the outskirts of the library. The light coming from dozens of torches showed everyone clearly.

Three Egyptian workers sat on the floor with one of my father's men guarding them with a rifle in his hands. There was one man who had been shot in the head. He lay sprawled on the floor, his blood staining the wood.

He must have been the guard Mr. Graves had mentioned.

The rest of my father's men had their weapons trained on two people, standing side by side. Mamá and Mr. Fincastle. A pile of knives, two pistols, grenades, dynamite sticks, and a rifle with a leather strap lay in front of his feet. I spotted Whit, still in disguise, directing a look of fury at Papá. It chilled my blood. He would risk his life to save mine. Fight tooth and nail, despite his recent near-death experience.

Slowly, I let my gaze fall on the one person I had been searching for ever since she had left me standing on the banks of Philae.

Mamá.

WHIT

The bloody idiot had brought dynamite down here. No, not just dynamite, but also grenades. I wanted to run toward Inez, but I forced myself to stay still, the gun steady in my hands. The men flanking me were restless, sweat dripping down their faces.

Nervous.

Painful memories pushed their way into my mind. Friends who had been just as nervous the moment before the first shot had been fired.

How the *hell* were we going to get out of this alive?

I was going to throttle my wife when this was over. Right after I kissed her senseless. If we made it out alive, I was never going to let her out of my sight.

From the corner of my eye, I caught Lourdes shifting her feet, and my attention flicked over to her. She met my gaze coolly. A sudden tension in her jaw revealed that she had recognized me. She dropped her gaze to the grenades and then flicked her eyes back to mine.

I gave her an imperceptible shake of my head. We were surrounded by water, the ground was rotting beneath my boots, and any blast would topple the columns.

It was ludicrous to consider it.

Then Mr. Sterling spoke, yanking Inez forward, his weapon lodged underneath her delicate chin. Anger burned through my body, as if I were lit from within, an inferno moments before an explosion. My hands shook from it.

Inez looked between me and Lourdes, unerringly seeing past my disguise—cap low on my head and a jacket that didn't fit properly. My wife would know me anywhere.

And in the second our eyes met, I could see everything she couldn't say out loud.

Fear for my life. Hope that we would survive the night. Trust that I'd stay by her side, no matter what happened. Love for me.

My hands stopped shaking, my entire being focused on one thing: I would not let her die. I would burn the world twice over to save her life.

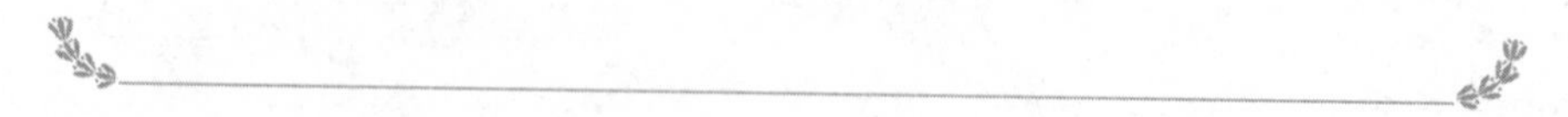

CAPÍTULO VEINTISIETE

Mamá's hazel eyes latched on to mine. She kept her face rigidly composed, but I sensed her frustration and anger. Some of it was directed at me. In her way, she had tried to save me, time and time again. But I had refused to be saved by her.

"Hola, Lourdes," Papá said, dragging me forward. His tone sounded almost conversational. It was only because I knew him that I could hear the subtle stab of anger. "¿Espero que estés bien?" Then he let out a queer little laugh. His breath tickled my cheek. "But I'm being rude speaking in Spanish. I trust you have been well?"

"Why don't you say what you came down here to say, Cayo?" Mamá said. "We can skip the pleasantries; I know you don't mean any of them."

"Where have you hidden her?" he asked softly. "If you tell me, we can avoid any more unpleasantness." He indicated the dead guard. "I will, of course, keep Inez with me to verify that you're telling me the truth."

Mamá's attention flickered back to me. "I know you received the tickets I sent you."

"Don't answer her," Papá said. "Lourdes, recall that I am not patient."

Her eyes flashed. "Oh, I remember."

"Where is Cleopatra?"

"She won't tell you," Mr. Fincastle snapped. Then he glanced at me, frowning slightly. His eyes drifted over my shoulder as if he was expecting to see someone else.

With a start, I realized who that would be.

"Are you looking for your daughter?" Papá asked. "I happen to know her whereabouts."

Oh no. I squirmed, but my father tightened his hold.

A muscle jumped in Mr. Fincastle's cheek. His face paled, and he appeared to brace himself.

"Her corpse can be found on Pharos Island. My daughter—well, presumably my daughter—killed her."

Mr. Fincastle looked to have been dealt a mortal blow. He staggered and whispered hoarsely, "You lie."

My mother looked at me for confirmation, her face draining of all color. When I nodded, she seemed to crumble, her knees shaking, shoulders dropping. I thought she would slump to the ground, but somehow, she remained standing.

"Ask Inez," Papá said. "Tell him what happened, hijita."

"She was crushed," I whispered. "Isadora fired at us first."

A devastated roar ripped out of Mr. Fincastle. He dropped to his knees, bellowing, moaning like an anguished animal.

"On your feet!" Mr. Graves yelled.

"I never should have sent Isadora to you," Mr. Fincastle screamed at me. In an act of lunacy, he dove for the pile of weapons. His hands were a blur of motion, moving quickly, as he grabbed one of the pistols and fired.

Mr. Graves staggered, then crashed to the floor. The wood splintered under his weight. Papá dragged me backward, cursing loudly in my ear. I dug my elbow into his side, and he howled, releasing me. I landed hard on my hands and knees, eyes watering from the impact. I flipped onto my back, kicking as he tried to reach for me again. Mr. Fincastle fired another shot, and Papá cursed again before ducking behind one of the columns, shooting over his shoulder.

One of his bullets rushed past my shoulder, smacking at a spot near my arm. More shots rang out, Mr. Sterling's men had joined the fight. Bullets streaked over my head, and I curled myself into a ball as terror filled my mouth, making it hard to breathe.

"Inez, run!" Mamá screamed.

I looked up, surprised by her warning. Mr. Fincastle was racing toward me at full tilt, a knife in one hand, a gun in the other.

"Charles, don't!" Mamá said, her voice tinged with terror and desperation.

But Mr. Fincastle ignored her, his whole attention fixed on me. He took aim—

His body jerked to a stop. His eyes widened, and he glanced down at the blood staining his shirt. He managed to look over his shoulder, an animalistic howl on his lips before slumping to the floor, his mouth open.

Behind him stood my mother, a smoking pistol in her hand. Tears streaked down her cheeks, and she let out a loud sob as she ran toward him. I stood, knees shaking, in shock that she had saved me.

"Mamá," I whispered, just as she said, "Oh, *Charlie*." She dropped to the floor, eyes red rimmed, tears streaming down her dusty face. Her hand shook as she reached for her dead lover.

"Mamá?"

"Don't," she said, clenching her eyes and refusing to look at me. "Go! ¡Sal de aquí!"

Papá rounded the pillar, pistol in hand. He stood triumphantly before us, a man on the verge of winning everything. The cold line of his mouth could have stabbed me through.

"Do you side with your mother, then?" Papá asked.

I tore my gaze from his gun and looked at Mamá, who still refused to meet my eyes. She was cradling Mr. Fincastle's head in her lap. "If you would have left Egypt, he would still be alive," she whispered. "None of this would have happened."

"It was always going to end like this," I said. "When you both declared war, did you really think there wouldn't be a cost? Did you really think there wouldn't be consequences?"

"Enough, Inez." Papá straightened his shoulders, visibly bracing himself. "*Choose*."

I shook my head. I'd been pulled into their bloody fight for long enough, and if I only had one more minute left to live, then I would live it for myself. "I choose *me*."

"Just like your mother did," he spat, then he rounded on Mamá. "You and your daughter are nothing to me," Papá said quietly, with no trace of Mr. Sterling's English accent. "I will kill her first, Lourdes, and while I'm the one pulling the trigger, her death is your fault, and no one else's. I hope your double life was worth it."

Papá shifted his stance, took aim. He stood not three feet away from me. His bullet would rip my heart in two. Behind him, in the distance, Whit and three of Papá's men were in a shooting match, ducking behind fallen columns, cursing loudly at each other. I wished I could have told Whit how much I loved him. That I forgave him for everything.

Whit fired another shot with his rifle, and one of the men went flying backward, something small falling from his hand.

"*Shit!*" Whit roared, snapping his head in my direction. "INE—"

BOOM.

My ears rang fully as I woke, disorientated, my cheek pressed to the wooden floor. Smoke billowed, wafting into my nose. I tasted smoke in my mouth. The sound of thunderous crashing echoed in the room.

I blinked, my vision slowly coming into focus. It took me several tries to stand, my limbs sore from my fall. My clothes were in tatters, hanging in long strips and burned off in some sections. Around me, the walls of the library shook in anger. And on my next inhale, the room quieted, the smoke disappeared, the columns were standing upright, lavishly painted in green and gold and fiery red. The arched entrances leading to various rooms were intact, the carvings detailed and beautiful.

I gasped, sure I was dreaming, knocked unconscious from the blast.

A slender hooded figure appeared in one of the doorways carrying a roll of parchment in her left hand. I'd seen her before, many times, and I realized where I stood.

I was in Cleopatra's memory.

She strode forward, pausing in front of each arched entryway, all painted and tiled in an array of glittering colors. I took a step, and then another, until I was close behind her. She walked farther into the library until she came to a room with another arched entryway. Like the others, writing in Greek was carved into the stone. If my father were with me, he'd translate what the words said. But I could only guess.

Cleopatra looked over her shoulder, her dark eyes passing through me as if I were a ghost. I supposed that I was. I'd been haunting her for months.

Then she pressed her fingers into different parts of the arch: First, a blue tile, veined in gold. The image of a serpent came next, followed by a press of a ruby-red tile. Then she carefully went to the other side and removed a tile that had a painting of Cerberus on it.

She was showing me the passage to the inner sanctum of the library.

Cleopatra slipped something off her finger, and with a start, I recognized it and stared down at my own hand.

It was the golden ring.

Cleopatra placed it in the space where the tile had been, fitting it perfectly on a raised circle. The space between the arch shimmered gold for half a second before returning to its usual ordinary state. Cleopatra slipped inside with me at her heels.

The room had high ceilings but was narrow. I could touch either side with my fingertips. The walls were divided into square-shaped cubbies, each packed with tightly bound rolls of parchment. In this space alone, there might have been thousands. Cleopatra brushed her index finger along the carved inscription on each partition, whispering several names I knew from my studies of great historical figures: Alexander the Great, Cicero, Archimedes, Thucydides, and Aristotle.

I gasped at the rolls, wishing I could pull each one out to read. But of course, I'd never be able to. So I forced myself to follow after Cleopatra, ignoring the nearly overwhelming urge to stand in place, just so I could marvel at this library, the most wondrous I'd ever known or seen.

Cleopatra knelt in front of a cubby, muttering under her breath, "Cleopatra."

This must have been her ancestor, the alchemist, a renowned Spellcaster. Much like the woman before me. She slipped her roll (the Chrysopoeia—it *had* to be) inside the cubby. Then she stood, turning to face me inadvertently.

I'd never seen her this close up. Dark eyes gleamed with intelligence.

Her skin was dewy with youth, rubbed in essential oils, her hair tucked under her hood, a few tendrils grazing high cheekbones. The curve of her mouth was steeped in determination and grit.

A woman beyond her time.

If only she knew of the legacy she'd leave behind.

Would it make her cry, to be reduced to a seductress of men? A temptress whose victories were diminished and forgotten? Part of me wondered if she would even care. This woman had a city to save, a throne to maintain, a name that had to endure the ravages of time.

She lifted her chin, squared her shoulders, and swept out of the room, using an exit on the opposite side of the arched entryway.

"Inez!" Whit yelled into my face. "Can you hear me?"

He shook me hard, and I coughed, the memory fading to the edges of my mind. I was back in the destroyed library, back in the fire and curls of smoke thickening the air.

"Yes," I managed, coughing again.

"We have to go," he said, snatching my hand. "*Now.*"

Behind him, a boulder fell, splintering the wooden floor apart. It crashed into the water below. Dimly, I heard the sounds of several people screaming, running back the way we had come.

Whit tugged and we ran through a narrow doorway. The floor shook beneath my feet as pillars fell like dominos around us. I looked back to find my parents behind us, my mother quickly running, my father hobbling after her, red-faced. His left cheek was splattered with blood, as if he'd been struck by debris.

We navigated the rooms as the walls shook and cracked. At some point, Mamá doubled back into one of them, snatching one of the rolled parchments. She didn't break her stride as she tucked it inside a shiny cloth. My father actually stopped and began stuffing his pockets with scrolls, whatever he could carry.

"Are you mad?" Whit bellowed over his shoulder. "Leave them! Leave them!"

But my father only slowed down.

My mother seemed to fall under the same spell because she, too, stopped to snatch more scrolls. The pair of them were no longer at war with each other, lost in their desperation to gather the priceless parchments.

"We need her," I gasped.

Whit shot me a furious glare but let go of my hand and then raced back for Mamá. He picked her up and carried her kicking and screaming to where I stood waiting. Together we rushed through the rooms of the library, Papá limping after us, carting a bundle of scrolls high in his arms.

From the corner of my eye, a narrow arch came into view. It was plain, the carvings long since smoothed away, but some of the tiles remained, though they were chipped and cracked. It was nothing like it had been, but I knew it all the same.

I raced toward it, nimbly climbing over boulders and darting around broken columns and loose papyrus that would serve as kindling for the raging fire.

"For the love of God, Inez!" Whit roared.

I stopped inside the arch, as if transfixed. "It's inside this room."

"What is?" my husband snarled. He'd released my mother at some point because he marched up to me empty handed. "Inez, I swear—"

"It's the Chrysopoeia, Whit," I interrupted, pressing on the tiles. The blue veined in gold, the serpent, the red tile now faded. I removed the tile with the three-headed dog and pulled the golden ring off my finger. The floor shook underneath my feet. We were running out of time.

"I know where it is," I said, staring at the spot I needed to place the jewelry in.

Another column crashed behind us, and I startled, coming to my senses.

This wasn't worth our lives.

Whit must have seen the hesitation on my face because he took the ring and placed it inside the vacated space. It still fit perfectly.

"I need it to make everything right between us," Whit said over the sound of the library coming apart at the seams. "It's the only way I can pay you back."

I looked into his face, streaked with dust, a bruise blooming across his cheek, his bottom lip bloody. "I thought you understood."

"Inez—"

"The money doesn't matter to me," I said. "The only thing that does is you, us, our family. *You* are the love of my life, and I will not lose you now."

He shut his eyes, his breath shuddering. When he opened them again, he stared at me intently, his hand coming to brush against the curve of my cheek. "I love you."

I gave him a watery smile. "You are the most precious thing in here, Whit."

"Sweetheart, will you marry me?"

I blinked at him in alarm. Perhaps something had struck his head, made him forget—

"I know we're already married," he said. "But I'm asking you again, Inez, this time for real. I want to do it properly. I want you to have flowers."

"Roses?" I whispered.

"In every color, if that's what you want." He pulled me close, and I tilted my chin upward, met his deep kiss, and then I smiled against his mouth and whispered, "Yes, yes, yes."

"This is very touching," came a voice from behind us. "But I'm afraid I still want that sheet."

My father and mother stood shoulder to shoulder, both looking as if they'd fought several wars, their clothing as tattered and scorched as mine. Papá's mustache was barely holding on, hanging crookedly. He had lost his spectacles, his padded belly.

But unfortunately, not his pistol.

He aimed it at me, and Whit instinctively moved, blocking Papá's view.

I had only seconds to act before my father stole him from me. I curved my fingers around Whit's leather belt, and I brought my hand to the level of the golden ring, perched where it was on the raised circle platform. With all my might, I yanked on Whit's belt, pulling him backward until we walked through the arched entryway. I snatched the ring in the same breath, and I felt the magic close around us.

Papá fired his gun, and the bullet streaked toward us. Whit lifted his arms to throw around me, but a loud crackling sound stopped his motion. The magic guarding the way inside had eviscerated the bullet.

I let out a triumphant yell—

Papá swung his pistol to my mother's temple. "I'll kill her if you don't give me the scroll, Inez."

My mother locked eyes with me. She didn't plead for her life, as if she knew that she'd be wasting her breath. She couldn't imagine that I'd want to save her. But she was wrong.

Without her, my uncle and Abdullah would never go free.

"I'll get it," I said.

Mother's lips parted, her eyebrows rising to her hairline.

The floors shook again as I turned, and Whit clenched his hands into tight fists. "We don't have time for this. There's only one way out of this room and—"

"Not true. There's an exit at the other end," I whispered. "Can you go and see if it's still passable?"

"I'm not leaving you alone—"

"Whit, *please*."

"A quick look and then I'll be back," he said waspishly.

He hurried forward as I dropped to my knees. Many of the cubbies were destroyed, but there were several still intact, the names of ancient engineers, philosophers, and Spellcasters carved into the wood. I found the name I was looking for: Cleopatra.

"I'm so sorry about this," I said under my breath.

The scroll was different than the others. It was thinner, and when I touched it, magic sparked, and the flavor of roses burst on my tongue. It was as if the magic spoke to me, whispering urgently in my ear.

This one.

The hair on my arms stood on end. I *hated* to hand over something that had been dear to Cleopatra. But my uncle and Abdullah needed me to come through.

"Inez, I'm losing my patience," Papá called out.

I rose to my feet, clutching the Chrysopoeia tightly in one hand, the golden ring in the other. The walk back to them seemed like it took hours, when it was only a matter of seconds. But no amount of time would be enough to prepare me for the sight of my ruinous parents, Papá with his gun and my mother glowering back at him. Her journal was filled with pages about Tío Ricardo and how she feared for her safety, worried about his criminal associations. She really had been writing about my father the whole time. Worried about her fate in his conniving hands.

To defeat him, she became like him.

And as they stared at each other in hatred, I knew, without a doubt, that *I* was nothing like them and never would be.

"I give the ring to you," I said to Papá, "and the Chrysopoeia, and Mamá leaves with me and Whit. Are we agreed?"

"Agreed. Is that it?" Papá's whole being now focused on the roll of parchment in my left hand.

Carefully, I unrolled it and showed him the sheet. It was exactly as Whit had said it would look like: the Ouroboros surrounded by Greek letters—detailed instructions on how to turn lead into gold.

"At last," Papá said. His face had lost all color except for the area drenched in blood from where he had been struck. He looked deathly ill, but a feverish excitement gleamed in his eyes.

"You need a doctor," I said over the noise of rubble crashing against stone. I flicked my gaze upward, gasping at the sight of a fissure growing in size. "The roof over our heads can't hold on much longer."

"Toss me the ring!"

I glanced at my mother. Her expression was of utter disbelief. It was that expression that made me give up the ring. It soared through the air, bypassing the magical barrier with ease, as it would since it was used in the creation of the spell.

"You first," Papá said to my mother.

"Coward," she said coldly, but she took a step forward, and then another. I watched without breathing, the air trapped at the back of my throat. Mamá walked through with no issue, and as my father followed after her, she surreptitiously reached for a charm hanging off her gold bangle.

"Stand by the wall," Papá said, pistol trained on my mother. She did, hands lightly clasped in front of her. "No tricks, Lourdes."

She was the picture of innocence. I would have believed her performance had I not seen her unclip the charm from her bracelet. My mother was up to something.

Whit came to stand next to me and muttered under his breath, "You were right. There is an exit."

"Give me the Chrysopoeia, Inez," Papá said loudly. "Now."

Mamá dipped her chin an infinitesimal amount. If I would have blinked, I'd have missed it. I stepped forward and gave it to him just as the walls quaked around us. Rolls of parchment fell off the shelves, and my mother used the moment to drop the charm onto the floor.

"What are you—"

Mamá stomped on it and jumped backward as it exploded into flames.

"Bitch!" Papá snarled, the flames growing in size, surrounding him. He shot his gun, and I dropped to the floor, the heat from the fire enveloping me.

"*Inez!*" Whit dragged me to my feet and then hauled me close to his chest as a section of the roof came down. "We have to go!"

"What about my mother?"

I stole a glance over my shoulder, catching sight of them fighting for the sheet. Papá had lost his gun but was tearing at my mother's hair.

"We have to go," Whit repeated, sweat dripping down the sides of his face. "This is not your fight anymore! It never was."

My mother kicked and clawed at Papá's face. Neither of them knew I was there. The fire reached higher and higher, blocking the sight of them. But I could hear their grunts of pain, the curses they hurled at each other.

Whit took my hand, and I let him drag me through the back exit and into a tunnel. We raced the whole way, our shoes slapping against the stone until we reached the canal.

"This should take us out to sea," Whit said.

"You don't know for sure?"

He winked at me. "Trust me."

Whit led me to the edge, and together we jumped into the Nile. The water was warm, and it swallowed me in its long arms, pulling me out and away from the destroyed remnants of the library. I knew I'd never see it again.

No one would.

The current pulled me under, dragging me to its depths, but Whit held on to my hand, helping me to the surface. I came up sputtering. The water swept over and around us, but still he didn't let go. He managed to pull me closer, wrapping his arm around my waist as the river yanked us along.

"I have you," he said. "I have you."

We were dumped into the harbor, near the Roman fortress Cleopatra had shown me earlier. It felt like an eternity had passed since then. Whit drew closer, gently brushing my tangled hair off my face.

"As much as I hated them, they were your parents," he whispered. "I can understand the wretched position you were in."

"Gracias, Whit," I said, my gaze moving past him and over his shoulder. We had come out of a sliver of rock, nondescript and ordinary. But I couldn't take my eyes away, somehow knowing in my bones that the river would send me one of my parents.

I didn't know which one had won the fight.

But I hoped, for Tío Ricardo's and Abdullah's sakes, it was my mother.

Dios, por favor. Let it be Mamá.

Please, please, *please.*

Whit tucked his index finger under my chin, and my eyes flickered back to his. They were a pale blue to match the waves gently prodding us to shore. "We should swim to the coast."

"I can't swim."

"It was implied that I'd help you."

I smiled at his aggrieved tone. "Can we wait five minutes?"

He narrowed his gaze at me. "Why, sweetheart?"

"Because my mother is going to come out of that canal any second."

His next words were impossibly gentle. "I don't think either of them made it."

"You're probably right," I said. "But I have to know for sure."

"Inez . . ." His voice trailed off before he gave me a nod. "Five minutes. I can't keep us afloat longer than that."

His legs were steadily kicking underneath us; I felt them brush against mine every so often. "Really?"

He rolled his eyes. "No."

I arched a brow.

"Fine. I am a *little* tired." He twisted his lips. "And hungry."

I leaned closer and kissed his cheek. "I promise to feed you falafels after this."

He ducked his head and smiled. A loud splash had us spinning toward the noise.

"*Please*," I said.

A moment later, Mamá's head appeared above the water. She caught sight of us and waved her arm wildly. "¡Ayuda!"

"I think we better help her."

"Ugh," Whit said.

Whit dragged us up the sandbank, and I got onto my hands and knees, coughing up seawater. He dropped Mamá next to me and then settled onto the ground on my other side, breathing heavily.

"If you make a run for it," he said after a moment, "I will catch you."

"You haven't changed, Whit," Mamá muttered.

I shifted around until I faced the rise and fall of the sea, and sat heavily on the damp sand. The waves crashed against the shore and the water reached my toes. Whit leaned forward slightly, looking past me to narrow his eyes at my mother. His wet eyelashes were pointed darts.

She glanced at him warily, her eyes flickering over his shoulder. Moonlight not only illuminated the shadowy outline of Alexandria, but also her calculating expression. I reached out to grab a hold of her arm.

"You're bleeding," I said, gesturing to the cut across her brow. "We ought to return to the hotel. Call for a doctor."

She waved her hand dismissively. "I'll be fine."

Whit pulled a small container from within his jacket and then reached into his holster for his gun. With quick efficient movements, he loaded his weapon. "Your daughter would like to spend more time with you. Are you really going to deny her?" he asked mildly.

My mother's eyes dropped to the revolver in his hand. "It won't work. That powder is useless by now."

Whit lifted his arm and pulled the trigger. The shot thundered harmlessly into the night sky. "Thank goodness for watertight containers."

The corners of my mother's lips turned downward. "You're certainly prepared."

"Endearing, isn't it?" I said.

"Is it?" she muttered, gathering her legs underneath her.

My mother was already planning her escape. She was already looking ahead at how to leave me, scheming and plotting for a move that would see her reunited with her treasures. "Where is Cleopatra?" I asked suddenly. "Where have you hidden the artifacts?"

My mother let out a choked cry as she stood. Her knees wobbled, but she somehow remained on her feet, wiping her eyes, and dripping water. "Is that all you care about?"

I slanted a look up at her, anger licking at my edges. "Abdullah and *your brother* are in prison." I stood also, my exhaustion swept away by my mounting frustration. "They are charged with a crime you committed."

"I'm afraid you will have to come with us," Whit said in that same light tone. He pointed the gun at her.

"You wouldn't shoot me, Whit," she said softly. "Not after I saved her life."

"Why don't you ask your daughter what I'd do?" he asked. "She knows me better than anyone."

"He won't aim to kill," I said promptly. "But he'll shoot you somewhere that will make escape near impossible without assistance. Perhaps in the leg so you can't run far."

Whit grinned, but his eyes were cold. If he were looking at me that way, I would have shivered. "See?"

Mamá twisted her mouth. "Perhaps a visit with a doctor would be wise."

Whit stuck close to her, watching her carefully as we made our way to the edge of the city. We walked a few blocks until he directed us down a street where a carriage and driver waited. I turned to look at him in amazement.

"How—"

"I followed Mr. Sterling's men to the entrance of the underground canals in this carriage. I paid the driver to wait—all night if necessary."

We climbed into our transport, Whit and I sitting side by side and facing my mother. He rested the gun on his left knee, palm curved around the handle. Keeping his eyes on her, he reached for my hand with his free one and interlaced our fingers.

I glanced at him. "I really thought you'd be irritated with me."

"Oh," he said, anger sparking in his blue eyes. "I'm bloody furious, darling." But then he lifted our clasped hands and pressed a soft kiss on the inside of my wrist. "I'm *also* glad you're alive. I lost years of my life watching you leave with Mr. Sterling"—he shook his head—"with Cayo."

"I didn't have a choice."

"Years of my life," he repeated. "Gone." Then he bent and kissed me, hard and quick. "Don't ever pull that shit with me again, Olivera," he whispered against my mouth. He'd said something similar to me months ago when we first met.

I gave him a small smile. Perhaps in another few months he'd finally realize that was just how I operated.

Mamá stared at the pair of us holding hands, her lips flattened. Before Egypt, her expression alone would have made me despair. Hearing her actual disapproval would have cost me several nights' sleep. But now I stared back at her steadily. I wouldn't feel bad for not meeting her impossible standards when *she* couldn't live up to them, either. Subconsciously, she must have known that. My father had demanded perfection from her, and she had crafted the perfect wife. She had created a cage all on her own, and my father was ruthless enough to use the key.

The carriage pulled up to the hotel. I went to open the door, but Whit's voice stopped me.

"Wait a moment, Inez." He handed me the gun, and I made a little noise of surprise at the back of my throat. "I'll be right back."

"You're leaving? Right now?" I asked.

Mamá narrowed her eyes at Whit. "He's planned something."

Oh, of course. I relaxed my shoulders and leaned against the cushion. Whit opened the door, climbed out, and then looked at me over his shoulder and winked. He turned his attention to my mother and in a hard voice said, "If you harm her in any way, I promise you will not like the consequences."

Mamá stiffened.

Whit closed the door, ran around the carriage, and disappeared into the hotel. Mamá peered out the window. She was like a cornered hare, skittish and nervous, eyes flicking left to right, looking for her chance to run. Then she looked at the gun in my hand and scoffed.

"Let's not pretend that you would actually pull the trigger, tesoro," she said, settling back against the seat, imitating my posture. "You are not a violent person."

"Nor am I a stupid one," I said quietly. "You wouldn't hurt me now after you've saved my life."

Her eyes clouded over. "Charlie."

"How did you two meet?"

She folded her arms across her chest. "Cayo hired him to help with operations. It began there."

"Did you know Papá was sick?"

She nodded. "It's why he wanted Cleopatra so badly. He believed her body would cure him."

"You will tell me where you've hidden her," I said. "*And* the cache."

She remained stubbornly silent.

"You'd let your brother die in prison?" I asked flatly. "Abdullah?"

Mamá lifted her chin, her face stony. "Maspero and his associates don't have enough proof to keep them there. You've caused nothing but stress, grief, and heartache since coming to Egypt. I think you can deal with the consequences of *your* actions."

"How dare you," I seethed.

"I dared to save your life," she shouted. "I killed Charlie. Do you have any idea what that cost me?"

"You marked Elvira for death," I yelled back. "Do you have any idea what that cost *me*?"

We stared at one another, breathing heavy, mirrors of each other. Same hazel eyes. Same band of freckles across the bridge of our noses. We shared a love for adventure, making plans, taking risks. We had both hurt people by the things we had done.

"I need you to be my mother," I whispered. "I need you to make it right."

She stared at me warily. "What does that look like? You'd see me in prison for the rest of my life?"

"I don't trust you to walk away from all of this," I said quietly. "Tradesman's Gate, stealing artifacts. I don't think you can give up the wealth it brings, no matter how much it twists your soul into someone I don't recognize." I inhaled deeply. "For everyone's sake, for my peace of mind, for Elvira—you belong in prison. And I need you to return Cleopatra and her cache to the antiquities department."

Her brows rose. "The one run by foreign agents? That one? Surely you can't be this naive. Do you honestly think it would help? Everything will be distributed to benefit the people with money, influence, and power. If you don't already know, those people aren't necessarily Egyptians."

Her words were a slap to the face. "So because the system is corrupt, your best choice is to play along? Why bother changing it?"

She shrugged.

I tried a different tactic. "There's a chance for future generations to enjoy and learn from Cleopatra's cache," I said. "But with *you*, there is no chance of that happening."

Mamá raised her arms to fix her hair, tucking strands back into her braid. She pulled one of her pins out and repositioned it into a different section. There was something practiced about her movement.

"That's enough," I said sharply, hand gripping the gun so tightly my knuckles turned white.

"In a minute," she murmured, another hairpin between her teeth. She pulled it out, her brows pulled into a severe frown. "I think this one is broken."

Her deliberate nonchalant tone put me on edge. My instincts screamed that she was up to some—

She bent the hairpin, flinging it into my lap. Smoke billowed, engulfing me in a thick plume. I clenched my stinging eyes. I tried to cry out but immediately began coughing. My hands reached for her blindly, but the door opened and she climbed out. I stumbled after her, still coughing, tears streaming down my face. There was a sudden yell and the sound of someone throwing a glass. It shattered when it met the ground.

"I warned you," Whit snarled.

He pulled me into his arms, and I wiped my eyes against his shirt. When the smoke finally disappeared, I lifted my head, expecting to see my mother, but I was met with another familiar face.

"Bonsoir, Mademoiselle Olivera," Monsieur Maspero exclaimed. "This is rather interesting, n'est-ce pas?"

I stared at him dumbly. "What are you doing here, sir?"

"I brought him." Farida, my cousin Amaranta, and even Tía Lorena were huddled by two men—whom I'd never seen before—carrying pistols. Both were pointed at my mother, who was busily mopping up her shirt, scowling at my husband.

"I threw lemonade at her," Whit said by way of explanation.

"Lemonade?" I repeated.

"I thought it would irritate her the most," Whit said. "Though you ought to be thankful I wasn't carrying a *scalding cup of tea*, Lourdes."

"Why did you have lemonade? Why is my family here? And Farida? And Monsieur Maspero? I'm so confused." I rubbed my forehead. "I feel as if I've missed something critical."

"Whit wrote me a telegram," Farida said, "telling me to inform Monsieur Maspero that if he wanted to know the true culprit behind Cleopatra's missing cache, then he'd better come to Alexandria. So of course, I set off to the department office, and by then, I had developed all of the photos from the auction we attended." She rummaged through her bag and pulled out a thick envelope. "We got here as fast as we could."

"So I have come," Monsieur Maspero said. He smiled ruefully. "I didn't realize that I would be escorting all these very"—he scrunched his brow—"*charmant* women."

I bit my lip to keep from laughing. No one living would ever describe Amaranta as charming.

"I had to bring the photographs," Farida said defensively.

"And I," Amaranta said coolly, "would not dream of missing seeing Lourdes arrested."

Tía Lorena coldly stared at her brother's wife. "Neither would I."

Whit and I exchanged a look. His seemed to ask, *Are you going to tell her about Cayo?* To which I mutely replied, *Not today.*

He nodded in agreement. He smiled at me, slow and tender, as conversation erupted loudly, my aunt yelling at my mother, Amaranta and Farida talking animatedly to Monsieur Maspero, who looked at them dazedly. He had probably never been addressed by two women so forcibly and sternly.

One voice rose above the din.

"This is ridiculous!" Mamá exclaimed. "You have no proof."

Farida pulled out the photographs from within the envelope and flipped through them before triumphantly holding one up for everyone to see. We all crowded around her to get a better look—save for the two men who still had their weapons trained on my mother.

It was a photo taken on Philae of Mamá sitting alone at a makeshift desk, completely oblivious to someone standing behind her practicing taking pictures with a portable camera. In the picture, Mamá was holding a square-shaped card.

An invitation to Tradesman's Gate.

Addressed personally to her.

WHIT

Maspero's men dragged Lourdes to the carriage. Inez stared determinedly in the opposite direction, her jawline tight, but her bottom lip quivered, betraying her grief. Lourdes looked at her daughter, as if willing to impart one last blow, but I moved to block the sight of my wife from her gaze. I wanted *my* face to be the last one she saw before being hauled away.

I held out my hand to help her climb inside.

"So gallant," she said mockingly.

But she clasped my palm, and as she took a step forward, she muttered, "Reach into my front jacket pocket."

I blinked and did as she asked. My fingers found parchment, rolled tightly and held together by a satin ribbon. I pulled it out and immediately transferred it to my own pocket.

"Is this—" I breathed, my heart pounding wildly. "Why give it to me?"

"Let's call it Inez's dowry," she said. "Look after her." Lourdes climbed into the carriage and settled onto the plush seat, her guards climbing in after her and settling on the opposite bench. She glared at them before dropping her gaze to her lap.

Monsieur Maspero slammed the door, calling up to the driver, "I will follow in another carriage." Then he turned to face me, his brows rising slightly. "What did she say to you?"

The roll of parchment burned in my pocket. "Inanities."

He nodded, called out a farewell to the group, and climbed into another waiting carriage. The drivers flicked their reins, horses neighed, and they were off. I stared after them, a roaring noise reverbating in my ears. And then I felt a cool hand brush against mine. I glanced down, blinking, into my wife's upturned face.

"Is it over?" she asked in a watery voice.

"It will be," I promised her, wrapping my arms around her shoulders. I kissed her hair as she settled against me.

She tilted her head and met my eyes. Hers were red rimmed, eyelids swollen. "Can we have cats?"

"*Cats?* Plural?" I asked, aghast.

"Who doesn't like cats?"

"I happen to love dogs," I said. Then I shook my head. I didn't know why I was arguing with her. I'd give her the bloody moon if she asked. "Inez, we can have as many of them as you'd like."

She lowered her head but not before I caught the soft smile on her lips.

"What do you want to do now, sweetheart?"

She considered the question. "Whatever we want."

PART FIVE

ONE THE ALL

CAPÍTULO VEINTIOCHO

TWO WEEKS LATER

Soft candlelight illuminated the dining table, which was laden with trays of expertly cooked, roasted, and braised meat and vegetables. Several bottles of wine had been opened and poured into thin-stemmed glasses. Satisfaction thrummed in every corner of my body. Seated around the table were the people I cared most about in the world, tucked away in a private room at Shepheard's.

Whit was on my left, his hand on my thigh underneath the snow-white tablecloth. At the opposite end of the table sat Porter next to his younger sister, Arabella. Whit had invited them for a visit, and much to his surprise, they arrived sooner than he'd expected *and* with several trunks in tow. Evidently, they were here for an extended visit, even going so far as renting a home near the hotel.

Arabella had won me over from the first. She had thrown her arms around me and thanked me profusely for turning Whit into a cat person. Within five minutes of conversation, we were talking about our favorite works of art, and she showed me a journal stuffed full of her gorgeous watercolors. She had a rare talent, my newest little sister.

I watched her discreetly from the corner of my eye as she took sips of wine from Porter's glass, her auburn hair shining like polished amber in the candlelight. Porter finally caught on to her antics and glared at Arabella, and I bit back a laugh when she dimpled back at him. But then her attention drifted to the handsome man to her right, and a deep blush bloomed in her cheeks. Whit's friend, Leo, didn't notice, but he'd curiously avoided meeting her eyes since he had sat down at the start of the dinner.

I got the distinct impression that he was actively trying to ignore her.

How *fascinating*. I wonder if—

"Don't even think about it," Whit muttered, following my line of sight. "He's too old for her."

"Not *that* old," I whispered with a wink.

He pinched my thigh, and I threw my napkin in his face. Across from me, Tío Ricardo and Tía Lorena argued in Spanish about his penchant for cigars.

"You are always surrounded by a plume of smoke," she complained. "Do you realize that in order to have a simple conversation with you—of course, no conversation with you is ever simple; *why* is that?—I must prepare myself for my hair and my clothes to stink of your deplorable habit?"

My uncle glowered at her. "Señora, a possible solution is not to engage me in conversation in the first place. How's that for simple?"

I smiled to myself, my attention flickering to Abdullah. Farida was piling his plate high with food. "No more," he protested weakly. "I couldn't possibly—"

"The roasted eggplant looks delicious," Farida said with a broad smile. "I insist."

"Well, if you insist," Abdullah grumbled. "I'd love more bread—"

"How about the tahini?" she said, her smile still fixed. "Vegetables first?"

Abdullah sighed, but then he chuckled fondly. Farida picked up her camera sitting at her elbow and snapped a photo of him smiling. Amaranta leaned close to her, asking, "May I take the next?"

Farida nodded, handing it over to her. "Take one of what you're going to be eating."

"My food?" Amaranta wrinkled her nose, looking down at her full plate. "Who would be interested in seeing that?"

"Some people would," Farida said, laughing. "Or no one, but it's a great subject to practice on. It won't suddenly sprout legs and move off the table."

The two had become good friends during their daily visits to the prison to check on Abdullah and Tío Ricardo. Amaranta held the camera in her hands and snapped a photo. Then she glanced in my direction, shifted the camera, and quickly took one of me.

"I wasn't ready," I protested.

"I know," Amaranta said coolly. "It will surely be the most unflattering image captured of you."

Whit let out a huff of laughter while I glared at my cousin from across the table. I contemplated throwing my glass at her, but it would be a waste of perfectly good wine. I sighed and picked up my fork instead, eager to enjoy this last meal with everyone before we all dispersed in different directions.

"Mr. Whit!" Kareem exclaimed.

My husband turned in his chair to face Kareem where he sat on his other side. "Yes?"

"Abdullah bought me three jars of honey," he said.

"So, he bribed you," Whit said, laughing. "Did he say that you could never eat the honey found in any tombs?"

Kareem nodded sagely. "I must not consume ancient relics."

"A wonderful motto to live by," Whit said, just as sagely.

Kareem frowned. "What's a motto?"

"It's an Italian word meaning—" Porter began.

The door opened, and I opened my mouth to order another bottle of wine, but it was not our server. Monsieur Maspero came in, led by a waiter. At the sight of all of us gathered, he flushed. I didn't have to examine each person closely to know that none of us looked particularly friendly or inviting.

"Oh," he said. "Pardon. I didn't realize—"

"What do you want, sir?" I asked coldly. I would never forgive him for what he'd allowed to happen to my uncle and Abdullah.

He shook his head, cheeks red. "Pardon my interruption. I can see that this is a family"—he broke off, brow furrowing in bemusement at Kareem's cheeky smile—"a family event. I only came by to let you know what has happened with the Lourdes affair."

A sudden quiet enveloped us. No more forks and knives clattering against plates, no more soft chatter or the sound of Farida's camera clicking. Whit's hand tightened on my thigh.

I inhaled deeply, nerves flittering deep in my belly, and said to the waiter, "Please bring an extra chair."

Monsieur Maspero stood awkwardly by the table, hands tucked deep into his pockets, as the seat was brought in and placed next to Abdullah.

"Lourdes has given up the location of Cleopatra and the cache entombed with her," Monsieur Maspero began. My eyes flicked directly to Abdullah's face. Dismay was etched in every groove across his brow. "She made a deal with Sir Evelyn and has since been removed from prison and placed under house arrest, where she will remain for the rest of her life."

Whit tensed, gripping the handle of his knife. "And how long will that last before she manages to escape?"

"There will be plenty of guards," Monsieur Maspero said defensively.

"As if she won't be able to bribe them," Tío Ricardo said dismissively. "My sister is a master manipulator and could charm a tree."

"Perhaps a return to prison is in order," Abdullah added. "There aren't so many entry points or opportunities to engage her guards in conversation."

"I tried," Monsieur Maspero admitted. "But Sir Evelyn insisted the lady have her comforts after revealing what she knew. But do not worry—I will do everything in my power to make sure an escape is impossible."

Next to me, Whit seethed in silence. Since my mother's arrest, we had had long conversations about everything that had happened since the day we met—and about long-kept secrets, his role under my uncle's employment. I knew he was thinking of when he'd overhead Sir Evelyn hiring a spy to observe my uncle's and Abdullah's movements. Up until now, we had narrowed it down to who he might have used.

It might have been my father, acting as Mr. Basil Sterling, or Mr. Fincastle in partnership with my own mother. With Sir Evelyn helping Mamá now, it was clear that he had some understanding with my mother and her lover prior to her arrest. They very well could have approached him with their idea to take the excavation site from my uncle and Abdullah. Or maybe it was Sir Evelyn's plan all along.

We'd never know for sure. What we did know is that Sir Evelyn now had access to one of the greatest historical finds in this century. One look at Whit's grim expression told me that he had come to the same conclusion.

"You must know that Sir Evelyn could have been working with Lourdes and her lover all along," Whit snarled. "Mr. Fincastle would have needed the manpower to overtake the excavation site!"

"The site not reported to the antiquities department?" Monsieur Maspero countered. "Come, come. This all ended for the best, I think. The artifacts are where they ought to be—in proper hands—and you're fortunate that Lourdes has taken full responsibility for the theft."

"*What?*" Ricardo asked.

Monsieur Maspero nodded. "She confessed it was her idea for the lack of transparency on where the team decided to dig. She insisted I release you and your associate." He splayed his hands. "And so I did, and now I have come to issue an apology for your arrest."

My uncle snapped his mouth shut.

"And for how they were treated?" Farida asked in a steely voice.

"Oui, ah, an unfortunate accident," Monsieur Maspero muttered. "I will endeavor to look into the matter and conduct a full investigation."

"There's no need," Abdullah said in a silky voice. "Perhaps a firman to excavate wherever we'd like next season?"

Monsieur Maspero's lips twitched. "I believe that might be possible." Then he pushed back his chair and stood. "Thank you for giving me a moment of your time during your dinner party. Out of curiosity, what is the occasion?"

"It is a farewell dinner," Tía Lourdes said. "We depart for Argentina tomorrow morning."

"Ah, then bon voyage," Monsieur Maspero said, and then he turned to look at me. "Egypt will be losing quite a jewel, mademoiselle. I hope that you will return one day?"

"Oh, I'm not leaving," I said cheerfully.

Whit made a circle with his thumb against my thigh. "We're staying in Egypt to work alongside Ricardo and Abdullah." He shot me a fond look, and I leaned my head against his shoulder.

"I'll be paying you a visit after our honeymoon to secure next year's firman," I said. "I believe we have our sights set on the pyramids."

Monsieur Maspero blanched, and I laughed in his face.

WHIT

Early morning light shone onto the surface of my worktable. Outside one of the many windows of my laboratory, the Nile River stretched for miles, feluccas and dahabeeyahs bobbing in its waters. Dimly, I heard Inez outside in the garden, calling for our recalcitrant cats, Archimedes and Memphis. They *hated* being told what to do.

Exactly like my wife.

I forced myself to pay attention to Cleopatra's Chrysopoeia as I stared at the Ouroboros, the snake continuously consuming and regenerating itself. Next to the sheet were stacks of chemistry books and older texts from alchemists who lived before me, attempting to achieve the impossible.

But that was the magic of alchemy. The transforming of one thing into another.

Copper into silver.

Lead into gold.

But right then, I was practicing the basic principles of alchemy on a common herb. I recited the three philosophical essentials to myself under my breath.

Sulfur (oil). Mercury (liquor). Salt (alkali).

Also known by what they represent: Sulfur, the soul. Mercury, the spirit. Salt, the body.

I swept the basil Inez had harvested from our garden earlier in the morning into a shallow dish, clearing up the area to complete the three main steps. First, separate, then purify, and finally combine these essentials to create a new harmonic substance.

If done right, I could apply this process to lead and, theoretically, create gold.

I stared at the flask where I had placed a handful of finely chopped fresh basil with half a cup of water to make a paste. Carefully, I added steam, watching as the scalding vapors rose into the condenser. A layer of oil formed on the surface of the water, the material principle of sulfur, otherwise known as the soul of the plant.

First separation done.

Now the plant had to ferment, which would take several long hours. Inez's laugh drifted into the room from the open window. She was still out in the garden, trying to find the damned cats. I smiled to myself as I left my makeshift lab.

I knew exactly how I wanted to pass the time.

It was the middle of the night and I was back in the lab. I'd left Inez sleeping, hating to leave our bed, but my gut was telling me that I was close to understanding Cleopatra's Chrysopoeia. As planned, the basil had fermented, or as an actual alchemist would say, the plant had died. It no longer had a life force to speak of. I distilled the watery mush until it eventually turned into alcohol, revealing the spirit of the plant.

The separations of the essentials were complete.

Onward to the last step—purification. I took the basil, drying it fully with a cloth to rid it of excess moisture, before setting it on fire, resulting in a gray ash. I smiled to myself, hands shaking with excitement. This was better than a full flask of my favorite whiskey. I carefully dumped the ash back into the flask of water, where it immediately dissolved after a brisk stir. From there, I filtered the liquid, where it would evaporate into a crystalized white salt.

The body of the plant.

I only had to recombine, or resurrect, the essentials in order to finish the process. Later, I would transfer the salt into an apothecary glass and pour the sulfur inside, followed by the mercury.

It would be my first elixir.

My attention drifted to the lead on my worktable. I would have to follow the same principles, the same steps, in order to transform the lead into gold. I walked to Cleopatra's Chrysopoeia, memorizing it fully, and as morning light filtered into the room, I began the noble art.

My eyes dropped to the tiny sliver of gold on the round dish, glimmering in the sunlight.

I'd done the impossible.

Did it mean I was an alchemist? I shook my head, feeling delirious, wondering how I was going to tell my wife that I could make back the fortune I had taken from her. The alchemical sheet sat in front of me, and I peered at it for the last time. I knew every line, every drawing, and every symbol by heart.

Now that I did, I had to figure out what to do with it. I would never keep something this precious, this *volatile*, in my life with Inez. Cleopatra's Chrysopoeia deserved to be protected, kept safe and far away from the people who might use it for ill.

There was only one person I knew who would know what to do with the sheet.

"Whit?" Inez said, opening the door while knocking against it softly. She carried Memphis in her other arm, and he looked indignantly at his means of transportation. "Are you all right?"

I looked up, blinking, disoriented. "I'm fine?"

She walked into the room, peering curiously at the table laden with flasks and glass bottles, my favorite books on chemistry, and stacks of papers filled with dozens of scribblings I'd made while working. She had tucked a white rose in her hair and the sweet fragrance drifted toward me as I smiled down at her. I had planted several rosebushes for her in our garden, and since then, I could count on finding flowers in unexpected places throughout our house. Hidden in the pages of my favorite book, slipped into a picture frame, or placed prettily on our dinner plates. Memphis went to swipe at a beaker, but Inez pivoted in time, preventing disaster.

"No, no, my darling," she cooed. "We mustn't destroy Lord Somerset's experiments."

"*Lord*—"

"You've been spending all of your free time in this room for two days," Inez interrupted. "I didn't think you'd work this much during our honeymoon." She wrinkled her brow, nose delicately sniffing. "It smells strange. What have you been doing?"

I stood up, swaying slightly and feeling weirdly light-headed. I had made gold. *Gold.* She looked at me in alarm, but I grinned at her as I pulled her close, kissing her cheek, her temple, her hair. The rose petals pleasantly tickled my nose. "Let's have breakfast, and I'll tell you all about it."

"It's dinnertime," she corrected mildly.

"Dinner, then," I said. I bent forward, tucking my arm under her knees, and scooped up my wife—and the damn cat—into my arms. She squealed as I carried her out of the lab while Memphis leapt out of her grasp with an impatient hiss. "Can we invite Abdullah to eat with us? I have something that belongs to him. We are going to celebrate."

"Yes, I'll send a note with Kareem." Inez raised her brows. "What are we celebrating?"

I leaned down and kissed her, once, twice, three times, before whispering against her mouth, "The rest of our lives."

EPÍLOGO

GASTON MASPERO

In his later years, he attempted to curtail the illegal exportation of Egyptian artifacts. In a now infamous act, he arrested the Abd al-Russul brothers, who were detained and tortured until they confessed to their discovery of a number of royal mummies. Despite this, he remained popular and went on to uncover the Sphinx, reconstruct the Karnak Temple, and manage the Bulaq Museum in Cairo. He died at the age of seventy.

SIR EVELYN BARING

Known later as Lord Cromer, he held his position as consul general of Egypt until 1907. His unseemly views would shape many of Egypt's policies, and his position all but guaranteed no roadblocks to any reforms he proposed, including his belief in Britain's prolonged supervision and occupation of Egypt. And thanks to the Granville Doctrine, Baring and other British officials were given the power to hire Egyptian politicians who supported British interests and directives. He eventually left Egypt at the age of sixty-six and died in 1917 when he was seventy-five years old.

SHEPHEARD'S

In 1952, the hotel was destroyed in the Cairo fire amid riots and political turmoil over Britain's continued presence in Egypt.

AMARANTA & TÍA LORENA

Much to Ricardo's horror, Lorena frequently visited Egypt, often bringing trunks filled with gifts that he never knew what to do with.

Amaranta married Ernesto. They had six children.

The youngest daughter followed in her aunt Inez's footsteps and became an Egyptologist (much to her mother's everlasting horror).

FARIDA

She opened her own portrait photography studio in Cairo, steps away from Groppi.

RICARDO & ABDULLAH

The two remained business partners until their old age.

Together, they discovered the tombs of
Alexander the Great and Nefertiti.

Not that either of them would ever admit it.

ARABELLA

Thanks to Whit's financial contribution, and Porter's protection against her thoughtless and selfish parents, she enjoyed a measure of independence and autonomy in England. Eventually, she ran away to Egypt and had her own adventure.

But that's a story for another time.

INEZ & WHIT

They lived in Egypt for the rest of their lives,
raising their twins, Elvira and Porter, while assisting
Abdullah and Ricardo with their excavations.

Elvira grew up to be one of the leading papyrologists of her time.

Porter studied photography, trained by his honorary aunt Farida.

ARCHIMEDES & MEMPHIS

Both lived long and happy lives and made plenty of discoveries in the garden.

But Memphis did, in fact, destroy several of Whit's beakers.

AUTHOR'S NOTE

The city of Alexandria has a long and layered history, and while *Where the Library Hides* is a historical fantasy, I wanted to work as many details as I could into the narrative. Alexandria really does have a system of underwater canals and passageways connected by ancient cisterns, which at one point numbered in the hundreds (Mahmoud el-Falaki counted seven hundred in his detailed map of the ancient city of Alexandria). They were described as underground cathedrals because of the vaulted ceilings, marble detailing, and columns topped with intricately carved capitals. After the British navy bombarded Alexandria in 1882, tourists ventured underground with hurricane lamps to explore the watery city of cisterns with its streets made of subterranean canals.

Speaking of Mahmoud el-Falaki, many present-day archaeologists and excavators owe their knowledge of ancient Alexandria to his pioneer work in creating a detailed map of the city, which otherwise would have been lost, thanks to modern urbanization. He was truly a Renaissance man, skilled in various professions: astronomy, engineering, mathematics, and science. Not to mention he was a researcher and cartographer *and* an excavator. His work was often dismissed in the English-speaking world, but modern archaeologists and historians have used his map of the ancient city of Alexandria over and over again in order to have a concrete image of what it would have looked like in antiquity.

In 1885, Alexandria was in a state of rebuilding after the bombardment by the British navy, and sections of the city, particularly near the coast, were still in shambles. However, there are two settings for which I took artistic license: the lighthouse of Alexandria and the Serapeum. The former was built by one of Cleopatra's ancestors and considered one of the seven wonders of the ancient world. It was made of limestone and granite and stood around 338 to 387 feet tall, and at the very top, there was an immense mirror that reflected sunlight during the day, while a fire blazed during the night. Sadly, several earthquakes destroyed the lighthouse of Alexandria, and the remaining base was turned into a fort during medieval times.

The Serapeum really was considered the daughter library of the Great Library of Alexandria. It was an enormous temple, and it housed the overflow of what was catalogued and stored in the Great Library of Alexandria. It was destroyed by Roman soldiers in 391, with only one pillar still standing today. However, there is an underground portion, and it was here where my imagination went into overdrive. It wasn't hard to connect this underground library to the city of subterranean canals flowing beneath Alexandria.

As for the Great Library of Alexandria, it was destroyed in a fire when Julius Caesar's soldiers set fire to ships docked in the port in an attempt to block Cleopatra's brother Ptolemy XIII from gaining access to the coast. It's estimated that forty thousand scrolls were lost in the disaster. Here is where I latched on to the idea of the secret library underneath the Serapeum where ancient scholars hid priceless scrolls in case another disaster occurred.

Cleopatra the alchemist was a real woman who lived possibly in the third or fourth century. She is credited as being one of the four women in the ancient world who could produce the philosopher's stone and was perhaps an inventor of scientific tools that helped forge a path to modern chemistry. There's debate as to whether her name was a pseudonym, but in the world of *Where the Library Hides*, I imagined her to be an ancestor of Cleopatra VII, and a mentor of sorts (despite having actually been born after Cleopatra VII).

And as for the Cairo prison, it really was an old military hospital, but it wasn't converted into a jail until 1886.

ACKNOWLEDGMENTS

I've dreamed about writing a book set in Egypt for as long as I could remember, since I was a little girl reading underneath the covers when my parents thought I was sleeping. The book you hold in your hands has been a labor of love from the beginning, and I can't believe it's time to thank everyone who came with me on this epic journey.

To Sarah Landis, my wonderful agent, who celebrated all my wins and showed up for me, again and again. A heartfelt thank-you to Eileen Rothschild, editor, friend, and cheerleader, for calling and texting every time there was good news (and there was a lot of it; we might have cried each time). Working with you on this duology has been a highlight of my career. Here's to the next three.

An enormous thank you to the Wednesday Books team, for all that you do, seen and unseen: Zoe Miller, Char Dreyer, Alexis Neuville, Brant Janeway, Kerri Resnick, Sara Goodman, Devan Norman, Eric Meyer, Cassie Gutman, and Lena Shekhter. This duology would not have been possible without all of your hard work, insight, and guidance. Once again, from the bottom of my heart, thank you. You all are wonderful. To the audio team, Ally Demeter, Maria Snelling, Isabella Narvaez, thank you for bringing this book to life.

For the guidance and help I received on all things Egypt: Adel Abuelhagog and Egyptologist Nabil Reda, thank you for answering all my endless questions. Once again, a big thank-you to Egyptologist Dr. Chris Naunton, who offered a tremendous amount of insight and guidance on ancient Alexandria.

To Rebecca Ross, my soul sister and critique partner, as ever, thank you for reading and brainstorming with me. Your friendship means the world to me. A million thanks to Renée Blankenship for reading this one at a drop of a hat. You're a wonderful beta reader. To my dearest friends and writing community, I'd be lost without your love and support. Thank you for reading and for cheering me on. You know who you all are. Sending you all a big hug and my eternal gratitude for your friendship. <3 <3 <3

I'm incredibly lucky to have wonderful support in my family and friends. They cheer me on, and celebrate my wins, and stick with me through the ups and downs, and all my deadlines.

To my parents, who always knew I'd grow up to be a storyteller. For Rodrigo, who never forgets to tell me how proud he is of me.

To Andrew, Alistair, and August, my precious family. You bring meaning and joy and hope to my life. The three of you are everything to me. All my love, forever and ever.

And to Jesus, you will always be the strength of my heart.